SERENDIPITY

By Janet Nissenson

Chapter One

September

Even at 8am it was already warm and humid, and Nathan Atwood was glad he'd forced himself to rise earlier than he would have preferred to start his eight mile run. As he ran through Central Park at a brisk pace, he noticed quite a few other runners, walkers, and cyclists, all undoubtedly anxious to beat the heat of a mid-September day in Manhattan and get their workouts done as early as possible.

He left the park and headed back towards the Plaza Hotel, where he was staying to attend the American Institute of Architects convention. The streets were considerably more crowded than they had been close to an hour ago when he'd started his run, requiring him to slow his pace and often dodge around people hurrying on their way to work. About a block from the hotel it got so congested that he gave up and slowed to a walk, conscious of the sweat pouring from his face and soaking his clothes, and he was grateful he didn't have to deal with this sort of weather on a daily basis.

Summers in San Francisco, where he'd flown in from yesterday afternoon, were much cooler and outdoor workouts not nearly so taxing. And while the streets around his office building back home could get quite crowded at times, they were nothing like the virtual mob scene that was Manhattan. This certainly wasn't his first visit here, but somehow he was never really prepared to deal with the masses of humanity he encountered in New York City.

But even with all the people hurrying this way or the other, Nathan still couldn't miss the extraordinarily beautiful woman walking his way. Heads turned in all directions as she passed, but she seemed oblivious - whether by intent or not – to the admiring male stares and jealous female glares sent her way, and she didn't make eye contact with anyone. Until she happened to glance up and meet his own enraptured gaze.

Time seemed to stand still for what was very likely just a few brief seconds, but to Nathan everything around him seemed frozen as he stared into those beautiful mossy green eyes. The brisk pace she'd been walking at slowed until she was almost standing still as they continued to stare at each other, as if there weren't dozens of other people rushing past them.

The beautiful stranger offered up a tentative smile, which he returned automatically, the sort of casual acknowledgement that people who find each other mutually attractive tossed out. But there was nothing casual about the instant and almost overwhelming reaction he was having to her, as he continued to hold her gaze steadily and her smile deepened. It wasn't just the physical awareness of each other, though that was certainly off the charts. Instead it almost felt as though he recognized her from somewhere, had been waiting for her to appear and already knew her intimately. As they continued to stare at each other, the woman's full, glossy lips parted, and he waited for her to say something.

And then just like that she was gone, continuing on her way, and he turned to watch her, wanting nothing more than to follow in her wake, find out her name, get her number, ask her out to dinner, fuck her senseless. But instead he merely watched her go, as he somewhat belatedly recalled that he was no longer free to do any of those things. Not since he'd become engaged to Cameron Tolliver less than a month ago.

But that recollection didn't erase the image of that flawlessly beautiful face from his mind as the day went on. As he showered and dressed in a light gray Prada suit, he remembered the way her structured white dress clung to a body with curves in all the right places. When he was getting coffee and a bagel at the continental breakfast buffet set up for the convention attendees, he pictured her perfect facial features – high, sculpted cheekbones, small, straight nose, plush, pillowy lips glossed in a soft rose, and those huge green eyes. To distract himself during the really boring opening presentation, he thought of her long, curling hair that fell more than halfway down her back, a light golden brown shade that reminded him of melted caramel. And the mental image of how her high heels had made her legs look endlessly long caused him to develop a hard-on at a most inappropriate time.

By the time the convention meetings had ended for the day and it was time to head to dinner, Nathan was mentally kicking himself for not following his initial instincts and running after his beautiful stranger. Now he'd never see her again and would probably regret it for a long, long time. He'd dated and slept with a lot of women in his thirty three years, but had never reacted quite this way to one of them before.

But it was likely all for the best, he thought, since he wasn't in a position to pursue this sudden obsession with a woman he'd passed on the street for maybe twenty seconds max. He did, after all, have a brand-new fiancée back home and it would have been really shitty of him to chase after another woman, no matter how gorgeous she was. Should he be worried that feeling this sort of strong attraction to another woman was a sign that perhaps he shouldn't have agreed to this engagement after all?

He and Cameron had been dating for just over two years, and she had started hinting about getting engaged less than a year into the relationship. He had put her off each time she brought the subject up, not at all sure he was ready to settle down, or that Cameron was the right one to settle down with. Prior to getting involved with her, he hadn't really done long term relationships, thoroughly enjoying a carefree state of unencumbered bachelorhood. He'd rarely dated the same woman more than a few times, and probably wouldn't have continued seeing Cameron much longer than that if it hadn't been for her persistence coupled with the fact that everyone else he knew seemed to be in a permanent relationship these days.

It had been a series of events that finally prompted him to get engaged. First, his younger brother Jared and his wife Brooke had had a baby boy earlier this summer, less than two years after they had married. Jared was a professional baseball player for the Colorado Rockies, and at age twenty-nine was a full four years younger than Nathan, who was the oldest of three sons. Not only was Jared the first of the boys to marry but now also the first to produce a grandchild. Nathan was quite aware that his parents had likely always expected him to be the first to do both given that he was the oldest. The marriage part hadn't really bothered him, especially since he'd thought Jared too young to get married. But the part about the baby had given him cause for reflection, especially when he saw how taken his parents were with their new grandson.

Then his younger brother Greg, who was beginning his final year of law school back in Michigan, had moved in with his longtime girlfriend Emma and there was talk of a Christmas engagement. And then, just a few weeks ago, Nathan and Cameron had attended the wedding of Kyle Philpott, one of Nathan's closest friends and former water polo teammates from their days at UC Berkeley. Kyle had been among the last of their circle of friends to tie the knot, leaving Nathan as practically the only remaining single one. He had started to feel like the odd man out, and to wonder if time was passing him by while all of his other friends were getting married and starting families.

Kyle's wedding, in fact, had been the catalyst in setting the scene for Nathan and Cameron to finally get engaged. Nathan had been pleasantly buzzed from all the free flowing booze, he'd been having a great time with so many of his friends who were in attendance, and Cameron had caught the bride's bouquet. She'd arrived back at their table clutching the flowers triumphantly, and quite boldly told him that he *had* to marry her now. To her utter delight, he'd agreed this time and she had immediately proceeded to call her parents, her sister, and half a dozen friends despite his pleas to keep the news to themselves for just a little while. But Cameron rarely listened to reason and frequently acted on impulse, and most of the time those impulses were ill-advised. He usually found her impulsiveness endearing but at other times – like the night of their engagement – it had been maddening. He had really wanted to keep the news to themselves for just a little while, especially considering how quickly the whole thing had wound up unfolding.

He'd been a little taken aback at the reaction – or, more accurately, the lack thereof – from his parents and siblings when he had called them with the news. Oh, they had certainly expressed surprise and offered him heartfelt congratulations, but he had sensed that none of them were over the moon about his engagement. He had received similar reactions from several of his friends, and in some cases – like Travis, his business partner – he had actually perceived a sense of disapproval. Small wonder, though, considering that Cameron and Travis didn't really get along and neither made much effort to conceal their mutual dislike.

As he headed into the banquet room that had been set for the evening's group dinner, he checked his phone for messages, sighing when he saw three missed calls and half a dozen texts from Cameron. He had called her during an early afternoon break, and the conversation hadn't been especially pleasant. She'd been peeved at him for the flight arrangements he'd made for this trip, in particular his return flight home. Because the convention didn't end until late afternoon on Friday, and he knew he'd wind up going out to dinner with a group of acquaintances, he had refused to get up early on Saturday to catch a flight back to San Francisco. Cameron had wanted him to escort her to one of those all-too-frequent high society functions that her parents always patronized, and often compelled her to attend as well. But his flight arrived in too late to make the charity ball, and she was none too happy about having to go alone. Nathan knew she still hadn't completely given up on convincing him to catch an earlier flight, and he hoped they wouldn't have yet another argument about it. He decided to wait until after dinner to call her back, wanting to enjoy the evening among old friends and business associates.

This convention was not only valuable for his career and business, but a bit of a getaway for him, too. Work had been incredibly busy this year, which was fantastic for the success of his firm but exhausting for him personally. The only vacation time he'd been able to scratch out so far had been a quick visit to see his parents in Michigan, and a couple of long weekends at Cameron's parents' second home in Lake Tahoe. He and Cameron did have a week's getaway to Maui planned for November but this week in New York City was a little breather just for him.

The rest of the evening passed by relatively quickly, and he was able to temporarily forget about the gorgeous woman he'd seen this morning. But she featured prominently in his dreams that night, though he couldn't remember any specific details when he woke up the next morning. Judging by the size of his morning erection, however, he figured they must have been juicy.

He chose to swim laps in the hotel's pool that morning rather than run since it was raining outside. He liked to mix up his workout rotation anyway, rarely doing the same thing two days in a row. Besides running and swimming, he also enjoyed mountain biking, rock climbing, and weight training. He'd always been a strong swimmer from the time he was a boy, which had evolved into water polo during high school and college. His years on the water polo team at Berkeley were some of the best times of his life, and the friends he'd made on the team continued to be his closest pals today.

The rain kept up for a good part of the day, preventing him from going outside, but the possibility of seeing his beautiful stranger was slim to none anyway. Still, he couldn't help but be disappointed when he ran again on Wednesday morning and didn't see her this time. The rain had stopped but the weather was hotter and muggier than ever. During a mid-morning break, coffee and tea were served as usual but a hot drink didn't seem very appealing given the rising temperature outside.

"I'm thinking of heading to the Starbucks down the street to get an iced coffee," said Nathan to Rick Marshall, an old friend and classmate from Berkeley, who was also attending the convention. Rick worked for a big firm in Chicago, and they typically saw each other at the convention each year.

"Sounds good to me. Actually, one of those frappuccinos they make sounds even better. I'll go with you," offered Rick.

The hot, humid weather enveloped them like a wet blanket when they exited the hotel. It was a mercifully short walk to the Starbucks, and the air conditioning inside was a welcome relief. There was a short line at the counter, but Nathan got his iced coffee fairly quickly. Rick's specially concocted caramel vanilla frappuccino took longer to prepare, so Nathan pulled out a chair at a table near the counter and sat down to wait. And saw his beautiful stranger sitting at the next table.

Her attire today was more casual than the classy white linen dress she'd worn the other day. This morning she wore a fitted white T-shirt that clung lovingly to those lushly full breasts he'd been fantasizing about for two days. The rest of her outfit consisted of a slim fitting navy skirt, a wide brown leather belt with a gold filigree buckle, and brown leather stiletto sandals with a sexy ankle strap. Her abundant fall of hair had been pulled back into a sleek ponytail, which emphasized those glorious cheekbones and huge green eyes. Her full, luscious mouth was glossed over in a shiny nude color this morning and he wanted to claim it in a deep, searching kiss so badly he couldn't think of anything else.

She looked cool and chic but incredibly hot at the same time. He wanted to lick her all over, starting with that deliciously fuckable mouth, and then traveling down that slender throat to those perfect tits. And that was just for a warm-up. Jesus, the things he wanted to do to her – spread her out on his bed, loosen that beautiful hair and run his fingers through it, then undress her slowly and savor her for hours, maybe even days. She was the sort of ultimate fantasy woman that most men never even got to see up close, much less do all of the dirty things on his sexual wish list to.

She was working on her tablet, and sipping what looked like her own iced coffee, and hadn't noticed him yet. Nathan was sure that someone as beautiful and sexy as she was had long ago perfected the knack of ignoring unwelcome attention; otherwise she'd have men hitting on her around the clock. But at that particular moment she happened to glance up and see him, and when she smiled in recognition, a warm glow spread over him.

"How are you this morning?" he asked, his voice huskier than normal as he smiled back at her.

Her green eyes sparkled in amusement, almost as if she sensed his uncertainty. "Pretty good, thanks. How about yourself?"

Her voice was soft and sweet and the sound made him hard. He wondered wildly if she would still sound that way when he made her pant and moan with arousal.

"Trying to stay cool in this heat," he replied, grateful that his voice now sounded normal. He raised his own plastic cup of iced coffee. "Looks like we had the same idea."

She didn't reply, merely gave him another of those sexy little smiles, and took a sip of her drink before returning her attention to her tablet. He shifted uncomfortably as he grew even harder, imagining those full, pillowy lips sucking his cock instead of the straw. He hadn't worn his suit jacket in deference to the heat, and hoped that his erection would subside enough to be able to walk out of here in a couple of minutes.

As if on cue, Rick appeared by his side, holding an oversized concoction swirled with caramel syrup and topped with a mound of whipped cream. It was more ice cream fountain treat than coffee drink, and Nathan had to suppress a shudder at the thought of how sweet it must taste.

"Ready to go?" asked Rick cheerily. "Almost time for the next session to start. We'll make it back just in time."

Nathan stood slowly, grateful to note that his erection had deflated just enough so that it wasn't tenting his trousers. "Sure, let's go." He hesitated for long seconds, willing his beautiful stranger to glance up again. When she didn't, he impulsively called out to her, "Have a good day."

She looked up then, her gaze locking with his, and smiled. "Yes, you, too."

Aware that Rick was staring at her, and then back at him, Nathan gave her a returning smile before ushering Rick out of the store. He wanted nothing more than to send Rick on his way and then go back inside, this time to find out her name and ask her to have dinner with him, not giving a shit if he was late for the convention or if he ever made it back at all. But then he thought again of Cameron and started walking back to the Plaza at a brisk pace, before he could change his mind and retrace his footsteps.

Predictably, Rick was full of questions. "Who the hell was that babe you were talking to? Damn, but she was fucking hot, Nathan. With a capital H-O-T."

He shrugged, not liking the way Rick was almost salivating. "Don't know. I passed her by on the street a couple of days ago and here she is again today. She must work in the area."

Rick shook his round, balding head in disbelief. "And you didn't get her name or number? With the way she was looking at you?"

Nathan tried mightily to seem nonchalant. "She wasn't looking at me in any special way, Rick. Women that look like her can pretty much have any guy they want."

Rick snickered. "Yeah, and she wanted *you*, dumbass. Only you were too dumb to do anything about it. You could be having the primest piece of ass I've ever seen sharing your bed tonight and you just walk away. If she'd been looking at me that way, we'd be halfway to my hotel room now."

Even though he had no right whatsoever to feel proprietary about his beautiful stranger, Nathan was still angered at the rather crude manner in which Rick was talking about her. Anxious to drop the subject, he waved a hand in dismissal. "Moot point anyway. I'm engaged, remember? No harm in looking but I'm not in any position to go farther than that."

"Never would have taken you for such a pussy, Atwood, especially after seeing you in action back in college," said Rick in disgust. "Hell, if I was married with three wives I'd still fuck that gorgeous babe if she gave me the come-hither sign. Don't be such a sap. You're a long way from home, buddy, and your fiancée would never know. Think of it as one final fling before settling down. And what a fling it would be. Damn, I'd cut off a couple of fingers just to get an up close look at those tits. They've got to be double D's."

"Stop it." Nathan was seething, and getting increasingly pissed off with every word Rick uttered. He didn't want his friend to cheapen anything about the beautiful girl he was becoming increasingly obsessed with. "Just drop it, okay? Yes, she's a fucking wet dream, and if I wasn't already spoken for I'd be back at that table trying to talk her out of her panties. But I'm not free to do that so let's forget it."

Rick shook his head. "Fine. But you're an idiot. Every other guy I know – single, engaged, or married – wouldn't hesitate to fuck her brains out, even if it was just once. Woman like that only comes along once in a lifetime, you know."

As the afternoon wore on, those words of Rick's continued to nag Nathan. Would he always regret passing up the opportunity to spend a night with his beautiful stranger? Because despite his denials to Rick, he had definitely felt a strong connection, a mutual attraction to the green-eyed beauty, and was very sure he would have succeeded in seducing her. There had definitely been something there, and she had felt it, too, he was sure of it. She had been every bit as aware of him as he was of her, and he wished like hell he'd had the nerve to linger at Starbucks awhile longer and talk to her at greater length.

But it was too late now, for he'd walked away from his only opportunity, and it was extremely unlikely he'd ever see her again. Or that she would even give him a second thought. She probably had guys calling her and asking her out all the time, and she sure as hell wasn't likely to dwell on a stranger who'd fumbled his best chance to approach her.

Chapter Two

Julia McKinnon gave herself yet another mental kick in the ass at how idiotically she'd behaved not once but twice now. Quite possibly the most gorgeous man she'd ever seen before had made it rather obvious that he found her equally as attractive, but what had she chosen to do about it? Oh, yes, walk away the first time and then give him the cold shoulder the second by turning her attention back to her iPad. And now the odds of seeing him for a third time weren't good. She'd overheard his short, pudgy friend – the one who'd frankly creeped her out with his lascivious grin – mention something about getting back to a session, so she assumed they were only in town for a meeting or conference of some sort. He was likely leaving town the next day or so, and she'd never see him again.

'Stupid, stupid, stupid, Julia!' she chastised herself. 'One of the very few times a man has actually interested you, and you basically freeze him out just like you always do.'

Her well-honed knack for ignoring men and their largely unwanted advances had developed at an early age. Julia had known that she was attractive from the time she was a small child, largely because everyone had told her so repeatedly. She could vividly recall any number of occasions when she'd been out with one or both parents – and her identical twin Lauren – and people had stopped them in the streets to comment "What beautiful children you have" or "Such gorgeous little girls". As she and her twin had grown older and started to mature, the attention had come from boys. She and Lauren had both developed boobs and hips by the tender age of thirteen, and their mother – Natalie – had made very sure that her daughters never took advantage of their beauty.

She'd been quite strict with regards to their clothing and makeup, nixing some of their choices as inappropriate, and making sure her girls always looked ladylike. That had been much tougher with Lauren, who to this day vastly preferred T-shirts, jeans, and hiking boots to the sheath dresses and high heels that Julia favored. But during their high school years Julia could quite clearly recall a number of occasions when her mother had forbidden her to wear a particular top that was too low-cut or clingy, or a skirt that was too short, or a shade of lipstick deemed too flashy.

And as far as boys were concerned, Natalie had been adamant that neither of her daughters gained a "reputation" as being easy or promiscuous. "Because both of you are so pretty, you're always going to have boys – and later on men – approaching you. You need to learn to be discriminating and careful, and not go off with every cute boy who smiles at you," she'd cautioned them more than once.

As it turned out, their mother had had very little cause for concern. Lauren had much preferred soccer, swimming, and her martial arts classes to dating, though she had somewhat reluctantly attended both of her proms at Julia's urging. Julia had been with Sam for all four years of high school, and even part of college, and had only had one other serious relationship since then – one that had not ended on an amicable note like it had with Sam. It had ended so badly, in fact, that she hadn't had a serious relationship since – and that had been over two years ago. There had been a couple of very brief flings with men she didn't care to think about anymore, and no one at all for almost a year now.

Her absence of a love life was certainly not for lack of opportunity. Everywhere she went men looked at her – and often tried to approach her – but she almost always ignored them, pretending they didn't even exist. Until two days ago when she'd spied the gorgeous man walking towards her on Park Avenue.

He'd obviously been out for a run, for his hair and face were damp with perspiration, his gray cotton T-shirt stained dark with sweat. But all she'd really noticed were those piercing light blue eyes, classically handsome features, and that beautiful head of thick, dark brown hair. The body hadn't been any hardship to look at either – tall and leanly muscled, well-defined biceps and slim hips. He looked like an athlete without having an overly-muscled body, or being too big and intimidating. His beautiful face and sculpted body had imprinted themselves into her memory banks immediately, even though she'd only seen him for less than a minute. She couldn't recall the last time she'd even given a man a second thought, much less daydreamed about him at inopportune moments.

When she'd seem him again earlier today, she had definitely noticed how hot he looked with the sleeves of his crisp white dress shirt precisely rolled back, and the way his dark gray suit trousers hung on his body. His clothes looked expensive, and Julia – who knew clothing and designers very well – guessed his suit to be Gucci or maybe Dior. She'd recognized the classic Piaget watch on his left wrist, noticing discreetly at the same time the absence of a wedding ring. His black oxford shoes had been buffed to a subtle shine, and he had looked every bit the suave, polished businessman he most likely was. Julia had a real weakness for a guy who could wear a suit really well, and Mr. Gorgeous – as she'd nicknamed him – certainly fit that bill. It was too bad that the weather had been so hot and he'd left his suit jacket off. She could just imagine how the undoubtedly well tailored garment would show off the breadth of his shoulders, and the dark gray color would compliment his blue eyes.

That she was seriously attracted to this man was without debate. The reason for it was something she couldn't explain as easily. Oh, he was undoubtedly gorgeous and sexy, and his smile could melt the panties off a nun. But Julia saw attractive men almost every day in Manhattan – and most of them tried to get her attention. There was something else about this one particular man that made him special, made her want to see him again, have dinner with him, kiss him, go to bed with him for hours, days, weeks. There had just been – *something* that had passed between them, not just an awareness but almost as though she recognized him, knew him in some inexplicable way, had been waiting for him for a very long time.

'Too late, stupid,' she told herself angrily. 'When are you ever going to learn it's okay to act on your instincts once in awhile?'

It was nearly time to leave work for the day, and she wondered hopefully if she might possibly run into him again. She began to tidy up her desk and workspace, though unfortunately there wasn't all that much to organize these days.

She worked as an interior designer at one of Manhattan's most exclusive firms. It had been a real coup for someone so young to land such a plum job, but of course she had Gerard to thank for that. Sadly, she also had Gerard to blame for the lousy situation she currently found herself stuck in.

Gerard Landreaux had been friends with Julia's aunt Madelyn – Natalie's twin – since their college days at the Fashion Institute here in New York. Gerard had majored in interior design, while Aunt Maddy had studied fashion merchandising. They had remained fast friends ever since, going on thirty years now. It had been Gerard – whom Julia and Lauren had met many times over the years during visits to Aunt Maddy – who had ultimately influenced her to pursue a degree and career in interior design, convincing her it was more stable and less subject to wide changes in trends than the career as a fashion designer she'd originally considered. And it had been Gerard who had obtained the internship at his firm for her once she'd graduated from Cornell three years ago, and had offered her a permanent job after that. He had been her mentor, her friend and her boss, not necessarily in that order.

He'd shielded her from the cattiness and outright hostility displayed by his business partner - Vanessa Bradshaw. The older woman had taken an almost instant dislike to Julia, and had advised Gerard against taking her on. Fortunately, Julia hadn't had much contact with Vanessa, working almost exclusively under Gerard's direction.

Julia had fretted once to Gerard, not at all understanding why Vanessa disliked her so. "I mean, I can't think of anything I ever did or said to make her mad. Why in the world does she hate me so much?"

Gerard had chuckled, shaking his close-shaven head. "Oh, sweetie pie, do you want a list? Let's see – it's because of your face, body, wardrobe, age, talent, personality. Oh, and let's not forget the design award you won last month. Van's been in this business almost twenty years and has never won a damn thing. You're in less than a year and you've already got clients singing your praises and being nominated for awards."

Vanessa was, from all accounts, not a particularly talented designer and most of her client base was referrals from her wealthy family. And it was her family money that had initially funded the design firm, the only reason Gerard had ever agreed to working with her.

Vanessa's hostility aside, working for Manhattan Interiors had been a dream job for Julia these past two and a half years. Gerard had given her some small but interesting jobs to start with, then, as her reputation as an innovative designer became more widespread, the jobs became larger and more prestigious. When she won three design awards in two years, Julia had become even more sought after.

And then everything had changed a little less than four months ago. Gerard's longtime lover – Theo – had left him abruptly for a younger man, and Gerard had gone a little crazy as a result. Stating very dramatically – in true Gerard style – that his heart was broken into a million pieces and that he couldn't bear to stay in New York where there were too many memories of Theo, he had promptly sold his share of the business to Vanessa, rented out his midtown apartment, and moved back home to New Orleans to lick his wounds. Gerard had been far too emotionally wrecked when he left to smooth things over for Julia with Vanessa, and she'd been left at the mercy of the older woman, now her sole boss.

And the changes had been immediate and unpleasant. The assignments Julia now received were small, boring, and not the least bit challenging, mostly redecorating the bedrooms or living rooms for uptown society matrons. Vanessa reserved the really good jobs for herself or the two or three other designers who chose to kiss her ass, something Julia flat out refused to do. But from what Julia had overheard, some of those jobs hadn't pleased the clients and there had been complaints. Business had also dropped off some since Gerard's departure, and Julia knew it had been his reputation that had brought in a lot of clients.

But the other increasingly unpleasant aspect of her job in recent months had had been the frequent and unwelcome presence of Vanessa's newest boyfriend at the office. His name was Philip and he quite frankly gave Julia the creeps. She supposed he was good looking enough, though in a dark, swarthy way with over-tanned skin and too-white teeth that didn't appeal to her in the least. He wore too much gel in his slick-backed black hair and an almost sickening amount of cologne. Coupled with all the gold jewelry he wore, and the open-necked silk shirts he favored that displayed too much body hair, he reminded Julia of an aging gigolo. And very, very unfortunately, he was also extremely taken with

Julia. Nearly every time he was in the office, he sought her out and made some very suggestive comment or worse, tried to touch her. Julia had become quite adept at evading him, or at least making sure she wasn't alone when he was around.

Philip's presence in the office earlier today had, in fact, been the reason why she had been in Starbucks this morning. She'd seen him enter the office and had hastily grabbed her things and exited through a back door. When she had returned over an hour later he'd mercifully been gone.

Between the lousy assignments she'd been getting, Vanessa's hostility, and Philip's unwelcome attentions, Julia was more than ready to move on. She had, in fact, recently begun to polish up her resume and started researching other firms both in New York and other parts of the country. She loved New York and had thoroughly enjoyed living here the past three years. She adored the shopping, the restaurants, the museums and shows, the almost constant hum of activity and excitement. She had loved Manhattan since she was a small child and had paid regular visits over the years to her grandparents and Aunt Maddy. It had always been a cherished dream of hers to live in Manhattan, and that dream had become a reality after her college graduation from Cornell in upper state New York. And even though her apartment on the Upper East Side was teeny tiny, though still outrageously expensive to rent, she loved it.

But she was also homesick for her family home in northern California, and for her parents, sister and friends. Her parents lived in Carmel, where Julia had grown up, and Lauren had a small cabin in Big Sur where she lived when she wasn't traveling all over the world for her job as a National Geographic photographer. Julia wouldn't mind in the least if a new job brought her to San Francisco or Los Angeles so she could be closer to home and see her family more often than three or four times a year. And she had never been crazy about East Coast weather – cold and snowy in the winter months, hot and humid in the summer, and somewhat unpredictable the rest of the time.

As she walked slowly down Park Avenue towards the bus stop, she couldn't help but keep a watch out for the gorgeous man. But even though she'd known it to be a long shot, Julia couldn't help the overwhelming sense of disappointment she felt when he didn't appear and hoped that he hadn't already left town. It would be just her bad luck to have squandered the perfect opportunity to talk to him earlier today, and then to never see him again. One of these days, perhaps, she would finally learn to act on her instincts, maybe even to be impulsive once in awhile. Julia vowed that if she was lucky enough to see Mr. Gorgeous again that she would definitely act on her impulses this time around – impulses that were compelling her to wind her arms around his neck and plant a long, slow kiss on that very sexy mouth.

Chapter Three

"Hey, Nathan. You're having dinner with us tonight, aren't you? Dave made reservations for eight of us at Tao."

Nathan glanced up from the tumbler of scotch he'd been sipping at the sound of Rick's voice. "Sure, why not? That sounds great. Let's end our week here with an awesome meal."

Rick clapped him on the shoulder. "That's the spirit. Come on, let's get another drink before we head out. Might as well enjoy the free booze while it lasts."

They were attending the cocktail party that marked the official end of the five-day convention. Nathan was more than a little sorry to see the week draw to a close, for it meant a return to the daily grind of his job and the various stresses that accompanied it. He loved his chosen profession, was proud of co-owning a very successful firm, and grateful for all of the opportunities that had come his way. But all that success came with a price, and sometimes he wished he could take a few steps back to more fully enjoy the fruits of his labors.

However, his well-deserved break was nearly over and tomorrow he'd be flying back to San Francisco and his normal, hectic routine. At least he would have Sunday to sleep in, unpack and relax before the work week began anew. Unless, of course, Cameron already had expectations to go out somewhere on Sunday, plans that she hadn't yet shared with him. That was a particular habit of hers, one he didn't like at all, and something she tended to laugh away, claiming she was so busy that he couldn't possibly expect her to keep track of so many appointments and social events.

He was finishing up his third drink and starting to feel pleasantly mellow when his phone rang. He scowled slightly when he saw it was Cameron, but began to walk to a quieter corner as he answered the call.

"Hi, babe!" she greeted a little too enthusiastically, and he groaned inwardly. It was the cheerful, almost over the top tone she used when she wanted something.

"Hey, yourself," he replied neutrally. "What's going on since I talked with you – oh, let's see – about five hours ago?" He had given her a quick call at lunchtime.

She giggled, another sure sign that she was getting ready to butter him up for something. "Nothing special. I just missed you. Thinking I should have come along on this trip after all."

Nathan had actually been the one to suggest she accompany him to New York, especially after she'd made a big deal out of his being away for almost a week. Cameron loved New York – the shops, restaurants, night clubs and Broadway plays – but she hadn't wanted to see all of that by herself while he was occupied with convention business. She had also had a previously scheduled show at the art gallery that she – well, technically her parents – owned and had felt obliged to attend.

"Well, there'll be other trips. Like Hawaii in a couple of months, for example. Look, I don't mean to rush you, Cam, but I'm supposed to leave for dinner in a minute with a group." Nathan in fact could see Rick motioning to him that they were ready to leave and he mouthed "I'll meet you guys there in a few minutes."

"Okay, babe, I won't keep you long. I just wanted to let you know there are still seats available on the 7:30am flight out of JFK tomorrow morning. You could be here by noon and still have plenty of time to attend the hospital benefit with me. I know you're headed out but I'd be happy to change your flight for you if you just give me your info."

Nathan was dumbfounded. After all of the conversations and arguments they'd had on this particular subject, here was Cameron still on it less than twenty-four hours before his flight left.

He closed his eyes, took a deep breath, and replied as calmly as possible. "Thanks for checking, but I'm not going to fly out that early. We've discussed this like – a dozen times at least. I'm flying out at 2:00pm tomorrow and that's it."

There was silence at the other end for long seconds before she finally answered. "You seriously wouldn't suck it up and give up a few hours sleep to catch that earlier flight? Babe, you know how much I want to attend this event."

He sighed, running a hand through his hair. "There's no reason at all you can't attend alone. Your parents will be there, your sister, a bunch of your friends."

"Yes, and everyone will have their spouse or a date. Think how I'm going to feel being the only one there alone."

"I'm sorry, Cam, but this isn't anything new. I arranged to attend this convention a long time before you ever mentioned this ball."

"But it's important, Nathan," she whined. "This is one of the top social events of the year. I'll look pathetic if I show up alone."

Nathan pinched the bridge of his nose, feeling the beginnings of a headache coming on. "You won't look pathetic, for Christ's sake. And frankly, every damned event you want to attend is one of the top ones of the year. You're going to have to start resigning yourself to the fact that you aren't going to be able to attend them all."

"And what's that supposed to mean?" she demanded. The mounting anger in her voice was evident. "You think that once we're married we should sit home every weekend like a couple of old people and rent movies and eat popcorn? How boring does that sound?"

In actuality, it sounded great to Nathan, vastly preferable to getting dragged to another black-tie event where the only purpose in attending seemed to be impressing Cameron's friends with her latest gown and flaunting her handsome boyfriend.

"Cam, this really isn't the time to have this discussion, okay? I'm going to be late for dinner if I don't leave now. I'll call you from JFK tomorrow before my flight leaves, all right?"

He was again met with a stony silence for long seconds until she finally replied in a brittle tone. "So that's your final answer, huh? You're still going to take the afternoon flight?"

"Yes," he answered in a tired voice. "I'm probably going to be up late tonight and no way can I get up early enough to make a 7:30am flight."

"Fine," she snarled. "Thanks for nothing. Good night."

Nathan cursed vividly beneath his breath as Cameron abruptly disconnected the call. Angrily, he shoved his phone into his jacket pocket, still in disbelief that she had called him on this matter yet again. He knew she was royally pissed off, and would be sure to let him know about it when he got home. At the moment, though, he really didn't give a shit. Cameron had pissed him off, too, and he was getting damned tired of always being the one to concede and compromise in this relationship.

He was angry enough to order yet another drink before the bartender could close things up for the reception, and bolted it down in three quick gulps. Rick and the others had left over five minutes ago so he headed for the hotel exit as swiftly as possible, his quick pace fueled by the simmering anger he still felt at the call from Cameron. He really, really disliked being manipulated or controlled, and he had begun to notice more and more as of late that Cameron was trying very hard – in her own subtle ways – to do both of those things. He was starting to re-think this whole idea of the engagement, wondering not for the first time if it had come about for all the wrong reasons. Probably because he hadn't had a lot of experience in this whole long-term relationship thing, he'd allowed her to take the lead on far too many things and he was starting to feel hemmed in and resentful. When he got home it was going to be way past time to iron out some important details and assert himself more forcefully in this relationship.

Nathan was still extremely pissed off, the anger making him want to lash out at something, to take his aggression out somehow, as he reached the revolving front doors of the hotel that left him standing on Park Avenue. He wondered briefly as he stood there if he ought to skip dinner and go swim a bunch of laps in the hotel pool to take the edge off. Deciding against that idea, he turned and began walking down the street when he saw her again.

She was walking at a leisurely pace in his direction and hadn't seen him yet so he had a few seconds to admire how exquisitely beautiful she looked this evening. Her dress tonight was a sleeveless, form-fitting sheath with a bow embellishment on the square-cut neckline. It was a luscious shade of pale pink that reminded him of whipped strawberry mousse. She wore those sexy stilettos again, these in a pale gray with a little space cut out for her toes, and she carried a large gray leather bag. As she drew closer, he noted that her glorious hair fell in long, loose waves down her back – no ponytail today – and that her kissable, lushly fuckable mouth was glossed over in bubblegum pink. She was classy and seductive at the same time, the perfect combination of lady and siren. She was doing another excellent job of ignoring all the admiring stares being sent her way, and he was half afraid she'd walk right by without noticing him.

But then, as though she felt his intense gaze upon her, she looked up and saw him and took his breath away once again with her otherworldly beauty. He couldn't recall a time in his life when he'd ever wanted something as much as he wanted her at this moment. He forgot everything else that had happened earlier – the nasty argument with Cameron, the fact that he was supposed to be joining a group of friends for dinner, that his flight back home was leaving in less than twenty-four hours. All he saw was her, and all he wanted was to talk to her, touch her, be near her somehow. If he didn't do it now, she would slip away forever, and he knew he would always regret it.

Nathan walked towards her slowly, and she stood rooted in place, watching him. Then he was standing right in front of her, close enough to smell the light fragrance of her perfume, to see the tiny flecks of gold in her big green eyes, to realize that even with her sky-high heels the top of her shining head barely came to his shoulder.

He had trouble finding his voice, much less think of something clever to say, so he merely smiled and said, "Hello, again."

She returned his smile, giving him a glimpse of her perfectly straight white teeth. "Good evening."

They stood in silence for several seconds, blue eyes locked with green, sharing a knowing smile, until Nathan said half-jokingly, "We've got to stop meeting this way."

That evoked a soft laugh from her. "Except that we haven't actually met, have we?" she asked pointedly.

He grinned. "You're absolutely right, but that's a situation very easily remedied. I'm Nathan."

That he chose not to offer up his last name was not a conscious decision on his part – it simply didn't seem necessary at the moment. He did, however, offer her his hand which she took carefully. Her hand was small and dainty, the skin warm and smooth, and he closed his own hand over it firmly.

"Julia," was all she said in response.

He drew her hand to his lips, pressing a soft kiss to her palm, pleased to hear the little indrawn hiss of breath she took. "Hello, Julia. So we finally meet. I was afraid I wouldn't see you again."

"Me, too," she confessed in a shy, sweet voice. "I've looked for you running the past few mornings. We must have kept missing each other."

Nathan was startled by her admission, and greatly exultant that she had evidently been thinking of him, too. "Well, I suppose it's fate that we happened upon each other again tonight, isn't it?"

She squeezed his hand gently. "Or simply good luck. Whatever the cause, I'm glad it happened."

He turned his cheek into her palm, enjoying the feel of her hand against his skin. "So am I. Would you like to get a drink?"

"Yes." It thrilled him that she agreed without the slightest hesitation. "I'd love to have a drink with you, Nathan."

The sound of his name on her lips enthralled him, not that he could be anymore spellbound than he already was. He couldn't tear his eyes from her, gazing back at her with an odd sense of wonder, almost as if this wasn't really happening. It seemed very important to him somehow to maintain physical contact with her, almost as though he was afraid she'd slip away as suddenly as she'd appeared, that all of this was just a wonderful dream, so he slid a hand to the small of her back as he guided her inside the hotel.

"Are you staying here?" she asked as they walked inside the lobby.

He nodded. "Is this all right? I thought about getting a drink in the Champagne Bar."

Julia looked pleased at his suggestion. "That sounds lovely. The Plaza is one of my very favorite places. I've been coming here since I was a little girl. You know - tea at the Plaza and all. I used to love reading the Eloise books when I was a child."

He slid his arm around her waist, holding her firmly against his side. "Then I'm glad I brought you someplace with happy memories. Because I intend to give you more of them tonight."

She gasped softly at the unmistakable meaning of his words, and her big eyes went even wider. He was afraid for a moment that he'd scared her off, had moved a little too fast. But then she simply smiled and rested her head on his shoulder, leaning into him, and he automatically tightened his arm around her waist.

Nathan stifled a groan at the feel of her soft, curvy body pressed to his, his hand splayed against her hip, and her full, round breast rubbing against his arm. He was incredibly aroused, and he hadn't even begun to do all the sexy, dirty things that he'd daydreamed about the past few days. Just being next to her, holding her close against his side, was more than enough to make him hard as stone.

As they were waiting to be seated, Nathan heard his phone ping, signaling an incoming text. Julia smiled at him.

"It's okay if you need to answer that."

He hesitated, then belatedly remembered that he was supposed to be meeting Rick and the others for dinner.

"I'm sorry, this will just take a minute." He withdrew his phone from his jacket.

The text was from Rick, short and to the point. *Where r u?*

Smiling, Nathan quickly typed in a reply. *Got a better offer. Sorry to miss dinner.*

As expected, there was a reply mere seconds later. *The hot babe from Starbucks?*

He kept his answer short and sweet. *Yup.*

The waiter arrived to show them to their table, so Nathan wasn't able to look at Rick's response until they were seated at a small, intimate corner table. He had to suppress a chuckle when he read *You lucky SOB. Go for it, buddy. I'll want details.*

He'd be damned if he would give Rick or anyone else the tiniest detail about anything that might happen with Julia tonight. He'd known from the first minute of seeing her that she was not a casual fuck, not by a long shot. She was a rare and precious prize, a woman that every other man in this hotel – hell, in this entire city – would give his eye tooth to have. Whatever might happen between them tonight would be kept entirely private, the memories his alone to cherish. Julia might be hot as hell but she was also very much a lady, and worthy of being treated as such.

They had been seated in old-fashioned high-backed chairs that provided them with privacy from the other patrons, virtually closing them off into their own secluded corner. At Julia's request, Nathan ordered for them – two glasses of Perrier-Jouet and a small plate of fruit and cheese. They sipped champagne and nibbled on the food in silence, content to simply gaze at each other across the space of the small round table that separated them. He watched her take a small, ladylike sip of her drink, imagining those same plush lips wrapped around his cock instead of drinking from the flute. He desperately wanted those slim, graceful hands touching him everywhere, wanted to slowly peel that delectable pink dress from her body and see what awaited him beneath. He longed to yank her onto his lap right here in the bar and kiss her senseless.

But he also wanted to take this slowly, to savor every minute he could have with her, to make this evening that he hoped liked hell he'd be spending with her something very, very special. So he tampered down his raging erection, forced himself not to wonder if she wore panties or a thong, and merely took her hand in his.

He used his thumb to trace over her slender fingers, noticing that she kept her nails neatly tapered and covered in a clear polish. He liked that look, never having been a fan of long, pointed nails covered in bright red gloss. He noted that she wore no rings, her only jewelry a pearl bracelet and a matching pair of dainty drop earrings. God, she was gorgeous, her skin dewy smooth and glowing with youth. He longed to press a kiss to one of her cheeks, and especially to that tempting mouth, but settled instead for her hand.

"Your skin is so soft," he murmured.

"Mmm, it's all the hand cream I use," she admitted. "It's become sort of an addiction."

He grinned. "Better hand cream than a more serious vice." He brought her hand to his face again. "You're exquisite, but I'm sure men tell you that all the time."

Julia's cheeks grew charmingly pink. "Not quite as often as you might think. And not always as suavely as you just did."

Nathan raised a brow. "Suave? I'm not sure I've ever thought of myself that way."

"Hmm, maybe suave isn't the best choice of words. Smooth, perhaps? Definitely charming," she added with a smile.

He smiled back at her. "And you are utterly delightful. You remind me of the fairytale princesses in a storybook my mother used to read to my brothers and me when we were very young. I don't remember the name of the book, I'm certain she must have given it away a long time ago. But I remember it had the most incredible illustrations – the colors and details were really special. And I remember thinking that the princesses couldn't possibly be real people because they were too beautiful for that. You look just like one of those storybook princesses, Julia."

She stared at him with wonder in her eyes, bringing their clasped hands to her cheek and turning her face into his palm, pressing a soft kiss there. "What a lovely thing to say," she whispered. "I think that's the most romantic thing anyone has ever said to me."

"It's true. You're almost too beautiful to be real." He brushed his thumb over her mouth until her lips parted. He slid the pad of his thumb inside her warm, lush mouth and hissed sharply when she sucked it deeper, her tongue wrapping around it. The sensation it evoked went straight to his groin, and he was instantly hard. He couldn't ever remember being this hot, this aroused before, and he hadn't even kissed or touched her yet.

The unspoken attraction between them was unmistakable. He had never come close to feeling this sort of instant bond with a woman, as though he'd known her for years instead of mere minutes. They stared at each other across the small expanse of the table, their fingers entwined. No words passed between them for long seconds, but speaking wasn't really necessary at this point. He knew from the look in her big eyes that she was every bit as aware of him as he was of her, and that she felt the same sort of irresistible physical connection. Her plush, glossy lips trembled slightly, and all he could think about was kissing her senseless, just before running his hands over the seductive curves of her lush breasts and that perfect little ass.

"Are you finished with your drink?" he asked hoarsely, painfully aware that his erection was straining against the fly of his trousers.

Julia picked up the flute and drank down the rest of the champagne smoothly. "I am now."

"Do you want another glass?"

She shook her head. "No, thank you."

"Dinner?"

Another shake of her head. "I'm not the least bit hungry. Not for dinner, anyway."

Nathan closed his eyes briefly, the husky, suggestive tone of her voice unbearably arousing, and the meaning behind her words unmistakable. "Then let's get out of here. I don't want to waste even one minute of this night."

He left several bills on the table, pushed back his chair, and helped her to her feet. He was tempted – oh, so tempted – to haul her into his arms and kiss her hard, but instead merely slid an arm around her waist and guided her out of the bar.

He whispered in her ear, "I hope you know I plan on ravishing you. For hours and hours. If that's not what you want, say so right now."

Julia reached up, giving the side of his neck an erotic little lick that made him gasp, before whispering back, "That's what I've been wanting since I saw you on the sidewalk four days ago."

Nathan groaned, burying his face in her glorious hair. "Come on then, baby. We've already wasted too much time."

✴✴✴✴✴

Julia was almost breathless with anticipation as Nathan escorted her out of the Champagne Bar and across the crowded hotel lobby. She'd been almost giddy with excitement ever since they had had yet another chance encounter out on the sidewalk a short time ago, grateful that her silent prayers had been answered and that they had seen each other again. She had been so afraid that she'd blown two such opportunities, and would never have the chance to see the breathtakingly handsome man again. As if to make sure he couldn't slip away from her, she laid a palm on his chest as he kept her close to his side. She could feel his body heat through the fine cotton of his shirt, as well as the steady beating of his heart. She knew her own heart was racing overtime in anticipation of what was yet to come tonight.

She had been well aware that by consenting to have a drink with him that she'd really been agreeing to much, much more, and that thought had thrilled her. This wasn't something she did – ever. The very few sexual relationships in her life had all been carefully considered and had taken at least a bit more time to develop. One-night stands were definitely not her thing, and going off with a virtual stranger wasn't something she'd ever contemplated doing prior to tonight. But then she'd never been as wildly, inexplicably attracted to a man before as she'd been to Nathan. She just knew somehow that if she didn't explore this overwhelming attraction she would always regret it.

Nathan paused before they reached the bank of elevators, looking suddenly thoughtful. "I just realized I don't have any condoms in my room. Do we need to stop at the gift shop?"

Julia shook her head. "It's okay. I just got a Depo-Provera shot a couple of weeks ago. And an exam, so everything's good with me."

He looked relieved. "I checked out clean at my last physical a few months ago, too, but I can still pick up some condoms if it makes you feel safer."

Impulsively, she reached up and pressed a kiss to the corner of his mouth, touched by his thoughtfulness. "No, don't. I trust you, Nathan."

His arm tightened about her waist and he made a harsh sound deep in his throat. "You're playing with fire here, baby. Let's get upstairs before I do something to get us kicked out of this fancy hotel."

They weren't alone in the elevator, joined by an older couple and two attractive, well-dressed women in their late thirties or early forties. Julia noticed the covetous glances they stole at Nathan, and she snuggled a little closer against him as if staking her claim and warning the two women off. If he was at all aware of them he gave zero indication, and only tightened his arm around her waist, nuzzling his face into her hair.

The women got off on the ninth floor, but not before throwing one final, inviting look in Nathan's direction. He paid them not the slightest attention, all of his focus on her alone, and this thrilled her. She was so hyper-aware of him at the moment – of his clean, masculine scent, the warmth of his body against hers, the hardness of his unmistakable erection as it pressed against her hip. If it wasn't for the presence of the other couple in the elevator, Julia would have been sorely tempted to pull his mouth down to hers for a long, wet kiss. She contented herself with resting her head against his broad shoulder, and clutching his arm against her side.

As the elevator stopped on the fourteenth floor, Nathan guided her out and down the wide, carpeted hallway to his room, his hand at the small of her back. He released her momentarily to fish the card key from his pocket and open the door.

"After you," he murmured, the first thing he'd said since before getting in the elevator.

Julia walked slowly inside the hotel room, hearing the click and lock of the door behind her. The designer in her would normally have noticed the furnishings, the colors, the layout of the room, but tonight none of those things interested her. Instead, what drew her attention was the magnificent view of Manhattan from the wide window, all of the buildings lit up as twilight began to descend on the city. She automatically dropped her purse on a chair and went to gaze out the window.

"What an amazing view," she said with a sigh.

She felt Nathan come up behind her, his hands drifting softly to her shoulders, pulling her back against his firmly muscled body. His breath caused the hairs at the back of her neck to stand on end, and she repressed the little shiver that wanted to ripple through her whole body.

"Hmm, I've been too busy the last few days to enjoy it much. And now I find myself too caught up in looking at you to pay the view any attention." He nuzzled his nose into her hair and she had to stifle a low gasp, already so aroused just by being close to him that she could feel the reaction deep in her core.

Julia closed her eyes as his hands slid down her bare arms to wrap around her waist, his fingers splaying over her belly as he pulled her even closer against him. "I like looking at you, too. So did those two women in the elevator."

He chuckled. "I didn't even notice them, so don't be jealous. You're the only woman I see, Julia, the only one I want. And I can't believe how lucky I am that of all the men you must ignore on a daily basis that you actually noticed me. And I'm going to make very, very sure that you don't regret singling me out of all your many admirers. In fact, I intend to make you forget any other man exists after tonight."

"Ahh." She gave a little moan as his lips traced a slow, delicious path up the side of her neck to her ear. His teeth tugged lightly on the lobe before his tongue traced slow, deliberate circles around the shell. His mouth continued to press soft, lingering kisses along her cheek, her jaw, coming teasingly close to the corner of her mouth. This time she couldn't repress the shiver that ran through her from head to toe and back up again, and she felt her nipples instantly grow hard in response.

"Do you want a drink?"

She shook her head at his whispered question, trying to suppress the little tremors that continued to ripple up and down her spine at his gentle but seductive kisses. "No. The only thing I want is you. I've wanted you since the first moment I saw you on the street outside."

Nathan groaned at her softly spoken words, running his hands through the long, silky strands of her hair. "God, you're so sweet, so open. I've never wanted anything as much as I want you, sweet Julia. Turn around now so I can kiss you, baby."

She willingly turned to face him, sliding her arms up around his neck a split second before his mouth claimed hers in a long, searching kiss.

Julia had never been kissed like that before – with a hunger so deep and profound it felt like he was consuming her. He threaded his hands into her hair, holding her head still as he feasted on her mouth – catching her full lower lip with his teeth, biting it gently, and then running his tongue over her upper lip before plunging it back inside her mouth. She clutched at his shoulders as her legs grew wobbly beneath the fierce demands of his deep kisses, and he began to bend her backwards against his arms. At first she didn't realize the low moans she heard were actually escaping from her own throat, the sounds increasing in volume as he continued to plunder her mouth with his tongue. He let out a low growling noise as she sucked at his tongue, every bit as hungry for him as he was for her. He was embracing her so tightly, pulling her so closely against his hard body, that her feet nearly left the ground.

He walked her backwards until she was pressed against the wall, still kissing her as he leaned into her, letting her feel the unmistakable bulge of his erection. She whimpered beneath his kisses as he deliberately rubbed himself against her cleft, where she was already so wet and ready she thought incoherently that she could come just like that with no further contact. Wanting more, she slid her hand to his crotch, palming him, almost recoiling at how huge and hard he felt.

Nathan groaned, grabbing her wrist. "Fuck. Don't do that. Not now. I'm too horny for you to be able to touch me like that, baby. And as good as this feels, I need to make it last as long as I can. So be a good girl and no touching until I say so." He drew both of her hands over her head, pinning them firmly in place against the wall as he kissed her again. She squirmed beneath him, more aroused than she could ever recall, and growing desperate to climax, needing more than he was giving her. It wasn't always easy or quick for her to have orgasms, but right now she sensed that it would take very little to send her spiraling over the edge. She couldn't ever remember being this wet, or her breasts feeling so swollen and achy, her nipples hard and pressing against the too-tight confines of her bra.

"Please." She barely recognized the throaty whisper as her own voice. "Oh, please, Nathan. I want you so much."

He was kissing her ear again, his tongue tracing erotic little patterns all around it while he continued to slowly grind his erection against the notch of her thighs. "Shh, baby. It's all right. I'm going to give you what you want soon. You're not ready yet."

She made an indecipherable sound of protest, wanting to grab his hands and bring them to her swollen, aching breasts or between her legs where she was throbbing with need, but he continued to hold her trapped in place. "I am ready. I'm so ready."

He chuckled, caressing her flushed cheek, holding her hands captive with just one of his own. "So impatient. So eager. We have all night, baby. Hours and hours to touch and kiss and fuck. Lots of time for me to make you come over and over again. I'm going to make you come harder and longer than you've ever imagined, Julia. You'll be totally ruined for anyone else after tonight."

She was panting now, his deeply erotic words a huge turn-on, not that she needed any further stimulus. Nathan smiled deliberately, his handsome features a darkly sensual mask. "Look at you, baby. So fucking hot, so turned on. And I haven't even touched you yet. Tell me, Julia. Are you wet?"

Her head fell back against the wall as she rasped out, "Yes. God, yes. Please. Nathan, I need you inside of me. Touch me, please."

He ran a finger down the bridge of her nose and across her lips. "Soon, baby. I promise. And it's going to be so good. I'm going to make you feel incredible, do all sorts of wicked things to this gorgeous body." He tugged playfully at the bow on the front of her dress. "This sexy little bow reminds me of unwrapping presents. Except that you're the best present a man could ever dream of." He slipped his finger inside her mouth, hissing as she ran her tongue up and down its length.

"You're going to do that to my cock later," he told her, his eyes glittering almost dangerously. "You're going to run that tempting little tongue up and down my dick before I fuck this sexy mouth and come hard down your throat."

"Let me do it now," she begged, as he withdrew his finger.

Nathan shook his head. "Uh, uh. Now it's time for me to start unwrapping my present."

He reached behind her, finding the zipper of her dress, and lowering it slowly, one maddening inch at a time. Julia's mouth quivered, and she was dimly aware that the moisture from her drenched underwear was beginning to seep down the insides of her thighs. She was growing desperate for relief, for release, and moaned softly as she rubbed her thighs together.

Nathan's hands on her hips stilled her frantic efforts. "No. Stop it, Julia. I know what you're trying to do. But I'm the only one who gets to give you an orgasm. Now, be a good girl and let me finish unwrapping my present."

She closed her eyes as he finished unzipping her dress before tugging the garment down her arms and past her hips until it hit the floor. He held her steady as she stepped out of it, and then drew her away from the wall as he looked at her, circling around her once, twice, until he was standing in front of her again.

Julia loved beautiful, ultra-feminine lingerie, and the set she wore tonight was one of her favorites. The pink and cream striped demi-bra, with the side insets of cream lace, pushed her already full breasts into centerfold-like proportions. The lacy pink boy shorts managed to be sexy and comfortable at the same time. Most of the year she liked to wear stockings – with or without a garter belt – but summers in New York were too hot and humid to comfortably endure hosiery so her legs were bare tonight. She offered up a quick thanks that she'd taken extra care the previous evening to shave and moisturize them, and had given herself a pedicure as well, painting her nails a dainty shade of pink.

Nathan still hadn't spoken but she could hear the ragged intake of his breath and slowly opened her eyes. He was staring at her transfixed, his mouth gaping open, his cheeks flushed. Her gaze dropped briefly to his crotch, where his erection looked about ready to burst the seam of his trousers. Her mouth went suddenly dry at the thought of that superb cock fucking her hard, riding her until she came over and over again, and she felt herself growing even wetter.

He spoke then, if one could call his harsh, almost guttural words speech. "Fuck, Julia. You're beyond beautiful. You're a goddamn fucking goddess. Jesus, look at you. I feel like I should kneel down and worship you."

Julia was almost shaking with need. "God, Nathan. Don't make me wait any longer. You're making me crazy."

He slid his hands up her bare arms, ignoring her impassioned plea. "Your skin is like satin," he whispered. "So soft, all pink and cream. Just like this sexy bra. I love the way it pushes your tits up, offering them up like some delicious dessert. I'm going to taste them now."

He pressed hot, open-mouthed kisses starting at the base of her throat, travelling across her collarbone, and finally down to the lush upper curves of her breasts. She gasped as his hands cupped her, his thumbs brushing over her taut, throbbing nipples. Julia threaded her hands into his thick, dark brown hair as he worshipped her breasts, running his tongue up and down the deep V between them. She clutched his head to her, elated that her hands were finally free to touch him, urging his mouth ever closer to her breasts.

"Ohhh, yes," she groaned, as he finally slid two fingers inside one shallow bra cup, finding the engorged nipple and twisting it. He repeated the action on her other breast until she was squirming, the sensation a heady mixture of pain and pleasure.

"Let me, baby," he murmured, reaching behind her to unhook the bra and letting the firm, creamy globes of her breasts tumble free into his eager palms. He lifted one lush, round breast up and took the hard pink nipple into his mouth, suckling her hungrily and drawing a long, low cry from her throat. Julia thought wildly that nothing had ever felt so good before, and she could happily let him feast on her breasts for hours. She was pretty sure that if he kept this up just a bit longer that she could come long and hard. Her breasts had always been super-sensitive and Nathan seemed to be very aware of this fact.

"Your breasts are beautiful, Julia," he breathed. "I love how they feel in my hands, how firm and full and soft. And they're very sensitive, aren't they, baby? I'll bet if I keep sucking these pretty pink nipples that you'll come, won't you?"

He licked one nipple, flicking his tongue over it hard and fast, then with maddening slowness. She was almost dizzy with sensation, more aroused than she could have ever imagined, every touch of his hands threatening to send her over the edge. She threaded her hands deeper into his thick hair, cradling his face against her breasts as he continued to suck her nipples, each hungry pull of his lips reverberating through her body all the way to her womb.

"Yes. God, yes. Keep doing that, please," she begged. "It feels so good, Nathan. Make me come this way, please."

"Don't come. Not yet," he instructed, and lifted his head from her breasts.

She almost cried out in frustration, needing release so badly, her body over-stimulated by his kisses and caresses. "Nathan, you have to - " she gasped, trying to pull his head back to her breasts.

"Hush, baby. I'm going to take care of you," he soothed. "Let's see just how ready you are."

He slid two fingers under the low waistband of her lacy boy shorts, dipping briefly into her navel, and then plunging into the slick, dripping wet folds of her slit.

Julia cried out while Nathan swore softly. "Fuck, baby, you're so wet and juicy. I want to lick up all that delicious juice, slide my tongue up inside you and eat you up."

He slid his entire hand inside her panties, cupping her with his palm. "But you've been a very naughty girl, Julia. You got these pretty panties all wet. Now I'm going to have to take them off of you."

Nathan sunk to his knees, hooking his thumbs in the waistband of the boy shorts, tugging them down her legs, and helping her step out of them. When she moved to kick off one shoe, he held her ankle still. "Leave them on," he ordered. "These sexy as fuck shoes. I want you wearing them when you wrap these gorgeous legs around me while I'm fucking you for the first time."

Julia's legs trembled, loving the way he talked dirty to her, as well as the way he was taking complete control of their foreplay, even dominating it. And then she was gasping, gripping his shoulders tightly as he slid two fingers back inside her, fucking her with them slowly and deliberately, as his thumb circled her ultrasensitive clit. The intense awareness and arousal that had been building inside of her ever since she'd met him on the street, and that he had been consistently stoking with his demanding kisses and expert caresses, suddenly burst to overflowing. The orgasm that flooded her body was the strongest and hardest she'd ever experienced, just as Nathan had promised. He wrapped his arms around her thighs, pressing his cheek against her belly, and held her as she continued to quiver in the aftermath.

"Damn, baby, you're so responsive," he said, almost in disbelief. "I barely had to touch you and you went off. Mmm, it's going to be fun to see how many times I can make you come. You're going to be wrung out by the time I'm finished." He nuzzled his face into the soft, damp tangle of her light brown pubic hair. "Time for round two."

She cried out helplessly, her hands tangling in his thick hair, as he licked at her slick, wet folds. He parted her swollen labia with his thumbs, holding her open as he licked her up like a cat would cream. Julia's breath came out in short, gasping pants as he continued to eat her out thoroughly, and she was half-afraid her legs would give out from under her. His tongue delved deep into the very core of her, thrusting in and out while one thumb skimmed back and forth over her clit, driving her crazy with the sensations. Then it was his tongue – that talented, wicked tongue - flicking over the distended little nub before biting down on it, sucking it hard, and this time she screamed his name as she came.

He slid back up her body, wrapping her in his arms and holding her close, soothing her as her body shuddered. "That's my beautiful girl," he crooned. "Such a sexy, responsive little temptress you are. And you smell and taste delicious, too. I want you to taste yourself, baby."

He kissed her then, a wet, open-mouthed kiss that bruised her already swollen lips. She could taste the salty muskiness of her own juices on his tongue and wound herself more closely against him. The realization that she was completely nude, save for her shoes, while he was still fully clothed, made her feel like a wanton harem girl, and she was more than anxious to get him naked.

Julia tugged on his tie. "You've got too many clothes on," she pouted. "It's not fair. I want to see you, too."

He shrugged out of his suit jacket, tossing it on a chair, and spread his arms. "Then undress me, baby. You're in charge now."

She smiled, liking that thought, and that she could tease and torture him with the same seductive slowness he'd just done with her. "Okay. First, let's get rid of this." She deftly unfastened his tie and let it fall to the floor.

"The shirt next."

She undid the buttons one at a time with deliberate slowness. Nathan's eyes were glittering, his breath starting to hitch as she continued her progress. She tugged the shirt from his pants and pushed it off him, gasping with delight as she bared his torso.

"What a beautiful man you are," she whispered, running her palms over the hard, defined muscles of his chest and abs, then back up his arms to his broad, strong shoulders and down to his bulging biceps. Julia leaned in and nuzzled the side of his neck, breathing in the clean masculine scent that was a combination of soap, shave cream and sweat. Imitating his previous actions, she trailed soft, moist kisses down his jaw and throat and continued past his chest. She ran her tongue over each flat male nipple, enjoying the sound of his indrawn hiss, and loving the feel of his heart beating in wild rhythm beneath her palm. Her hands moved to his back, her fingers splaying over the muscles she found there, as her mouth continued its descent until it stopped at his waist.

"Now these." She tugged at the waistband of his trousers. "Let me," she instructed as his hands would have begun to unbuckle his belt.

Nathan kicked off his shoes and toed off his socks as Julia unbuckled his belt with aggravating slowness. He growled a warning as she rubbed her breasts against his bare chest, the erect nipples boring into his hot skin. Smiling naughtily, she unbuttoned his pants and began to slide the zipper down very, very carefully, its rasp the only sound in the room save for Nathan's increasingly ragged breathing.

She tugged the fine fabric down his legs as she knelt, waiting for him to step out of his pants, before taking a page from his book of seduction and running her hands up the back of his well-muscled calves and powerful thighs until she reached his crotch.

His cock was standing at full attention, pushing at the too-tight confines of his dark blue briefs. Julia smiled up at him, elated to see the glitter of his light blue eyes, the flaring of his nostrils, the dark flush on his cheeks, and knew that he was immensely aroused. She slipped her fingers inside the low waistband of his underwear, and glanced at him with big, innocent eyes.

"May I?" she asked huskily.

He bit his lip. "You may do whatever the fuck you want, baby, as long as it involves my cock being inside that hot mouth of yours within the next twenty seconds."

"Tsk, tsk. So impatient," she scolded mockingly. "Where's your control? I thought you wanted to take this slow."

He grabbed a handful of her hair and yanked her head back, staring down at her with a dangerous smolder in his eyes. "You have no idea how much control I've had to use tonight. I was ready to come when I kissed you the first time, and I've been on the edge every minute since," he whispered gutturally. "Now be a good girl and do what I asked you to do when you were licking my finger."

Julia felt a thrill go through her at the commanding, domineering tone of his voice, liking this side of him and finding it incredibly arousing. "Yes, sir," she murmured in what she hoped was an obedient voice.

She peeled the snug fitting underwear from his body, freeing his enormously erect cock. Julia licked her lips as she ran her slender hands lightly over his pulsing length, but it was more than enough to make him jump and his breath to expel in a long, slow hiss. At the first flick of her tongue over the broad head of his penis, Nathan groaned. She ran her tongue up and down the heavy, thick length of him, long, slow strokes followed by quick, butterfly-like flutters. A thick drop of pre-cum oozed from the tip and she daintily licked it off before plunging her tongue deep into the slit.

"Fuck!" cursed Nathan vividly, his hands threading into her hair. "Open your mouth, Julia. This isn't going to take very long, baby."

Her lips parted and a second later he thrust himself hard into her wet, welcoming mouth. The head of his dick battered against the back of her throat and she had to force herself not to tense up as his thrusts grew deeper and faster. His harsh groans were the most erotic sound she'd ever heard, and she felt herself growing wetter, her nipples hardening. She slid one hand to lightly fondle his swollen balls, and that slight pressure was more than enough to send him over the edge, crying out her name and holding her head still as he spurted hot, salty cum into her mouth, filling her until she had to swallow. She couldn't swallow all of it fast enough, and could feel his semen escape from her lips, running down her chin until she could wipe it off.

She sank to the floor by his feet, her head resting on his thighs as he shuddered repeatedly from his release. Then Nathan slid to the carpeted floor beside her, gathering her into his arms.

"You are extraordinary," he whispered into her hair, pushing the damp strands from her forehead and pressing kisses to her temple. "Gorgeous and sexy and you respond so beautifully, baby. And you make me crazy for you. I don't think I could ever get enough of this hot body." He slid his hand up her hip all the way to one full, swollen breast, his thumb brushing over the nipple.

Julia bit her bottom lip, her head drooping to his shoulder as be bent and licked the other nipple. She rubbed her palm over his taut, defined abs. "I feel the same way. I'm ready for more." She leaned in and pressed a kiss just below his ear. "Take me to bed, Nathan. I need you inside of me."

Chapter Four

Nathan grew instantly hard at her sweetly murmured words, despite the fact he'd just spilled himself almost violently into that sexy mouth of hers mere minutes before, coming harder than he could ever remember doing. He scooped her up into his arms and carried her the short distance to the big, king-sized bed, tumbling them onto the plush pillow-top mattress. Julia wound herself around him, her arms about his neck, legs tangling with his, and those spectacular breasts crushed up against him. He groaned at the feel of all that creamy, satiny skin entwined with his, and bent his head to claim her mouth in a long, leisurely kiss. She kissed him back with a little "mmm" sound, which he found really, really sexy. Her tongue made arousing little licks at his mouth, driving him half-mad until he gripped her chin and held her still so he could kiss her harder. Everything about this woman was so fucking sexy, from her face to her body to the little noises she made, and especially in the way she kissed and touched him. He'd never, ever been this aroused before, this hungry, and felt the overwhelming urge to lose himself in her for as long as he possibly could.

He slipped his hand down her body, past the adorable little curve of her belly, and into the soft nest of her pubic hair. He was pleased that she didn't shave or wax that area, not particularly liking when women did that. He preferred it when they were natural like Julia, and especially when their sweet, delectable pussies were as slick and hot as hers.

She gasped as he slid two fingers inside of her and he smiled. "Mmm, so sweet and juicy already," he crooned. "Like a ripe peach. I'd love to taste you again, baby. But first my cock wants a turn."

She smiled sultrily. "Then I think it should have one. A nice long turn. And speaking of long."

"Jesus Christ!" he gulped, as her small, slim hand took hold of his dick and began to stroke him slowly, with tantalizing precision. She ran her hand up and down the entire length of his cock, cupping his balls, then sliding up until her thumb could flick over the slit at the head. He was so hard that it was difficult to remember he'd just had a mind-blowing orgasm mere minutes ago. But Julia was so hot, so arousing, that he feared he could never get his fill of her, that he'd be perpetually hard just by being next to her.

He rolled her underneath him, then rose up on his knees, pausing to gaze down at Julia and how beautiful she looked – her glorious hair splayed out on the pillow; eyes heavy-lidded with desire; her mouth half-open as she breathed in shallow pants; those round, tempting breasts thrusting up at him; her legs sweetly parted in welcome. Nathan groaned, and ran a hand down from her throat, between her tits, over her belly, to her thigh, noticing that her creamy skin was flushed pink with arousal. He lifted one leg over his shoulder, running his hand down her calf to where she still wore the sexy gray stilettos.

"I want to fuck you this way," he told her bluntly. "Tell me if it's too deep."

In reply, Julia merely took hold of his cock and guided him to the slick opening to her body. He needed no further invitation, and slid inside of her in one smooth stroke. She gasped as he buried himself as deeply inside of her as possible, and he closed his eyes, remaining completely still for long seconds as he savored the feel of his bare cock sheathed in her hot, tight core. She felt like wet velvet around him, and it was the absolute best feeling in the entire fucking world.

He grit his teeth fiercely, almost afraid to move. "God, you're so tight around me, baby. Tell me if I'm hurting you this way."

Slowly, he began to move in and out of her, withdrawing about halfway before easing back in. From Julia's little moans of pleasure each time he did so, he guessed it felt as amazing to her as it did to him. With each slow, measured thrust he filled her a little more, until he was buried to the root, fully sheathed inside her of her enticing body. Then, as he deliberately slid back out almost to the tip, she startled him by lifting her other leg over his shoulder, crossing her ankles one over the other behind his neck.

"Fuck," he hissed, as he slid all the way back inside of her, burying himself to the balls. This position brought him so deep inside of her it felt like they were co-joined.

"Oh, baby," he murmured, running his hands up and down her legs. "You are so hot, you feel so good, so tight. Nothing has ever felt this fucking good before. I need to fuck you harder, Julia, but it's so deep this way. I don't want to hurt you."

She locked her ankles tighter around his neck, pulling him in even deeper. "You won't," she whispered. "Come on, Nathan. Do me hard and fast."

He let out a long, low groan before sliding his hands under her buttocks and lifting her slightly off the mattress. He pulled out of her nearly to the tip of his cock, only to slam back into her hard. She screamed and he hesitated, but only briefly before gradually picking up the pace of his thrusts. He stared down at her face, watching for any signs of pain or discomfort, but only saw the sensual pleasure etched on her features. Her eyes were tightly shut, her cheeks flushed pink, her lush mouth a perfect 'O'. She was gripping handfuls of the bed linens, holding on tight as he rode her hard. She was so beautiful it made his chest hurt and all of a sudden it was critical for him to share eye contact.

"Look at me," he ordered. "Open your eyes, Julia, and watch me."

Obediently, her big eyes fluttered open and she gazed up at him with a dazed expression. "Nathan," was all she could summon up, but the sound of her sweet, husky voice was all it took to send him teetering to the brink. Sweat poured freely from his brow as he fucked her like a madman, his body pistoning in and out of her in a frenzy, desperate now to bring them both to fulfillment.

"Oh, God, oh, God!" she cried, just before he felt her tight little cunt convulse around him, her head falling back in surrender as she let the orgasm rocket through her. The sight of her release was all he needed to send him into oblivion, and he called out her name in one long, drawn-out moan as he spilled himself into her, his body shaking with the force of his climax.

Nathan felt like he'd just run the fastest mile of his life as he collapsed onto the bed next to her, his arm flung limply over her torso. Both of them laid that way for several minutes, too wrung out to speak or think, or do anything but let their heart rates slowly return to normal. He'd never, ever, had sex that intense before, couldn't remember ever coming so hard, and had never felt quite as satisfied and replete as he did as this particular moment. Even now, his body was still shuddering with the force of his release, his legs shaking and his breathing labored. He was both physically and emotionally drained, and yet he still felt an overwhelming sense of hunger for this beautiful, sensual creature whose limbs were still entwined with his.

He heard Julia give a little sigh of contentment, and he opened one eye to watch as she turned on her side towards him, burrowing into the pillow. Her eyes were shut, and she looked exhausted, though a satisfied little half-smile played around her lips. Unable to keep his hands off of her for long, he reached over to caress her hip before capturing her mouth in a soft, sweet kiss.

She opened her eyes, and the look of slumberous desire in them made his breath catch in his throat. She stroked his cheek with one slender hand, and he couldn't resist pressing a kiss into her palm.

"That was – " she paused, giving her head a little shake. "I've never had sex like that before. It was – consuming."

He eased her head to his shoulder, kissing her forehead. "It was fucking amazing is what it was. I've never come that hard or that long before, Julia. Like my life force was being sucked out of me."

She ran her index finger over his jaw and then up over his mouth. "You were right earlier," she said quietly.

"About what, baby?"

She rose up on an elbow and gazed down at him. "About ruining me for other men. I can't imagine ever feeling like that with anyone else but you. I've never - "

He tilted up her chin when she looked away shyly. "Never what?"

Her eyes were shining and her mouth trembled a little. "I've never had such intense orgasms before," she whispered. "It – I don't often have orgasms, actually, it isn't easy for me to come. I always figured it was me, that I just wasn't responsive enough, or that somehow I was doing something wrong. But it's so different with you. You've already made me come three times tonight, almost without any effort at all, and each one was stronger than the last." She leaned down and kissed him. "Thank you."

Nathan groaned and enfolded her in his arms. "Oh, God, Julia. It was my pleasure as much as yours. And you are the sexiest, most responsive woman I've ever known. If you haven't been able to have orgasms easily in the past, it certainly wasn't because of you." He buried his face in her hair and murmured, "And this night is far from over. I plan on giving you more orgasms, sweet Julia. As many as you can stand."

She wound her arms and legs around his, trying to get as close as possible. "Mmm, that sounds delightful. But I think you're going to have to feed me before you try. I feel like a wet noodle right now. I'm not sure I can move, much less stand up."

He grinned. "And you've worn me out, you insatiable little minx. So let's get ourselves fed so we can play some more."

✳✳✳✳✳

Julia shook her head as Nathan offered to refill her glass yet again with the deliciously chilled Prosecco he'd ordered from room service to accompany their meal.

"No more for me, thanks. I'll be too sleepy in a few minutes if I have any more to drink."

He raised a brow, and filled his glass with the sparkling wine instead. "Well, we can't have that, can we? I still have plans for you while the night is young."

Her nipples instantly hardened beneath his white dress shirt that she'd pulled on when their food had arrived. A quick glance at the bedside clock showed that it was barely ten o'clock, and she wondered briefly how many more times he could reasonably be expected to perform tonight, given that he'd already come hard twice this evening. With her limited past experiences, she'd never had a lover who was good for more than two orgasms in one night. By the way Nathan's blue eyes had begun to glitter, however, she had a feeling – a very, very good one – that he was more than ready for the next round.

The food he'd ordered – an interesting potpourri of a Portobello mushroom flatbread pizza, lobster mac and cheese, and white and milk chocolate covered strawberries – had done wonders to revive her after their very physical and exhausting lovemaking. She'd had just enough Prosecco to feel a slight, pleasant buzz, while still being extremely aware of the gorgeous, half-naked man seated just across from her.

And as she gazed at Nathan across the small corner table where they sat, she felt herself growing wet again, her nipples hardening merely from looking at him. He looked ridiculously sexy wearing just a low-slung pair of sweat pants, his beautifully defined chest and shoulders bare. His thick brown hair was mussed, and the dark stubble on his face lent him a rather roguish look. He was, as she'd told him earlier, a beautiful man in both face and body, and she couldn't tear her eyes from him. She resisted the urge to lick her lips as her gaze continued to rove over his muscular arms and torso, before dropping to his crotch where his erection was already beginning to tent his pants. Evidently just looking at her was enough to arouse him, too.

He watched her in an almost predatory manner as he sipped his wine slowly and deliberately, neither of them saying a word. His gaze traveled from her tousled hair and flushed cheeks to her trembling mouth before dipping to her chest. He smiled knowingly at the sight of her nipples poking unmistakably against his shirt, but only refilled his glass yet again, emptying the bottle this time. Julia was nearly quivering in arousal as he continued to sip his wine leisurely, seemingly in no hurry whatsoever to satisfy his rather obvious need for her body. When he finally finished the last of the wine, he set the glass down and pushed his chair back from the table.

"Come here."

The softly spoken words were a command, not a request, and Julia got to her feet slowly, walking over to his chair on shaky legs. She tried not to shiver at the intensity she saw in his eyes, their gazes remaining locked as she stood in front of him. She was helpless to say no to him, to resist whatever he told her to do. This was all new to her, for the few previous lovers she'd been with had all treated her like she was something fragile and delicate. But she knew instinctively that she wouldn't be able to deny Nathan whatever he wanted from her, and already had firsthand experience with his physical, demanding lovemaking. He had her spellbound, and she would do his bidding eagerly.

"Take the shirt off."

A bit clumsily, she unbuttoned his shirt and let it pool at her feet, standing before him proudly nude. She suppressed a satisfied smile when she heard his sharp inhale, knowing that the sight of her naked body was arousing him.

Nathan's hands settled on her hips, pulling her closer towards him before skimming up the sides of her torso to cup her breasts. Julia couldn't stifle her gasp of pleasure as he kneaded her breasts roughly, twisting the nipples until she was whimpering in arousal.

"I love your tits," he whispered as he pressed a kiss in her cleavage. His tongue flicked over an already erect nipple. "And I love that they're real. I hate fake boobs." He cupped them in his hands again, their fullness overflowing his palms. "For such a little thing, you're really stacked, baby."

Nathan had been surprised to realize how petite she was when she'd finally taken off her shoes. At barely five foot three she almost always wore high heels, since they not only gave her added inches but made her legs look longer, too.

She looped her arms around his neck, holding his head to her breasts as he licked her nipples. "Hmm, sounds to me like you're a breast man. Lucky for me I've got what you want."

He smirked, running his hands down her back to cup her ass. "Honey, you've got everything I want, and I want everything you have – tits, ass, legs – there isn't one part of you that isn't perfect."

He slid one hand to cup her vulva, drawing a low moan from her as he slipped two long fingers inside of her. "Mmm, nice and juicy. Your cunt is perfect, too. Tight and hot and wet. I want this sweet little cunt riding my cock."

Nathan quickly divested himself of the sweat pants. He hadn't bothered with underwear so his cock sprang free, fully erect and seemingly even longer and thicker than before. Julia licked her lips, reaching out a hand to stroke him, but he gave her a playful swat.

"Don't. I want to make this last, and it'll be over awfully quick if you touch me. Now, do what I ask or I might have to spank this pretty little butt. Turn around."

Once again, the commanding tone of his voice excited her and she was quick to obey. She turned her back to him as he grasped her by the hips. A little unsure of what he intended, Julia uttered a cry of surprise as he lowered her hips down until he was able to thrust deep inside of her. She sat on his lap, straddling his thighs with her back to his chest as he fucked her from that position. He kept an arm wrapped around her waist, holding her in place as he urged her to ride him. She moaned when his fingers began to stimulate her clit, circling the hard little nub over and over.

"Come on, baby. I want you to come for me again, Julia. Your hot little cunt feels so good riding my cock this way. I love being so deep inside of you, filling you up all the way. I'm going to come so hard inside of you, baby, give you all of me. Christ, you're so beautiful."

His lips burned hot against her skin, tracing a slow, sensual trail from behind her ear down the side of her neck and back up to her jaw. Julia was almost mindless with the sensations he was stirring up in her body, building and building until she felt herself drawing ever closer to another climax. She braced her hands on his muscular thighs, arching her back and letting her long hair tumble about his shoulders. His continued thrusts were long and slow and so deep that she whimpered from the almost painful fullness. She could feel every thick, throbbing inch of his cock buried deep within her as she rocked back and forth, savoring the delicious pleasure. She felt completely surrounded by him, every one of her nerve endings being stimulated in one way or another – his lips capturing hers in a deep, searching kiss; his fully engorged penis embedded deep inside of her core, stretching her to accommodate him; his chest pressed against her back, while one hand expertly stroked her clit and the other was busy fondling her swollen breast and pinching the taut nipple. He aroused her unbearably, deliberately, unceasingly – until everything exploded and she fell apart right there on his lap, the orgasm shattering her into thousands of tiny pieces where summoning a single coherent thought was beyond her reach.

Nathan was quick to follow her to nirvana, shouting her name over and over as he poured himself into her, filling her with hot, thick semen, the volume so copious it seeped down her legs in spite of the fact their bodies were still tightly co-joined. He kept his arms wrapped around her torso, holding her in place as his body continued to shake in reaction, his face buried in the curve of her upper back. She was dimly aware of his teeth raking over her skin as he struggled for some semblance of control, then gave up the battle as he slumped back in the chair in total surrender.

Julia was limp and exhausted when he finally scooped her up and carried her back to the bed. She was vaguely aware of being sweaty and sticky, especially between her thighs where his cum had seeped down, but was too content and sated to even think of moving so she could wash. Nathan wrapped her in his arms, pulling the duvet over them and kissing her softly on the lips.

"Go to sleep now, baby. I think we've finally managed to wear each other out. For now, anyway."

She cuddled against him with a little sigh of bliss, her eyes so heavy she couldn't keep them open a minute longer.

✳✳✳✳✳

When she woke again, sleepy and disoriented, she took a quick glance at the bedside clock which now read two a.m. Aware of the sudden need for the bathroom, Julia gingerly slid out of the big bed, not wanting to wake Nathan. He'd rolled onto his back, one arm sprawled out to the side, and the duvet pushed down to bare the top half of his body.

She tiptoed quietly to the spacious, well-appointed bathroom and took care of her needs. She took a few extra minutes to wash off her makeup, grimacing at the sight of mascara streaks beneath her eyes, and also washed away all the residual stickiness between her legs. The glasses of wine she'd consumed had left a dry, stale taste in her mouth so she quickly rinsed it out with the complimentary bottle of mouthwash she found on the sink.

Naked, she slid back into bed, noticing that Nathan had kicked even more of the duvet off now, baring him below his navel. Julia licked her hips, hungry for a look at the narrow ribbon of dark hair that started at his torso and kept travelling down the length of his body. When she pulled the covers further down, exposing his genitals, she felt the stirrings of arousal in her body. Nathan wasn't the only one who got turned on by the sight of nudity – gazing at his male beauty was doing the exact same thing to her.

His skin was lightly bronzed, and she wondered if he ran without a shirt since he didn't appear to have any visible tan lines. The definition of his biceps and triceps spoke of a dedicated weight training regimen, though he wasn't overly bulky. He didn't have an ounce of spare body fat, especially on his abs which were rock hard and mouthwateringly detailed. He had that sexy V shaped line where his lower abs met his hip flexors, more proof that he did a lot of targeted weight training and was undoubtedly in fantastic physical condition. His legs were long and leanly muscled, his calves having the same sort of definition as his arms and shoulders.

Knowing she should let him sleep, but unable to resist at the same time, she straddled his legs and bent her head until her lips could reach his cock. She began to lick him with long, slow stokes up and down his length. Nathan shifted on the bed, moving his head from one side to the other, but remained asleep. Seeing his cock begin to gradually harden and grow, her actions became bolder – taking the very tip of him into her mouth and sucking, while her hand began to move up and down his thickening length, stroking, pumping. At his initial groan of pleasure, Julia felt her nipples harden, her breasts swell. Her arousal building rapidly, she kept sucking his cock while her hand slid back to lightly fondle his testicles. When he gasped, his eyes opening slowly, she took him fully into her mouth and began to increase the tempo of her movements.

"Christ, that feels good," he croaked. "Keep it up, baby. Keep sucking my cock hard. Oh, yeah, just like that."

His hips began to move as he thrust his cock in and out of her mouth, fucking it eagerly. She was using both hands now, one continuing to stoke his rigid penis while the other cupped his swollen balls. Her mouth moved wetly up and down his ever-expanding length, as she flicked her tongue over the slit at the tip before sucking just the head into her mouth, then repeating her actions.

Nathan was thrashing wildly on the bed, his arms splayed out to the sides and clutching the mattress as he bucked his hips up in sync with her mouth. Julia loved seeing him so out of control, so completely aroused. She glanced up briefly to watch his face – his eyes were tightly shut, his head falling back against the pillows, his cheeks flushed a dark red and his mouth hanging open as he panted. Then she returned her full attention to pleasuring him, sucking him deeper and stroking faster and faster until he groaned.

"I'm so close, Julia. God, what you do to me. Oh, fuck, I'm coming!"

Her lips closed around him as he came, her throat working frantically to swallow the hot, salty semen. When he it was over, he flopped back on the bed, well and truly spent, while she daintily licked him dry. Then she slid back up his body and wrapped her arms around him. He nuzzled her neck, drawing her close against his heated body.

"Wow, that was incredible, baby," he murmured. "To what do I owe such an unexpected treat?"

She ran a hand over his broad, firmly muscled chest. "I woke up, saw you lying there all naked and yummy, and you just looked good enough to eat. So I did."

Nathan laughed and pressed a kiss to her temple. "Such a dirty, naughty girl. I'll bet you're wet, aren't you?"

She gasped when he didn't wait for an answer, and merely slid his hand over her belly, thrusting two long fingers deep inside where she was most definitely wet.

"Ahh, you are a naughty girl, aren't you?" he crooned. "Did giving me a blow job excite you? I can already tell it made your nipples hard."

Julia moaned as he spread the creamy moisture from her cunt around her outer labia and her clit. He repeated this action again and again – fucking her with his talented fingers and then coating her vaginal lips and clitoris with the resulting liquid. She began to rock her hips back and forth with the movement of his fingers, rubbing herself against his hand.

Nathan claimed her lips in a hot, sumptuous kiss, his tongue voracious as it swept through her mouth. His free hand cupped her breast and she whimpered with pleasure beneath his hungry kisses.

"Your tits are so swollen, baby," he whispered against her lips. "They get all full and hard when you're excited. I'd love to make you come just by playing with these beautiful tits."

Then his hands moved to grip her hips as he slid down her body, his head disappearing between her legs. He looked up at her, a lascivious smile on his lips. "But I can't resist licking up all this delicious juice first."

Julia cried out wordlessly at the first touch of his skillful mouth. He licked, sucked, thrust, bit, then repeated it all over and over again, until she was wild with arousal and need, so close but not quite there, squirming madly beneath his knowing, tormenting mouth and tongue. He continued the sensual torment for what seemed like an eternity, bringing her oh, so close to bliss only to back off at the last second. She felt wet, hot tears trickling down her cheeks, so aroused and so needy for an orgasm that it was nearly unbearable. Finally, he thrust two fingers deep inside of her core, fucking her rapidly, and sucked her clit at the same time, and she came powerfully, the pleasure going on and on. Julia's cries were low and weak, so spent from the force of the orgasm he'd just given her that she couldn't summon up the strength to move.

She was fast asleep in seconds, not even aware when Nathan tucked her close to his side and re-covered them both with the duvet.

Chapter Five

It was still dark outside when Nathan woke, groggy from too little sleep and too much alcohol. But his head was pounding and his mouth so dry he could barely swallow, so he forced himself out of bed and stumbled into the bathroom. He found some Advil in his toiletry kit, and tossed three back with a full glass of water. After seeing to his other needs, including brushing his teeth, he walked back into the bedroom.

He smiled sleepily as he viewed the disarray of clothing strewn about the room. He liked things tidy and in their place, so it was intuitive for him to begin picking up articles of clothing and neatly placing them on a chair. As he reached for each item of Julia's, he couldn't resist taking a curious glance at the labels.

Whatever it was she did for a living, it had to pay extremely well, because everything of hers was designer and expensive. The exquisite pink sheath dress was Moschino, size six; the sexy gray stilettos Yves Saint Laurent, also size six. Her gray bag was Bottega Venetta. He fingered the cream lace on her Victoria's Secret bra, flipping the tag over to read the size – 32DD – and smiled. The little lady in his bed wasn't so little in certain places, and he had to stifle a groan just thinking about those lushly full tits.

The pink lacy panties, however, eluded him for the moment and he was too drowsy to continue looking for them, sliding back into bed instead. But as tired as he was, he couldn't resist pulling the duvet from Julia's prone body carefully, baring her to his gaze.

He longed to touch her, to run a hand over the gentle curve of her hip or the sweet cheeks of her ass. Her legs weren't long but were beautifully shaped, not skinny but leanly muscled. She had dainty, adorable feet, the toenails painted the same shade as her dress. Her skin was flawless, without a single freckle or mole to mar its creamy perfection.

Nathan smiled at the teeny little bulge of her tummy, finding it exquisitely feminine. He was glad she didn't have the rock-hard, six-pack abs that some women at his gym seemed obsessed with achieving. He liked that Julia was slender and shapely but still soft and a tiny bit round. And, of course, there was the part of her body he seemed the most obsessed with – her breasts. He loved their round, high fullness, how they reminded him of big, pink pearls.

He couldn't stop himself from rubbing his thumb over one soft pink nipple, manipulating it until it stiffened. In her sleep, Julia made a little sound of pleasure, and his hand grew bolder, cupping her breast. He was more than a little astonished to find himself growing hard again, figuring that she'd wrung the very last drop out of him with that soul-stealing blow job. He'd never come close to having this much sex in such a short span of time, would have never believed it physically possible, and could only reason that Julia was the cause. She was such a giving, responsive lover and certainly the hottest, sexiest woman he'd ever met. It was small wonder that all he had to do was look at her glorious body and become instantly erect.

Fully aroused now, he lowered his head and took her nipple in his mouth, suckling her hungrily. As he moved to the other breast, he felt Julia stirring beneath him, heard her soft groan of pleasure, felt her hands sliding into his hair.

He lifted his head, one hand still fondling a breast. "I'm sorry to wake you," he whispered. "I just can't keep my hands off of you. I guess I'm addicted."

She smiled sleepily. "Mmm, we have the same addiction then, because I need another fix, too. I don't think I'm ever going to get enough of you."

Nathan slid behind Julia, turning her on her side and lifting one leg over his. She gasped when he entered her from that position, his chest spooned against her back. Their lovemaking this time was slow and careful, and infinitely tender. He captured her hand, their fingers entwined, as she arched her head back to meet his sweet, searching kiss. This time was in sharp contrast to the frantic, physical fucking they had done earlier, so much that Nathan's chest ached from the beauty of it. They fit together so perfectly, their slow, sensuous movements in complete sync with each other, like this was a beautiful, dreamy dance.

Even their orgasms this time were quiet, though still deeply satisfying. He stayed buried inside of her as they fell asleep, unwilling to withdraw from her and break contact. Just before sleep claimed him again, he thought drowsily that he'd never felt so satisfied or content before.

✳✳✳✳✳

Nathan woke reluctantly, far too warm and comfortable to even think of opening his eyes. He yawned sleepily, his brain still too fogged over to be able to really summon a clear thought, and his body too limp and thoroughly relaxed to move. He closed his eyes again, willing himself to fall back asleep, but now his brain and body were gradually beginning to awaken and become aware of his surroundings.

He was snuggled deep into the plush mattress of his hotel room bed, his head burrowed comfortably on one of the thick pillows. The crisp, clean scent of the bed linens was pleasant but there was a different scent that was making his nose twitch and a smile to play about his lips. This scent was of a very light floral fragrance, one that was not familiar to him, but that he knew instinctively he liked a lot. He nuzzled his nose to breathe more deeply of the scent, feeling his cheek brushing against something soft and silky. As he came more fully awake, he was suddenly aware that his arm was wrapped around a warm, curvy body, his leg covering a shapely, feminine limb.

Nathan blinked once, twice, before opening his eyes fully and glancing down at the enticing female body curled up trustingly against his side. A body that most definitely did not belong to his fiancée. A body that he began to all too vividly recall had done wicked, enticing things to him last night and early this morning, a body that he'd come to know intimately in a very short period of time, and that was even now tempting him to tumble back onto the mattress and sink inside of.

It all came rushing back to him like a tidal wave – his argument with Cameron, the amount of liquor he'd belted back in a very short time frame, meeting the beautiful girl he'd been obsessed with for days out in front of the hotel, inviting her back inside for a drink, and the resulting hours and hours of hot, consuming sex they'd engaged in.

'Ah, fuck," he groaned beneath his breath, careful not to wake Julia. "What the hell have I done?'

Cautiously, he began to ease himself away from her an inch at a time, desperate not to wake her. She mumbled sleepily but only burrowed further into her pillow as he slowly eased himself out of the bed. He stood by the foot of the bed for long seconds, running his hand alternately through his hair and then over his jaw, trying to make some sense of what the hell had happened the previous evening. Had he really seduced this beautiful, sweet girl while knowing full well that he was already engaged and had to fly back home today? Nathan simply couldn't fathom how he'd done something so thoroughly rotten, how he could have intentionally taken another woman to bed when he had a fiancée waiting for him back in San Francisco. He'd never been that kind of guy, had always been honest with the women he'd dated. Sure, he'd had his fair share of one-night stands but never when he was already dating someone else. So what the hell had possessed him last night to suddenly start acting like Prick of the Year? He struggled to calculate exactly how much alcohol he'd consumed last night, but knew it hadn't been nearly enough to cloud his judgment that badly. Unfortunately, he'd known exactly what he'd been doing by enticing Julia into his bed and then had taken full, despicable advantage of her passionate capitulation. And that unquestionably made him the biggest dog-faced bastard in the history of mankind, seriously in need of a major ass-kicking.

As quietly as possible, he gathered up some clean clothes and slipped noiselessly into the bathroom. He showered, shaved, and dressed in record time, badly needing some alone time to get a hold of himself and then figure out what the hell to do next. There was no way he was just going to ditch Julia – sneak out of the room like a spineless jerk without explaining or apologizing. He might have acted like the world's biggest asshole last night but he wasn't about to make things that much worse by just leaving like a thief in the night. But he did need coffee – and more Advil, judging from his pounding headache – and at least a few minutes to get his shit together before manning up.

He exited the bathroom as quietly as he'd entered, grateful to see that Julia still slept peacefully, and hastily found his shoes, wallet, and room key. As he headed for the door, though, he couldn't resist sneaking another peek at her, if only to assure himself that she was every bit as beautiful as he'd thought. Nathan closed his eyes, overcome at the sight of her gorgeous face in repose with her pink cheeks and soft, lush mouth slightly parted as she breathed in and out. The image of that fairytale princess from his old childhood storybook came to mind, but Julia in the flesh was a hundred times more beautiful than any of those illustrations. Her glorious mane of caramel colored curls tumbled carelessly about her bare shoulders and his fingers itched to run through the long, silky strands again.

Instead, his grit his teeth and opened the door carefully, knowing he'd need the biggest cup of coffee he could find before facing her again. Maybe one with several bracing shots of whiskey in it.

✳✳✳✳✳

Julia winced as she turned over in the unfamiliar bed, feeling the soreness in seldom used muscles. The drapes had been drawn, blocking out most of the bright sunlight streaming into the room, but not enough to hide the fact that it was definitely morning. She opened one eye a crack, just enough to see it was slightly before nine a.m.

Memories of the previous night – and early this morning – began to surface, one after the other, until she didn't know which one to recall first. She smiled dreamily as the decadent splendor of the last fifteen or so hours replayed itself over and over in her mind. She'd never had sex that physical, that demanding, that *raw* before. No one had ever talked to her like Nathan had, the dirty but thrilling things that he'd whispered to her all night long. And she had never even come close to having that much sex in such a short period of time, hadn't dreamed it was even possible to get a man hard that many times. And it went without saying that she had never had even one orgasm as intense as the multiple ones Nathan had wrung out of her.

She stretched luxuriously, feeling very lazy and satisfied, like a big cat. It was then she realized she was alone in the huge bed, the covers shoved back on Nathan's side. Trying not to panic or make assumptions, she slowly sat up and looked around the hotel room.

Relief washed through her when she noticed his suitcases lined up against the far wall, his jacket laid across a chair. She hadn't actually believed that Nathan could have done something as unconscionable as sneaking out of here without a goodbye, or a discussion of where they went from here. There was no way, she told herself firmly, that someone who'd been so wonderful, so tender and caring, would be capable of doing something like that. After what they had shared last night and this morning, Julia couldn't imagine that this would turn out to be just another one night stand for him. It certainly was much, much more to her. She was already a little in love with him, already missing him, and trying really hard not to start thinking about what happened next. There were so many things she didn't know about him – where he lived, what he did for a living, not to mention his last name. It was obvious he didn't live in New York, and she thought it was fortunate that she had already begun to think about moving out of the city for at this moment she thought she would gladly follow him to the ends of the earth.

Thinking that he had to be in the bathroom, Julia padded naked across the carpeted room, only to frown again when she found that space empty as well, though evidence remained that he'd showered sometime this morning.

Fighting back a growing sense of unease, Julia turned on the shower taps and grabbed a towel and one of the hotel bathrobes. Not wanting to take the time to wash and dry her long hair, she piled it into the complementary shower cap before stepping into the shower. The hot, steamy water did wonders for her sore muscles, and the soap smelled wonderful as she washed. She could have lingered for awhile in that huge shower, but she was anxious to see Nathan. She dried off quickly and wrapped herself in the plush robe. After restoring some order to her hair, and using another swig of mouthwash, she tentatively opened the bathroom door and was relieved beyond description to see that Nathan had returned.

He was standing over by the window, where he'd opened the drapes to let the full morning light flood into the room. He was sending a text and hadn't noticed her yet, so Julia allowed herself a moment to drink in his splendid male beauty. He was more casually dressed this morning, in dark jeans and a fitted gray T-shirt. His thick brown hair was neatly brushed and he'd shaved, leaving his handsome face smooth. He was frowning slightly in concentration as he tapped out his text, and she was determined to replace that frown with a very happy smile.

"Good morning," she said in a husky voice as she padded over to him on bare feet.

He glanced up, abruptly setting his phone aside. The rather somber expression on his face should have been cause for concern but Julia was too happy to see him to think much about it.

"Good morning," he replied quietly. "I brought coffee and some pastries. They're over on the table."

She smiled at him sultrily, sliding her arms around his neck and pressing her body flush against his. "Thank you. But I need a good morning kiss first."

Julia pulled his head down to hers and kissed him, a sensual, open-mouthed kiss, and tasted the inside of his mouth with slow, deep licks. At first, Nathan seemed to merely accept her kiss almost passively, and then suddenly he groaned and hauled her into his body. The neckline of her overlarge robe fell open and Julia, needing to feel his hands on her, brought his fingers to her nipple. He obliged by tweaking the already hard little peak between his fingers, eliciting a moan of pleasure from her throat.

Abruptly, Nathan broke the kiss and placed his hands on her shoulders, holding her away from him at arm's distance. Julia raised puzzled eyes to his.

"Nathan, what's wrong?"

His gaze dipped to where the robe had parted, revealing the full length of her nude body, before he closed his eyes. "Fix your robe, Julia. I can't think straight with you looking like that. All I can think about is fucking you again."

Her mouth quivered at the harsh, almost impersonal tone of his voice but she complied, tightening the belt so that the robe covered her from neck to ankles. "Please tell me what's wrong," she said quietly.

He opened his eyes, looking relieved to see her covered, and took her by the elbow. He led her over to the same table where they'd eaten late last night. "Sit down, Julia. I wasn't sure how you took your coffee. I hope cream is okay. There's sweetener there if you use it. And you should eat something, help yourself." He gestured to the tall white bag on the table.

She shook her head. "I'm not hungry. Please talk to me, Nathan. What's wrong?"

He took the opposite chair. "Have your coffee first, then we'll talk."

Julia's hand shook as she stirred sweetener into her coffee and then took a sip. Her stomach was starting to churn with unease, and she had a terrible premonition about what was to come. There was no trace left of her sexy, passionate lover of the previous evening, and she knew she didn't want to hear what he was going to say during their "talk". But Nathan remained stubbornly silent, looking off in the other direction until she'd finished about half of her coffee. By then tears were already spilling from her eyes, and she had to choke back a little sob.

That small sound brought his head back around, and he groaned to see her wipe tears from her cheeks. "Oh, baby. Why are you crying?" he asked tenderly, brushing her hair back from her face.

She closed her eyes as the tears continued to fall freely. "Because you're about to tell me this was all a terrible mistake, and that it should never have happened, aren't you?" she whispered brokenly.

"Look at me, Julia." The commanding tone was back in his voice, and she was powerless to resist him as she opened her eyes. His gaze upon her was compassionate, but there was a firm set to his mouth and jaw. "You're partly right," he told her gently. "What happened last night shouldn't have. I should never have allowed myself to even approach you. But to call the most incredible night of my life a mistake is completely incorrect."

Julia felt like her heart was splintering into thousands of tiny shards. "I don't understand, Nathan. Why shouldn't it have happened? We were obviously both attracted to each other, right from the very first time I saw you coming back from your run."

He made a harsh sound. "Attracted is too mild a word for what I felt for you, baby. Obsessed is more like it. I thought about you constantly, kicked myself a thousand times for not running after you that first day, and getting your number. But the reason I didn't is the same reason why I have to say goodbye to you now, Julia. I'm not free to be with you, baby."

Shocked, she stood up abruptly, pushing herself away from the table. "Oh, God, you're married? Oh, no. God, no. How could I be so stupid again?" She covered her face with her hands, weeping like a child.

Nathan tried to take her in his arms, but she walked away from him. "I'm not married, Julia," he said quietly. "Even I wouldn't be that much of an asshole. But I am in a long term relationship and very recently engaged."

Anger surged through her as she turned to face him. "Like that's much better?" she hissed. "How could you, Nathan? What a fool I am, a stupid, stupid, fool. I actually believed we had something special but all you wanted was a good long fuck before you flew home to your fiancée. You bastard."

He paled visibly at her angrily spoken words. "It wasn't like that, Julia. Not even a little bit. I certainly didn't come to New York thinking I was going to have a final wild fling. If you recall, I didn't even bring condoms with me."

She was so angry and upset – both with him and herself - that she was shaking. "Then exactly how was it, Nathan? If you were engaged and obviously had no intention of ever seeing me again after today, why did you let it go so far?"

"Because I couldn't help myself," he whispered harshly. "You were so goddamned beautiful, like a dream, like that fairytale princess I told you about. And I let myself be a total asshole and use you because I was selfish and greedy, and I just fucking wanted you. I'm sure you must hate my guts right about now."

Julia shook her head. "I should. I should be screaming names at you right now, throwing things, cursing you. But I'm just – sad, Nathan. Last night was so amazing for me, like a beautiful, living dream. I've never, ever considered going off with a man I just met and didn't know anything about, but I couldn't help myself. I was so attracted to you, wanted to be with you so badly. And now - God, I don't even know your last name! I don't do things like this – one night stands – and now I just feel dirty, like some nasty skank you picked up in a bar."

He was at her side in an instant, dragging her into his arms and burying his face in her hair. "Jesus, baby, don't say things like that!" he told her in alarm. "Julia, you are the finest, most precious woman I've ever met. Don't ever think of comparing yourself to some cheap slut. I know you wouldn't just go off with any man you meet, and I could tell it had been awhile since you'd been with someone. Don't you dare cheapen what happened last night. It was the best night of my life."

She raised tear-filled eyes to his. "Then why are you leaving me? If it was so good between us, then why can't we keep seeing each other?"

He rested his forehead against hers, heaving a sigh. "It's not that simple. I know I've acted like a bastard – cheating on my fiancée and using you. But I've been with her for two years, Julia. What kind of an asshole would I be to ditch her just because someone else came along? I should have tried harder to resist you. But now because I was weak I've hurt you and betrayed someone else."

Julia felt lightheaded, and held on to his forearms to stop herself from collapsing. "Are you in love with her?" she whispered faintly.

He groaned. "Don't, Julia."

She pushed herself away from him and began to search for her things. "You're right. Of course you love her. Why else would you be engaged? Where are my clothes?"

"Over there on the desk chair. Julia, listen to me. "

She ignored him and walked over to where she saw the pink dress. A strange sense of numbness had begun to seep into her bones, an awful feeling of cold and dread, and she couldn't stop the shivers that rippled through her body. Almost without being aware of her actions, she dropped the robe from her shoulders, barely hearing the indrawn hiss of Nathan's breath behind her as her nudity was displayed. Like a robot, she pulled her bra on and then frantically searched around for her panties.

"Where are my panties?" she asked, her voice high and panicky. "They aren't with the rest of my things. I can't walk out of here without them."

Nathan's voice sounded behind her but she didn't pay him any attention as she searched for her missing underwear. "Julia, take it easy, baby," he soothed. "It's okay."

She sobbed and shook her head. "No, no, it's not. I can't find them, Nathan. I can't leave here without panties on. Only bad girls do things like that and I'm a good girl. I never do naughty things."

"Jesus, stop it." He pulled her into his arms, pushing her face into his shoulder. "Calm down and I'll help you find them."

She pushed away from him. "No, I need to go. I can't be here with you." Resigning herself to walking out of there sans underwear, she pulled her dress on, awkwardly zipping it up behind her while shoving her feet into her shoes. Angrily, she dashed away the tears that blinded her and grabbed her purse, stumbling towards the door.

A door that Nathan was blocking, his back pressed against it so that she couldn't leave. She refused to look at him, her hair falling forward to shield her flushed, tearstained face.

"Julia, look at me, please." The commanding tone of his voice had been replaced with an almost desperate plea. "Baby, please."

Her head shot up angrily. "Don't call me that," she hissed. "I'm not your baby. I'm just some stupid, naïve girl you banged last night. You're flying home today to the woman you really care about, so don't waste your fake endearments on me."

His shoulders slumped, and an expression of unbelievable sadness crossed his face. "Julia, I am so sorry. I never meant to hurt you like this. I wish there was something I could say or do to make it better."

She raised huge, tear-filled eyes to his. "Just let me go, Nathan. Please open the door now."

But he ignored her, instead sliding his hands into her hair. "Let me take you downstairs, get you a cab. I need to know you're going to be okay."

Julia placed her hands over his, trying in vain to dislodge them. "No. I want to leave now. Alone. Don't make this harder."

He brushed his thumb over her lips. "Then kiss me goodbye. A kiss to remember."

She tried to turn her head to the side, but he held her still as his lips claimed hers one final time. His kiss tasted of hunger, of desperation, but mostly of farewell. Julia refused at first to respond, remaining passive beneath his hungry mouth, but then she gave a little moan and kissed him back, clinging to him as though she never wanted to let go.

He released her then, stepping away from the door, looking as though he were struggling to speak. Not able to bear another apology, Julia yanked open the door and simply walked away before she could run back into his arms and beg him to never leave.

Chapter Six

January

"Julia, how wonderful to see you again. Please, come in and have a seat. Did you want Courtney to get you some coffee or tea?"

Julia shook her head as she walked inside Travis Headley's office and took a seat at one of the chairs facing his desk. "No, thank you. Courtney was already kind enough to ask but I'm fine. And it's lovely to see you again, too. It's been over two years, I think."

Travis nodded as he sat down next to her rather than behind his desk, taking her hand in his. "Yes. I was in Manhattan for the Thanksgiving weekend two years ago. We had dinner together with Gerard and Maddy before your family flew in for the holiday."

Travis had been another of Gerard's protégées, having originally been a student of his at the Design Institute. Gerard had on occasion presented workshops and seminars at his alma mater, and he'd been impressed with Travis' talent and vision. Like Julia herself, Travis had spent a year interning at Manhattan Interiors after graduating from college but had left New York for the West Coast soon thereafter. He had made it a point over the years, however, to keep in close touch with Gerard via email and phone calls and had made several visits to New York.

Julia had met Travis for the first time about five years ago when she was still in college. She'd traveled down from Cornell to spend a long holiday weekend with Aunt Maddy, and Travis had been in town at the same time to visit Gerard. Travis knew Maddy as well, so it had been only natural for all of them to meet for dinner one evening.

There had been a couple of other meetings since that first one, and Julia had hit it off with him each time. Like Gerard, Travis was openly gay, but in a more discreet, less dramatic manner than the older man. In his early thirties now, Travis favored tailored business suits like the light gray one he wore today, and could just as easily have been a lawyer or executive as the interior designer he was. He was the co-owner of a very successful architectural design firm here in San Francisco, in charge of the interior design division of the company while his partner managed the architectural side. And Julia was keeping her fingers crossed that she would soon be one of their employees.

Travis seemed in little hurry to discuss the business at hand, however. "How is Madelyn these days?" he asked of Julia's beloved aunt.

"Relieved that the holidays are over, of course. It's crazier than normal at the store then." Madelyn Benoit was the head buyer at Bergdorf Goodman, one of Manhattan's most exclusive, high-end department stores.

Travis nodded, his admiring gaze taking in the beautiful dress of cream cashmere that Julia wore today. With its crisscross neckline and slim pencil skirt, it managed to be both businesslike and ultra-feminine at the same time.

"I see Auntie is still keeping her favorite niece well dressed. Another Donna Karan?" he asked, naming one of Julia's favorite designers.

She shook her head. "Ralph Lauren. And yes, there are definite and numerous perks to having Maddy for my aunt."

Madelyn had never married, and had no children of her own, so she had always showered her adored nieces with affection and gifts. She had worked in the fashion industry for three decades, and as a buyer for about half of that time. In her current high profile job, she frequently received samples and overstock from all manner of designers, especially when she attended the twice-yearly Fashion Week in cities like New York, Paris, Milan and Hong Kong. It was always far too much stuff for her to use personally, and even after distributing goods to her staff there was plenty to ship to her sister and nieces. And since Lauren favored a much more casual wardrobe, the bulk of the dresses, skirts, shoes, and bags went to Julia. It was a very fortunate thing, too, because there was no way Julia could have ever afforded to buy such high end pieces on her own salary. She made good money as an interior designer – or had, at least – but it still wasn't nearly enough to afford the outfit she had on today. And she had a real weakness for designer goods, so she was eternally grateful she had Aunt Maddy to make frequent contributions to her clothing addiction and therefore avoid having sky-high credit card bills.

Travis' gaze dropped to her feet, shod in cream suede Giuseppe Zanotti peep-toe stilettos. "Love the shoes, too. But you always were a very stylish young lady. Even when you were in college I don't recall you ever wearing jeans and flats."

She gave a mock shudder. "Jeans are for tomboys and flats for old ladies. Besides, both of them make my legs look too short."

He grinned, looking very boyish with his well-styled wheat blond hair, fair skin, and trim build. "Well, you look sensational, honey. You must have to beat men off with a stick."

Julia sobered and made a dismissive movement with her hand. "Actually, I'm kind of off men at the moment. You know the old saying 'fool me once shame on you, fool me twice shame on me'. Or the other old saying – 'men are assholes'."

Travis lifted a brow. "Well, I can see we'll have to have a *loong* talk one of these days. Sounds like you've got some interesting tales to tell. But in the meanwhile let's talk about the possibility of you working here." His expression turned serious.

"Gerard told me a little about what happened with that witch Vanessa but I'd like to hear your side."

Julia sighed. "You mean why she fired me and then proceeded to call every design firm she could think of to blacklist me?"

Travis listened intently — and with empathy — as she related the story that had filled him with outrage when Gerard had first filled him in. One evening last October Julia had been in the office working late when Vanessa's slimy boyfriend Philip had accosted her. The office had been deserted and no one had heard her scream when Philip had torn her blouse, slapped her across the mouth hard enough to draw blood, bruised her hip, and cracked three of her ribs as she'd fought him off.

It had been a mixed blessing when Vanessa — who had arranged to meet Philip at the office — had arrived and heard the commotion, rushing into Julia's office in time to stop Philip from hurting her further. He of course had tried to blame the whole thing on Julia, claiming she'd been flirting with him and leading him on for months. And, despite the fact that Julia was curled up in a ball, bleeding, bruised and sobbing, Vanessa had chosen to believe Philip and had fired Julia on the spot.

Vanessa's anger and jealousy had gone far beyond merely firing her, however, and she'd done her damndest to prevent Julia from getting another job. That was when Julia had called Gerard, hoping to move to New Orleans and work with him again. But his new firm was still getting off the ground, and there was barely enough work to keep him afloat, much less to bring on another designer. Gerard had, however, contacted Travis who coincidentally was looking for a new designer and here Julia was.

Travis's mouth had tightened into a grim line as she had related her story. "I always knew Vanessa was a royal bitch — that's one of the reasons I never took a permanent job with Gerard. But I never imagined she could be quite that mercenary. I hope you pressed charges against her slimebag boyfriend."

Julia shook her head. "Aunt Maddy was very upset with me when I refused. She came to pick me up that night after I called her but I just didn't see much point in pressing charges. Vanessa's family has piles of money and she would have probably hired some shark of a lawyer to get Loverboy off. I just wanted to forget the whole nightmare."

"Is that why you left New York?"

"One of them," she admitted. "But to be honest, I'd been thinking of moving anyway. New York is wonderful but I've left some other bad memories back there, too. It's been nice to be back in California and especially to be spending time with my parents and sister."

She'd been staying at her parents' home in Carmel since just after Thanksgiving, having given up her apartment in Manhattan and shipped all of her belongings out here. Everything she owned was currently in storage inside her father's workshop.

"Did you tell your family about what happened?"

Julia nodded. "Only because Aunt Maddy threatened to do so if I didn't. My dad was furious, he still wants to press charges, but I've convinced him not to. And Lauren swears she's going to beat the crap out of both Vanessa and her boyfriend the next time she's in New York. Considering that she still takes kung fu classes on a regular basis, I'm a little worried about that."

Travis grinned, having heard multiple stories about Julia's fierce twin sister. "And what did your mother do?"

She sighed. "Mom didn't say anything, just held me and let me cry things out. It was a rotten few months for me, Travis, going back to something that happened in September."

"Ahh. Does that have anything to do with the 'men are assholes' quote?"

She laughed. "It has everything to do with it. But I've tried really hard to move past it, so can we not discuss it right now?"

"Your wish is my command. How about we take a look at that portfolio you've brought along instead?"

For the next half hour or so, they poured through Julia's design portfolio, with Travis asking questions, making comments, and listening to her responses. They talked for awhile longer about some of the other projects she'd handled, what types of assignments she could expect to be given here, and about current design trends.

At the end of it all, Travis was regarding her with a half-smile. "So I assume you'd live in the city if you got this job?"

She nodded. "Luckily there's a great little place that just became available in my friend Angela's building. She lives in this amazing Victorian in Lower Pacific Heights. I've been crashing with her the past couple of nights."

"Any other job offers you're considering?"

Julia bit her bottom lip uncertainly. "Nothing serious, no. There's a small firm in Atlanta that I've had a phone interview with, and a place in Minneapolis who just emailed me this morning. But both of those are just straightforward home interior shops, nothing like what you were just describing."

Travis waved a hand in dismissal. "Ugh, Atlanta. From a boy who grew up in Florida, trust me when I say you'd hate summer in the Deep South – all that humidity and those nasty bugs. Yuck. And Minnesota? Honey, all that wretched snow and probably no Neiman Marcus or Barneys within a hundred mile radius. No, you can't even consider either of those offers because you're coming to work for me."

She stared at him in shocked surprise. "Just like that? I mean, don't you have to think about it for awhile? Or – or discuss it with your business partner or something?"

"Yes, just like that. No, I knew almost before you walked in the door that I would hire you. And, no. Nate and I don't interfere with who the other hires. So, if you'll do us the honor, Ms. McKinnon, Atwood Headley would very much like you to be their newest interior designer."

Julia smiled, really smiled, for the first time in months and couldn't contain her happiness, almost giggling in reaction. "I would absolutely adore working here with you, Travis. Given our connection through Gerard, this feels like the perfect fit for me. I know I'm going to be very happy here."

Travis stood and extended his hand to her. "Welcome aboard, honey. Now, give your new boss a hug, why don't you? You know with me it's not going to be any form of sexual harassment if I touch you."

She did giggle then as she gave him a quick, affectionate hug. "Thank you, Travis," she told him, suddenly serious. "You don't know how much this means to me. I was afraid for awhile that I'd never be able to get a decent job again."

"Vanessa's influence isn't as far reaching as she'd like to believe with that overinflated ego of hers," declared Travis. "And from what I hear her business isn't going so well these days. A lot of clients were very loyal to Gerard — and also to you — so with the two of you gone things are drying up. Plus, Gerard is so pissed over what happened to you that he's working on damaging her professional reputation with as many people as he can."

She nodded. "He told me that. It really isn't necessary, you know. I'm just glad to be out of that awful situation. Ever since Gerard left it was hell for me to work there."

Travis's mouth tightened. "Having interned there for a year and seeing how Vanessa operates, I can certainly empathize. But that's all in the past now. You're going to love working here and I'm going to start throwing stuff at you right away. How soon can you start?"

"Hmm. Today is Tuesday, Would next Monday be okay? I think I can sign the lease on the flat today – the landlord is holding it for me until Thursday – and then convince my dad to haul all my stuff up this weekend."

He grinned. "A woman of action. I like that. It will serve you very well here because things move fast. Monday would be sensational. Let's take you over to Personnel so you can fill out mounds of boring paperwork. I'll introduce you along the way to as many people as I can. You'll never remember names, of course, but I guarantee they'll all remember you. Especially how good your ass looks in this dress."

Julia gaped at him in mock horror, then shared a laugh with him. "I know. Gay boss, straight employee, no sexual harassment."

"Just paying you a compliment, honey. Hell, I'm practically like your brother. But there are a couple of the guys you do need to watch out for. I'll make sure you know who they are." He shook his head. "Too bad Nate is already spoken for. The two of you together would have been awfully pretty. And I can't stand his fiancée. But that's a long story, one we'll share over a bottle or two of wine someday. Come on now, let me go show you off."

Atwood Headley was a much bigger firm than Manhattan Interiors had been, largely because of the architectural arm of the company. Between architects, designers, and all the support staff, there were over a hundred employees. It seemed to Julia that during their whirlwind tour of the office Travis must have introduced her to at least half the staff. She knew he was right and that she'd never remember anyone's name come Monday, apart from Travis, of course, and his admin assistant Courtney.

Julia thought the oddly dressed girl was what Olive Oyl would look like if she suddenly went hipster. Courtney was tall and painfully thin, with super skinny arms and legs, and long, lank hair dyed a bright orangey-red. Travis had whispered that this was a new shade – last week it had been cotton candy pink. Courtney wore a very strange assortment of clothing that looked vintage/thrift shop – but not in a good way – accented by leopard-print flats and red-framed eyeglasses that clashed badly with her current hair color. The fashionista imbedded deep within Julia could have wept at such a horrific assault on the eyes, but Courtney seemed like a sweet girl and was very kind, despite her scary sense of fashion.

In fact, everyone she met was very kind and welcoming, though more than a few of the men had either gaped at her open-mouthed or stared at her breasts. The two men in particular that Travis had warned her against – one an architect, the other a landscape designer – had both definitely flirted with her. But Julia had long ago mastered the art of the firm but subtle put-down, and was quite certain she'd made it very clear to both of them that it was to be a business only relationship.

One of the last stops they made before Julia was to spend an hour or more filling out personnel forms was at the office of Travis' partner – Nate Atwood. Seated just outside of the office was a petite woman who looked to be in her mid-to-late forties. Her nameplate identified her as Robyn Reynolds, and she was all eager smiles as Travis introduced her to Julia.

"Welcome to the fold, Julia," she told her warmly, clasping her hand. "You're going to love it here. We're all like a big family."

Travis put an arm around the older woman's narrow shoulders affectionately. "And Robyn's the mama of our family. Nate and I stole her away from the firm we both worked at when we decided to spin off on our own."

If Courtney was Olive Oyl, then Robyn was Tinker Bell. Small and sprightly, her chestnut hair was cut in a stylish pixie and there was a smattering of freckles across the bridge of her nose. She wore a wrap dress of dark burgundy wool and black suede ankle boots.

"I'm sorry that Nate isn't in today so you could meet," apologized Robyn. "He's on a job site up in Napa all day. Lousy day for it, too, with these scattered showers."

Travis turned to Julia. "The Napa site is the resort hotel I mentioned to you earlier. It's one of the first projects you'll be assigned to, so you'll be working closely with Nate on it."

Julia nodded. "I'm really looking forward to doing the design for that one. It's amazing that you have the Gregson Hotels as your client."

Gregson Hotels were known worldwide as an ultra-luxe brand of both city hotels and sprawling resort properties. The headquarters for the North and South American properties was located in San Francisco, and Atwood Headley had already completed several projects for the company. By coincidence, Julia had worked on a remodel project for one of their Manhattan hotels last year, and she was thrilled at the opportunity to work on such a high profile account again.

A couple of hours later, as she finished her tour of the office and filling out an endless stack of new hire forms, she headed back to Angela's flat with a sense of satisfaction. Finally, after several months of so many bad things happening to her, it seemed that all the dark clouds were starting to blow away. Julia was more than ready to forget the heartache and disappointment she'd known in New York and begin a new, happier chapter of her life here in San Francisco.

✳✳✳✳✳

Nathan was running late, and operating on too few hours of sleep, as he walked briskly to his office. Fortunately, his condo was just three blocks from the office, one of the main reasons he'd bought the place four years ago. He liked the convenience of being so close to his job, even if the modern high-rise building wasn't exactly to his taste. But he certainly didn't plan on living there forever if he had his way about it. Convincing Cameron to eventually move out of the city and into his idea of a dream home across the bay in Tiburon, however, was something else entirely.

It was because of Cameron that he was both late and tired this morning. They had spent a three-day weekend up at her parents' luxurious vacation home in Lake Tahoe, skiing and socializing with her family and their wide circle of friends. Nathan had wanted to head back to San Francisco late morning yesterday to beat the traffic and have some time to relax before the work week began on Monday. But Cameron had wheedled and cajoled, wanting to stay for lunch and spending extra time with some friends she hadn't seen in awhile. It had been very late afternoon by the time they had left, and a drive that should have taken about four hours quickly doubled due to all the traffic. Nathan had been stressed out from driving in bumper to bumper traffic and in poor weather conditions, knowing the whole while that he had a busy day at the office. To make matters worse, he'd been away Monday through Thursday of the previous week on a business trip to southern California, and thus hadn't been at the office all week. The amount of work he was going to have to get caught up on gave him a violent headache just thinking about it.

Cameron was maddeningly oblivious to such matters, since her own job as the owner of an art gallery was far less stressful and demanding. Business at the gallery was typically slow at this time of year, and she was an expert at delegating as much work as possible to her employees. He was certain that she would sleep in quite late this morning while he was making do with less than five hours of sleep.

Nathan sighed as he pressed the elevator button for his floor. He really had to start setting his foot down with Cameron about all of these social functions she insisted on attending. It seemed that pretty much every weekend was packed with one thing or another, and that he rarely got a say in what they did. Or, rarer still, actually got to relax and unwind occasionally. It had been especially hectic over the holiday season, and things hadn't seemed to settle down all that much in the resulting weeks.

He waved hello to Becca, the pretty Asian receptionist, and somewhat sleepily greeted several other employees on his way to his office. He grinned at Robyn, who was already hard at work like the whirlwind of activity she was.

"Well, you look like hell," she said by way of greeting, in a manner that spoke of years of familiarity. "Good thing you're clutching that extra large coffee. I'm guessing by the dark circles under your eyes that you'll be needing a refill soon."

"Good morning to you, too, Mrs. Reynolds," he chuckled. Robyn was a combination of admin assistant, bossy big sister, and close friend. Convincing her to come work for them had been the best move he and Travis had made when they'd taken the plunge and decided to start their own firm nearly ten years ago.

"I take it you got back later than planned from Tahoe last night," she commented as she resumed checking through email.

Nathan rolled his eyes. "That's the understatement of the year. You know, if I liked driving through snow and ice I'd have gone back home to live in Michigan after college."

Robyn shook her head. "Hon, you need to start setting your foot down with your woman. She's got more social engagements than the Queen of England."

"Yeah, I know. But not today. Is everything ready for my meeting at ten?" he asked.

"Of course. And I have all of your notes from your trip last week ready. Thanks for the email draft, it was a big help."

He nodded. "Good. Anything else going on around here that I need to know about? I didn't get a chance to talk to Travis at all last week. Everything okay on his end so far as you know?"

"Very okay. His new designer started last week so he's over the moon about her. And what a darling girl she is. I'm sure you'll meet her later."

The very last thing he was concerned with was meeting one of Travis' new employees, already having way too much of his own work to deal with. Nathan rolled up his sleeves and got right to it, going through his mail and email from the previous week, and looking over his notes and sketches for the client meeting this morning. The morning flew by rapidly, and he worked without interruption, even when Robyn brought him another cup of coffee.

His meeting was due to begin in about fifteen minutes, so he started putting away files and other items in his desk in preparation. Nathan hated a cluttered, untidy desk, especially when he had clients in his office. He spun around in his desk chair so he could re-file several folders in the credenza behind his desk, and stopped short when he accidentally tried to stuff a folder into the wrong hanging file.

He stared at the lacy pink underwear he kept hidden away in the file. Absently, he fingered the fragile lace between his thumb and forefinger, resisting the urge to pull the panties out and bury his face in them. Angrily, he shoved them back into their hiding place, and slammed the credenza drawer shut.

He'd found the panties tangled in the bed sheets as he had left the hotel room that turbulent morning last September, and hadn't been able to leave them behind. He'd stuffed them into his laptop case, intending to get rid of them when he arrived home. But then he'd seen them again at work while unpacking his laptop, and still hadn't been able to throw them out.

Nathan had dealt with the tremendous guilt and regret he'd suffered after that night in New York by repressing it all. Each time memories of that night began to surface, he'd pushed them away, refusing to let himself remember – or worse, to imagine what could have been.

Once, when the guilt had overwhelmed him for a few minutes until he'd found the strength to fight it off, he'd had the wild idea of returning to New York to try and find her. He could have simply loitered outside the Plaza Hotel for hours on end, hoping she'd walk by. Or haunting the Starbucks where they'd met in the event she should drop in.

But of course he had never acted on such a crazy impulse. Even if he had by some minor miracle been able to find her again, he was quite certain she would have either ignored him completely or smacked him across the face. God knew that was the least he deserved for what he'd done to her.

And while he'd more or less been able to squelch thoughts of Julia and the sex-filled hours they'd spent together while he was awake, his dreams had been another matter. He'd been haunted more than once with explicitly detailed dreams about her. He wasn't able to recall specific details, but he'd always woken from them with a painful hard-on and a frantically beating heart.

Of course, he'd felt even guiltier over how he'd betrayed Cameron and had been trying – albeit unknown to her – to make it up to her ever since. That was the primary reason he'd agreed to attend so many parties, receptions, dinners, and other events with her these past few months, and had been treating her like a queen. Fortunately, Cameron remained blissfully unaware of his infidelity and had been delighted at his acquiescence and indulgences.

Their lives had been a virtual whirlwind since last September. In October, her parents had thrown them a lavish, high society engagement party. They had gone on their two-week vacation to Hawaii in early November. And then there had been the dizzying array of holiday events, almost nonstop since Thanksgiving through New Years. Now Cameron was starting to throw herself into wedding plans, even though the date they had agreed on – Valentine's Day of the following year – was a long time from now. But he knew to expect an extremely over the top affair – no expenses spared on her parents' part – and that it very likely would take more than a year to plan it all.

At five minutes to ten, the two employees who were working with him on this particular project arrived at his office. Jake Harriman was an associate architect, and Brent Wilson an apprentice, not even a year out of college. Nathan liked working with both of them, for they had good energy, good chemistry, and some innovative ideas. The only real problem he had with them was that Jake was an incessant talker, and a real ladies man, so that his conversations were usually about the girl he'd banged the previous evening. And Brent was an impressionable puppy dog who thought Jake was a great role model and hung on his every word, especially when it came to recounting his sexual exploits.

As usual, Jake was prattling on about some babe as they settled themselves at the oval table in one corner of Nathan's spacious office. Nathan, who'd been fighting off both fatigue and a growing headache, really wasn't in the mood to listen to Jake's latest bawdy tales but didn't seem to have much choice in the matter.

"So did you see what she was wearing this morning?" Jake asked Brent, as they both began to set out their meeting notes and materials.

The younger man shook his close-cropped reddish blond head. "No, but I'm guessing it was something sexy."

Jake groaned. "Sexy? That's putting it mildly. This woman is a fucking wet dream, every single day. So get this. Today she's wearing this little black skirt that shows off that gorgeous ass, and this blouse – can't tell if it's silk or satin – but it looks like someone poured cream all over those big tits."

Brent's voice seemed to go up an octave as he asked excitedly, "What about the shoes? More of those fuck-me stilettos?"

"Oh dude, today's are the best ever," said Jake, smacking his lips. "Black, pointy-toes, high heels – and fuck me sideways – ankle straps. And – swear to God – she's wearing these sheer black stockings with a fucking seam up the back. She might as well have 'Do Me' written on her forehead."

Nathan frowned. Normally he didn't mind Jake's dirty stories, but his associate's tongue was practically hanging out of his mouth. "Hey, manwhore," he referred to Jake jokingly. "Who are you talking about anyway? This woman sounds way too hot for you."

Jake grinned. "A dude can dream, can't he? And we are talking about the smoking hot new designer Travis hired. She started last week."

Nathan raised a brow. "And you've fucked her already? I hope like hell you're keeping it discreet. We've talked about this, Jake. No more sexual harassment lawsuits, okay?"

Brent smirked. "He hasn't even scored a date with her. She gives him the brush off every time he tries. Dude, I told you, she's probably got some actor or model for a boyfriend. You may think you're irresistible but she's out of your league."

Jake shrugged. "Hey, no harm in trying, is there? I figure if anyone in this office has a shot at getting a date with her, it's me.

And I don't see any of the other losers here making any progress, either. So you haven't met Walking Wet Dream yet, Nate?"

Nathan rolled his eyes. "Christ, is that what you're calling her? Better not let that charming nickname get out. And no, I haven't met this so-called goddess yet. I've been too busy since I got here to even take a piss."

"Well, I'm sure you'll meet J-"

Jake was interrupted by the buzzing of the intercom from the front desk, and Becca announcing that their client had arrived. Nathan went to personally meet and escort him back to the office.

The meeting went extremely well – Jake and Brent instantly putting aside their bawdy conversation and becoming all business. As soon as the meeting ended, Nathan shooed them out of his office, not in the mood to hear anymore about this new designer they were both panting after. He just hoped that Manwhore Jake didn't have to be reprimanded again for flirting too blatantly with a female employee.

He grabbed a quick lunch with Damien Suarez – a friend he'd made years ago at the health club they both belonged to – before heading back to the office. On impulse, he decided to swing by Travis' office, just to check in – and maybe, if he was being honest - quiz him about this hot new designer that the men in the office were all lusting after.

He grinned at Courtney, noting that her crazy eyeglasses today were purple with pink polka dots. Amazingly they were probably the most conservative part of her outfit. "New hair color?" he asked.

Courtney fingered the red-orange strands. "Yes, but I'm bored with it already. I'm thinking of something less bright, more Goth. Like purple."

Nathan chuckled. Most people in the office didn't get Courtney, thinking her too freaky with her ever-changing hair color and odd wardrobe, but he'd liked her spunky personality and offbeat sense of humor since Travis had hired her over two years ago.

"Well, knowing you, it won't be boring. Travis busy?" he asked, nodding his head towards the half-open door to his partner's office.

"He's just finishing up with Julia, but I'm sure he won't mind if you go in. Have you met her yet?"

Nathan froze at the mention of *that* name. He shook his head, telling himself his reaction was unfounded. There had to literally be tens of thousands of women in this country with that name. It was just some unfortunate coincidence that their newest employee shared the same name as the woman who'd rocked his world off its axis last year.

"Is she the new designer I've heard about? If so, then, no, I haven't met her yet. But she's evidently made quite an impression on Jake and Brent," he replied wryly.

Courtney smirked. "A mannequin would make an impression on that slut Jake. Apparently he's in a big snit because Julia won't give him the time of day. He's dreaming if he thinks she'd ever look twice at him anyway. Travis told me one of her old boyfriends is an NFL quarterback."

Nathan raised a brow. "Well, now I'm curious. Time for me to meet this supposedly irresistible female."

"You won't be disappointed. Hey, I'm a girl – a *straight* girl despite all the lesbian cracks I know people make about me – and *I* think she's hot."

He was chuckling at Courtney's candid outspokenness as he knocked briefly on Travis' door, then walked in before his partner could invite him.

Travis glanced up from his desk chair at the unexpected interruption. "Yes, do just barge in, Nate," he drawled sarcastically.

"Don't forget you only own half of this place, and that you've crossed the border into my territory."

"Sorry to interrupt. Courtney seemed to think it was okay to come in," he said sheepishly.

Travis clucked in annoyance before beckoning him in. "Fine. We're just about done here anyway. Come on in and meet my absolutely brilliant new designer. You ought to see what she's come up with already for the Gregson project. Julia, meet Nate Atwood, the less creative half of this place. Nate, this beautiful being is Julia McKinnon."

Nathan walked to the far right of Travis's desk just as the woman seated in one of the high-backed chairs facing the desk stood and turned towards him. The hand he was extending her way froze in mid-space, and he could only stare in mingled shock and panic at the woman he'd last seen fleeing his hotel room in Manhattan in tears. The woman that Jake had been lusting after this morning was, by some bizarre and unfortunate quirk of fate that he couldn't begin to fathom at the moment, Julia – *his* Julia.

By the look of horror on her face, and the way she paled, this was as much of a shock to her as it was to him. The hand she placed limply in his was trembling, and he released it immediately.

"I – it's a pleasure to meet you, Mr. Atwood," she stuttered in a barely audible voice.

"And you, as well, Julia," he replied stoically, following her lead. "Except you must call me Nathan. We're not formal here."

Travis was looking at the two of them oddly. "You both look like someone just died," he drawled, a hint of his Southern accent noticeable. He rose to his feet, studying them carefully. "Have you two met before or something? I'm getting some really odd vibes here."

Julia shook her head emphatically, while Nathan chimed in a bit too enthusiastically, "No, Travis. Everything's fine." He gave Julia a polite smile. "I've never met Ms. McKinnon before, though I've been hearing a great deal about her around the office." His gaze dropped to her feet, noticing the sexy ankle straps of the shoes that Jake had mentioned. Absently, he wondered if those erotically sheer black stockings were pantyhose or – fucking hell – held up by garters. Aware of his face flushing, he returned his gaze to her face, which held a terse, almost angry expression.

"I thought for a moment that Nathan looked familiar," replied Julia tightly, "but now I realize he's a total stranger to me." She turned to Travis. "Are we finished here? I need to do some more work on the Garibaldi remodel."

Travis nodded. "All done for now, sweetie. We'll meet again tomorrow. And you and Nate should probably get together in a day or so to start going over interiors for the Napa resort. I have mentioned he's the lead architect on the project, haven't I?"

Julia glanced briefly, reluctantly, at Nathan and nodded. "Yes, of course. We'll talk soon, I'm sure – Nate."

He frowned. "I actually prefer Nathan. Travis is one of the few people to annoy me by using Nate. And, yes – we'll be meeting very soon, Julia."

She bit her bottom lip, glossed over in a shiny mocha shade, before hurrying out of Travis' office. Nathan watched her leave, noticing the way the elegant black wool skirt did in fact cling lovingly to the high, sweet curve of her ass. He cursed her silently for wearing those sexy as fuck stockings, with their naughty back seam, and fumed that he was far from the only man in this office to be turned on by them. He was furious to realize that the hot babe Jake and Brent had been frothing at the mouth about this morning was Julia. He wished now that he'd popped Jake in his filthy mouth, that -

"So are you going to tell me what the hell that was all about?" demanded Travis.

Nathan closed his eyes, forcing himself to push all of that shit to the depths of his memory, repressing it once again. He turned back towards Travis, feigning nonchalance. "What are you talking about?"

"You know exactly what I'm talking about, asshole. You looked like you saw a fucking ghost when you met Julia. Explain."

Nathan shrugged. "She's hot. I didn't expect that. I mean, Jake was getting a hard-on talking about her this morning but he gets aroused looking at video game babes. I was just startled to realize how pretty she really is."

"Hmm, that sounds like a huge load of bullshit to me, but we'll play it your way for now."

Nathan took a seat in the chair Julia had just vacated, noticing that traces of her light, flowery perfume remained. 'So tell me about our newest designer. She seems a bit young to be assigned to the Gregson project."

"She is, only twenty-five, but one of the most talented designers I've ever met," defended Travis. "Top of her class at Cornell – which, as you know, has one of the best architecture and interior design programs in the country. Then an internship followed by two years at Manhattan Interiors, the same place I did my internship at. In her first two years she's already won three design awards, and was nominated for two others. Coincidentally, Julia's already done some work for the Gregson group. Last year she did the designs for one of their Manhattan hotel remodels."

Nathan nodded, satisfied with her credentials. "So how did you find her for this job? Resume, headhunter?"

Travis regarded him curiously. "Why so interested? You usually don't care much about my staff."

"I'm interested when they've been assigned to work on what's arguably this firm's biggest project to date," retorted

Nathan. "I'm still not clear why you aren't the lead designer on the Napa resort."

"And I've told you half a dozen times that hotels aren't my thing. I find very little inspiration when every single guest room has to look basically the same. Plus, I have four other big projects going on right now. Julia is perfectly suited for this job. And Ian will adore her."

Ian Gregson was the Managing Director for the Americas division of the worldwide hotel chain, and despite his very elevated position in the company, he took an active role in the development and remodeling of all the properties under his umbrella. He was also single, very good looking, and certain to find Julia extremely attractive.

Nathan's mouth tightened into a thin line at the thought. "Fine," he told Travis abruptly. "I'm willing to at least see what her ideas are. But if I don't think she's experienced enough I want her replaced. This project is way too important."

"You worry too much," scoffed Travis. "Julia will do just fine. And she's such a sweetheart, very easy to work with. Not to mention," he added with a gleam in his eye, "very easy on the eye as you've already mentioned. It shouldn't be any hardship at all for you to work with her."

'Oh, if you only knew, buddy" said Nathan to himself as he returned to his office. 'Working with Julia is going to be the hardest thing I've ever had to do, given what happened between us in New York. Unless, of course, I can talk her out of working here and find her a job somewhere else.'

Chapter Seven

Julia was shaking so hard by the time she reached her office that she feared she might collapse. She grabbed the edge of her desk for support and gradually eased herself into her chair. Still trembling uncontrollably, she bent over at the waist, hiding her face in her hands, and struggled to take deep, calming breaths like the ones she practiced so faithfully in her daily yoga classes. After several minutes of this, she felt a bit more in control and was able to think in a more rational manner, not the panicked alarm mode she'd been in ever since realizing that Nate Atwood – the co-owner of this firm and Travis' business partner – was by some horrendous twist of fate the same Nathan who'd fucked her senseless last fall.

She'd cried for days after leaving his hotel room, a myriad of emotions ravaging her thoughts – sadness, anger, longing, hurt. One minute she'd be furious at his betrayal, the next she'd be wishing with all her heart that she was back in his arms. The sex – she refused now to call it lovemaking – had without question been the best she'd ever had, the orgasms he'd given her with such ease the strongest she'd ever experienced. The whole night she'd spent with Nathan had been almost dreamlike in its beauty, in the perfect synchronicity she'd had with him.

Her heart and her spirit had both been badly broken after that night for she'd recognized that if things had been different a relationship between her and Nathan could have been amazing. She'd connected with him on so many different levels, even without knowing anything about him. She had fallen into a deep depression after that night with him, a condition that had only been made worse by the unfortunate series of events that had befallen her afterwards – the attempted rape by Vanessa's boyfriend, her subsequent firing and difficulty in finding a new job, the tough but necessary decision to leave New York and move back home. Her parents had been deeply concerned about her during her stay with them, and Lauren had done her damndest to get her to open up about what had upset her. Under duress, not to mention the affects of too many shots of single malt Scotch, she'd finally sobbed out part of the story to her twin, but hadn't revealed the name of the lover who'd broken her heart. Julia had been too mortified to admit to her sister that she didn't even know his last name, and Lauren had already been on the verge of a rampage as it was.

And now fate had brought them together again, a fact she was having a great deal of trouble coming to terms with. How had she never put two and two together and figured that Nate was evidently a nickname for Nathan? Why, when applying for this job, had she never bothered to research Atwood Headley's website, where a photo of Nathan would have certainly been included? And how were they going to manage to work together after what had happened in New York? Though judging by Nathan's cool, composed reaction to "meeting" her in Travis's office, he was going to have no problem in maintaining a strictly professional manner in her presence. He had certainly appeared to handle the shock far better than she had.

Julia was more than a little miffed at this realization, wondering how he could appear so formal and unaffected by meeting again when she herself felt torn apart, her stomach churning bitterly. She knew she'd done a very poor job of disguising her shock and dismay at seeing him again, and it must have been her own reactions that had raised Travis' suspicions. She wondered what if anything Nathan might have said to him after she left, though she highly doubted he would ever discuss what had happened last September with anyone. But it was certainly possible that even now he was telling Travis they had met before, and that working together was going to be an impossibility. God, what if Travis decided he couldn't offer her a job after all? She'd just signed a year's lease on her new flat, moved all of her things up, and was starting to settle in. Would she even be able to find another job here in San Francisco if it came to that? She was just going to have to hope that Nathan kept quiet about what had happened last September, and realize that he had as much to lose as she potentially did if the truth was revealed.

Somehow she summoned up enough focus to return to the project she'd been working on earlier today. She'd missed working, loving the design work she did. It was her own form of artistic expression, her particular individual talent in a family comprised of artists of one sort or another. Her father – Robert – had himself been an architect of great renown until he'd explored another passion of his – designing and building furniture – and made that his primary focus. Her mother was the world famous painter Natalie Benoit, whose landscapes and seascapes graced the walls of many top galleries and private collections. Natalie didn't paint much anymore, devoting most of her time to the world class gallery she herself owned in Carmel instead. Natalie's twin Madelyn had been a fashion designer at three different houses in New York, Paris, and Milan before turning her focus to merchandising. And Julia's twin Lauren was a professional photographer, graduating at the top of her class from UCLA's film school before being recruited by National Geographic.

Julia was also something of an artist, certainly not on the same scale as her mother, and she preferred sketching with pen and charcoal to painting. She'd spent many peaceful hours while staying with her parents the past several weeks drawing and dabbling, with the incredible views from the oceanfront home in the Carmel Highlands her father had designed and built serving as inspiration. Robert had framed several of those sketches for her, and she'd hung them in her new office.

Once again blissfully absorbed in her work, the shrill ring of her office phone startled her. Since she'd only been here a scant week, she'd had very few calls so far.

"Julia McKinnon," she answered professionally.

The caller didn't identify himself but she knew his voice intimately. "We need to talk," Nathan stated bluntly. "I want you in my office at 5:45 this afternoon. Is that a problem for you?"

She almost flinched at the terseness of his tone, the barely repressed anger that simmered at the surface. Her spine stiffened, outraged that *he* would be mad at *her* considering the circumstances, but she only replied stiffly, "Not a problem. I'll see you then."

He disconnected the call without further comment, and she replaced the receiver, her hands beginning to shake again. Damn the man for having this effect on her, for rattling her otherwise perfectly composed nature, she thought in annoyance.

A quick glance at her watch revealed that there was still nearly an hour until she was to meet Nathan. Most people – herself included – typically left the office between five and five-thirty, so she assumed he'd chosen the slightly later time to ensure they weren't seen together. She struggled to focus on her project now, her concentration once again shattered because of Nathan. After several fruitless minutes, she gave up and carefully put all the materials away. Julia was a neat freak, very fastidious about putting everything back into its proper place, and having a tidy work space. It was like that at her apartment as well - everything perfectly put together and organized, especially with her clothes, shoes and bags.

She spent the remaining time until her enforced meeting with Nathan by answering some emails she'd been too busy to deal with lately – to Aunt Maddy, Gerard, Sam, and Lauren, who was currently climbing some mountain peak in Tanzania for a photo assignment.

At precisely 5:40pm, she powered down her laptop and stored it away, then walked in what she hoped was a confident and assured manner toward Nathan's office. She was relieved to see that Robyn was gone for the day, as were most of the others in the office.

Julia stood silently in the doorway of Nathan's office for long seconds, watching him unobserved as he worked. Her heart ached in spite of her better judgment as she took in his gorgeous face, the thickness of his rich, dark brown hair, the way his pale blue dress shirt strained across his broad chest and shoulders. She remembered in vivid detail how well defined his pecs and biceps were, how warm his skin had been beneath her hands and lips, how he'd groaned when she'd taken him into her mouth and -

He glanced up then and saw her, and their gazes locked in much the same way they had that very first time on Park Avenue. This time, though, he didn't smile at her, merely beckoned her inside almost brusquely.

"Close the door behind you, and take a seat. I'll be right with you." His voice was terse as he finished whatever he was doing on his computer.

Julia walked slowly into his office and sat in one of the chairs facing his desk. She gave the office a quick, assessing glance, liking the overall space with its gleaming hardwood floors, the natural light that streamed in from the windows, the big mahogany desk, and the various pieces of art. She might have added a slightly edgier, more modern vibe to what was overall a rather traditionally decorated room, but couldn't fault the design per se.

She was studying the various framed certificates hung on the wall above his credenza – his diploma from UC Berkeley, his certification from the AIA, awards he'd won – when he finally spoke.

"How did you find me?"

Julia's head swung to meet his gaze in disbelief. "Excuse me?"

Nathan leaned back in his desk chair, regarding her across the wide expanse of mahogany, with an expression of barely checked anger. "Come on, Julia. You don't really expect me to believe that your working here is some sort of wild coincidence, do you? The only logical explanation is that you somehow found out who I was and where I worked, and was lucky enough that there was a job opening. The only real coincidence is that you happen to be an interior designer and that I co-own an architectural design firm."

She stared back at him, appalled by his arrogance. "Are you kidding? Even assuming that I was able to figure out who you were – Mr. No Last Name, No Occupation, No City of Residence – why would you think I'd *want* to see you again, much less work with you?"

He shrugged, but his composure looked a bit less cocksure than it had. "Revenge, obsession. Maybe a little of both."

Julia smirked. "Really? You think I somehow managed to find out your name – by what means I have no idea – then stalked you several thousand miles across the country because I wanted to get back at you? Or worse, because I craved another fuck? Sorry, you weren't *that* good."

Nathan's eyes narrowed and shot out sparks of light blue fire. "That's not what you said that night."

Enraged, she got to her feet, leaning over his desk. "As I recall, both of us said a lot of things that night. But one of us intentionally neglected to say the one thing that would have instantly put a stop to everything else – something along the lines of 'by the way, I'm already spoken for'."

He winced at the angry lash of her words. "I deserve that, I suppose. But that still doesn't explain how you found me or why you followed me cross country."

She let out a rather undignified hoot of laughter. "For real, Nathan? You've still got me pegged as some *Fatal Attraction*-like stalker? Well, think on this one. I'm normally not a vain person, but I'm not naïve, either. I know I'm hot. Men have been telling me that since I was twelve. If I wanted a man that badly all I'd really need to do would be to walk inside the nearest bar or club or even a grocery store, and let nature take its course. It would take little to no effort on my part to get whatever man I wanted. And he sure as hell wouldn't be one who's already taken."

Julia could almost see steam rising out of his ears as he, too, surged to his feet and glared at her.

"Then explain to me how this could have happened," he demanded. "If you didn't know who I was, and you didn't come here because of me, how and why are you here?"

Aware that her legs were shaking again, she sank back to her chair and took several deep, calming breaths. "I needed a job, and I knew Travis through a mutual acquaintance," she explained quietly. "We spoke on the phone and arranged for me to interview with him. And here I am. Nothing more sinister or complicated than that."

Nathan frowned, clearly not satisfied with her explanation. "Why would a native New Yorker just pull up stakes and move clear across the country for a job? I would have imagined there were plenty of design jobs in Manhattan. And why did you need a job in the first place?"

She clasped and unclasped her hands nervously, not really wanting to have this particular conversation with him and knowing she'd need to choose her words carefully. "I'm actually a native Californian. I grew up in Carmel, and my family still lives there. I only lived in New York for a few years after college. And I'd been thinking of moving back to the West Coast for awhile. Things at my job hadn't been comfortable for months."

"Go on. Why did you leave your old job?" He sat back down in his chair.

Julia sighed, silently damning his persistence. "My boss hated me. Call it professional jealousy, who really knows, but she never wanted to hire me from the beginning. Her former partner was the one who hired me on, and mentored me. Has Travis ever mentioned someone named Gerard?"

Nathan nodded. "Of course. I've actually met Gerard once or twice when he came out here for a visit. He was your boss?"

"Yes. He and my aunt were classmates in college and remained friends. Gerard brought me on as an intern right after I graduated, and then hired me full time. Things were great until he had a bad breakup and decided to leave New York far behind, including his share in the company. Then everything sort of went to hell very quickly."

"This boss of yours – the one you claimed hated you. Just out of curiosity, how old is she?"

Julia shrugged. "Early to mid forties, I'm not exactly sure. Why?"

He gave a short, humorless laugh. "And you really wonder why she disliked you? I'm sure professional jealousy was a big part of it – Travis told me you've already won several design awards. But I'm just guessing she was also wildly jealous of you as a woman. As you so succinctly phrased it, you're hot. If your former boss was almost twenty years older than you I doubt she enjoyed being reminded of that fact every day."

She felt her cheeks flush. "I'm not sure her reasons for disliking me really matter. The point is that she basically made working there extremely unpleasant for me and I'd been thinking about finding another job for some time before she - "

Her voice trailed off, unwilling to reveal any more information.

"Before she what?" he persisted. "Did she fire you, Julia? And be honest. You know I can find this out very easily from Travis, and I know you're smart enough not to have lied to him about something like this."

She nodded, keeping her eyes downcast, afraid of giving too much away if he saw her face. "Yes, she fired me. And made it very, very difficult for me to find a job anywhere on the East Coast. Vanessa knows a lot of other designers and made sure to spread the word quickly that they shouldn't even consider hiring me. Moving back to California soon became my best option."

"You realize you're avoiding the real question, don't you? You need to tell me why she fired you, Julia. Again, I can find out the truth from Travis but I'd rather hear it from you."

She closed her eyes, having been afraid all along that he would insist on knowing this information and not at all eager to re-hash the trauma she'd suffered yet again. "Please, Nathan. It's not something I really want to talk about, okay?"

"Too bad. If you got fired for the wrong reason, then as the co-owner of this company I damn well need to know about it. And if I'm not satisfied with the reason, I'll insist that Travis release you."

Julia gasped, her gaze flying up to his. "You'd really do that? My God, I know you don't want to work with me, but you have no idea how hard it was for me to find a job, Nathan. I had to move back in with my parents for the past couple of months while I was looking for a new position. Please don't take this away from me."

His expression softened at her plea but he was still insistent. "Just tell me, Julia. How bad can it be? I mean, if it was something really bad like embezzlement I'm guessing your ex-boss would have pressed charges.'

She shook her head. "No, it wasn't anything like that. It was – oh, God, this is really hard for me. I've tried to just forget about it." To her horror, she felt tears begin to trickle hotly down her cheeks and she brushed them away impatiently.

Nathan's expression turned to one of concern, almost alarm. "Jesus, what the hell happened? How bad could it have been to make you cry?"

Once again she refused to meet his eyes, staring down at the floor as she haltingly related the story about the night Philip had attacked her in the office. She kept the details to the bare minimum but Nathan heard enough of the sordid tale to push himself away from his desk and surge to his feet in a rage.

"What's this fucker's name?" he demanded as he began to pace back and forth behind his desk.

She was sobbing quietly by now, her whole body quivering as she wrapped her arms around her midsection. "Philip. I'm not sure of his last name. It's Russian or Czech, something long and complicated. What difference does it make?"

"Because I'm about five minutes away from booking a flight to New York, finding this guy, and cutting his balls off," Nathan said harshly. "How badly did he hurt you, Julia?"

She covered her face with her hands, trying vainly to stem the flow of her tears. "Nathan, please. I really don't want to talk about this anymore. It's obviously very upsetting to have to relive that night again."

He walked around the side of the desk to kneel in front of her, his hand cupping her cheek, his thumb brushing away her tears. "I'm sorry, baby. Sorry that I wasn't there to prevent something like that from happening, to protect you, to kick that bastard's ass into the Hudson River. Just answer this one last question, and then I promise we'll never talk about it again."

Her bottom lip quivered and he clasped her hands tightly in his as she shook her head. "God, this is hard. I still have nightmares sometimes."

He pressed a gentle kiss to her forehead. "It's okay, baby. You're safe now. No one is going to hurt you again. Now just tell me what I want to know and the subject will stay closed after that."

Julia took a deep breath before murmuring in a barely audible voice. "He – he split my lip. My jaw and cheekbones were bruised. One black eye. Three cracked ribs. Scratches and bruises in too many places to count. That's about it."

"So he never actually –"

"No." She cut him off. "It never got that far. Vanessa interrupted him before anything could happen."

Nathan made a harsh noise. "You don't call getting beaten and broken anything? Jesus, I hope like hell the fucker is rotting in some jail cell right now."

She shook her head. "No. I didn't press charges. I just wanted to forget it ever happened and leave New York as soon as possible."

He stared at her in disbelief. "Are you fucking kidding me, Julia? You just let him walk away without any consequences? And then let that bitch fire you because her boyfriend's a rapist?"

Julia shuddered. "It was a living nightmare, Nathan. One I wanted to wake up from and forget as quickly as possible. I didn't want to deal with police, attorneys, trials. Vanessa has piles of money, she would have hired a top lawyer for him and gotten the charges dismissed, and I would have had to go through all of that trauma for nothing. No, I made the decision to just walk away and I don't regret it. Now, it's time to stop talking about this. For good."

He brushed her hair back behind her ear, gave a brief nod, and then stood. "All right, if that's what you wish. We won't discuss it again." He took a seat behind his desk. "But what we do have to discuss is how in hell you and I are going to be able to work together given the circumstances. After all, I'd be a complete and total bastard at this point to force you out wouldn't I?"

Her voice choked. "Oh, God. You'd really do that? Please, Nathan. I need this job more than you can even imagine. I'll do whatever it takes to keep working here."

"Relax, Julia. I'm not going to fire you. I did have thoughts of trying to find you a job at different firm here in town, but I doubt we could pull that off without having to tell Travis about what happened last September. And, not to borrow that ridiculous Las Vegas cliché, but whatever happened in New York definitely has to stay in New York. Have you discussed it with anyone?"

"Just my sister. But I never mentioned your name. And I didn't tell her much, though being twins she always knows when something's upsetting me."

Nathan's eyes widened. "You have a twin? Identical?" At her nod he shook his head in disbelief. "Christ, there are actually two women who look like you? That's unbelievable. But to get back to what I was saying, you never mentioned any of this to Travis, did you?"

"No, of course not. And I don't plan on discussing it with anyone else. I'm fully aware that you could get me fired very easily, Nathan, so I will definitely be a model of discretion," she said quietly. "I pride myself on being a complete professional at work. You don't have to worry about me ever acting inappropriately. Just please give me a chance to prove myself. I'm actually a very good designer and I'm thrilled to have such a fantastic opportunity like this one."

"Let's be perfectly clear here, Julia," he stated firmly. "No discussion or reference to meeting in New York to anyone. Not even the slightest hint of flirting or impropriety between us. We are to have strictly – very strictly – a business only relationship. If you can agree to that, then I'm willing to give this a try on a trial basis. Otherwise, I'll make some calls and try to find you another job close by."

She shook her head."No, that won't be necessary, I assure you. I agree completely with everything you just said. It won't be a problem to work together, I promise." She glanced down at her clasped hands again. "If I'd had even the slightest suspicion that the Nate Atwood who Travis kept mentioning was actually the Nathan I'd met in New York, there's no way I would have taken this job or even interviewed for it. I'm not here to make trouble for you, or make working conditions difficult. I'll do whatever is necessary to be able to keep working here."

"All right, then. Let's hope that we can keep things professional." He paused a moment before continuing on, somewhat awkwardly. "There's just one more thing. This might be a little touchy but it has to be said. At some point in time – whether it's here in the office or at an outside function – you're likely to meet Cameron, my fiancée."

Julia couldn't help the little shudder that passed through her body. "Most likely, yes."

"I've got to ask you. Please don't say anything to her about what happened. I know I treated you badly, Julia, but none of that was her fault. Don't take it out on her, okay?"

She stared at him in hurt disbelief. "You really think I could be that vindictive? I guess we don't know each other very well at all, do we? Don't worry, Nathan. I won't rat you out to your fiancée. After all, you're just my boss now, aren't you?"

He exhaled deeply. "Thank you, Julia. I know I deserve your anger but taking it out on Cameron won't solve anything."

She stood, fighting back a fresh onslaught of tears. "I'm not that sort of person, Nathan. Besides, doing something like that would only further ruin the memory of that night for me. And for me, at least, it was the most special night I've ever known."

Nathan groaned. "God, Julia. Don't -"

She held up a hand. "Don't say anything more, okay? Right now it's as though that night happened to two other people a long time ago. Let's just leave it buried in the past. Now, if that's all, I'd like to leave now."

He nodded, unable to meet her gaze. "Yeah, that's it. You can go."

Julia felt the hot tears threatening to spill over again so she turned and left without another word, wondering if she was kidding herself that she could actually work with Nathan under these circumstances. She just knew that she didn't have any other options but to at least give it a try, even if it meant having her heart broken all over again.

✳✳✳✳✳

Nathan was practically shaking as Julia left his office, and headed immediately for the cabinet where he kept an assortment of liquor and glasses. He pulled out the bottle of twelve-year old Macallan and poured himself a healthy portion, not bothering with either ice or water. He tossed half of it down in one gulp, badly needing the fortification it would hopefully provide him. The last time he'd been this shook up had been on that damned plane ride home after having left a heartbroken Julia behind in New York.

He wanted to fling the heavy crystal tumbler against the wall and watch it shatter into tiny pieces as he tried to imagine how upset and terrified she must have been after almost getting raped in her own office. He slammed the glass down on his credenza, struggling for control as he recalled her tearful sobs and trembling hands while choking out the story of what had happened. And despite his promise to her that they wouldn't speak of the incident again, all he really wanted was to book a flight back to New York, find this bastard and pummel him into a bleeding, broken mess. All he would need to do was call Travis' friend Gerard – Julia's old boss – and find out the last name of the fucker who'd hurt her so badly. It would be just that easy.

But then, as the whiskey began to have its desired effect, he started to calm down and think more rationally. He couldn't call Gerard and ask him such a question without betraying his past with Julia, and he wasn't naïve enough to believe that Gerard wouldn't immediately turn around and share this information with Travis. And God knew his business partner already suspected something fishy was going on. Travis was a nosy bastard, always probing and prodding, and loved to gossip more than a little old lady. And given the animosity that existed between Travis and Cameron, there was no way in hell he could risk the knowledge that he and Julia had had a passionate fling getting out. Travis would find some way – discreet or not – to plant doubts in Cameron's mind and then all hell would break loose.

'Fuck it all," he muttered, plopping down onto his desk chair and slumping against the high, padded back. 'What a goddamned fucking mess. How in hell am I going to be able to work with her every day, especially when she looks like that?'

Julia was ten times more beautiful than his recollections of her, and seeing her in the flesh again had made him excruciatingly aware of how much he still wanted her. Four months apart had done absolutely nothing to dim the stunning physical attraction they shared – it had flared to instant and burning recognition the moment he'd met her eyes again.

He tortured himself by wondering if she already had a new boyfriend out here in California, and how many men she'd been with in the months since he'd met her in New York. He saw red as he recalled the almost haughty manner in which she'd coolly informed him that she could have pretty much any guy who caught her fancy, and didn't have to waste her time on someone like him. What made matters so much worse was the fact that she was absolutely right. Julia could conceivably date a different guy every night of the week for a month, and have her pick of who she liked best. Or simply start over again with a fresh batch.

He'd probably just made a huge ass of himself, therefore, by insinuating that she was still pining over him and laying down rules about keeping things professional between them. Hell, she'd probably been so pissed off at the way he'd treated her in New York that she had forgotten about him before his plane left the ground. And then she'd likely hit up one of the many bars or clubs in Manhattan and found some attractive guy who wasn't already engaged – a guy who'd probably worshipped her and treated her like the goddess she was.

No, he thought angrily. It wouldn't be Julia he was going to have to worry about to keep things professional between them. *He* was the one who was going to have to make a superhuman effort to keep his fucking hands off of her, and somehow remember that he was engaged to another woman. The way he looked at it, he sure as fuck had his work cut out for him.

Chapter Eight

February

After a month on the job at Atwood Headley, Julia had quickly learned the telephone extensions of the key personnel in the office. Thus, she recognized the incoming call as being from Robyn, Nathan's super-efficient assistant.

"Good morning, Robyn. How are you today?" she said as pleasantly as possible. The older woman had been exceedingly kind to Julia since day one.

"Just great, hon. Listen, the boss asked me to tell you that the Gregson meeting has been moved up by fifteen minutes, so be ready to leave here around nine-thirty. Is that okay?"

A quick glance at the clock on her computer shoved it to be just after eight-thirty. "Yes, that's fine. I'll meet Nathan by the elevators then."

"Perfect. Talk to you later."

Julia sighed as she hung up the phone. Over the past few weeks, anytime Nathan needed to communicate with her it had either been through Robyn or via email. Any face to face meetings they'd had – primarily about the Napa hotel project – had also been attended by at least one other person, usually that idiot Jake Harriman who spent most of the meeting staring at her tits. Nathan had certainly fulfilled his part of their bargain – acting like the perfect gentleman, always professional, always distant. Julia had a hard time reconciling his current behavior with the seductive, flirtatious, and passionate man she'd met in New York. No doubt, she thought unhappily, he was only sharing that particular side of his personality with his fiancée.

Being around Nathan on an almost daily basis had been far more difficult – and heartbreaking – than Julia could have imagined. She'd always been a sucker for a man who could wear a suit really well, and Nathan wore his collection of tailored designer suits – Armani, Prada, Gucci, Dolce & Gabbana – far better than most. He had a good eye for color – no doubt he had something of an artistic side given his chosen profession – and always paired his suits with perfectly coordinated shirts and ties. Her particular favorite was his black pinstriped D&G, especially when he teamed it with a crisp white shirt and dark red tie. She loved the way the beautifully cut jacket emphasized the breadth of his shoulders and back, and how the trousers fell just so from his slim hips.

Each time they met, her fingers itched to run themselves through all that thick, dark brown hair. She longed to see those beautiful light blue eyes twinkle at her, his sinfully full mouth to smile at her just once – *really* smile, not just one of those brief, polite acknowledgments that one might bestow on a total stranger. He never once asked her a personal questions, how her weekend had been, or complimented her on her appearance.

And yet, he did all those things and more to nearly everyone else in the office, male and female. She'd seen him give Becca, the receptionist, a wide grin and compliment her bright red sweater. Just two days ago he'd asked Jake the Jerk – and his sidekick Brent the Bonehead – about their weekends and had listened as each described in excruciating detail what they'd done. He'd even teased Courtney about her latest hair color – this one a bright electric blue. But with Julia herself, it seemed he was doing an exemplary job of acting like she didn't exist beyond her sketches and designs for the Napa hotel.

He had, in fact, been a bit harsh with his critiques and she'd had to re-do a number of the designs several times. She had agreed with a few of his suggestions, but on most of the others she'd really felt like he was nitpicking and intentionally making things challenging for her. But she was determined to succeed here and had made every change he'd requested without complaint or argument.

She was working harder and putting in more hours than she had at Manhattan Interiors, but also felt more artistically fulfilled and satisfied with her work. There was more variety, more challenges, and more demands but she found those things had also lit a spark in her creative side, and in her opinion she was producing some of her best work right now.

Julia was actually grateful for the long hours she'd been working, a welcome diversion to her continuing infatuation with Nathan. In the six weeks or so since she'd moved to San Francisco, her day to day life had fallen into a busy but satisfying routine. She rose early enough to make it to a 6:00am Ashtanga yoga class at a studio close to her flat. She was at her desk beginning her work day by eight-thirty, and often worked past six in the evening. She cooked dinner for herself most nights – and occasionally for Angela when she could persuade her upstairs neighbor and girlhood friend to actually eat something. Weekends thus far had been spent doing household chores, laundry, shopping, more yoga, and dragging Angela to an occasional movie or dinner out.

One thing she did *not* do was go trolling in clubs or bars as she'd bragged to Nathan about. That had never been her scene and the only one-night stand she'd had in her life had been Nathan. And while San Francisco was proving to be little different from New York in terms of how many men stared at her or tried to hit on her, Julia was in absolutely no rush to have a steady man in her life. She tried to tell herself it was just because she had been so busy – settling into her new flat, getting to know her way around the city, and of course the many demands of her new job. But deep down she knew it was because she was too attracted to Nathan to want to settle for someone else, even though the attraction certainly seemed one-sided at this point.

Pride had demanded that Julia look her absolute best every single day at work, and she went out of her way to always wear stunning clothes and shoes, make sure her makeup was flawless and her hair perfect. She didn't consciously think about flaunting herself in Nathan's face, as though to remind him of everything he was missing, but knew that was likely the real motivation. She spent hours every weekend getting her outfits ready for the upcoming work week, making sure shoes and bags and jewelry were all perfectly coordinated with her dresses and skirts. But for all that Nathan commented or appeared to even notice, she might as well be wearing baggy jeans and shapeless sweatshirts every day.

The worst times, though, had been when she'd tearfully imagined him with his fiancée, making love to her as passionately and skillfully as he had done to Julia back in New York. Julia assumed that Nathan's fiancée was a beautiful, sexy woman since someone as mindblowingly handsome as he was could easily have his pick of any female he wanted. She recalled how obsessed he had been with her boobs, and guessed that his fiancée must have an equally impressive rack. Julia wondered if the woman was blonde or brunette, tall or petite, what she did for a living, and if Nathan took as much pleasure in her body as he appeared to have done with Julia's. Tears came to her eyes once again as she realized how much she missed him, longed for him, and how it made her physically ache just to be near him and know she could only look and not touch ever again. Angrily, she forced herself out of her melancholy and returned her focus to her work.

It was chilly outside today with a cold wind blowing, so she'd dressed warmly in a light gray James Perse dress with elbow-length sleeves. The soft fabric was shirred from waist to hem, emphasizing her curves without being too clingy. Because the cross-front bodice revealed just a bit too much cleavage, she'd wrapped a gray and black print scarf around her neck to fill in the gap. She wore her favorite shoes – black Christian Louboutin pumps with sky-high heels – and carried a black Gucci tote bag. She'd curled her hair into long, loose waves, and taken extra care with her makeup to achieve the smoky gray eyes and pale pink lips that she knew were her best colors.

She was standing in front of the elevators and just starting to shrug into her Azzedine Alaia gray wool princess coat when she felt a hand on her shoulder, helping her into the coat, and heard a voice that said, "Here, let me."

Her answering smile froze on her face when she saw that it was Jake helping her with the coat, and not Nathan, who was just walking into the elevator lobby, an impassive expression on his handsome face.

"Thank you," she told Jake neutrally.

As usual, he was grinning from ear to ear, and she quickly buttoned the coat up so he couldn't stare at her breasts again. "Oh, my pleasure, Julia. You look beautiful today, once again. You're wearing my favorite shoes, you know."

Julia gave him a small smile in return, making a mental note to shelve the black Louboutins for a few weeks. But it likely wouldn't do much good with Jake, for he seemed to think she looked gorgeous no matter what she wore. Unlike Nathan, who never said one word about her appearance.

"Ready to go?" was all he said in a brisk voice. "Do you have everything you'll need?"

Julia indicated the large black case she was carrying. "Everything's in here, yes."

He pressed the elevator button that would take them straight to the garage level. "We'll drive. It's freezing out today and I doubt you could walk fast enough in those shoes anyway."

There was a tight, almost disapproving set to his mouth when he said that, and Julia now felt a bit foolish with her choice of footwear. She hadn't assumed they would be walking to the Gregson corporate offices since they were more than a mile from here. Not that it would have done her much good to wear different shoes, anyway, since pretty much every pair she owned had at least a four-inch heel.

"Do you want to take my car, Nate?" offered Jake. "I don't think the three of us are going to fit in your Beamer unless Julia sits in my lap. Which is just fine with me, by the way."

Julia rolled her eyes at his latest innuendo and ignored his eager smile. God, she was really going to have to put the kybosh on his constant flirty behavior soon. Jake was harmless enough, and she certainly didn't feel threatened by him like she had that creep Philip, but he was still annoying as hell.

Nathan remained expressionless as he checked a text on his phone while the elevator continued its descent. "Not a problem. I drove the Lexus today, so plenty of room for all of us."

"Aw, too bad," replied Jake as he playfully slipped an arm around Julia's waist. "I was looking forward to sharing my seat."

She firmly removed his hand from her waist and took great pleasure in hearing him yelp when she bent his little finger back. "Keep your hands to yourself. And your adolescent comments, too."

While Jake nursed his sore hand – and undoubtedly bruised ego – Julia stole a quick glance at Nathan and swore she saw the ghost of a smile playing about his lips. But then the elevator doors opened on the garage level, and the three of them walked the short distance to where a dark blue luxury SUV was parked.

"Jake can ride shotgun," she declared, not wanting to be that close in proximity to Nathan. Even from here she could smell the scent of his light cologne, feel the warmth of his skin. She was so attracted to him that she almost ached with the wanting, especially since she was forbidden from touching him the way she longed to do. Keeping her distance was a wise move.

Nathan held the back door open for her as she slid her case and purse inside. Julia eyed the high step up into the car dubiously, wishing her dress wasn't quite so formfitting, but then shrugged and hoisted herself up into the car. Predictably, her dress had ridden up in the process and she automatically began to pull the hem down, catching Nathan's gaze in the process. His eyes dropped to where the dress had crept up, revealing a glimpse of a lacy silver gray garter clipped to the top of her sheer, pale gray stockings. His jaw slackened momentarily before he tore his gaze away and abruptly shut the door. Julia couldn't help but feel a small sense of satisfaction to know that he'd noticed her lingerie, and she hoped rather naughtily that he'd keep thinking about it all during their meeting.

Jake prattled on about some TV show he was watching during the short drive to the Gregson offices, but he was the only one talking, seemingly oblivious to the awkward silence that existed between Julia and Nathan. When they arrived at the parking garage, Nathan handed the keys over to the valet before hurrying over to open Julia's door for her, somehow beating Jake to the punch.

"Here, watch your step," he cautioned as he offered Julia his hand.

She took it lightly, grateful for his assistance as she stepped down from the SUV in her high heels. Before she could reach back in for her case, he was doing that for her.

"I'll take it," he assured her. "It's a lot heavier than I thought, you should have had one of us carry it down for you."

She shrugged. "It's not so bad. But thank you."

Julia noticed with satisfaction that Jake kept a careful distance from her as they exited the elevator from the parking garage to the main lobby of the building. Conversely, Nathan kept a light hand on her elbow, guiding her through the busy throng of people entering and exiting the main lobby until they were inside a crowded elevator car. It was the first time he'd made even the tiniest bit of physical contact with her since they'd met again, and she forced herself not to read too much into his almost impersonal gesture.

The Gregson Hotel Group's American headquarters encompassed four full floors of this high-rise building, with the executive offices and meeting rooms on the twentieth floor. Julia found herself wedged into a corner of the packed elevator, with Nathan right beside her. When the woman in front of her turned slightly to rummage in her oversized handbag, she gave Julia an unintentional bump that pushed her back against Nathan.

His free hand instinctively grasped her forearm to steady her. "Easy," he murmured in her ear.

Even through the wool of her coat she could feel the warmth of his hand, and she had to resist the urge to lean against him. The longing she felt to be in his arms again, to kiss him and be naked with him was almost overwhelming at times. She wondered how he could be so unaffected by her, how he could act like a completely different person than the man she'd had such mindblowing sex with in New York. But it was becoming more and more apparent that their time together hadn't meant anything to him, and maybe even that it hadn't been the first occasion he'd cheated on his fiancée. She forced that particular thought from her mind, for it only further ate away at the memories she had of that magical night, cheapening them to a greater degree.

The elevator doors opened into a spacious, elegant reception area with marble floors, a trio of pale mocha sofas arranged around a round glass-topped table, and a gleaming walnut reception desk. Nathan announced them to the receptionist – a cool, pretty blonde who smiled at the two men with an air that spoke of familiarity. She didn't spare Julia a glance, something Julia had grown used to over the years. Most women found her threatening in some way or another, especially if there were men in the vicinity, and it was one reason she had only a few close female friends.

Within two minutes, a slim young man of medium height wearing a conservative dark brown suit and wire-rimmed glasses walked briskly into the reception area. He was unsmiling and looked all business. Julia couldn't imagine ever trying to crack a joke around him.

He extended his hand first to Nathan, then to Jake, before turning to Julia. He did a bit of a double-take before introducing himself. "I'm Andrew Doherty, Mr. Gregson's PA. You must be Ms McKinnon. We've all been looking forward to meeting the new designer for this project."

She shook his hand, a little surprised at his firm, assured grip. He gave off something of a nerdish-vibe, but the brown eyes behind the glasses were sharp and intelligent, and she doubted he ever missed a detail.

"A pleasure to meet you. And please, call me Julia."

Andrew gave a brief nod of acknowledgment. "Let's head back, shall we? Everything is ready for you, and I'll just let Mr. Gregson and the others know you've arrived."

Andrew ushered them down a long, plushly carpeted hallway past half a dozen or more private offices to the left and cubicle workstations to the right. They turned right at the end of the hallway and were shown into a large, spacious conference room. One wall of the room was floor to ceiling windows that let in some much needed light on this rather gloomy, overcast day. The square conference table was huge and polished to a shiny rosewood patina. At least two dozen plushy upholstered chairs had been placed along the sides and at either end.

At one end of the room a wall to wall built-in credenza had been set with a complete coffee service, fresh fruit, and pastries, everything beautifully arranged. Closer to the other end of the room, several display easels had been set up.

"I assume this is where we should sit?" Julia asked Nathan, indicating the chairs closest to the easels.

He nodded. "Yes, Ian always sits at the head of the table here, and he prefers us close by. Do you need any help setting up your presentation boards?"

She shook her head as she began to shimmy out of her coat. "No, thanks. I've got it. I just need my case."

"Here, let me," he offered, as he helped her out of her coat. Julia's breath hitched at the feel of his hands on her shoulders as they eased the gray coat off. "I think there's a coat rack around here somewhere."

"Oh, I'll be happy to take that for you, Mr. Atwood," said a soft, feminine voice.

Julia glanced up as a beautiful, shapely blonde girl walked into the room, her arms filled with a stack of folders. She set them on a corner of the table before taking Julia's coat.

"Thank you, Tessa," replied Nathan with a smile. "Julia, this is Tessa Lockwood, who works here for Ian and his staff. Tessa, I'd like you to meet our new interior designer, Julia McKinnon."

Tessa, whom Julia guessed was a couple of years younger than herself, smiled sweetly, her big blue eyes kind. "It's nice to meet you, Ms. McKinnon. What a lovely coat this is. Your dress, too."

Julia's discerning eye immediately pegged the black and white checkered wool skirt and black turtleneck sweater Tessa wore as inexpensive, most likely from a discount chain store. But when you had the sort of tall, curvy body the blonde girl did you looked good in most anything, expensive or otherwise. Julia smiled at her almost reassuringly. "Thank you so much. And please call me Julia."

Tessa's cheeks pinkened, and she swept an arm to the back of the room. "Please, help yourselves to coffee and such. I'll be back in just a minute or two. The others are on their way."

Jake make a smacking sound with his lips as Tessa hurried from the room. "I'd like to help myself to a nice big bite of her. Next to Julia, she's the best looking thing I've seen in a long time."

Nathan rolled his eyes. "Keep it under lock and key there, lover boy. And forget about Tessa – she's a married woman."

Julia's eyes widened. "Really? She's so young."

Nathan shrugged. "Don't know the story there. All I know is that Gigolo Jake here needs to back off."

"That's okay," replied Jake with a grin. "I'd rather have Julia anyway."

Nathan flashed him a warning glare, but Julia was more than capable of sticking up for herself. "Well, news flash. Julia would rather *not* have you, so give it a rest, okay? I may have to work with you but that doesn't mean I have to put up with your constant flirting," she retorted.

Jake smirked. "Probably all for the better. I couldn't afford you, anyway."

She gasped at the same time that Nathan angrily cautioned, "Watch it, Jake. I can pull you from this project in a flat second."

"And what the hell did that last comment mean, anyway?" demanded Julia. "Are you trying to imply – "

Jake waved a hand in dismissal. "Of course not. All I meant was that you like a lot of expensive designer clothes. Those shoes you have on – six or seven hundred bucks, right? I know Travis isn't paying you *that* well."

Julia put her hands on her hips. "So – what? I must have a rich sugar daddy supporting me? Not that it's any of your business, asshole, but I have an aunt in the fashion business who sends me stuff. Now – end of discussion. I've got a presentation to set up."

She wasn't sure who looked more shocked by her outburst – Jake or Nathan. But it didn't matter because both of them shut up and swiftly finished helping her set up the display easels with the various designs they were presenting today to Ian Gregson and his team.

Within minutes, a dozen different people – men and women – began filtering into the room. Nathan did his best to introduce Julia to them – a Director of Marketing, a Facilities Manager, a Project Manager, and so forth – but she knew she'd never remember most of their names or titles at this first meeting. Until Ian Gregson entered the room, and she knew that no one could ever forget that name or face.

He was a tall, broad-shouldered man who instantly commanded attention and respect. Julia guessed him to be in his late thirties, possibly even early forties, and he was one of the most strikingly handsome men she'd ever met. Not in the same classically handsome, dreamy way that Nathan was, but in a more rugged manner that was at odds with his conservatively tailored black suit. Ian was also dark haired but the style was cut shorter and closer to the head than Nathan's luxurious mane. Power rolled off this man in waves, and Julia felt more than a little intimidated by him.

But his hazel eyes twinkled at her, and his firm mouth curved up in a smile as Nathan introduced them. He clasped her hand in his for long seconds, gazing down at her from his vastly superior height.

"It's a great pleasure to meet you, Julia," he told her in a crisp British accent.

She smiled up at him with what she hoped was her best professional look. "The pleasure is mine, Mr. Gregson. It's a privilege to work for the Gregson Group again."

Still clasping her hand, Ian led her to the chair right beside his and held it out for her. "Ah, yes. I understand you're responsible for the remodel of our hotel on the Upper East Side in Manhattan. I was given a brief tour the last time I was in New York, and as I recall it was quite impressive." He slid her chair in once she was seated. "And you must call me Ian. Mr. Gregson always sounds like my father."

Julia knew from having done her research that Ian's father – Edward – was the CEO of the company, and that Ian's two brothers – Hugh and Colin - were Managing Directors of the European and Asia Pacific regions respectively.

Nathan was seated to her immediate left, and as she caught his eye when he took his seat, she was puzzled at the frown he directed her way. She had no idea what he could possibly be displeased about already, given that the meeting had yet to begin. Julia gave him a little shrug and returned her attention to Ian.

To call the man dynamic was the understatement of the century. When Ian Gregson spoke, every person in the room seem mesmerized and paid him complete attention. Julia couldn't properly explain what it was about him that commanded such attention, for he didn't speak in a louder than normal voice, nor did he dominate the conversation, yell, demand, or intimidate. In fact, Julia thought him to be one of the best listeners she'd ever met.

No, Ian Gregson just had charisma, bucket loads of it, and both men and women were drawn to him. Even Nathan, who was himself an extremely dynamic and charismatic man, was giving Ian his rapt attention, and Julia sensed it had little to do with the fact that the Gregson Group was his biggest client.

When it came time for Julia to present her design boards, every eye in the room was fixated on her. She ought to have been nervous, for this was by far the most important project she'd ever worked on, but instead she was in her element as she went through each board and deftly answered each and every question that arose.

Julia had to contain a smug smile of satisfaction when Ian expressed some doubts about three of the four designs that Nathan had made her re-do. She was surprised when Nathan offered up, "I believe we have a second idea for each of these. Julia, did you bring the alternate designs with you?"

A raised brow was the only sign she gave him to acknowledge his quick-thinking cover-up. To the rest of the group, she merely smiled and replied, "Yes, I did happen to bring them along. Thank you for reminding me, Nathan."

Julia forced herself not to gloat, or even to look in Nathan's direction, when Ian and the others nodded their approval of her original designs. It made Julia wonder if Nathan had forced her to alter them just to be a hardass and exert his control over her.

One of Ian's managers – a charming, older Frenchman who had recently transferred to San Francisco from the European headquarters – was trying to make a comment about one of the designs but was struggling a bit with the language barrier. Julia had noted from previous comments he'd made that his English wasn't terribly good, leading her to guess he had likely worked in one of the firm's French hotels or resorts before transferring to the London offices.

The man – Henri was his name – tapped his fingers on the table impatiently. "I cannot think of the English translation – it is a saying we have in French – ah, I am so stupid today."

Taking pity on him, Julia told him in perfect French, "*Dites-moi que vous voulez dire*," or in English "tell me what you want to say."

Henri's face lit up, and every pair of eyes at the table was focused on Julia. "*Ah, la belle femme parle le francais*," he said joyously. He then spoke to Julia in rapid French, happy to be able to convey his thoughts properly.

She easily translated to English the commentary he had made on the design for the hotel lobby before moving on to the next design board. Once she was finished, it was Nathan's turn to update the group on some modifications for the original building design that they had apparently requested at a previous meeting.

Julia used the break to rearrange some of her notes, and to discreetly observe the faces and reactions of the group gathered around the conference table. Nathan was an engaging speaker, and kept everyone's rapt attention, especially that of an older, well-dressed blonde woman who stared at him with ill-disguised interest. Julia knew from the frequent questions and interruptions the woman had made that her name was Morgan Cottrell, and that she was the Business Development Manager. She was quite attractive and well-kept, but Julia guessed her to be at least ten years older than Nathan.

She told herself angrily that she shouldn't give a damn if some cougarish woman kept smiling invitingly at Nathan. It certainly wasn't any of her business or concern – she ought to be leaving that up to Nathan's fiancée. But she still couldn't stop wishing she had the nerve to tell the overly eager Morgan to button up her blouse a bit higher, and to stop trying and interest Nathan in her impressive but undoubtedly fake cleavage. After all, hadn't he told her back in New York that he hated fake boobs? It had been right before he'd licked her nipple, causing it to harden much as it was doing right now. Stifling a soft moan, Julia turned her attention back to Nathan's presentation.

Forcing herself to look at anyone but Morgan and observe the older woman's blatant interest in Nathan, she stole a quick glance to her right at Ian and was surprised to see his gaze directed not at Nathan – who was still speaking – but at the back of the room. Her interest piqued, Julia waited a few moments before discreetly following the line of Ian's vision, and then she smiled knowingly to herself.

The beautiful blonde girl who'd been so sweet and helpful earlier – Tessa – was seated quietly in a back corner of the room, though not at the table itself. It seemed her purpose in being present was to not only take notes but also to make sure the coffee service and food stayed well stocked and tidy. Tessa's head was bent as she wrote in her notebook, and thus she remained unaware of the look her boss was giving her. But Julia had seen that particular look many times on a man's face, and wondered briefly how a commanding, powerful man like Ian dealt with the fact that the girl he was lusting after was a married woman and therefore unavailable to him.

The meeting wrapped up twenty minutes later and Julia spent a few extra minutes chatting with several of Ian's team who approached her, including Henri who was delighted to converse in his native tongue. At some point, Ian joined in their conversation and he was nearly as fluent in French as Julia was.

From the corner of her eye, Julia spotted Nathan, who appeared to be trying to find a polite way to disengage himself from Morgan. The older woman was practically rubbing herself against him she was standing so close, and laughing flirtatiously. Torn between feeling that Nathan could take care of himself and didn't deserve her sympathy, and a raging need to pull Morgan's dyed blonde hair from her scalp, she settled for somewhere in between.

Excusing herself politely from Henri, she walked to where Morgan was nearly shoving her fake tits into Nathan's chest and placed a feather-light touch on his arm.

"I'm so sorry to interrupt," she said in her sweetest voice, "but we really do need to head back to the office. I have a client due to arrive within the hour, and I believe Jake does as well."

Nathan looked at her with an expression of such gratitude that she couldn't help but beam at him, while Morgan looked like she wanted to claw Julia's eyes out.

"Yes, you're quite right," agreed Nathan eagerly. "You'll have to excuse us, Morgan. I'm sure we can continue our conversation another time."

Morgan pouted prettily, a ridiculous expression for a woman of her age. "Oh, damn, and I was going to offer to buy you lunch, Nathan. Do you have an appointment, too?"

He shook his head. "Not until later, but I'm the chauffeur today so I need to get my staff back to the office. Another time perhaps."

"Of course." She would have reached over to give Nathan a hug good-bye – which Julia thought quite unprofessional of her – but he was already grasping Julia's elbow and moving away.

Julia gave her a dazzling smile. "It was lovely to meet you, Ms. Cottrell. I'm sure we'll all see one another again soon."

Morgan gave her a tiny smile in return, which made her overly-Botoxed face look tight and pinched. "Yes, I'm sure we will."

Nathan whisked her away before Morgan could say another word, whispering in her ear, "Thank God. I owe you one for that."

She arched a dainty brow at him. "I'll keep that in mind when I need a favor."

Ian clasped her hand tightly in both of his as they bid him farewell, a warm smile lighting up his otherwise austere features. "What a delight it's going to be to work with you, Julia," he said with enthusiasm, then gave Nathan a quick wink. "You've got a real treasure here, Nathan. I hope you and Travis treat her well. Not only beautiful but extremely talented as well."

Nathan gave him an answering smile. "Yes, I think we're well aware of Julia's talents."

A little shiver went up her spine at his softly spoken words, and she wondered briefly if he was referring to talents she possessed outside of the workplace. She remembered how he'd praised one particular talent of hers – one that involved her lips around his cock.

Her cheeks flushed at the naughty direction of her thoughts, and she barely heard Ian telling her half-jokingly, "Well, if they don't treat you right, my dear, come and see me straightaway. I'd be honored to have you working for my company."

"That's very kind of you," she replied, "but all is quite well at the moment."

Ian's expression sobered at that particular moment, his smile gone, and Julia instantly pegged the cause as the reappearance of sweet, shy Tessa.

"I've brought your coat, Ms. McKinnon," she said demurely. "I didn't want you to forget it."

Julia reached for her coat but Nathan beat her to it, holding it as she slid her arms inside. "Thank you, Tessa," she told her gently. "And thank you for helping us out today."

The blonde girl's cheeks pinkened adorably. "It was my pleasure," she murmured, before hastily making her exit.

The drive back to the office was brief, and fortunately Jake was on his best behavior. Julia hoped fervently that her earlier chastisement would have some permanent affect on him, and that he'd stop his flirting and suggestive comments. She certainly didn't want to cause trouble for him, but she also wouldn't hesitate to complain to Travis if the innuendoes didn't stop soon.

Jake did turn to face her during the drive but only to comment, "So you speak fluent French, huh? Where'd you pick that up from?"

She shrugged. "My mother's parents were French Canadians from Montreal. They moved to New York City before my mother and aunt were born but always spoke French to them. I learned from my mother and also from my grandparents when I'd visit them."

"Huh. So you'd already spent a lot of time in New York as a kid?" asked Jake.

"At least twice a year from the time my sister and I were little. It's great to be a kid in Manhattan — the Macy's Thanksgiving Day Parade, all the museums, tea at the Plaza Hotel."

Julia added that last bit in deliberately, curious to gauge Nathan's reaction at the mention of where they had spent such a memorable evening. But aside from gripping the steering wheel a bit tighter, it didn't seem to faze him.

Jake had picked up on a different subject matter, though. "Sister? Is she older or younger?"

She rolled her eyes. "Older by five minutes. We're twins."

"Really?" Now Jake's interest had really been piqued. "You mean there are two gorgeous babes that look like you walking the planet? Well, if you aren't interested in me maybe twin sis would consider going out with me sometime."

Julia hooted in a rather undignified manner. "That's hilarious. Trust me when I say there's no way you could handle my sister. She's — um — a tough cookie."

She was saved from further inquisition about Lauren when Nathan pulled into the garage of their building. But she was still smiling to herself at the mere thought of feisty, ballsy Lauren with smarmy Jake and his clichéd come-ons. Lauren didn't even glance at men who wore suits and ties. Her type was either the outdoorsy sort in cargo pants and hiking boots, or tattooed rocker guys with piercings.

As they exited the elevator on their floor, Julia moved to take her case from Nathan but he waved her off. "I'll take it to your office for you," he offered. "There's something I want to talk to you about anyway."

Julia nodded in agreement but was more than a little nervous as they walked to her office side by side. Was he going to reprimand her for bringing her original designs, thinking that she'd meant to show him up? Was he displeased with her presentation today?

Nathan set the case down on her desk while she hung up her coat. He was studying the framed charcoal sketches on her wall when she turned to face him.

"These are fantastic," he said sincerely. "Carmel, right?"

"Yes. My parents' house has some incredible views from the deck. Endless hours of inspiration."

"You did these?" he asked incredulously. He peered at them more closely, noticing the way she signed all of her artwork — *JMcK* — in the lower right corner.

She nodded. "Back in December when I was staying with them. Just to pass the time."

Nathan ran his finger over the middle frame. "You've missed your calling, I think. You're a very talented artist. Have you ever displayed your work?"

She shrugged. "Occasionally my mother will claim a piece for her gallery, but I hardly have time anymore to sketch or paint. Do you draw?"

He smiled faintly. "Not for years. I've got an easel and paints stashed away somewhere, but I'm like you – too busy with work these days to indulge. And I'm nowhere near as talented as you."

Julia deposited her purse into a drawer of her credenza and tried to sound nonchalant. "What did you want to talk to me about? I really do have a client coming in soon."

"This won't take long," he told her, not bothering to take a seat. "Bottom line is very simple – don't flirt with Ian Gregson anymore."

Of all the things he could have said, that was likely the most unexpected. She stared at him in bewilderment. "What? When was I flirting with him?"

He shook his head, clearly annoyed. "When weren't you? Come on, all those little smiles and the way your voice got all soft and breathy? I know he's a good looking guy and quite a catch, but he's our best client and you aren't going to mess up what's been a very good working relationship."

"You have got to be kidding," she said in disbelief. "Let me assure you I'm very well aware of how important a client he is. Not only am I also unwilling to jeopardize that professional relationship, but I have a personal policy of *never* getting involved with clients. Even if they are six four with huge shoulders, Armani suits and British accents."

Nathan did not look pleased at her succinct description of Ian. "Well, it sure as hell seemed like you were flirting with him to me. And he liked you plenty, given the way he kept looking at you."

Julia smiled cattily. "You sound jealous. Need I remind you that's not your prerogative?"

He made a low, harsh sound. "I realize that, yes. Were you trying to make me jealous, Julia?"

She scoffed. "Hardly. I don't make it a habit to beat my head against a brick wall. And to stress the point – I was not flirting with him or him with me."

"But you think he's an attractive man apparently."

She gave a roll of her eyes. "Are we really having this conversation? Yes, Ian Gregson is a hunk. He's also rich, powerful and charming. A real catch, as you said. He also happens to be obsessed with that pretty blonde admin assistant."

Nathan frowned. "You mean Tessa? Ian wouldn't mess with her. Not only is she way too young for him but she's married."

Julia laughed. "I doubt Mr. Prim and Proper would hit on a married woman, either. That doesn't mean he doesn't think she's hot or stares at her when he thinks no one's looking. I assure you he certainly didn't look at *me* that way. Now, are we through with the lecture? I've got to get ready for my meeting."

He still didn't look convinced but gave a small shrug. "Fine. Just keep it professional, okay? I'm not going to risk losing a client because you decide he's new boyfriend material."

His words hurt, that he could be so callous and uncaring, and she felt the overwhelming urge to lash out in return. "What makes you think I don't already have a new boyfriend?" she challenged. "I believe I told you that wasn't a problem for me."

He was visibly taken aback by her retort, and Julia could swear he actually looked hurt. But then he simply shook his head and muttered, "Whatever. Have a good meeting."

And then he was gone, leaving Julia to gaze after him, once again fighting back unshed tears.

✳✳✳✳✳

Nathan was *not* in a good mood when he returned to his office, barely acknowledging Robyn as he passed her by. He spent a few minutes checking his email and voice mail before pushing himself away from his desk in irritation to go stare out the window.

Even though the meeting with the Gregson group had gone remarkably well, it had otherwise been a shitty day. It had started on his drive to work with a phone call from Cameron. He'd known immediately from her high-pitched, overly sweet voice that she wanted something.

"Hi, babe. Are you at the office yet?" she'd asked cheerily.

"Not yet. I'm surprised you're awake this early." It had been just before eight and Cameron was not known to be an early riser.

She'd yawned. "Just got up, still in my robe. But I had a text a few minutes ago from that wedding site I told you about up in St. Helena. They can see us this morning at eleven and I was really, really hoping you could get away with me. We could get lunch afterwards."

Nathan had sighed. Cameron was full throttle into wedding planning now, and coming to a decision on the site was at a critical junction. She and her uber-controlling mother kept going back and forth between a big city wedding at one of the fancy hotels, or holding it at an estate or winery in the Napa Valley. Cameron was currently favoring the latter.

"Cam, I'm sorry but that isn't going to work for me today," he'd told her gently but firmly. "We have a meeting with the Gregson group mid-morning and it's going to last a couple of hours or more. I can't cancel or re-schedule with Ian, you know that."

Cameron was well aware of how important a client Ian was, but even that didn't stop her usual wheedling. "Well, of course you can't do either of those things with him," she agreed. "But is there a real reason you have to personally be there? Can't the rest of your team handle it?"

He'd been as patient as possible while explaining that no, he really needed to be there. "Besides, it's not a whole team of people today. Just myself, Jake, and Julia."

"Who's Julia? I've never heard that name mentioned before," Cameron had inquired.

Nathan had hesitated, choosing his words carefully, not wanting to give her even the tiniest hint of his past with Julia. "She's Travis' newest designer. He hired her after the holidays."

"And he gave a brand new employee the Gregson account?"

He'd forced himself to sound as nonchalant as possible. "She replaced the designer who'd worked on the project initially so it was a natural transition. Plus, apparently she's done some work on one of the Gregson hotels in Manhattan. Anyway, this is her first meeting with Ian and he specifically requested that I be present. I'm sorry, but can we go to St. Helena another day?"

There had been more back and forth, and it had been frustrating because Cameron never seemed to get it that he couldn't just drop or delegate something on a whim. It was different for her, since her role at the gallery was almost more of a figurehead. Her staff – well paid and well trained – did the vast majority of the work and she actually spent little time there. To Nathan, it seemed the major part of Cameron's job was to host artist shows and receptions and socialize with the patrons.

He'd ended the conversation rather abruptly, knowing she was annoyed with him but unable to let it interfere with his day. But the phone call had irritated him and started his day off on the wrong foot.

His pissy mood had intensified when it was time to leave for the meeting with Ian. The first thing he'd seen upon walking towards the elevator was Jake helping Julia on with her coat, and quite obviously relishing the physical contact. Then Jake had made that comment about her shoes, and Nathan had had to stifle a groan.

He was *very* familiar with those goddamned Christian Louboutin black stilettos. Julia wore them often and every single time he saw her in them he had a hard-on that lasted for an eternity. He certainly didn't need Jake calling his attention to them and making matters worse.

And then Jake had continued his almost nonstop flirting with Julia. It had angered Nathan to the point where he'd almost been ready to punch out his associate architect until Julia herself had quite capably put him in his place. He'd been both relieved and absurdly pleased with her at the same time.

But then the torture had continued when she'd stepped up into his SUV and bared enough leg in the process for him to catch a glimpse of her lacy garter. He'd felt like someone had kicked him in the chest, unable to look away from that delectable bit of lingerie until she'd discreetly tugged her dress back down. It hadn't helped one bit, though, for all he'd been able to think about for the next half hour was the fact that she was wearing a garter belt and stockings and probably did most days. That knowledge only added more unnecessary fuel to the ongoing fire that burned inside of him each time he imagined Julia without her clothes on.

Next he'd had to suffer through more than two hours seated right next to her at Ian's conference table. Close enough to small her perfume, her shampoo, the scent of her soft skin. That gray dress had clung to her tits like a lover, defining their firm, round perfection. She'd thankfully worn a scarf to fill in the neckline but every so often she'd moved the right way and he'd get a tantalizing glimpse of cleavage. And each time he did his cock would get a little bit harder.

It had only gotten worse when Julia stood to give her presentation. Then he'd had to observe how that damned dress hugged the sweet, high curves of her ass, and how hot her legs looked in those sheer stockings. And, of course, it was back again to those cockteasing shoes.

And it really, really hadn't helped to notice that every man in the room was also enjoying the view. Even Ian, who was always a perfect gentleman, the model of proper British decorum, didn't bother to disguise his appreciation for the very tempting picture Julia presented. Nathan didn't care if Julia was right and that the woman Ian was really interested in was young, pretty Tessa. Ian might want the luscious admin assistant but he wouldn't have refused Julia, either.

But the straw that had broken the camel's back – what had put him over the top into this incredibly foul mood – was Julia's mocking comment about already having a boyfriend. That had been his worst fear since seeing Julia again last month – that she'd followed his lead and forgotten about New York, had moved on and found someone else. God knew she was right in that it would be the easiest thing in the world for her to get a man. If she'd wanted Jake, for example, who happened to be a good looking guy, all she would have had to do was snap her fingers and he'd be on his knees like a well-trained lapdog.

Most of the time, Nathan congratulated himself on maintaining the very professional relationship he'd insisted on having with Julia. He'd been careful as hell not to be alone with her, had made sure all of their meetings and interactions had occurred with at least one other person present. He'd discussed nothing personal, hadn't touched her in any way, and continued to do a very good job at repressing the memories of their night in Manhattan.

Today, however, he'd faltered a few times – touching her, albeit lightly, with a hand on her elbow or helping her with the coat; being alone with her in her office where he'd praised her artwork and then somehow eased into a discussion about her personal life. He couldn't – wouldn't – let any of those things happen again. God knew it was a daily struggle to keep things professional as it was – he didn't need any added temptation.

And Julia was everything tempting, everything forbidden. Christ, the way she dressed every single, fucking day was enough to drive a man insane. She looked like a model, always perfectly put together and coordinated, only she was far more beautiful and sexy than any model he'd ever seen.

Her angry comment to Jake about an aunt in the fashion industry explained why she had such an extensive and obviously expensive wardrobe. It had been a relief to learn that some man at some point hadn't been the one to gift her with the seemingly endless supply of figure hugging sheath dresses, pencil skirts, silk blouses, and high heels. Always, always, with the erotic high heels. He wondered if she even owned a pair of shoes with less than a four-inch heel. And now that he knew she wore stockings – fuck him blind – it was going to take even more of a superhuman effort not to shove her up against the nearest wall and grind himself against the cleft of her thighs.

He'd gone through the tortures of hell the past few weeks since Julia had begun working here. His willpower was being tested on a daily basis, and at times he thought he would go insane with the effort. Or come in his pants, as he'd feared he might one day last week when Julia had looked especially hot. If he closed his eyes he could still picture the sexy black lace sleeveless top, ass hugging gray wool skirt, and sky high gray pumps. He'd been positive he could see glimpses of a black lace bra through the top, even though it was fully lined. Her stockings that day had seams up the back, and he'd wanted to fall to his knees and lick her from ankle to thigh before lifting that skirt and burying his face in her sweet, juicy pussy.

"Shit," he muttered, realizing he had a raging hard-on again.

Nathan honestly didn't know if he could keep this up – working with Julia, seeing her every day, wanting to fuck her constantly. The worst part was that he couldn't talk to anyone about it. No one but he and Julia knew what had happened in New York, and he had to make sure it stayed that way. He knew Travis probably still suspected something, but so far his partner hadn't confronted him again.

Common sense would indicate that if he was this obsessed with a woman who wasn't his fiancée that he ought to end the engagement to said fiancée. But Nathan simply couldn't bring himself to hurt Cameron that way. He cared about her – correction, *loved* her – and was committed to marrying her. They had been together for two years now, and he couldn't even think about how shitty it would be to just give up on all they had shared, the relationship they had worked on building, just because the hottest woman he'd ever seen was back in his life.

And Cameron was most assuredly a hot, beautiful woman herself. Granted, she was much different than Julia both in looks and personality, but certainly attractive in her own right. She was older than Julia, of course, approaching her thirty-fifth birthday in a few months. She was actually almost two years older than Nathan himself. And, while he knew she'd been completely faithful since they'd started dating, he also knew she'd been with a lot of men – a *lot* of them – before him. Even if she hadn't already talked at length about some of her past relationships and sexual exploits, her experience had been readily apparent in her aggressiveness in bed, in the things she said and did, most of which were exciting but some that were actually a huge turnoff. She enjoyed not only initiating sex between them but controlling it, and often resisted his efforts to take the lead.

Unlike Julia, who had submitted so sweetly to the dominant behavior he liked to unleash at times. Oh, he definitely was not into any sort of BDSM – though the thought of blindfolding and binding Julia was certainly appealing – but he certainly preferred to be the controlling partner in bed.

"Dammit!" He was at it again, remembering the hot sex he'd had at the Plaza Hotel, how responsive Julia had been, how eager and easy to please, how tight her juicy cunt had been. Without being told, he sensed somehow that there hadn't been very many men in her life. In spite of her gorgeous face and centerfold body, she seemed reserved, almost shy around men, though that could just be the defenses she'd built up out of necessity.

And she'd been a total pro about this whole messed up situation, certainly living up to her end of their bargain. She barely looked at him most of the time, and had never once tried to strike up a conversation that could be deemed the least bit personal. From what he had observed and also had reported to him from other employees, she worked her butt off, spending long hours in the office and turning out some admittedly stellar work, and got along famously with all the other employees. He had been ridiculously proud of her talent, and knew he'd acted like a total bastard by forcing her to re-do some quality work. He still didn't know what had compelled him to be such a hard ass that day, especially when he knew Ian would prefer the original designs. Perhaps it had just been a way for him to exert his dominance over her when he couldn't very well do the same in the bedroom with her again. And she'd proven her professionalism yet again by not giving him a gloating "I told you so" look when Ian hadn't liked the sketches she had re-done. Instead, Julia hadn't missed a beat and simply took out her original designs which she'd probably known all along were exactly what Ian had in mind.

He wished like hell he could talk to someone about this dilemma, but all of his friends and family knew Cameron and he wasn't about to put one of them in the position of having to lie to her. It had been difficult enough for him to keep the truth from her – he wasn't going to consciously force someone else to have to do the same.

No, he was just going to have to toughen up and stop thinking so much about Julia. Cameron was his fiancée, the woman who'd been in his life for two years, and he wasn't enough of a bastard to just shove her aside for a younger model on a whim.

Fortunately, he was due to fly to Colorado on a business trip next week, and he hoped the time away would provide him with some much needed breathing room. And a reprieve from wondering what sort of sexy outfit Julia was going to wear each day to torment him.

Chapter Nine

March

Cameron Tolliver was feeling pretty much on top of the world on this sunny afternoon in early spring. This morning at the gallery she'd been able to finally get a long sought after artist to agree to a show next month. Then had come the phone call from the event planner at the hotel that she had finally decided on for her wedding reception telling her that yes, her first choice of dates was available after all. To celebrate, she had treated herself to a massage and facial at her favorite day spa, where as a steady client they'd served her a delicious salmon salad and crisp glass of Pinot Grigio. Now, feeling relaxed and mellow, she was on her way to Nate's office to drop off his ticket to the ballet tonight. The only sour note in her day thus far was the fact that he couldn't meet her for dinner first due to a late client meeting he'd had scheduled for weeks, and would have to meet her at the ballet instead.

Nathan, she thought confidently, was going to have to start delegating more of his duties at work. It was beyond ridiculous that the partner of one of San Francisco's most successful architectural design firms had to work so many hours and do as much traveling as he did. Cameron knew for a fact that Nathan had any number of other architects on staff that he could re-distribute work to, leaving him more time to relax and travel for leisure. She certainly didn't want a husband who was going to have to work late on a regular basis or couldn't go on vacation when it suited him. After all, she owned her own business and pretty much did what she pleased. There was really no good reason why Nathan couldn't do the same.

Cameron smiled to herself as she thought again of what a catch Nathan was. He was by far the handsomest and most charming man she'd ever dated – and she'd dated a lot over the past twenty years. After two broken engagements, she had begun to despair that she'd ever fall in love and get married, and then she'd met Nathan and her hopes had been renewed.

Oh, it had taken a lot of time and work to get him to finally make a commitment to her, but it had all been worth it. As all of her girlfriends told her often, Nathan was a real prize. Cameron had absolutely no intention of letting him slip away, or allowing anything to ruin their weeding next February. She'd waited way too long for happiness, and it was well past time for her to finally get what she deserved.

She smiled back at the attractive older man who gave her an admiring glance as he passed her by. She walked with the confidence of a woman who knew she looked good. At five foot nine, she was taller than average but that only served to call more attention her way. With the help of a stylist, she knew the best way to dress her slim, almost angular figure. Unfortunately, no amount of weight training or exercise had been able to put much muscle or definition on her naturally thin arms and legs, so she seldom wore short skirts or sleeveless tops. And while she loved her slim hips and super flat stomach, her stylist tended to steer her away from anything too form fitting, wanting instead to give the illusion that she had more curves.

Therefore, most of her business outfits were similar to what she wore today – beautifully tailored black pleated trousers, a silky white blouse, and a short, fitted black jacket. The push-up bra helped give an impression of cleavage above the two buttons of her blouse she'd left undone. She gave off an air of both power and control, the modern businesswoman, while still looking sexy and feminine.

She'd just had her hair cut and colored about a week ago, and knew the shiny blonde chin-length bob looked amazing. It still bothered her that she had to keep her hair this short, knowing that Nathan really preferred long hair, but it had been on her hairdressers' advice. A natural brunette, Cameron had been bleaching her hair to a pale Nordic blonde shade since she was sixteen years old, and all the years of harsh chemicals had begun to take their toll. Her hairdresser – one of the very best in the city – had cautioned that her hair was thinning dramatically and to keep it any longer than its current length would draw attention to that fact. She'd nixed the idea of extensions, knowing that Nathan disliked artifice and had made non-complimentary comments about a couple of her friends who'd had them done.

Cameron strode confidently into the reception area of Nathan's office, not even bothering to glance over at the little receptionist. As the owner's fiancée, she felt very at ease walking anywhere in the office, and certainly didn't need support staff to announce her presence.

She went directly to Nathan's office, pausing briefly to give Robyn a perfunctory smile. "Hi, Robyn. I assume he's in? I've got something to drop off."

The older woman gave her a polite smile in return. She was always professional, always pleasant, but Cameron sensed that Robyn didn't really like her for some reason. A fact that didn't bother Cameron in the least, because she also considered Robyn to be support staff and not worthy of her attention.

"Actually, he's in the small conference room right now," corrected Robyn. "You can leave whatever it is with me if you'd like."

Cameron waved a hand in dismissal. "No need. I'll just pop my head in. Is he with clients?"

Robyn shook her head. "No, he's meeting with Jake and Julia about a project. I'm sure he won't mind if you stop in for a minute."

Cameron's spine stiffened at Robyn's implied suggestion to keep her visit brief. "Well, of course, he won't mind. What man wouldn't want to see his fiancée whenever possible?"

Nathan's assistant gave her a tight little smile as she returned her attention to whatever mundane task she'd been working on. Cameron frowned as she walked down the hall to the conference room, not really liking the somewhat superior air Robyn tended to adopt at times. She really didn't understand why Nathan thought Robyn was such a terrific PA, since the older woman seemed just a bit too confident and arrogant given her position in the firm.

The door to the small conference room was closed, but the blinds on the large window facing out to the office floor were raised so that Cameron had a clear view into the room. Nathan and Jake — who Cameron thought was terribly cute with his flirting and continual flow of compliments — were seated at the table with their backs to her and evidently studying some sketches that had been propped up on display stands around the room. Standing next to one of the stands was a young woman that Cameron assumed was the Julia that Robyn had mentioned. Then Julia turned to face the two men so Cameron could get a good look at her.

Cameron froze in her tracks, unease bubbling up inside of her at a rapid boil. The young woman inside the conference room was — unfortunately — undeniably beautiful. With an inexplicable anger that simmered beneath the surface, Cameron swiftly took in the girl's long, nearly waist length hair of a light brown shade, the stunning perfection of her face, and her curvy body. She wore a fitted sheath dress of navy lace that had little flutter sleeves. There was no way — with her own slim, straight frame — that Cameron could ever wear something so form-fitting.

The younger woman was wearing killer shoes, too — nude peep-toe platform pumps — Louboutins by the signature red soles.

Cameron's stylist had advised her away from stilettos, cautioning that they drew attention to her thin legs and skinny calves. Plus, a four-inch heel would have made her slightly taller than Nathan, which didn't bother him but bugged her.

It shouldn't have bothered her that this young, very attractive woman was working in her fiancé's office, for Cameron was extremely confident about her own good looks. But then she caught the way Nathan – *her* Nathan – was gazing discreetly at the other woman's rounded ass and lush breasts and rage consumed her. Without further ado, she barged into the conference room without as much as a knock.

Three pair of eyes turned her way immediately, but Cameron was only focused on Nathan. He stood abruptly, a surprised look on his face. Quite intentionally, she walked over and placed a welcoming, open-mouthed kiss on his lips.

She smiled at him, her hand caressing his cheek. "Hey, babe. Why so surprised to see me? I told you I was going to drop that ticket off."

Nathan was unsmiling as he gently removed her hand, giving it a little squeeze. "You did, but I thought you were going to call first. Or leave the ticket with Robyn when you knew I was in a meeting."

"Oops, sorry!" she giggled. "You know how impulsive I am, babe, always spur of the moment with me. I was right in the area so I just popped in. *Sooo* sorry if I interrupted." She gave Jake a little wave. "Hey, sweetie. Nice to see you again."

Jake grinned and walked over to give her a quick peck on the cheek. "You, too, gorgeous. You're looking spectacular as always."

Even though she knew Jake was something of a manwhore, and flirted with almost every good looking woman he met, his compliment was still flattering and she smiled at him warmly. "You big flirt," she scolded. "And in front of my fiancé, too."

Jake winked at her. "Some men have all the luck, you know. Like the boss man here."

Cameron finally, reluctantly, turned her attention to the woman – Julia – and offered up a faint smile. "Hello. I don't believe we've met before."

Julia returned the smile, gazing at her politely with big green eyes, and extending her hand. "No, we haven't. I'm Julia McKinnon, one of the interior designers here. It's a pleasure to meet you."

The younger woman's voice was soft and melodious, and Cameron took an instant and fervent dislike to her. For some peculiar, unknown reason, she felt threatened by this woman, and her hackles rose up defensively. "Cameron Tolliver, Nate's fiancée. But I'm sure you've already figured that out." She gave Julia's small hand the barest of shakes before abruptly turning her attention back to Nathan. "Are you finished here, babe? I was hoping to talk to you for a few minutes."

Nathan hesitated, glancing uncertainly at his two employees. "I suppose we're just about done. Jake – Julia – anything else to add?"

Jake shook his head. "I'm good. I'll leave you two lovebirds alone. Good to see you, Cameron."

Julia paused, watching Jake leave the room before turning to Nathan. "Um, we still had the design for the wine bar to review, but I can just leave that one here for you to look at. Just let me gather up my things and I'll be on my way."

Cameron tried to ignore how gracefully the other woman moved about the room picking up her sketches, especially in those towering heels. Even with the sky-high Louboutins, Julia was still a few inches shorter than she was, making her feel like a clumsy giant. It was not a pleasant feeling, and Cameron glowered at Julia as if to hurry her along.

Before Julia could exit – her arms filled with design boards – Nathan called her back. "Wait. Can you leave the one of the deluxe suite as well? I wanted to look at that one again."

"Of course." Julia quickly located it and placed it back on its stand. She gave Cameron a brief smile. "It was nice to meet you, Cameron. I'm sure we'll see each other again soon."

Cameron had never felt less like smiling but forced herself to reciprocate. "Yes, I'm sure we will."

Nathan was frowning at her once Julia left. "Don't you think you were a little bit rude just now?"

She shrugged. "Not particularly. What did you expect – that I was going to gush about her dress and invite her out for lunch?"

"No," replied Nathan sternly, "but I think you could have been a bit more pleasant."

Cameron made a gesture of dismissal. "Whatever. Look, both of us are busy so let me give you the ticket. I just remembered I've got a client due in within the hour."

Nathan took the ticket she handed him. "How come you never remember appointments? You've got two assistants and a Blackberry."

She laughed. "You know I'm a scatterbrain, babe. It's one of the things you love about me. Just too many things going on between work and the wedding." She reached up to press a brief kiss on his mouth. "I'll see you at the ballet later. Don't be late. And text me when you're leaving the office, okay?"

"Sure, no problem. Didn't you have something to talk to me about? That is why you interrupted my meeting, wasn't it?" he asked pointedly.

"No, just dropping the ticket off," she replied breezily. "Nothing else that can't wait until tonight."

Nathan sighed, "I really wish you had just left the ticket with Robyn, then. Jake and Julia and I actually did have more to discuss."

Cameron huffed. "Well, excuse me. I thought you'd welcome the interruption to see your fiancée. But I guess you were too busy staring at Miss Tits and Ass, weren't you?"

He gaped at her. "What are you talking about? I was *not* staring at Julia. You're being ridiculous."

"Am I?" she challenged. "You're not going to try and bullshit me by denying that she's pretty, are you?"

He shook his head, running a hand through his hair. "Jesus, Cameron. Let's not do this now, okay?"

She gave a short, humorless laugh. "No, I think this is exactly when we should do this. Are you trying to say you haven't noticed your little designer is attractive?"

"Of course I've noticed," he replied impatiently. "Julia's a very pretty girl. She's also my employee. *Only* my employee. *You're* my fiancée, Cameron. Now if you've finished with whatever you're accusing me of, I do have other work to do, including looking at these designs."

"Fine. We'll pretend that you weren't staring at her ass in that tight dress. Does she dress like that every day?" she asked cattily.

Nathan made an impatient sound. "Do I look like a fashion consultant? How am I supposed to know? I don't even see her most days. So stop acting like a jealous shrew."

"Jealous!" Cameron spat. "Of *that*? Why in the world would I be jealous?"

"Exactly," he replied calmly. "Why would you? You have zero reason to be jealous of anyone. Now, come on, you don't want to be late for your meeting."

He gave her a brief kiss and began escorting her out of the room until she stopped to glance over the two design boards that Julia had left behind. Cameron wrinkled her nose in distaste.

"I don't like these at all," she declared. "And I'm sure Ian won't, either. Your little designer's going to be doing some major re-working here."

Nathan looked annoyed at her admittedly petty comments. "For the record, she's not *my* designer, she works for Travis. And second, Ian happens to love these designs. Julia only made some very minor modifications to them, this will likely be the final product."

Cameron shrugged. "Well, I wouldn't want her designing anything for me based on these. Just not my taste, I suppose."

But the air of carelessness she assumed blew away like smoke in the wind as she left Nathan's office. The feeling of being on top of the world that she'd had when entering the building a short time ago had faded rapidly, and she was now in a vile, vicious mood. She resisted the urge to kick something, to shove a passerby into the side of a building, to scream at the top of her lungs.

Cameron couldn't put her finger on it, but there was something – some niggling little feeling that all was not as it should be – and it had to do with Julia McKinnon. Cameron considered herself a very confident, poised woman but five minutes in the presence of the younger woman had rattled her badly.

'Just how young is she?' thought Cameron wildly. Julia's flawless complexion still bore that dewy youthfulness that Cameron could no longer achieve, even with frequent facials, microdermabrasions, Restalyne injections, and expensive skin care products. And Julia had those incredible cheekbones that no amount of cosmetics could fake. Cameron had resorted to having cheekbone implants done almost ten years ago, but she was reluctantly aware they didn't look all that natural.

And of course the little bitch would just have to have all that long, thick hair when Cameron was having to contend with her own thinning locks. She did much prefer her own pale blonde shade to whatever color one could call Julia's hair. It was a well known fact that men always preferred blondes.

Cameron continued to fume during the cab ride back to her gallery as she recalled – reluctantly – how the form fitting navy lace dress had clung to Julia's shapely hips and ass. She thought snidely that the girl's big tits had to be fake. There was no way they could be that perfect and still be natural. One of Cameron's great disappointments was that own boobs were so small. She always wore padded push-up bras to give the illusion of cleavage but there was no way to disguise the fact that she was flat-chested when her clothes came off. She had first considered getting implants when she was barely in her twenties, but her mother had gotten wind of the idea and had been horrified that she would even consider doing something so crude and trashy. And when she'd mentioned the idea to Nathan in recent times he had made his distaste for anything fake well known. Conversely, Cameron was well aware that Nathan – like most men – loved big boobs, based on comments he'd made to his friends when he didn't think she was listening.

It was little wonder, then, that all of her old insecurities came rushing to the surface at the thought of this young, beautiful and tempting girl working in such close proximity to Nathan. Cameron had worked very hard to look like she did, having procedures done that most people didn't know about, especially not Nathan. Her appearance now was a source of pride for her, and she knew she'd never looked better. But it had only taken a very short while in the presence of that little bitch to feel like the awkward, unattractive girl she'd once been and had vowed never to be again. Cameron did *not* like revisiting those feelings and swore that little Julia would never be allowed to make her feel that way again.

✳✳✳✳✳

Julia was struggling to hold it together as she walked back to her office after being hustled out of the conference room. It was very obvious that Nathan's fiancée was a supremely confident woman used to getting her way in all things. Even if it meant putting a premature end to what had actually been a pretty important meeting. But what enraged Julia even more than Cameron's lofty attitude was the fact that Nathan had allowed her to get away with it.

'He was probably afraid I'd start tattling on him,' she thought angrily. 'and wanted to hustle me out of there before I could say anything.' It hurt that he could think so little of her, especially when she'd vowed not to betray him.

Unless, of course, he was afraid that *he'd* be the one to give something away. But no, Julia dismissed that rather wild idea quickly. Nathan had given her zero indication over the past couple of months that he ever gave her a second thought, and treated her more distantly than ever.

As she put away the design boards in their designated files, she thought absently that Cameron Tolliver wasn't what she'd expected. For one thing, Nathan's fiancée was several years older than expected, mid-thirties instead of the late twenties Julia would have assumed. And she was much taller and slimmer than Julia would have guessed, her hair a lot shorter, too. But there was no denying that Cameron was a very lovely woman who certainly knew how to dress. Julia recognized the cut of her pants and jacket as Armani, had noticed her dramatic makeup, perfect manicure and expensive jewelry.

Of all days, thought Julia glumly, not to be wearing one of the many designer dresses or skirts in her wardrobe. Not all of her clothes were courtesy of Aunt Madelyn. Her aunt, in fact, had taught her years ago to mix high end pieces like the Louboutin pumps with less expensive items, such as the pretty navy lace dress she'd bought online from a women's apparel website for less than seventy dollars.

"It's all about accessorizing, darling," was one of Aunt Maddy's favorite sayings. "That and having the figure to look good in anything, which you and your sister were fortunately blessed with."

Being both petite and busty, however, didn't always make it easy for things to fit properly, and Julia was extremely grateful that she'd learned how to sew when she was still a girl. Her Grandmere Vivienne had been a seamstress, a very talented one at that, and she'd taught Julia and Lauren how to do hems and seams. Well, she'd at least taught Julia since Lauren had been more interested in her camera or sports or getting into trouble to bother learning the finer parts of operating a sewing machine.

Julia gave a little shrug, not really sure why she gave a damn about how she looked today. She certainly didn't care about impressing Nathan's fiancée, and Nathan himself seemed completely oblivious to whatever she wore. Julia wondered peevishly if he'd even notice if she strutted through the office wearing just her underwear and high heels. Not that it should matter any longer, she thought with a sigh. It was very obvious that he only thought of her as an employee, and that Cameron was the woman in his life. She needed to stop being such a silly, sentimental goose, forget all about that night in New York, and find someone new.

The thought of trolling singles bars or clubs made her feel queasy, though, so there was no way she was going to find a guy that way. Maybe she'd call Sam and ask if he had a friend he could fix her up with. Even though he lived in Arizona now, he was sure to know a lot of guys in the NFL. There were also a couple of guys in her yoga classes who seemed nice enough, though the one with the long hair and tattoos was more Lauren's type than hers. Maybe all she really needed was a few dates with a hot guy to get Nathan out of her system and clear her head. She made a mental note to give Sam a call tonight. Even though he was currently dating some Australian supermodel, they were still friendly and kept in regular touch.

"Why so serious, hunny bunny?" teased a familiar voice.

Julia glanced up and smiled at her boss as he hovered in the doorway. "Just thinking about the best way to snag a new boyfriend."

Travis looked very interested in this topic and took a seat in front of her desk. "Ooh, men, my favorite topic. And sweetie pie – I wouldn't think you'd have to worry about that ever. It's like buying shoes at DSW – just find something you like among thousands of pairs on the shelves and take them."

She laughed, grateful for his perpetual cheeriness. "Not quite that simple. I'm picky, after all. I mean, I'm not desperate enough to go out with Jake, for example."

He shuddered. "Thank God. You can do *sooo* much better than that idiot, sweetie. I'm sure we can find a nice guy for you. In fact, I might have someone in mind."

Julia regarded him warily. "No offense, but I only date straight guys. Bi-sexuals are off the table, too."

Travis looked offended. "Not all of my friends are gay, you know. I mean, Nate's one of my closest friends and he's the straightest guy I know."

At the mention of Nathan's name, Julia instantly tensed up. "That's true. Look, let's table this discussion for now, okay? I'm not sure I ought to be talking to my boss about looking for a new boyfriend."

He grinned. "Oh, but it's such a fun topic. However, I'll put it on the back burner, sweetie. Speaking of Nate, did he like the re-designs?"

She nodded. "Just fine, I think. Except we got interrupted before he could look at a couple of them. His, um, fiancée showed up."

Travis grimaced. "Ah, so you've met the she-devil, have you? I don't see any claw marks on you so I trust everything went well?"

Julia gave a small shrug. "She wasn't brimming over with friendliness, if that's what you mean. She was rather distant actually."

He hooted. "You're being polite, hunny bunny. Cameron Tolliver is a raging bitch, and I'm guessing she wasn't happy at all to meet you. Or realize how closely you work with Nate. When the she-devil feels threatened, her hackles really rise up."

"Oh, please. I have no idea why she'd be threatened by me. She's a beautiful woman. And she's the one wearing his engagement ring, not me. I just work with him, that's all."

"Hmm, that doesn't mean Nate isn't checking out all of your – er – assets as often as possible. Being engaged doesn't automatically turn off a guy's radar, you know. And I've always said that he was making a huge mistake in marrying Cameron."

Julia's curiosity was not piqued. "Why do you say that?"

Travis grinned. "Interested, are we? Well, that's a discussion that might take awhile. Maybe like this weekend. Anton and I should take you to dinner."

Anton was Travis' partner, whom Julia had met a couple of times already. He was a slight, dark-haired, half-Asian man who worked as a personal shopper at Neiman Marcus, and absolutely adored Julia. They had talked fashion for hours the last time they had met.

"Actually, I owe you guys a dinner," admitted Julia. "Why don't you come over Saturday night and I'll cook for you? And by cook, I mean preparing the meal from scratch, not ordering takeout."

"So you're gorgeous, artistic, fashionable *and* you cook? Hmm, maybe being gay isn't what it's cracked up to me. I might give Anton the boot and date you myself," he teased.

She giggled, her good mood restored with his rather outrageous humor. "Oh, but you'd break poor Anton's heart. And lose that great discount he gets you at Neiman Marcus."

Travis looked horrified. "Oh, God, I can't lose that discount, can I? Guess I'll have to hold onto the boy. But seriously, sweetie, dinner at your place sounds awesome. We'll bring the wine. Around seven sound good?"

She nodded. "Perfect. And I'll see if I can pry Angela out of her hidey-hole. I swear that girl is in training to become a nun. If I ever meet that guy who screwed her up this bad I'd – um – unleash Lauren on him!"

"Ah, Kung-Fu Twin. I still have to meet her, you know, see if all those stories can possibly be true."

Julia smiled. "Oh, they're all true. And I've only scratched the surface, told you some of the tamer stories. My sister has packed a lot of living into twenty-five years. Hopefully she'll visit soon. I saw her last month when I went to Carmel for President's Day weekend but she's on the road again now. Somewhere in Central America, I think."

"Well, got to get back to work, sweet pea. But dinner on Saturday sounds fabulous. We'll have a *loong* talk about the she-devil."

She shrugged. "That's not necessary. I mean, I don't really think we should be gossiping about her."

Travis rolled his eyes. "Of course we should. I assure you I've never met anybody who deserves to be dissed more than that witch. And I have some real dirt on her, things that even Nate doesn't know." He grinned at the sudden interest on Julia's face. "Ah, now I've got your attention. Trust me, its good stuff."

＊＊＊＊＊

As it turned out, Angela did not come for dinner on Saturday but it wasn't because she chose to closet herself away again. It was one of her niece's birthdays, and she felt obliged to drive down to Carmel for the weekend to attend the party. Julia knew that Angela disliked going home and only did so when absolutely necessary. Mrs. DelCarlo – Angela's mother – was quite a piece of work, and if she were Julia's mother she knew she'd spend as little time as possible with her.

Julia's flat was small but charming, with its original hardwood floors, bay windows, and high ceilings. The main room was a shared living/dining space, with her antique oak dining table and matching chairs arranged on the end closer to the kitchen. She had set it with bright, beautiful Provence-style linens in yellows and blues. A vase of spring flowers sat in the middle of the table. She'd chosen the hand-painted ceramic dishes she'd bought a few years ago at a crafts fair in SoHo, and accented the setting with cobalt blue glasses from Cost Plus. The country French table décor would go nicely with the rustic French meal she'd prepared – ratatouille with eggplant she'd bought fresh at the Ferry Building Farmers Market just this morning; a divine smelling cassoulet with chunks of chicken and tiny white beans; a loaf of crusty artisan bread and a platter of assorted olives, peppers, and other antipasti. For dessert she'd baked one of her famed tortes – this one with beautifully fresh Anjou pears.

To Julia, cooking was yet another form of artistry, and she took as much pride in it as she did her design work or drawings. She loved to entertain, though she preferred small, intimate groups to a large crowd. It was a holdover from her childhood and youth, for her parents had frequently hosted the same sort of small, casual gatherings at their home. They had a lot of friends, most of whom were artists, musicians or writers, and a party at the McKinnon home had never been boring. In addition to being one of the greatest artists of her generation, Natalie Benoit was also an incredible cook and hostess and had instilled a love of cooking into at least one of her daughters, passing on many of the recipes she'd learned from her own mother.

Julia had dressed casually – for her, anyway – in a long-sleeved V-necked black top and a cute A-line skirt in a black and white stripe with a wide black belt to cinch in her waist. What passed for flats for her – little black sling backs with a kitten heel – completed the relatively inexpensive outfit she'd pieced together.

Travis and Anton arrived promptly at seven, with not one but two bottles of wine plus a box of decadent chocolate truffles. After exchanging hugs, Julia gave them the brief tour of her flat.

Travis nodded in appreciation of how she'd decorated the small living/dining space. "I knew there was a reason I hired you," he teased. "You've made a small space look almost twice its size. And I love all the little touches of color here and there. I should have known your own personal space would be something special."

Anton was admiring the exquisite seascape that graced the wall over the small brick fireplace. It was one of Julia's mother's finest pieces and one of Julia's most cherished possessions, not just for its considerable monetary value but for the sentimental one as well.

But for both men the real attraction in the flat was Julia's clothes closet. Though the bedroom itself was on the small side, it did boast a sizeable walk-in closet that she had taken great care to arrange her extensive wardrobe in.

Anton pressed a hand to his chest as he gazed at the contents of the closet, an enraptured look on his pale, bespectacled face. "Oh, honey, I think I've died and gone to fashion heaven! And I'm really, really thinking how unfair it was that I wasn't born female."

Travis gave him a mocking little frown. "Hey, watch it. I'm not into girls, or even cross-dressers."

Anton patted his lover's arm. "Never fear, dear. I was just having clothes envy here. Sweet pea," he said to Julia, "you have an amazing set-up here. Color coordinated, all your shoes and bags in perfect little rows, so neat and organized. No wonder you always look so smokin' hot."

Julia and Travis shared a look, and he shook his head. "Oh, God, maybe we should have shown him this after dinner. Now you'll never get him out of your closet."

They laughed at his little joke, but Anton only groaned in mock horror. "Dear boy, you know I've been out of the closet since I was thirteen. Maybe even younger."

Julia watched in amusement for a couple more minutes as Anton crooned over her racks of dresses, coats, shoes, and other apparel. He gasped over the Diane von Furstenberg boat necked navy dress, cooed when he pulled out the Gucci wrap-front dress in taupe, ran his finger lovingly over the Giuseppe Zanotti poppy red patent leather pumps, looked longingly at the Versace black leather tote.

Anton grinned at her. "This would be more fun than dressing a Barbie doll. But you don't need my help, sweetie. You should have been a fashion consultant or designer instead of playing with furniture."

She chuckled. "Yes, but this way I get to do both. Come on, let's break open that bottle of French burgundy you brought. How did you guys know I was cooking French food?"

The three of them had nearly polished off a whole bottle of the fine French wine even before dinner was served. Fortunately, Julia had set out a plate of cheeses and pates along with a thinly sliced baguette so they weren't drinking on an empty stomach. A very fleeting memory of sitting in the Champagne Bar at the Plaza Hotel with Nathan sipping champagne and nibbling on fruit and cheese came to her before she firmly willed it to the archives of her brain.

Travis and Anton were very amusing company, and they lavished praise on her dinner, eating heartily as the second bottle of wine began to disappear. They insisted on helping her clear up the dishes – fortunately her small, old fashioned kitchen did have a dishwasher – and begged her to hold off on dessert for awhile until they could make room in their very full stomachs.

The men sunk into her comfy sofa upholstered in a butter yellow fabric patterned with tiny blue flowers, while Julia curled up in her favorite chair – a big, overstuffed armchair that had been her grandmother's. She'd begged for it when her grandparents had passed away, having many happy childhood memories of her and Lauren cuddling with either Grandpere or Grandmere and having stories read to them in French. She'd had the chair recovered in a vivid emerald green, which was one of the pops of color Travis had mentioned.

Travis' eyes twinkled with mischief. "So now that we're all comfy and pleasantly tipsy, I promised Julia that we'd share all the juicy gossip we know about the future Mrs. Nathan Atwood."

Anton whooped. "Oh, me first, me first! After all, I was the one who kept pouring Cosmos down the throat of Cameron's friend at the engagement party. What did it take for her to spill the beans – four or five drinks?"

"I think it was three and a half, actually, "said Travis dryly. "Girl could not hold her liquor too well. By Cosmo number five, she wasn't holding anything back."

Julia took a small sip of her wine, feeling oddly not in the mood for this discussion. "I didn't realize they had an engagement party. Not many people have those nowadays, When was this?"

"Back in October sometime - mid-month, I think. And Cameron's parents are very old-school, old money kind of people," explained Travis. "Daddy is the CEO of some big company here, Mommy is from filthy rich money, so they only want the best for their little girls. So of course they threw Cameron and Nate this huge bash, held it at the Gregson Hotel on Nob Hill. Very lavish affair."

Anton nodded in agreement. "You would have thought it was the actual wedding. No expense spared, and at least three hundred people. And I swear Travis and I were the only non-heteros in the place."

"Well, that shouldn't have been a surprise, considering Graham Tolliver has given hundreds of thousands of dollars to the campaigns to defeat gay marriage," sniffed Travis. "He's a homophobic, ultraconservative, NRA ass kissing prick. And his evil she-devil of a daughter is just like him. Cameron hates the two of us."

Julia frowned. "Why does Nathan tolerate that? I mean, besides being business partners I was under the impression that the two of you were close friends."

"We are, hunny bunny. But that doesn't mean Cameron has to like me. Oh, she's very polite in front of Nate, always careful not to make a scene or show her cards. But Anton and I aren't blind. We see the way she looks at us, and we've both overheard her making homophobic slurs. It's pretty obvious that she hates our guts, and she's found every excuse in the book not to socialize with us. Every party or event we've invited her and Nate to they've either declined or he's attended solo."

"Hmm. So is this the so-called dirt you told me you had on her?" inquired Julia.

Both men laughed riotously. "Oh, God, not even close," guffawed Anton. "That's like the least of it, sweetie. Who cares if some stuck-up bitch doesn't like us? We've got plenty of friends who do."

Travis pulled his phone out and started scanning for something. "Here, I think the best way to tell you is just to show you."

Anton peeked over at the phone. "Ooh, are you trying to find the Facebook photos? Awesome!"

"Found them. Here, let Julia have a look. Now, as you flip through them, let me narrate so you know what you're looking at. And for a little background, Anton and I met one of Cameron's oldest and surprisingly dearest friends at the engagement party. A dear if not drunk lady by the name of Stephanie — what's her last name, Anton?"

"Norris," supplied Anton helpfully. "They've been friends since the third grade, though if Cameron knew everything that Stephanie told us that would be the end of it."

Julia reluctantly took Travis's phone and gazed at the photo on the screen. It was a bit grainy, looking almost twenty years old, and was of a skinny, brown-haired girl who wasn't especially attractive. She wore an ill-fitting dress of pale pink that did nothing to flatter either her nonexistent figure or her pale coloring. The girl had a rather large nose, sunken cheekbones, and a somewhat pointy chin.

She shook her head. "I don't get it. Am I supposed to know who this is?"

Travis smiled triumphantly. "That, sweetie pie, is the she-devil herself – Miss Cameron Tolliver – at her sweet sixteen birthday party. What a doll, huh?"

Julia stared at the photo harder, trying to find any trace of the polished, attractive woman she'd met two days ago. "No way is this Cameron. She looks completely different."

Travis perched on the arm of her chair and took the phone from her. "Ah, but this is just the start of our little photo tour. You'll start to see the progression of the changes as we go along."

She watched closely as Travis flipped from one photo to the next, explaining as he went along. "Okay, here's a year later. Cam's obviously had a hell of a nose job because it's about half the size it was. "

He flipped to the next photo, where Cameron was now a blonde. Subsequent photos showed the changes after a chin job, cheekbone implants, collagen injections to her lips, and a much improved fashion sense and makeup application. If Julia hadn't seen the transformation occur over the approximately seven year time frame in the photos she would never have believed it.

"Wow, she's really a different person now, isn't she?" she commented.

Anton smirked. "Except she should have kept going and bought herself some tits and ass. Hey, I know dudes with bigger boobs than hers. And my perky little butt fills out a pair of jeans better than her flat old booty."

Julia almost choked on a sip of wine at Anton's outrageous comments. Travis patted her on the back until she was able to grin at Anton with watery eyes.

"You are so bad," she admonished. "Both of you. Now, how did you come to acquire these photos? I'm just assuming Cameron didn't give them to you."

"Well, of course not," replied Travis. "I'm sure she'd be furious and mortified to realize anyone has seen them. Dear friend Stephanie was kind enough to share them with us at the boozy engagement party. She has them posted on her Facebook page with about five thousand others. And of course Anton and I are now good buddies with her on Facebook."

She shook her head. "How is Cameron not aware these are posted on a social networking site? I can't imagine she'd be very happy about them."

"Well, duh, of course not. As for why she hasn't noticed them – did I mention there were five *thousand* or so photos? One would need to know where to look. And Stephanie was only too happy to point us to the right folder. Apparently there's some animosity there between the girlhood friends."

"I told you what that was about," scolded Anton. "You never listen. Stephanie is still pissed off at Cameron because she slept with some guy that Stephanie really liked. And apparently that wasn't the first time that happened. All this before she met Nathan, of course. She isn't stupid enough to risk losing him by cheating now."

Travis grinned, thoroughly enjoying this gossipy hen fest. "And we're not even telling her the really juicy parts. Nate is not Cameron's first fiancé apparently. She's been engaged two times before. Guess she's really hoping that old three times a charm adage will come true for her."

Julia couldn't contain her surprise. "Two other times? What happened? Is she divorced or something?"

Anton shook his head. "Never made it to the altar. According to Stephanie, the first time Cameron was engaged she was about twenty-eight. All the wedding plans made, everything ready to go. Then – boom! Less than two months before the big day her fiancé gets arrested for big time embezzlement and hauled off to jail. Apparently he's still serving time."

"That's terrible. She must have been wrecked over it," sympathized Julia.

Travis chuckled. "Didn't take her too long to get over it apparently. Within a year she had another guy on the hook. They got engaged around the time she turned thirty. But this one didn't take, either. No particular reason that Stephanie was aware of, dude just got cold feet and broke things off."

"So by the time she met Nathan a couple of years ago she must have been getting awfully desperate," piped up Anton. "Over thirty years old, seeing all of her friends get married, including her younger sister who's already got one kid and another on the way. Cameron's biological clock must be ticking awfully loud."

"Biological clock?" mocked Travis. "Sorry, but no way can I ever imagine that bitch being a mother. She might have Nate fooled but Anton and I see right through her."

Anton grinned at his partner. "But you have a gift, sweetie. Have you told Julia about it?"

Travis grinned. "Anton thinks I'm sort of psychic. At first I thought he meant psycho, and of course I am a little bit crazy, most of us artistic types are. But, no, he's positive that I can see things other people can't, predict stuff even."

Julia smiled. "And what do you think?"

He shrugged. "I must say I'm awfully good at *Jeopardy* and *Wheel of Fortune*. And I've been pretty lucky with predicting who's going to win *American Idol* or which desperate chick the *Bachelor* is going to choose. But I think the only real gift I have is in reading people. I've just got this knack for seeing past the pretenses people put up to who they really are."

"That's a pretty cool gift," she agreed. "You do seem very perceptive. And you think that Cameron isn't who she really appears to be?"

Travis frowned. "I don't think that. I *know* it for a fact. There's other stuff – more personal stuff that Stephanie told us. If Nate knew - "

Julia blinked. "How drunk did you get this girl anyway?"

Anton gave a little giggle. "A couple more Cosmos and she would have either passed out or tried to give me a blow job." He wrinkled his nose in distaste at the latter thought. "But she was pretty plastered and not holding anything back. For example, Cameron's gotten knocked up twice and had two a- "

She held up a hand. "Okay, let's stop here. Travis is right, this is starting to get into things we really shouldn't be discussing. I'm guessing Nathan may or may not know this stuff, and either way he wouldn't appreciate us talking about it. I'm going to make coffee now and set out dessert."

They lingered over French-pressed coffee and the pear tart, which turned out better than ever, for another couple of hours. Not another mention was made of Cameron, Nathan, or even the office. Except towards the very end of the evening, when Travis and Anton were about to leave.

"Don't forget that next Thursday we have the dinner to attend at Taverna Francesca," reminded Travis.

The restaurant had recently been extensively remodeled, and Atwood Headley had done all of the structural and design changes. Next Thursday was a special re-opening dinner, and since the restaurant owners were well-known locals who had several establishments in the Bay Area, quite a few dignitaries and celebrities were expected to attend. Julia really hadn't been involved with the design since it had all taken place prior to her arrival in San Francisco, but the owners had already expressed interest in having some of their other restaurants re-designed. Not to mention the handful of brand-new places they were considering opening. Travis wanted Julia to meet the owners and their development team.

She nodded. "I'm looking forward to it. The place looks pretty formal from the pictures I've seen, so I assume the dress code will be, too?"

"Oh sugar. I know exactly what you should wear," exclaimed Anton. "The red Donna Karan. Exquisite. It will be perfect, trust me. And those sexy red Valentino shoes with the bow."

Julia knew the dress he was talking about and smiled in agreement. She'd loved the dress since unpacking it from Aunt Maddy's latest shipment, and had been looking for an occasion to wear it.

"Who else is supposed to attend from the office?" she asked, fearing she already knew the answer.

Travis grimaced. "Well, Nate will be there of course since he did the structural design. And unfortunately that means he'll have to bring Cameron with him. The associate architect on the project will be there as well. I think it was Eric Chiang, so probably him and his wife. Along with the three of us here that should be everyone."

Anton patted her on the shoulder. "Why don't you bring a date? Just call one of the hundreds of names in your little black book."

She laughed. "No little black book and definitely not hundreds of names. In fact, sad as it sounds, I can't think of anyone to ask."

"Girl, that's just wrong," clucked Anton. "You should be out with a different hot guy every night. Travis and I are going to get you out clubbing where you can meet some new blood."

"Hmm. Would I be wrong to assume that those clubs you go to are gay bars?" she asked wryly.

"Oh. Right." Anton looked chagrined. "Well, I'm sure I can find someone. Maybe one of my clients at Neiman Marcus. One of my *straight* clients."

She chuckled. "It's okay. I really don't want to take someone I've just met to a business dinner. I doubt he'd have a very good time. And I'm fine going by myself. How about the two of you be my escorts for the evening?"

Travis gave her a good night hug. "That sounds wonderful. Anton and I will make sure to fend off any attacks from the she-devil. If you wear the Donna Karan she's going to be so jealous she'll start chewing her fake fingernails off."

Anton, too, gave her a hug. "Dinner was spectacular, sweetie Thank you for such a great evening. And I'm looking forward to that yoga class tomorrow. I hope your teacher doesn't kick my ass too badly. "

Julia gave him an answering grin. "She probably will. Sasha is an amazing teacher, easily the toughest I've ever had. You're going to love her class even if you might be crying at the end of it."

Though she was still devoted to her 6:00am weekday Ashtanga yoga class, she liked to sleep in on weekends, and had heard about a super tough Vinyasa class on Sundays that she had recently started attending. With the help of several glasses of wine, she'd managed to convince Anton to try the class out tomorrow morning. Travis, who claimed to be the least flexible person in San Francisco, had tactfully declined to join them.

During the short taxi ride from Julia's flat to their home in Cole Valley, Travis and Anton were both gleeful as they plotted their strategy for the dinner on Thursday.

"We're going to push so many of Cameron's buttons that her elevator will have to stop at every floor," joked Travis.

Anton rubbed his hands together in anticipation. "Payback's a bitch, isn't it? And it couldn't happen to a bigger bitch, in my opinion."

"And maybe if we push her hard enough – subtly, of course, can't be too obvious – Nate will see what she's really like underneath all that phony sweetness. Cameron's not the right woman for him, and she's nowhere near good enough for a guy like him."

Anton sighed, resting his head on Travis' shoulder. "He'd look awfully good with Julia, don't you think? Both of them are so gorgeous. Can you even imagine the babies those two could have together?"

Travis looked at his partner oddly. "Strange that you should bring that up. From the first time those two met in my office, I could swear sparks flew. But it was more than that, almost as if they already knew each other. Oh, both of them denied it like crazy but I know chemistry when I see it."

Anton patted him on the arm. "Well, you are the best at reading people, dear. I still swear you're psychic. So if you think there's something between those two then it's probably true. Ooh, how romantic! Forbidden, tragic love. He really wants her but he's promised to someone else, while she's hopelessly in love knowing he can never be hers. My heart aches for both of them."

Travis shook his head. "Stop reading those crappy romance novels, okay? I mean, it's obvious you're gay, you don't have to turn into a pussy to boot. And I never said they were in love with each other, though it's fairly obvious Nate thinks she's hot."

Anton rolled his eyes. "*I* think she's hot. I'm guessing if you and I got drunk enough, we could probably even get it up for her. Nathan probably gets a hard-on for her when he's stone cold sober. I can just imagine his reaction when he sees her in that red dress."

Chapter Ten

Nathan knew the exact moment Julia walked into the restaurant. Not because he could actually see her right away, but because every male head in the place turned to watch her entrance. And when she did come into his view, he thought he'd have a heart attack on the spot for she'd never looked more beautiful, more tempting, more forbidden.

The sexy red dress made her look like a siren, with its cap sleeves, draped neckline, and the way the fabric clung to her breasts and hips. The hemline had a tiny slit just above the knee, concealing more than revealing, but just that slight hint of leg was much more of a turn-on that if the dress had been slit to the thigh.

Stilettos, of course, these of red satin with a teasing little bow near the open toe. She wore more makeup than she normally did at the office, her kissable, plump lips glossed in a deep red. Her glorious hair tumbled down her back in thick, lustrous curls.

Once again, she looked like both the sophisticated lady and the sultry temptress at the same time, and Nathan imagined that every straight man in the place was dying to fuck her. And he was grateful for the fact that Cameron was running late as usual, because there was no way he could have hidden the fact that he was practically drooling at the sight of Julia right now.

He'd been dismayed and concerned when Travis had very casually mentioned a few days ago that Julia would be here tonight. At first he'd argued the idea, rationalizing that Julia hadn't been involved with this particular project. But he'd had no comeback for Travis' calm, reasonable response that Julia would certainly be working with the clients in the very near future and ought to have this opportunity to meet them. He couldn't very well have continued to argue the matter without betraying his attraction to

Julia, especially when he suspected that his business partner was already well aware he found her extremely alluring.

Julia stood poised at the entrance to the vast bar area where the pre-dinner cocktails were being served, looking around uncertainly. Nathan's fists clenched tightly when he saw the way at least a dozen men were staring at her, and for once she seemed uncomfortable with all the attention she was getting. But then she looked up and saw him and the smile that lit her face went straight to his groin. He started walking towards her, quickening his pace as he went, determined to reach her before someone else could approach.

When he stood directly in front of her, she touched his arm lightly, still smiling. "Thank God for a familiar face. I never imagined there'd be so many people here."

He took her hand and gave it a reassuring squeeze. "You don't like big parties?" Large, splashy social events like this were what Cameron lived for. He'd grown used to them as a necessary evil to build his business.

Julia shook her head, drawing his attention to the ruby and diamond drop earrings she wore. "Not particularly. I like smaller groups much better. This is sort of intimidating."

"You should have a drink to relax." He beckoned a waiter over. He had yet to order a cocktail himself, figuring he should wait for Cameron, but he suddenly felt in dire need of some fortification.

"What would you like?" he asked her when the waiter arrived.

"Glenlivet on the rocks, please," she told the waiter. "Preferably the 18-year if you have it."

The waiter couldn't take his eyes off of Julia and nodded automatically. "Of course, miss. We definitely have that."

Nathan thought wryly that even if they didn't the young, besotted waiter would gladly offer to run out to procure it for her.

He cleared his throat until the waiter turned his way, a flustered look on his face.

"Oh, sorry, sir. I'm – I didn't mean to ignore you. What can I get for you?"

Nathan grinned. "Actually, the same thing as the lady ordered. Excellent choice, Ms. McKinnon."

As the waiter hurried off to fill their orders, Nathan regarded Julia curiously. "I wouldn't have pegged you as the single malt Scotch type."

She laughed softly. "My father is a Scotsman, after all, even though he's lived in the States since childhood. And I don't always drink Scotch. It just seemed like a good night for it, what with the fog and damp outside."

"Ah, I see. So if you were in – say, Mexico - right now you'd be drinking margaritas? Or Mai Tais in Hawaii?"

Julia grinned. "Sure. And sangria in Spain, mojitos in Miami, wine in Napa."

He chuckled, enjoying this little game. "Let's see what else we can think of. Sake in Japan. Guinness in Ireland, vodka in Russia. And, of course, champagne in France."

Julia froze, and he could have kicked himself for his thoughtless reminder of that night at the Plaza Hotel. But then she merely shook her head and murmured, "No. I only drink champagne when I want to be seduced."

He made a low, feral sound in his throat and would have yanked her against him, kissing her senseless, if they hadn't been surrounded by almost two hundred people. He was saved from having to think of a reply by the arrival of the waiter with their drinks.

Julia took a small, dainty sip from hers, while he bolted down half his drink in one rather ungainly gulp. There was now an awkward, uncomfortable silence between them, and he was trying desperately to get his emotions under control. Her comment about seduction had made his head spin, and all he could think about was sitting across from her at the Champagne Bar in the Plaza, holding her hand and imagining all of the naughty things he was going to do to her. Nathan closed his eyes for a brief moment, wishing with all his might that the two of them could be magically transported back to that exact same table.

He was saved from the awkward silence by the arrival of Travis and Anton, who both gushed over Julia and how gorgeous she looked. Anton in particular couldn't stop fussing over her.

"Oh, my God, girl. I *told* you this was the dress, didn't I? You look like sin. Travis, isn't she just breathtaking?"

Travis, always the more subdued of the pair, merely smiled and gave Julia a peck on the cheek. "Always. I would say red is your color, sweetie, but I've yet to see a color that doesn't look good on you." He turned to Nathan. "What do you think of our gorgeous girl tonight?"

Nathan met Julia's gaze head on. "That she always looks gorgeous, but especially tonight."

Her cheeks pinkened. "Okay, that's enough, all of you. You're going to make my head swell if you keep this up."

Anton giggled. "Honey, I'm guessing you're making half the men in this room swell up right now. Different head, though."

Travis and Nathan groaned at his innuendo, while Julia just laughed and gave him a playful swat. "You're *sooo* bad! Do you always say such outrageous things?"

Travis smirked. "Can't take him anywhere, no telling what he might say. Now behave yourself, Anton. There are a lot of important people here tonight and they aren't going to appreciate your naughty mouth."

"Speaking of important people, you should introduce Julia to Aaron and Lance before they get too busy," suggested Nathan.

"They're right over there." He pointed to the co-owners of the restaurant.

"Good idea, we'll head right over." Travis took Julia by the arm. "You coming with us, Nate?"

Nathan shook his head. "I'd better give Cameron a call and see where she's at."

"Running late again?" asked Anton, making a tsk-tsk sound. "I swear that girl is going to be late for her own wedding! Speaking of which, have you two set a date yet?"

Nathan caught Julia's eye briefly, frowning when he saw the crestfallen look on her face before she turned away. "Valentine's Day next year," he told Anton, wishing like hell the subject hadn't been brought up.

Travis seemed to sense his unease and tactfully pulled Anton away with him, giving Nathan a glance of part sympathy, part irritation. Nathan could only wonder what the hell that particular look was all about.

It was too loud in the bar to be able to make a phone call so he sent Cameron a quick text instead. While waiting for her to reply, he spied Eric Chiang and his cute wife Karen entering the bar and waved them over. As they chatted, Nathan couldn't help but keep an eye on Julia as Travis introduced her to Aaron and Lance. Both of the restaurant owners were known players, though he was fairly sure Lance was married. It didn't seem to matter, though, since both he and Aaron were almost shoving the other out of their way to get closer to Julia.

Jealousy and possessiveness raged through Nathan like a fast moving wildfire, and he wanted to hurry over to where she stood and claim her in front of all these people. But the fact that he couldn't do exactly that gnawed at his guts and made him want to punch something. He knew he was being an unreasonable ass about the whole situation, but he wasn't able or willing to let go completely. He was the one who'd turned Julia way, who'd made it very clear that Cameron was the only woman in his life. Julia was free to date or fuck whoever she wanted, and he had absolutely nothing to say about it. So he found himself caught in the intolerable situation of not being free to claim her for himself but not wanting anyone else to have her, either.

'I'm so fucked,' he muttered to himself in disgust, motioning the waiter over for another drink.

✳✳✳✳✳

Cameron was well on her way to getting very, very drunk, but she figured she deserved it given the way her evening had gone so far.

Oh, it had started out quite well, no debate there. She'd spent several hours this afternoon getting ready for tonight's dinner, knowing there would be a lot of local dignitaries and most likely media in attendance. She had left work early to allow plenty of time for all her primping – a mani-pedi, getting her pale blonde roots touched up and her hair blown out, and even having a professional makeup application done. Back at her condo, she'd tried on half a dozen outfits before deciding on the black Stella McCartney. The sequined fabric skimmed lightly over her slim frame, the elbow-length sleeves helping to hide her skinny arms. The shoes had taken longer to decide on, as she didn't want to appear as tall as Nate but also didn't want to wear anything too dowdy, either. She'd finally chosen the black Marc Jacobs pumps with the silver kitten heel and buckled strap. Dangling diamond chandelier earrings and a wide diamond cuff bracelet finished the outfit, and Cameron knew she looked damned good.

She had entered the crowded bar area of Taverna Francesca feeling like a million bucks, until she'd noticed that most of the attention in the room – the *male* attention, anyway – had seemed to be focused on the one person she really hadn't wanted to be here tonight – Travis' little bombshell designer Julia.

Cameron had seethed inwardly as she'd observed the little bitch, provocatively attired in a fitted red dress that she could never even consider wearing herself. Julia continued to attract attention as she was introduced to one group of attendees after another. Cameron had made a rather unpleasant face upon noticing how Travis and his little faggot lover Anton were fawning over Julia, laughing and conversing like they were all the best of friends. Travis had been making it a point, it seemed, to introduce Julia to every good looking man in the room, whether they already had a woman on their arm or not. Cameron had silently cursed the pair, whom she knew detested her as much as she despised them, and had grit her teeth to observe Julia holding court like she was a fucking queen or princess.

But what had really pissed her off was when she finally located Nathan in the crowd of people, only to observe how he was following Julia around the room, the lustful interest in his gaze unmistakable. Cameron's cheeks had flamed with anger, and she had stalked across the crowded room towards her fiancé, determined to bring his attention to *her* instead of that little bitch.

Nathan had confirmed her suspicions by looking more than a little guilty when she'd appeared at his side. He'd given her a quick kiss and made sure she had a drink, but she could tell he was definitely distracted by something. In fact, it seemed to her that he'd been a little distracted for months now, almost as though he were going through the motions. Whenever she'd asked him about it, he had blamed it on work or being tired or dismissed her concerns altogether. But she knew something was off, especially with their physical relationship. Sex, which had always been a strong part of their relationship, had become more and more infrequent, and had seemed rushed and almost impersonal when it did occur. There had even been a few times when Nathan hadn't been able to maintain an erection, or become aroused at all.

The natural assumption, of course, was that he'd been cheating on her, but she had refused to let herself believe that. However, after observing the way Nathan had been following Julia around the room with his eyes, she was beginning to have some real suspicions now. Could he possibly be banging that little bitch? It would explain his withdrawn behavior these past few months, their bland sex life, and other oddities she'd noticed. She made a mental note to herself to pay closer attention to Nathan's habits and maybe even stop by the office more frequently to observe any interactions between him and Julia.

Cameron's mood had not improved once they were seated for dinner, since their tablemates included Travis, Anton, and Julia, along with Eric and Karen Chiang, and a very attractive gray haired man in his fifties who introduced himself to everyone as Jackson West, the owner of the winery whose vintages were being served at tonight's dinner.

From the very beginning of the meal, Travis and Anton had taken control of the conversation, and their very favorite topic of discussion had been Julia. During the first two courses, everyone at the table had been obliged to hear one or the other of them prattle on about what a great cook Julia was, how beautifully decorated her flat was, how kick-ass she was at yoga, no surprise considering that she had been a teacher of the practice during college. Cameron learned – reluctantly – that Julia had graduated from Cornell, had interned and then worked at one of the top design firms in Manhattan, and had lived in a tiny studio in the Upper East Side.

Cameron wasn't sure which of these facts angered her more. She couldn't cook at all, had always had hired staff to look after her while living with her parents, and nowadays she liked to joke that her favorite thing to make for dinner was reservations. She'd never really used the kitchen inside her professionally decorated apartment. She hated yoga, claiming that it wasn't really a workout and that she needed something much tougher to challenge her, like kickboxing or spinning. The truth of the matter was that she wasn't the least bit flexible and was also somewhat uncoordinated, but she'd never admit either of those facts to anyone.

The knowledge that Julia had attended an Ivy League school had really touched a nerve. For most of her life, Cameron's parents had pushed her to excel at school and get good grades so that she could attend a school like Harvard or Yale or Stanford. But she had generally disliked school, and had goofed off and partied a lot in high school. No number of private tutors to bring her grades up or improve her SAT scores had helped. Neither had any of her parents multiple social and political connections, or their monetary donations. By pulling a lot of strings, Cameron had managed to get accepted to USC but she'd dropped out after her freshman year due to academic probation. She'd eventually obtained a degree in art history from a small liberal arts school in Manhattan, but her father had set his foot down about her living there after graduation. He'd been willing to set her up in the gallery, but only if it was in San Francisco. He had wanted both of his daughters close by and under his control as much as possible. No matter that Cameron had always dreamed about living in Manhattan, which she considered a far more vibrant and exciting city than San Francisco. When Graham Tolliver made up his mind about something there was no denying him, and Cameron had grudgingly returned to San Francisco after college.

At one point in her life Cameron had fancied herself an artist, but had been told by more than one of her teachers that she simply didn't have that sort of talent. She had settled for learning enough about art and artists to carve out a career as a gallery owner, and the Union Street establishment was quite successful. Travis had even bought several pieces from her recently for design projects, and one of those pieces was currently gracing a wall in the restaurant this evening.

Travis made sure to call everyone's attention to the piece, complimenting Cameron on her choice. "I think that turned out to be an excellent selection," he told her. "I'm glad we went with the still life instead of the abstract, much more fitting with the décor."

She nodded warily, a bit unsettled with this rare compliment from him. "I agree."

Travis gave her an odd little smile. "Tell me, Cameron. What was the name again of that artist who did those magnificent landscapes hanging in your gallery? The ones you told me weren't for sale?"

"You mean the Benoits? Her full name is Natalie Benoit and you're correct - those pieces aren't for sale. They're part of my personal collection, pretty much my most prized pieces," she replied firmly.

Julia started visibly and shot Travis a quizzical look, but he only continued to regard Cameron calmly. "Well, you won't believe this amazing coincidence. The woman you told me was one of your favorite artists of all time happens to be Julia's mother."

Cameron felt like she'd taken a punch to the solar plexus, unable to catch her breath or think of anything to say in response. She had only to look at the expression on Julia's face to know it was true. She quickly reached for her wine glass and bolted down the rest of its contents before refilling it to the brim.

Jackson turned to Julia with great interest. "I'm not much of an art expert, but even I've heard of Natalie Benoit," he gushed. "And lucky enough to have attended one of her shows about a decade ago. Your mother has incredible talent."

Julia smiled up at him. "Yes, she does. She doesn't paint much anymore, since she's already begun to develop some arthritis in her fingers. She devotes most of her time to her gallery nowadays."

"Oh, that's the Spindrift Gallery in downtown Carmel, isn't it?" asked Karen. "Eric and I have been in there a couple of times. They always have such a magnificent display. I've read that it's one of the top galleries in the country."

Eric snapped his fingers. "It just occurred to me, Julia. If your mother is Natalie Benoit, isn't she married to Robert McKinnon?"

Nathan looked startled. "The architect?" He gaped at Julia. "Your father is *the* Robert McKinnon?"

Julia nodded. "Yes, though he rarely does design anymore. He prefers to build things these days – decks, furniture, cabinets."

Nathan seemed fascinated by this revelation, and Cameron was furious that all of his attention now seemed to be focused on Julia. He and Eric peppered her with questions about her father, who apparently was some highly regarded architect that both men had studied and tried to emulate while back in college.

"I would kill to meet him someday," said Eric. "Any chance he might pay you a visit soon?"

Julia shrugged. "My parents aren't big city people. They love living in Carmel and don't venture away from there too often. But I might be able to persuade them to come up for a visit one day."

Travis gave Cameron a huge, very satisfied grin. "Well, wouldn't that be something? Eric and Nate could meet their idol, and perhaps Cameron hers."

Cameron would have gladly spit in Travis' twinkling, humor-filled eyes at that moment. She knew now that he had brought all of this up deliberately to rub her nose in the fact that the artist she had idolized for years was the mother of a woman she saw as a rival. The knowledge stuck like a thorn in her side, and she had to clench her fists to keep from tossing her wine at his smugly triumphant face.

She finished off her wine, and discreetly motioned a waiter over, asking him to bring her a dirty martini. She'd had two already before dinner, plus four glasses of wine since, but needed the alcohol badly to steady her nerves that were all but screaming at this point.

Karen unknowingly poured salt into Cameron's already gaping wound by asking Julia, "Are you an artist like your mother, then?"

Julia laughed softly. "There is no one like my mother. Her talent is otherworldly. I draw and paint a little as a hobby, nothing more."

"She's being modest, Karen," chimed in Nathan. "There's a series of charcoal drawings in her office that she swears she did on a lark, and they're incredible."

Cameron felt like kicking Nathan under the table, and pulling Julia's hair. The fact that her own fiancé was now singing the little bitch's praises made her stomach clench. And how the hell much time was he spending in her office anyway? Her palm began to twitch with the need to hit something, someone.

When the waiter arrived with her martini, she drank it down like it was lemonade, drawing a raised brow from Nathan.

"Easy, there," he said in a hushed tone. "What the hell's the matter with you, anyway? You haven't said two words all evening and you've been belting drinks back like a sailor on shore leave."

"What's wrong?" she hissed. "What the hell do you think is wrong? I'm fucking sick of hearing about how fucking wonderful that little bitch is. All of you might as well be kissing her perky little ass."

"Keep it down!" he urged in a low whisper. "And ease up on the booze, Cam. Maybe we should order you some coffee."

Defiantly, she poured herself another glass of wine and swallowed half of it at once. "I'm fine," she bit out. "Now can you act like my fiancé for the first time tonight and try to change the goddamned subject at this table?"

✳✳✳✳✳

In actuality, it was Julia who tactfully changed the subject when she asked Jackson more about his winery, a topic he was only too happy to expand upon. That only worked for a little while, however, before he began to ask her and Travis questions about potential re-design ideas, not just for the tasting rooms but for two of his personal residences.

Julia was well aware of the murderous glares she'd been receiving all evening from Cameron. The blonde hadn't even said hello to her when they had all taken their seats earlier, nor had she said a single word to her since.

And she had absolutely no idea what sort of little scheme Travis and Anton had cooked up between them, but it was quite obvious to her that something was up. She'd given Travis a couple of little nudges under the table, and frowned at Anton more than once when they had persisted in making her the subject of conversation. It made her very uncomfortable to find herself the center of attention, for she was normally a rather private person. She'd spent almost half her life trying *not* to call attention to herself, and wasn't very happy that the two men were now doing just the opposite.

The waiters had cleared away the main course and were starting to bring coffee around in preparation for dessert. Julia figured this would be a good time to visit the ladies room, and excused herself quietly. She happened to catch Nathan's eye as she stood, and was conscious of him watching her as she walked away from the table.

She'd been more than a little on edge all evening with Nathan seated directly across the table from her. Very aware of the presence of his fiancée by his side, Julia had been extremely careful to keep any conversation with him brief and polite, and had avoided looking in his direction as much as possible. But despite her best efforts, there had been several times when their gazes had collided and held until one or the other had looked away abruptly.

It was killing her to see him with Cameron, to covertly watch the other woman touch him, whisper to him, to know that she would be the one sharing his bed tonight. Julia didn't know if they lived together or not, but it was difficult to believe they didn't have frequent and very physical sex. Nathan had been such a hungry and demanding lover during their one night together that she knew he'd need to fuck often and hard. She bit down on her bottom lip to stifle its trembling, and refused to let herself picture him screwing Cameron as well and as eagerly as he'd done her. It was obvious from his skill and his dominance in bed that he had a lot of experience, certainly far more than she did, and she realized that there had likely been quite a few women in his life. That realization made her doubt even more that the night they had spent together had really meant anything to him other than another notch on his belt.

The ladies room was mostly empty when she walked in, with one woman washing her hands and one of the stalls occupied. The woman at the sink looked up and smiled at Julia.

"I love your dress," she gushed. "We're sitting at the table next to yours, and I've been admiring it all evening. Lucky you to have the perfect figure for it."

Julia smiled gratefully at the woman, who was in her early fifties and garbed in a stylish ivory wool pantsuit. "Thank you. You're very kind."

The woman, who had close-cropped auburn hair, finished drying her hands. "Oh, to be your age again and have every man in the room panting at your feet. Watch out for that one at your table in the black suit, dear. He looks like he wants you for dessert."

With a wink, the older woman left and Julia locked herself inside an empty stall. Going around the table in her head, she flushed as she realized the only man in black was Nathan. The woman must have been mistaken, though, for surely Nathan wouldn't have been looking at her in *that* way, especially with Cameron glued to his side and watching his every move.

She was alone in the bathroom while washing her hands until the door opened and Cameron strode purposefully into the room. The blonde's gait looked a little unsteady, and as she drew closer Julia recoiled from the smell of alcohol on her breath. Cameron's hazel eyes were furious, spitting fire, and her mouth was twisted into a tight, angry line.

Julia looked at her uncertainly. "Have they served dessert yet? I was hoping to get back in time. The desserts here are supposed to be fabulous." She hoped wildly that she didn't sound too forced in her effort to be pleasant to the other woman.

But Cameron was evidently in no mood to make polite small talk. "You fucking little bitch," she snarled angrily. "I hope you and your fucking little queer friends are having a good old time making me look like an idiot tonight."

Julia gasped, unprepared for the harshness of both Cameron's words and tone. "I don't know what you're talking about," she ventured. "No one is trying to do that to you."

Cameron smacked her hand against the granite topped sink. "That's exactly what's happening. I'm well aware that Travis and his little pet hate my guts, and they know the feeling is mutual. This is their twisted little way of sticking it to me. They want to make me look bad in front of Nate. But it won't work."

"I'm sure that's not - "

Cameron gave her a sudden, vicious shove, cutting her off. "Shut up! I'm sick of hearing you talk tonight, sick of seeing you looking at *my* fiancé like a lovesick calf. You've been sending him little suggestive glances all night, thinking I wouldn't notice. He's *my* fiancé, Julia. *I'm* the one he loves and is going to marry. Leave him the fuck alone!"

Julia gaped at her, one hand propped against the wall to steady herself. Cameron might be thin but she was also tall and strong, as evidenced by the push she'd just given her. "I'm well aware of that. Nathan is my boss, that's all. And I don't poach on other women's territory."

Cameron's eyes narrowed dangerously. "Oh, but I bet you'd like to, wouldn't you? He's awfully yummy to look at, and *sooo* good in bed. You can't tell me you don't want him to fuck you? Or has that already happened? Have you been fucking my fiancé, you little bitch? Have you?"

Julia flushed. "Stop this. I think you've had too much to drink and - "

Crack!

The sound of Cameron's palm making contact with her mouth reverberated though the cavernous bathroom. Julia whimpered in pain and pressed a hand to the corner of her mouth, startled to see blood staining her fingers. She'd noticed the massive ring on Cameron's engagement finger earlier, and realized it had just cut her lip.

Memories of the night when Philip had tried to rape her came rushing back, for he'd struck her across the mouth in much the same manner, also drawing blood. Julia was shaking, tears running silently down her cheeks as she turned away from Cameron, afraid another blow would fall.

But Cameron seemed content to lash out with words alone. "Stay the fuck away from Nate," she threatened. "If I catch you looking at him again tonight, you'll be sorry. He isn't interested in you, bitch, so leave him alone."

She stormed out of the bathroom then, slamming the door shut behind her. Julia clutched the granite countertop, her legs trembling like crazy. She forced herself to take several long, deep breaths, afraid she was going to throw up or pass out. Hoping desperately that no one else came into the bathroom, she grabbed a paper towel and wet it before pressing it to her mouth. The bleeding stopped fairly quickly but her lip was swollen and sore, and she winced when reapplying as much lip gloss as she could stand to camouflage the cut. She dabbed under her eyes with a tissue to dry her tears and hoped her eye makeup wasn't destroyed. After brushing her hair, she forced herself to return to the table, though it was the very last thing she felt like doing. She wasn't about to give Cameron the satisfaction of driving her away, or letting the evil witch think she was afraid of her.

But something in her face must have betrayed her, for Travis frowned instantly upon seeing her and whispered urgently in her ear, "What the hell happened to you? Have you been crying?"

Julia bit her lip and turned her face away from the others to whisper back. "Can't talk now. I'll tell you about it later."

She was silent and subdued for the remainder of the evening, which fortunately ended sooner than later. She was more than happy for Cameron to take control of the conversation, especially since the nasty bitch was quite obviously well on her way to being sloppy drunk, and making an ass of herself in the process. Even Jackson murmured to Julia, "Looks like someone's been enjoying my wine a little too much."

Julia absolutely refused to glance across the table where Cameron and Nathan were seated, even though she felt the almost continual force of Nathan's gaze upon her. As drunk and obnoxious as Cameron was quickly becoming, Julia wouldn't put it past her to make a scene if she caught Julia looking at him again. She kept her gaze downcast and hoped no one tried to engage her in conversation.

Travis, with his famed sense of intuition, seemed to have put the puzzle pieces together fairly quickly, and fortunately wrapped things up and made their excuses to leave as soon as dessert was finished.

"I'm sorry to eat and run, everyone, but Julia and I are meeting a client at 8:00am in the office tomorrow," he explained. "We all need our beauty sleep, especially me, so we'll bid you good night." He pulled Julia's chair out and helped her to her feet. "And I promised Julia that we'd all share a cab home."

Julia could have thrown her arms around her boss and kissed him, but settled for uttering a subdued "Good night" to everyone at the table, without singling anyone out.

Jackson set his napkin down on the table and stood. "Let me walk you out," he offered. "We still need to exchange business cards." He placed a hand on the small of Julia's back and steered her out of the room, with Travis and Anton trailing just behind. Normally Julia would have shied away from such contact, but for some reason Jackson's light touch was oddly comforting tonight.

She managed to hold it together until the three of them were safely ensconced in their cab, and then she lost it, sobbing onto Travis' shoulder while Anton squeezed her hand comfortingly. She managed to choke out what had happened in the ladies room between sobs.

"I'm going to make sure Nate knows what just happened," warned Travis. "In fact, he's getting a text as we speak."

"No!" Julia put a hand over his. "Please don't. Let's just leave him out of this."

Travis' mouth firmed. "No. His bitch of a fiancée assaulted my employee at a business function. She's fucking lucky I'm not calling the police right now."

"Travis, please. I don't think Cameron would have acted that way if you and Anton hadn't acted like the co-Presidents of my fan club. What were you two thinking anyway?"

Anton grinned. "That we'd piss her off real good. But I guess we pushed a few too many buttons."

"Yeah, that elevator went all the way to the roof," said Travis wryly. "I'm sorry, sweetie. We were just trying to rile her up a little, get back at her for all of her previous nastiness. And also trying to get her Dr. Jekyll side to surface so that Nate could see she wasn't the sweet Miss Hyde she pretends to be."

Julia sighed, gingerly probing at her split lip. "Well, I think that part at least was successful. Too bad I'm going to have a fat lip as a result."

✳✳✳✳✳

Nathan was furious when he arrived at the office early the next morning, his mood not helped by the fact that he'd had precious little sleep. By the time he'd dropped a falling down drunk Cameron at her condo and driven back to his place, it had already been close to midnight. And then sleep had not come easy to him after the tumultuous events of the evening.

He couldn't say who he was more pissed off at right now. The candidates included Travis and Anton for whatever little scheme they'd cooked up to antagonize Cameron; at Cameron herself for drinking so much and very nearly making a scene; or at that sly old bastard Jackson West for daring to flirt with Julia all night and then having the nerve to actually touch her. West was more than twice Julia's age, had been married and divorced three times, and was a notorious womanizer. The fact that he had engaged Julia in a discussion about doing some design work annoyed Nathan greatly, for the last thing he wanted was to give the horny old bastard multiple opportunities to associate with her.

But he was perhaps the angriest at himself for not having spoken up last night when Julia had returned to the dinner table clearly upset about something. He knew that Cameron was somehow involved, for his fiancée had arrived back at the table a few minutes earlier, looking very smug and satisfied. She had quite obviously said something to rattle Julia, but he had been too afraid of riling Cameron up in public to confront her about it.

It certainly wasn't like Cameron to get so completely wasted. Oh, he'd seen her drink quite a bit before and even get plastered, but last night her drunkenness had turned ugly. She'd puked on the sidewalk just outside her building, staining her dress and shoes, and had immediately gotten sick again once inside her condo. He'd helped her get cleaned up, and made sure she took some Advil before leaving, rather appalled that she had wanted him to stay the night. The mere thought of sleeping in the same bed with her after her actions had made his skin crawl. She was sure to be pissed off at him this morning, especially when coupled with the vicious hangover she must have.

Recalling Travis' comment about having an early client meeting, Nathan made sure he was waiting for Julia inside her office by 7:30am. He needed to talk to her privately for a few minutes and get her side of the story. Cameron had been in no shape last night to discuss what had happened, and Nathan hadn't been in the mood for the argument that was sure to occur when they did eventually talk it out. It didn't take a rocket scientist to realize that Cameron was extremely jealous of Julia, and he wasn't the least bit anxious to discuss her with his fiancée. Cameron was a highly perceptive person, and if she prodded and pushed hard enough he was very much afraid that she'd uncover his attraction to Julia and what had happened between them in New York.

While waiting for Julia in her cozy, tidy office, he studied the grouping of framed photographs artistically arranged on her credenza. One was of an attractive older couple that he knew to be her parents. The woman bore a great resemblance to Julia, and he recognized the dark haired man as his idol, Robert McKinnon. He was still in disbelief that Julia was his daughter, and that he hadn't associated the two before now.

There was a photo of Julia's mother and another, more sophisticated woman who looked just like her, and Nathan assumed this was the aunt who supplied so much of Julia's scintillating wardrobe. Twins evidently ran in the family.

And there were three different photos – the frames hinged together – of Julia and her own twin. One had been taken when they were both young girls – already beauties – with three Australian Shepherd dogs snuggled between them. He smiled at this one, for the girls obviously loved their dogs, judging by the way they cuddled them close. He'd grown up with dogs, too, mostly Labradors, and missed having a pet of his own. Then he grimaced as he thought of the tiny, yappy dog owned by Cameron's mother. He was a nasty, temperamental little thing that Mrs. Tolliver insisted on dressing in ridiculous articles of dog clothing and bejeweled collars.

The second photo was of both girls in cap and gown at their high school graduation. The final photo looked more recent, and had been taken at Christmastime, evidenced by the decorated tree in the background. Two identical pair of green eyes gazed at the camera, though it was easy to tell the girls apart. Julia was dressed up in a silky blouse, wool skirt and high heeled boots, while her twin wore a bulky sweater, jeans and sneakers.

He checked his watch – now reading 7:40am – and frowned, wondering if he'd understood Travis correctly, or if their meeting was even here at the office. He had just decided to swing by his partner's office when he heard the clicking of high heels in the hallway outside. Julia froze in the doorway of her office as she stared at him in surprise.

She was still wearing her coat, of black and white checkered wool with large black buttons, and those sexy black Louboutin stilettos. Her face was as flawlessly made up as usual but she looked pale and tired.

"What are you doing here so early?" she asked quietly as she hung up her coat and set her purse and laptop case down. Beneath the coat she was simply but elegantly attired in a white button-down blouse cuffed at the elbows, and a black pleated skirt, this one a little fuller than her typical pencil style.

"I wanted to talk to you before your client meeting," he explained.

She looked puzzled for a moment, and then shook her head. "Actually, there's no meeting. Travis must have made that one up on the spur of the moment so we could leave a little early." She stood behind her desk, arms crossed over her middle as she looked at him. "What did you want to talk about?"

Nathan shut the office door and locked it. "I want you to tell me what the hell happened last night after you came back to the table. You looked like you'd just seen a ghost, while Cameron looked like the cat that swallowed the canary. Did she say something to you?"

Julia didn't answer him for long seconds, and refused to meet his eyes, her head turned slightly away from him. "You haven't already asked her these questions?"

He gave a short, mirthless laugh. "Kind of hard to carry on a conversation with someone when they're upchucking in the gutter. Let's just say she wasn't in the mood for talking last night, and neither was I."

She maintained her stubborn silence for a bit longer before stating quietly, "I think you should talk to her. I don't imagine she'd appreciate knowing you were in my office right now."

"What the hell is that supposed to mean?" he burst out. "Did she warn you away or something? Exactly what did she say to you last night?"

Julia looked up at him, and he was alarmed to see the shimmer of tears in her eyes. "Not a whole lot that made sense. But she did accuse me of sleeping with you, or at least wanting to sleep with you."

He closed his eyes, fearing that something like this had been bound to happen sooner than later. "What did you tell her, Julia?" he asked harshly.

She stared at him angrily. "What do you think I told her? Not the truth, for God's sake! I told you before, Nathan – I won't betray you. She won't hear about what happened in New York from me." She turned away, as though she couldn't bear to keep looking at him. "All I told her was that you were my boss and that I didn't poach on men who were already taken."

"What else did she say?" he persisted. "You seemed way too upset, and she looked far too pleased with herself from the little you've told me."

Julia gave a careless little shrug. "Does it really matter, Nathan? I mean, all you care about is whether or not I've kept your secret and I did. I have. So let's just forget about last night and get to work, okay?"

He placed his hands on her shoulders and turned her around firmly to face him. "No. Not until you tell me the rest, because I know there's more. And believe it or not, I care about more than just keeping secrets. I care about your feelings too, Julia. So, please, tell me what really happened."

She shut her eyes, stubbornly refusing to look at him, and took a deep breath before murmuring in a barely audible voice, "She warned me to stay away from you, that *she* was your fiancée, and that if she saw me looking at you again I'd be sorry."

Nathan cursed softly when he noticed a single tear tracking slowly down her cheek, and he wiped it away with his thumb without giving it a thought. She tried turning her head away again, but he held her still, gripping her chin between thumb and forefinger. "What else? I can tell you're leaving something out."

She shook her head, but more tears fell from her eyes, and she brushed them away impatiently. "No, there's nothing else."

"Then why are you crying?" he pressed. "Tell me all of it, Julia." He wiped away a tear that had trailed down to the corner of her mouth, only to recoil when she whimpered in pain.

"Ow," she cried, trying to dislodge his hand on her chin, but he only gripped it tighter.

"What's the matter?" he asked urgently. "Did I hurt you? Let me see." Gently, he probed the side of her mouth, noticing for the first time how swollen it was beneath a thick coat of dark berry lip gloss. "Jesus, what happened here? It looks like someone hit you."

And then, realization washed over him and he groaned, pulling her into his arms.

"It was Cameron, wasn't it?"

Julia didn't reply to the question that was really more a statement of fact, but did give a tiny nod against his chest. She rested her palms lightly on his shoulders as he held her gently, his hand stoking her hair.

"I'm sorry," he whispered. "I would never have let her touch you if I'd been there. She was drunk and pissed off and jealous.

That's no excuse for slapping you, but I've never known her to become violent before. Let me take a look at it."

Julia reluctantly let him examine her swollen lip more closely, and he frowned when he noticed the still open cut. "Did she scratch you with her nails or something? I wouldn't have thought her strong enough to draw blood."

"No, it was her ring. Her, um, engagement ring. It's so big that it split my lip when she slapped me."

He felt anger surging through him. "You should have hit her back."

She covered her face with her hands, and he felt her trembling in his arms. "I was scared," she confessed faintly. "It brought back bad memories. From that time in my old office."

She didn't elaborate, but he knew exactly what she meant. She'd been flashing back to the night that fucker had tried to rape her, when he'd hit her and bruised her. Nathan was furious at himself that he hadn't been there to protect her, either in New York or last night.

He caressed her cheek tenderly, pressing a gentle kiss to her forehead. "It's okay, baby. Everything's okay. That bastard can't hurt you anymore, and I'll make sure Cameron leaves you alone from now on, too."

She nodded, but kept her eyes downcast, the tears still streaming down her cheeks. Overwhelmed with the need to protect her, to comfort her, he threaded his hands into her thick, silky hair and tilted her head back. His lips touched her cheek, whisper soft, soothing her, trying to dry the tracks of her tears. As he continued to press soothing kisses along her cheeks and eyelids, she grew calmer and her sobs began to subside. She lifted huge eyes the color of wet moss to his, her lips parted as her breath started to slow down, and he groaned at the tempting, delectable picture she presented. Then, as though it were the most natural thing in the world, he bent his head, claiming her full, lush mouth in a searing kiss. She made a little "mmm" sound deep in her throat that went straight to his groin, and he yanked her against him, his arms wrapped around her back, practically lifting her off the floor.

Julia wound her arms about his neck, kissing him back with an almost desperate ardor, her hands in his hair. His tongue sought entrance to her mouth, and she welcomed it, meeting it with her own. His hands slid from her back to the sweet curves of her ass, holding her still as he rubbed the hard ridge of his erection against the cleft of her thighs. She moaned beneath his kisses, her hands sliding inside his suit jacket to clutch handfuls of his crisp pearl gray shirt.

Gasping for breath, he reluctantly broke the kiss, only to move his lips to the side of her neck. He shuddered with arousal as she licked his chin, the corner of his mouth, his lips. Christ, it had been so long since that night he'd fucked her into oblivion, since he'd held her and kissed her this way. She had haunted his dreams for months, aroused him just from being in the same room, and he'd wanted her more than he could even try to put into words. He was already so hard that his erection pressed painfully against his trousers, afraid that he would lose it at the slightest touch of her hand.

"You smell so good," she whispered, nuzzling her nose against his cheek. "I want to lick you all over, eat you up."

Nathan growled, spinning her around and shoving her up against the wall. Julia gasped as he simultaneously cupped her full, lush breast with one hand and lifted one of her legs to wrap around his hip with the other. He ran his hand up under her full skirt, hissing when he found the frilly garter attached to her silky stockings.

"Fuck, you're wearing those goddamn stockings again," he groaned. "Do you just wear all these cockteasing things to torture me? Let me see."

He pulled her skirt higher until he could see the sexy black garter clipped to the sheer hosiery, then followed the length of her leg down to those shoes that had given him so many hard-ons.

"You're so fucking sexy," he hissed. "Every time I see you, every goddamn day, all I can think about is ripping whatever you're teasing me with that day off this delicious body, touching these beautiful tits, these fabulous legs, your gorgeous little ass."

Julia was panting as he ran his hands over her body, squeezing her breasts, pinching her nipples, cupping her ass cheeks, sliding up and down the length of her leg. "I want you, too," she breathed. "So much. I want to throw myself in your arms every time I'm near you. I miss you so much, Nathan."

"Sweet Julia," he groaned. "I can't get you out of my mind. And it drives me crazy to have to watch other men look at you, to listen when they talk about how hot you are. When that dirty old man touched you last night I wanted to punch him in the face. I can't stand the thought of anyone else putting their hands on you. Especially here."

She cried out as his hand slid all the way up her leg to the crotch of her lacy little panties. He cupped her through the silk, finding the fabric soaking wet. Pushing the crotch aside, he swiftly thrust two fingers up inside her wet, tight cunt.

"God, look at how juicy you are," he whispered, his tongue tracing around her ear. "So tight and hot. Do you know what it does to me to know I can get you this wet so quickly?"

"Ohhh." She released a long, low moan as he fucked her with his fingers, first with slow, deep thrusts, then with faster, shallower ones. When his thumb moved to circle her swollen clit, she shoved her fist into her mouth, stifling the erotic whimpers coming from the back of her throat.

He was so hard he feared he'd come in his pants just from watching the glorious spectacle that was Julia as she climaxed against his fingers, her head falling back against the wall, her mouth opened in a silent moan. He pulled her mouth to his, kissing her savagely as he continued to stimulate her ultra-sensitive cunt.

"This is mine," he muttered hoarsely, cupping her vulva possessively. "I don't want anyone else touching you here. Or anywhere else for that matter."

Julia gasped and stiffened in his arms before unexpectedly gripping his rock hard erection through his pants. He was startled at her sudden move but couldn't help the groan that escaped his lips at the feel of her small hand on his immensely swollen prick.

"Really, Nathan?" she asked angrily. "Does that go both ways?" She stroked along his length and he shuddered in reaction. "Does this only belong to me? You aren't going to fuck your fiancée with it anymore?"

Stricken by the hurt and anger in her voice, he grasped her wrist and reluctantly pulled her hand from him, even though his body was screaming for release. Shamed, he turned from her and took several long, deep breaths.

"That's what I thought," replied Julia quietly. "You might want to fuck me but she's still the one you're with, the one you're going to marry. Don't touch me again, Nathan. You don't have the right anymore."

He nodded, willing his erection to subside enough for him to walk to his office. "I'm sorry, Julia. I was way out of line. It won't happen again, okay?"

From somewhere behind him he could hear the sound of her weeping, and it broke his heart. It was an unpleasant reminder of how upset, almost incoherent she'd been that morning in New

York when he'd told her he was engaged. He turned back, reaching for her as she sobbed into her hands.

"Don't cry, baby. I'm such an asshole. I'm not worth your tears," he pleaded.

Julia shoved him away, grabbing a wad of tissues from the decorative box on her credenza, and wiping her eyes and nose delicately. "Please just go, okay? I have work to do. And this is *not* going to happen again, understand? I'm tired of being used. You *are* an asshole – I should have remembered that before I let you touch me."

Her words stung like little pieces of broken glass, but he couldn't fault her for saying them. "I'll leave you alone, Julia," he whispered. "I'm sorry."

He walked out of her office without a backward glance and kept on going, like a robot, until he reached his own office. He slammed the door shut, not really caring if anyone else in earshot had arrived yet, and emitted several vicious curses. There was a neat stack of file folders on the corner of his desk and he knocked them all to the floor in one fell swoop. He took his suit jacket off with sharp, jerky motions and flung it onto the sofa, before pacing angrily around the room over and over again.

Finally he plopped down in his desk chair, banging his head against the surface of his desk several times. "Goddammit!" he swore in a low voice. "Fuck, fuck fuck! How the hell did I just manage to make an already shitty situation into a complete and total clusterfuck?"

He'd started out the conversation with Julia intending only to find out what had gone down last night between her and Cameron. He hadn't expected anything more serious than some catty sniping on Cameron's part, enough to upset Julia but nothing over the top. The last thing he'd anticipated was that Cameron had physically harmed Julia, and shook her up so badly.

And when he'd seen the tears trickling down her cheek, his only intent in embracing Julia had been to comfort and console her. He sure as hell hadn't planned to kiss her as though he wanted to eat her alive, and most definitely hadn't figured on touching her body, much less fingering her to an orgasm right there against her office wall. And then he'd had to go ahead and make that domineering, possessive statement about how she belonged to him and no one else. He didn't blame her in the least for being pissed off, for he'd acted like a total dick to her once again.

Nathan gave himself a few minutes to calm down before picking up his discarded files and restoring order to them. He hung his suit jacket up in its usual place before opening his office door.

Robyn was just arriving, and took one look at his face before shaking her head. "So it's going to be one of *those* mornings, is it? I should go get myself a double espresso right now. Or maybe a tequila shot."

He smiled faintly, rarely able to resist her perennial good humor. "Sorry. I just had a rather upsetting conversation a little while ago. Give me some time to get over it, okay?"

She shrugged. "Sure, whatever. So how was the dinner last night?"

His smile faded abruptly. "Don't ask." He checked his watch. "Speaking of which, I'm going to see if my dear partner has dragged his ass in yet. He has a few things to answer for."

Robyn called after him as he stalked away. "Should I call Courtney and warn her to duck for cover?"

※※※※※

Travis had been expecting Nathan to drop in sometime this morning, and to also be in a foul temper. So when his partner strode purposefully into his office unannounced, slamming the door behind him, he didn't even glance up from the designs he was studying.

"What the hell kind of juvenile little game were you and Anton playing last night?"

Travis calmly set the design boards aside, and glanced up at a very pissed-off Nathan, smiling broadly. "Well, good morning to you, too, sunshine. A bit hungover, are we? No, wait, that would be your oh so charming fiancée who fits that bill."

Nathan pounded a fist on Travis' desk. "What were you two thinking anyway? Why did you deliberately antagonize Cameron that way?"

Travis raised a pale blond brow. "Who says we were trying to do that? All I intended was to have some pleasant dinner conversation, that's all. It's hardly my fault if your fiancée couldn't handle not being the center of attention for once."

Nathan plopped down in a guest chair, glaring at his partner. "It wasn't bad enough to keep praising Julia all night – she went to Cornell, she speaks fluent French, she was a yoga teacher during college, she's such a great cook. But the kicker was when you told Cam the artist that she'd admired and raved about for years was Julia's mother – that kind of put her over the edge."

Travis' eyes blazed angrily, a rare emotion for him. "Yes, and I saw the aftermath of that edge Cameron fell over. You weren't in that cab last night when poor Julia was shaking like a leaf. Your girl really walloped her, it wasn't just some little smack on the cheek. And don't blame me. Cameron's a grown woman, after all, and ought to have better control over her emotions. And the fact that Natalie Benoit is Julia's mother is public knowledge and would have come up eventually."

Nathan sighed, rubbing a hand over his weary face. "I know it would, bizarre coincidence that it is. There're an awful lot of coincidences involving Julia, matter of fact."

"Like what?' asked Travis curiously.

Nathan shrugged. "I don't know. Like the fact she did design work for the Gregson Group in New York. Or that the two of you shared a mentor."

"That's not a coincidence That's merely a situation that brought her out here in the first place. If I hadn't already known her via Gerard it's highly unlikely she'd be working here now. So what else is a coincidence?"

Nathan waved a hand in dismissal. "Nothing, I guess. Forget I said anything."

"All right." Travis returned his attention to the stack of design boards. "Well, if you've finished scolding me for being a naughty boy, I'd like to get back to work now."

"Why did you do it?"

Travis frowned in annoyance. "Because I damned well felt like it, that's why. Your charming fiancée hasn't been quite so charming to Anton and me. You know darned well she can't stand us, that she despises gays in general. Which considering she lives in one of the gayest cities in the world, and works in the art world, is sort of mind blowing. And I won't even discuss her prick of a father."

"Yes, please, let's not. I have to see the old bastard at some fucking boring party tomorrow night, and that will be soon enough."

"Well you might want to keep the Princess away from those dirty martinis," drawled Travis. "Evidently someone can't hold her liquor as well as she thinks she can."

"She was just pissed off and jealous," Nathan replied dismissively. "She hardly ever drinks like that, and especially not when her parents are around."

"If you say so. I'm not really sure why she'd be jealous, though. Cameron seems like the most confident woman I've ever met."

Nathan hesitated. "She is, but I think she feels threatened by Julia somehow."

"Really? Can't imagine why. Unless it's because Julia is younger, hotter, and is actually nice to people. Or maybe it's just because Cameron sees the way you stare at Julia's tits, like you know what they look like naked."

Nathan flushed a bright red and looked shocked, his mouth gaping open. "I don't do any such thing."

Travis laughed heartily. "Oh, you sure as hell do. I may be gay and don't look at women the same way, but lust is lust, buddy. And you've got it in spades for my girl. You've got to do a much better job at hiding that from your fiancée, though. Discretion, Nathan, discretion."

Nathan had the good grace to appear disgruntled. "Well, how the hell do you expect me – or any red-blooded hetero man – to keep from staring at her when she dresses that way?"

Travis frowned. "There's nothing wrong with the way Julia dresses. She's classy all the time, no cleavage or see-through fabrics, nothing too short or clingy."

"None of that matters. She just wears all of these form fitting dresses and skirts, and those fucking high heels. I'm only human, you know. Can't you get her to wear baggy clothes and flats?" he pleaded.

Travis looked alarmed. "Oh, hell no am I having *that* conversation with her! She may be a friend of a friend but that doesn't mean she can't claim sexual harassment . Besides," he added with a wicked grin, "her amazing good looks and that smokin' little bod have helped us get an awful lot of business lately. Including a very promising lead with Jackson West just last night."

"That fucker," cursed Nathan, not looking at all pleased. "Rumor has it that he likes pretty girls less than half his age, and that he's got the money to buy whatever sweet young ass he wants." He pointed a warning finger at Travis. "You'd better keep him the hell away from Julia. Get his business but put another designer on the job. I don't want her anywhere near that bastard."

Travis guffawed. "*You* don't want her near him? Last time I checked Ms. McKinnon worked for *me*. Why do you give a shit who she works with anyway?"

"I own half this business, remember?" challenged Nathan. "If one of our employees gets harassed by a client it affects me, too. Just do us all a favor and assign someone else to work with that douchebag West."

"You've got the hots for her yourself, don't you?" challenged Travis.

"No, that's not it," Nathan insisted. "Just because she's attractive doesn't mean I want to fuck her. And – hello – have you forgotten? Engaged man here."

"Oh, right. I did forget, excuse me," replied Travis sarcastically. "You're so blissfully in love with Cameron that you couldn't possibly be attracted to someone else? Sorry, my mistake. Now look, as fun as this conversation has been, I really do need to work. Close the door on your way out, will you?"

Nathan glared at him for long seconds, as though he wanted to say something else, but finally threw up his hands in frustration and stormed out just as he'd stormed in, slamming the door behind him.

Travis chuckled with unmitigated glee. 'Engaged my ass. He could be engaged to a dozen different woman and he'd still want Julia,' he thought to himself. 'Well, he certainly has something to think about, doesn't he?'

And with that very pleasant thought in mind, Travis got back to work.

Chapter Eleven

Late April

Julia ignored the good looking man who turned and gave her a wolf whistle as she passed him on the street. After the upsetting encounter with Nathan in her office several weeks ago, she'd sworn off men yet again, and just wasn't in the mood to deal with what Travis jokingly referred to as her cheering section.

She had thrown herself into her work even more than usual this past month, spending insanely long hours at the office. When she wasn't working she was at yoga, often taking two classes a day to work off the stress, and spent the remainder of her time cooking, shopping, or rearranging her closet – again. She'd made two trips to Carmel and Big Sur to see her parents and sister, desperate to keep busy and not allow herself even a moment to think about Nathan.

God knew he'd done a bang-up job of pretty much ignoring her these last few weeks. If he'd treated her professionally and somewhat coldly before the make-out session in her office, he was positively non-communicative and icy now. She hadn't been assigned to any new projects that Nathan was also involved with. Instead, Travis and Olivia, one of the other designers, were working with Nathan on two new accounts, while Julia had been assigned to a project with Eric as well as working on several design-only accounts. That left only the Gregson hotel project, and Nathan had been leaving Jake to deal with most of the contact with Julia on that one.

She was certainly getting his message loud and clear. It was to be strictly business between them from now on, and as little business as possible. Julia was well aware that Nathan avoided her, even taking the long way around so he wouldn't have to walk past her office. Last week she'd happened to be in the same elevator with him, and aside from a curtly nodded "Hello" he hadn't looked at her or said another word.

And while she understood his need to keep contact with her to a bare minimum, it hurt like hell to have him treat her like a stranger. 'For God's sake,' she thought 'he had his tongue down my throat and his hand inside my panties and he acts like he can't stand to be within ten feet of me.' She couldn't help but feel cheap and used, shuddering as she recalled how quickly she'd come against his talented fingers, how desperately she'd clung to him, and how eagerly she'd kissed him. Both times that she'd been with him – in New York and in her office – she'd been wrecked physically and emotionally after he'd left. And yet, stupidly, Julia feared that she would continue to be drawn to Nathan, to succumb to the pull she felt towards him, and to let him have his way with her whenever he chose.

No man had ever had this sort of affect on her. Certainly not Sam, her first love. He'd been kind and caring and sweet. They had grown up together, been each other's first, and even when things had ended between them during college they'd been able to remain good friends.

Initially with Lucas she'd been dazzled by him. He had been older, of course, and his suave sophistication had swept her off her feet. But then she'd found out the truth about him, the secrets he'd been keeping, and she'd broken things off immediately. Lucas had kept pursuing her, but his lies had shattered her faith in him, and she'd steadfastly refused to see him again. He'd finally gotten the hint and left her alone.

In some ways, the situation with Nathan was all too similar to her failed relationship with Lucas, except that this time she was too weak and too attracted to forget about him. The fact that he belonged to another woman troubled her, of course. She didn't condone cheating – had certainly learned a hard lesson about that with Lucas – but feared that she just couldn't turn off her feelings for Nathan. When she'd been with him in New York, she hadn't known about his fiancée until it was too late. She had already spent the most incredible night of her life with him and fallen hard. And try as she might, she was discovering that love wasn't something you could just stop feeling, or that you could turn off such a strong physical attraction like a light switch.

The sensible solution, of course, would be to find another job so that she didn't have to worry about seeing him every day. But it wasn't easy to find a job in her field, and certainly not one with such a prestigious firm. There was always Ian Gregson's standing offer to work for his company, and lately she'd begun to give it some serious consideration. Though the old "out of sight, out of mind" adage certainly hadn't applied in the months between last September and meeting Nathan again in January. It didn't give her great confidence that it would work this time, either.

She stopped at the corner, waiting for the traffic light to change, and looked straight ahead despite the very interested gaze of the tall, dark-haired man to her right. 'Maybe I should have worn a coat after all' she thought tiredly. It was a very pleasant spring day, and since the client's office she'd just walked from was only three blocks away, she had left her jacket back at her desk. Julia supposed it was her dress that was attracting what seemed like more attention than usual today. It was one of her favorites – something Aunt Maddy had received during last fall's New York Fashion Week – but the weather hadn't been right for it until today.

It was Narciso Rodriguez, who she thought knew how to dress curvy women better than almost anyone. This creation was of a deep coral shade, another pencil-skirted dress with a square neckline and cap sleeves. She'd teamed it with taupe peep-toe Louboutins and a Tory Burch clutch in the same shade. Julia knew the coral was a good color for her, setting off her golden brown hair and creamy skin, but was now a bit self-conscious of all the male stares she was getting as a result.

Her spine stiffened as she recalled Nathan's comments about her outfits, how he'd sounded almost angry about the way she dressed. She'd even tried dressing more demurely for a few days, in lower heels and less form-fitting attire. But after a few sarcastic comments from Travis, like "Are you in mourning or something", "Forget to pick up the dry cleaning?", and "My grandmother has shoes like that", Julia had defiantly decided to wear what she damned well pleased from now on. In fact, she'd even gone to extra lengths to wear the most figure flattering and alluring things in her vast wardrobe. Whether Nathan noticed or not, she'd at least had the satisfaction of knowing she looked awesome.

The light changed and she stumbled very slightly stepping off the curb. The dark haired stranger on her right immediately slid a hand to her elbow to steady her.

She glanced up at him with a brief smile. "Thank you. I'm fine now."

But as they walked across the street, tall, dark and handsome kept his hand on her arm. The smile her gave her was purely carnal, and she couldn't help the little frisson of awareness that shimmered up her spine. He was certainly one of the most attractive men she'd ever seen.

"My pleasure," he said in a deep voice. "In fact, why don't you let me buy you a drink? You know, to steady your nerves."

Julia laughed, but gently disengaged her arm from his grasp. "My nerves are fine, thanks. As for the drink, it's a bit early in the day for that, don't you think?"

The stranger shrugged as they reached the other side of the street. "It's lunchtime. Barely. Or we could get coffee. It doesn't matter to me."

She smiled, shaking her head. "I don't think so, thanks. I need to get back to work, I'm afraid. Have a nice day."

"Wait." He grasped her elbow again as she began to walk away. "Can I give you my card at least? In case you want to take a rain check on that drink?"

Julia hesitated. She normally blew off overly aggressive men like him, but her battered ego did feel in need of some bolstering right now. She took the proffered card. "Thanks again. I really have to go now."

She felt his dark eyes on her ass as she walked into the building, and suddenly felt in better spirits than she had for weeks. Maybe she was being an imbecile to keep pining after a man who was already taken but who kept sending her mixed signals in spite of that fact. There were a lot of attractive, eligible, *available* men out there for the taking, and maybe it was well past time for her to start trying some on for size. Like the hottie who'd just passed her the card still folded in her palm.

There was an older couple waiting for the elevator when she approached, and she returned the friendly smile both of them gave her. The man – who she surmised to be in his early sixties – looked strangely familiar but she didn't think they had ever met before. The woman, who was probably a few years younger, looked incredibly well kept for a woman of her years. Both were well dressed and looked fit and trim.

As they stepped inside the elevator, the woman looked at her admiringly. "That is such a beautiful dress, dear. What a perfect color for you. But you're such a pretty little thing I'm guessing you look good in anything."

Julia warmed to the woman instantly. "Thank you so much. What a lovely thing to say."

The man grinned. "You'll have to forgive my wife. She's nearly always talking to strangers but she doesn't mean to be so forward."

His wife gave him a playful swat on the arm. "Stop that, Michael," she scolded. "This young lady is going to think I'm crazy or something."

"Or something," teased Michael, before clutching his arm as his wife socked him again, harder this time.

Julia smiled at their obvious affection for each other, finding it similar to the easy, close relationship her own parents shared.

"I see we're headed to the same floor," she commented politely. "Are you clients of the firm or just visiting someone?"

"Oh, we're here to visit our son, dear," replied the woman eagerly. "Do you work here, too?"

Julia nodded as the elevator stopped and the three of them exited. "Yes. I've been employed as an interior designer here since January."

The woman looked delighted at the news. "So you work for Travis, then? I've always said that boy had excellent taste. What's your name, dear?"

Julia extended her hand, heedless of the small card that fluttered to the floor. "I'm Julia McKinnon."

"Alexis Atwood," replied the woman with the short, stylish dark blonde bob. "And this is my husband Michael. I'm sure you must know our son – Nathan."

Julia was startled at this revelation but managed to compose herself enough to shake hands with both of Nathan's parents. No wonder Michael had looked familiar – he bore a striking resemblance to his son, though his thick hair was almost completely gray, and his eyes an even lighter shade of blue.

"It's so nice to meet both of you," she told them sincerely. "So you're here for a visit?"

Alexis nodded. "Yes, we're out from Michigan for a week to see Nathan. And our middle son is going to be in town for a few days as well. Did you know Nathan's brother Jared was a professional baseball player?"

Julia shook her head, not even knowing until now that Nathan had siblings or that he was from Michigan. They hadn't exactly spent a lot of time exchanging family histories. "I wasn't aware, no. You must be very proud of him."

"Yes, absolutely," agreed Michael. "Jared is an outfielder for the Colorado Rockies. The team will be here to play the Giants starting tomorrow. This way we get to visit our two oldest sons at the same time."

"Our youngest – Greg – is attending law school in Michigan. The only one to follow in his father's footsteps," lamented Alexis.

So Nathan's father was a lawyer. Judging from the way both he and Alexis were dressed – not to mention his Omega watch and her stunning gold jewelry – he must be quite successful. Julia was pleasantly surprised at how friendly and down to earth they both seemed, not at all like some of the very wealthy clients she dealt with.

"Well, you have three very successful sons, then," commented Julia.

Alexis beamed. "Yes, and a darling grandson, too. Jared and his wife Brooke have an eight month old. Alas, no girls yet. Hopefully one of my sons will present me with a granddaughter someday."

"Well, with Nathan and Cameron getting married next year, hopefully more grandchildren will follow soon," added Michael.

Julia's smile froze on her face at the mention of Nathan's wedding. And she wasn't sure if it was her imagination or not, but the beaming smile on Alexis' face seemed to fade rapidly.

"One can hope," replied Alexis quietly. "But I'm not counting on my oldest son giving me grandchildren anytime soon."

Julia regarded Nathan's mother curiously, sensing – or perhaps hoping – that Alexis wasn't thrilled with the prospect of having Cameron as her new daughter-in-law. But then Alexis quickly changed the subject and quizzed Julia about her own family and background. She was delighted to learn that Julia had a twin, and over the moon when she heard that Aunt Madelyn was the head buyer at Bergdorf Goodman.

"Well, I can see where you get your fashion sense from, dear," she gushed. "I love clothes, too."

Michael rolled his eyes. "Yes, I can certainly vouch for that. As each of my sons has moved out, Alexis has taken over their bedroom closets. She could open her own department store."

Alexis gave him another playful swat. "I can't help it," she confessed. "My shopping addiction is a holdover from my modeling days. Oh, nothing major, mostly catalogues and local stuff. And it was a very long time ago, of course."

Julia noted Alexis's tall, slender figure, perfect makeup and hair, and smiled. "You still have the look, you know. I can totally imagine you strutting the catwalk."

Alexis was absurdly thrilled at the compliment, giggling like a girl, and giving Julia an affectionate little hug. "You are the sweetest little thing besides being beautiful. How lucky your mother is to have not one but two girls like you."

At the sound of heels clicking on the foyer's tile floor, Julia glanced up to see Nathan heading straight towards them. After the initial look of surprise on his face at seeing her in his mother's embrace, it was swiftly replaced by an expression Julia couldn't quite place – annoyance, irritation, maybe even a bit of panic. Whatever it was, he wasn't pleased.

Julia gently disengaged herself from Alexis's arms as Nathan strode into the foyer. Alexis smiled at her son and gave him a hug.

"Hello, darling. Your father and I were just having the most delightful conversation with Julia. I suppose we lost track of time," she apologized.

"I was wondering where you were," Nathan told her. "I should have guessed you'd be busy making a new friend." He turned and gave his father a quick hug. "Dad isn't doing a very good job at keeping you under control."

Michael chuckled. "Like I've ever been able to do that, son! You know how your mother gets at times."

Nathan looked at Julia expectantly. "I hope my parents haven't been making pests of themselves. They were supposed to have met me in my office ten minutes ago."

Julia shook her head. "Not at all. And I'm sure they didn't mean to keep you waiting."

"It's my fault," exclaimed Alexis. "I was just so taken with this pretty little thing that I kept hounding her for more details about herself. I hope you don't think me a nosy old lady, Julia."

"Not at all," reassured Julia. "I enjoyed meeting both of you. You should probably be off to lunch, though. Nathan seems a bit impatient."

Alexis wrapped a hand around Nathan's arm and leaned her head on his shoulder. "Oh, he's no fun sometimes! Indulge your mother, Nathan, you don't see me all that often." Her eyes lit up all of a sudden as she beamed at Julia. "I know. Why don't you join us for lunch, dear? I'm sure it's too early for you to have already eaten, and I would love to continue chatting with you."

Julia was startled at her impromptu invitation and stammered, "Um, I really don't think that - "

Before she could finish her sentence, Nathan interrupted. "She can't join us for lunch, Mother, because she has a client meeting with Travis in half an hour. Isn't that right, Julia?"

Julia almost recoiled from the terseness of his tone, not to mention the angry expression on his face. "Y-yes, I do. In fact, I need to get some things ready for it, so if you'll please excuse me."

She turned to walk away, but Alexis held her back. "Wait, dear. I just wanted to say how much I enjoyed meeting you. Will we see you again during our visit? Maybe we can have coffee together."

Julia gave her a warm smile, wondering how Nathan could be such an asshole sometimes when his mother was such a sweetheart. "I've enjoyed meeting both of you, too. And I'm sure we'll see each other again here at the office before you leave." She tactfully didn't mention having coffee together, knowing that Nathan wouldn't like that idea. It hurt her to the quick to realize he didn't want her anywhere near his parents, and was already pissed off that she'd spent time talking with them. The excuse about a nonexistent client meeting that he'd just invented was just a flimsy way of keeping her away from them.

Julia blinked back a tear or two as she started walking away, until Nathan called her name.

"Did you drop this?" he asked, holding out the business card she'd forgotten all about. He glanced at the name, which she hadn't even bothered to do yet.

It was on the tip of her tongue to tell him to just throw the card away, but she was so hurt and angry at his abrupt dismissal that she reached out a hand for it.

"Yes, I did. Thank you."

Nathan frowned as he looked at the card again before handing it to her. "A client?"

She shook her head. "No. It's – personal. Someone I'm meeting for drinks later."

She was oddly pleased to see the look of displeasure on his face.

"I see," he replied tightly. "New boyfriend?"

She gave a careless little shrug. "Perhaps. It's too soon to tell. Thanks for the card." To Alexis and Michael she said, "Enjoy your lunch. It was lovely to meet you both."

She walked directly to her office after that, and put her things away, still holding the stranger's business card. She was almost ready to throw it away before deciding with a sigh that she ought to at least know his name, just in case Nathan asked her about him.

Tall, dark and handsome's name was Todd Bryant, and he was the Chief Operating Officer of a hedge fund. Julia stared at the card for long seconds, debating whether to throw it out or throw caution to the wind and call him.

In the end, she merely tucked the card into her desk drawer, too timid to actually pick up the phone but oddly reluctant to completely ignore the stranger's invitation, either.

✳✳✳✳✳

Nathan glowered when he pulled up Todd Bryant's detailed profile on Linkedin later than afternoon. He'd committed the fucker's name to memory after glancing at his business card twice before handing it over reluctantly to Julia.

He had hoped that the guy Julia was meeting for a drink – and most likely a lot more – was a total loser, someone she'd quickly decide wasn't worth her while. But it seemed that Mr. Bryant was the exact opposite – quite a catch.

At thirty-six years old, Bryant was more than ten years Julia's senior, but judging from the guy's admitted good looks Nathan guessed that the age difference wouldn't bother her in the least. The guy was smart as hell, too – undergrad at Harvard, MBA in Finance from Wharton. He'd lived in San Francisco for about seven years, presumably moving out here from New York where he'd last worked to take the job at the hedge fund. The guy was single, and his hobbies included sailing, tennis and skiing.

'Great, just fucking great' thought Nathan sourly. Not only was Todd good looking, smart, and undoubtedly rich, he had the Ivy League education and years of living and working in Manhattan in common with Julia. There was no reason at all why the two of them wouldn't hit it off big time. Nathan scowled as he pictured them together – Todd with his dark good looks and Julia with her golden brown hair and creamy skin. Todd's mouth was probably watering right now at the thought of running his hands over all of Julia's luscious curves – her hips, ass, thighs, those round, perfect breasts.

Nathan groaned when he realized he was getting hard again just thinking about her. She'd looked delicious today in that figure-hugging coral dress. He'd longed to cup that sweet butt in his hands, to bend and press a kiss to the glimpse of cleavage bared by the neckline of the dress. Instead, once again, he'd been a total asshole to her, treating her with the cool standoffishness that he'd had to work so hard on sustaining these past months.

He hadn't meant to be such a prick to her, but he'd panicked when his well-meaning but interfering mother had invited her to lunch. It just figured, he thought tiredly, that his mother would meet Julia and be so completely enchanted by her. Alexis had continued to ask question after question about Julia during lunch, until Nathan had told her in exasperation that she knew more about the woman than he did. That had finally silenced Alexis, but he knew it hadn't stopped her fascination with the girl Nathan himself was enthralled with. If he'd allowed Julia to come to lunch with them, he wasn't at all sure that his wily mother wouldn't have suspected there was something between them. And that had been his main motivation in ensuring she didn't join them.

Conversely, Alexis had never seemed to warm up much to Cameron, at least not like she'd appeared to do so quickly with Julia. His mother was always charming and kind to Cameron, but he'd never sensed even the slightest sort of bonding or friendship between the two women. Of course, a lot of that was Cameron's fault, for she saw any woman as a threat to her relationship with him – even his own mother. And Cameron was very close to her own mother, and didn't seem at all inclined to forge a similar sort of bond with Alexis. Cameron always hedged about going back to Michigan to see his family, or to Colorado to see Jared and Brooke. She'd reluctantly conceded to paying a visit with him for a week last summer, but had refused to do the same at Christmas, preferring to remain in San Francisco with her family. It had given him cause for concern for the future, hoping that Cameron would be agreeable to splitting the holidays between their respective families. They definitely needed to get those sort of details ironed out, and sooner than later, before they became an issue in their marriage.

Nathan and his parents were having dinner this evening with Cameron and her mother and father. Cameron's father had insisted on dining at the private yacht club he belonged to, and of course Graham Tolliver always got his way. Nathan didn't have a problem per se with the club, though he didn't think the food was particularly good and the atmosphere was a little too stuffy for his taste. He couldn't imagine, for example, his rowdy group of former water polo teammates in such a formal setting. The guys tended to get a bit raucous when they had a few, behavior that would surely be frowned upon here.

As he pulled the Lexus SUV into the parking lot, he remembered to caution his parents. "By the way, don't say a word to Cameron about meeting Julia today. She, er, doesn't care for her."

Alexis gave a little gasp. "Now how can that be? Julia is the sweetest girl. Why doesn't Cameron like her?"

"I'd be willing to bet she's jealous of her," observed Michael. "But we'll do as you ask, son. Alexis, keep that mouth of yours closed, understand? We don't want to cause any trouble for Nathan."

"Fine." She sighed in resignation. "And I still don't understand why you rushed her off today, Nathan. I don't believe that nonsense about a meeting. You just didn't want her to go with us."

"Mom, it's not that simple, okay? She's an employee and it's really not a good idea for her to be socializing with her boss and his parents."

Alexis frowned. "I thought Travis was her boss. And it was just a casual lunch, Nathan. I think you're overreacting, dear."

"And I think you're butting into things that don't concern you," retorted Nathan. "Now, come on. Let's go inside, shall we?"

It wasn't the first time that Michael and Alexis had met Cameron's parents so everyone was relatively at ease during dinner. As usual, Graham dominated the conversation with his deep, booming voice and know-it-all attitude. Nathan didn't like his future father-in-law very much, especially the way he needed control over everything and everyone in his life. He'd ordered the wine tonight, for example, without asking anyone else's opinion, and had proceeded to tell everyone at the table what the best entrees to order were. When Alexis had tentatively mentioned ordering the shrimp scampi, Graham had made a loud noise of disapproval, telling her the cook did a terrible job with them here.

Intimidated, Alexis had rather meekly relented and ordered the salmon instead.

Nathan was largely silent throughout the meal, for when Graham didn't have the floor it belonged to Cameron or her mother Elaine, who talked incessantly about wedding plans. Nathan watched his mother struggle to maintain a polite expression on her face throughout the evening, knowing how much she loved to talk herself. His father, on the other hand, wasn't doing such a good job of hiding the irritation he felt as the Tollivers controlled the conversation. Nathan felt badly for his parents, knowing they were both too well mannered to interrupt, and wished the rather uncomfortable evening would come to a blissfully quick end.

As dessert and coffee were eventually brought out, he couldn't help but wonder if Julia's parents were much different than Cameron's. He remembered Julia's comment that they disliked going to the city and preferred to remain close to their home in Carmel. And then he wondered why in hell he was even giving a second thought to two people he'd never met, and likely never would.

His mother didn't hold anything back during the drive back to his condo, going on and on about what a pompous ass Graham was, and how rude Elaine was and how Cameron hadn't even asked her opinion about any of the wedding plans. His father, well used to Alexis' little emotional outbursts, kept mostly quiet except to tell Nathan, "You need to be careful of that man, son. He's the sort that likes to walk all over people and always get his own way. And I'm sorry to say this but I think Cameron takes after him in certain ways. Don't let yourself be controlled that way, Nathan. I didn't raise my boys to take orders from other men, or women for that matter."

Nathan sighed. "I know, Dad. It's a tricky situation is all. Cam and I need to hash a few things out sooner than later. Her overbearing father is only one of them."

In the backseat, his mother was muttering under her breath, but Nathan didn't miss part of what she was saying. "Don't know what he sees in that girl. He's too good for her in my opinion."

He knew better than to argue with his mother when she started talking to herself so he tactfully said nothing.

＊＊＊＊＊

His brother Jared had flown into town with the rest of his team the night before, and they had a full day off before starting a four-game series with the Giants. It was a welcome opportunity for the two of them to enjoy a leisurely lunch with their parents at a tapas restaurant near Nathan's office.

The balmy late April weather was continuing so Alexis had begged to sit at an outdoor table on the expansive front patio. Back home in Michigan the weather was still too chilly to even think of eating outdoors, so she was enjoying this rare opportunity while in San Francisco. Over a multitude of shared small plates and a pitcher of Sangria, the pleasant conversation and relaxed atmosphere was a welcome relief from the stilted, uncomfortable dinner with Cameron and her parents last night.

Nathan knew he'd been lucky to have such terrific parents and the most amazing childhood a boy could want. He'd grown up in the affluent community of Bloomfield Hills, and even though Michael could have easily afforded to send his sons to expensive private schools, he and Alexis had been firm supporters of the local public school system. Alexis had been the perfect mother, volunteering at school events, chauffeuring her boys to and from athletic practices and games and play dates, and encouraging the boys to invite their friends over to their home. Their house – a big, sprawling place that his parents still lived in – had been filled with laughter and good times. He couldn't ever remember his parents having a really serious argument, and though he, Jared, and Greg had certainly had their fights and disagreements, overall the three boys had been very close all their lives.

Athletics had been encouraged during their childhood and teens, and each boy had chosen a different pursuit. Nathan's had been swimming and later on water polo, and he'd been good enough to get an athletic scholarship to Berkeley. Jared, of course, had always been crazy about baseball, and had played college ball at Arizona State. Greg's passion had been cross country and track, and he'd run both at the University of Michigan.

Nathan missed his family — which included grandparents, aunts, uncles, and cousins — but kept in close touch with them as often as possible. He paid at least two visits a year back home, once during the summer and again at the holidays. In turn, his parents came out to California once or twice a year.

"I do wish Greg had been able to make the trip," Alexis said wistfully. "Maybe we should have waited until June to visit."

Jared shook his head. "I told you, Mom. The team won't be back in San Francisco until August. Besides, you're bringing the Gregster along when you come out to Colorado in July. I'm not sure I can stomach too much brotherly love."

Alexis gave him a playful swat. "Oh, stop that. You know you love seeing your brothers. And I know we'll be visiting you and Brooke and my darling little Damien soon. But Nathan isn't certain he can fly out, so all of us might not be together."

"I'll try, Mom," he assured her. "No guarantees, though, okay? I've got a bunch of projects going on right now, and I've already promised Cameron to spend the Fourth of July up at her parents place in Tahoe. I don't know if I can take any more time off in July."

She patted him fondly on the cheek. "I understand, darling. I just miss my boys, that's all. And I'm so afraid when you get married next year that we won't be seeing you as often."

Nathan frowned. "Why do you think that?"

Alexis gave a little shrug. "Well, Cameron is obviously very close to her own family, so there are bound to be times when there are conflicting events. That's all."

He was saved from having to think of a suitable reply by the arrival of their waiter with several more plates of food. He was absorbed in making a selection from the various dishes spread out on the table, not paying the slightest attention to any of the people walking by on the sidewalk just on the other side of the patio. So he started in surprise when his mother exclaimed happily, "Oh, look, dear. Isn't that Julia walking this way?"

Nathan glanced up automatically at the mention of *that* name, and gulped when he realized his mother was absolutely correct. Julia was walking down the street in her usual steady but measured pace, and once again every man in radius was staring at her in stunned admiration. She looked as breathtaking as ever, in yet another of her classy but sexy as hell outfits. Today's ensemble was a sleeveless white silk dress with black polka dots and a black patent leather belt. Black buckled heels and a matching tote coordinated with the dress. Oversized black sunglasses obscured the upper part of her face.

As she walked closer towards the restaurant, Alexis called out to her and waved. Julia seemed as startled to see them as he had been to spot her, but she approached their table with a tentative smile.

Alexis reached over the low concrete wall that separated the dining area from the sidewalk and clasped Julia's hand. "I knew that was you the second I spotted you," she told her, smiling brightly.

"All that beautiful hair, and the way you walk. I'm so happy to see you again, dear."

Julia pushed her sunglasses to the top of her head, revealing the rest of her face, and Nathan heard Jared mutter under his breath, "Holy crap!"

"It's nice to see you again, too," replied Julia politely. "Hello, Mr. Atwood," she nodded to Michael. "Nathan." Her gaze rested uncertainly on Jared, who immediately surged to his feet and proffered his hand.

"Jared Atwood," he introduced himself. "The middle and best looking of the brothers."

Julia laughed and shook his hand. "A pleasure." She glanced at their table. "Well, I'll let you all get back to your lunch. Enjoy the beautiful weather."

But Alexis wasn't so easily deterred. "Why don't you join us, dear? We're just having tapas so there's more than enough to go around."

"Yes, please, have lunch with us," urged Michael. "We'd love to have you sit with us."

Nathan kept his face deliberately impassive, not wanting to give Julia any encouragement to join them but also not willing to be scolded by his mother again for being rude. Fortunately, Julia must have sensed his reluctance and shook her head.

"Once again, I'm afraid I have to decline," she said gently. "I'm meeting someone for lunch about a block from here."

"Todd?" asked Nathan tersely.

She stared at him in bemusement, her green eyes wide. "Who?" Then she flushed. "No, not him. I'm meeting Angela, who I went to high school with. She lives in the flat above me."

"That's so nice that you've kept in touch and stayed friends all these years," gushed Alexis. "Is Angela an interior designer, too?"

Julia smiled. "Actually, she's a stockbroker. And I'm sorry to dash off, but I'll be late to meet her if I don't leave now. Enjoy your lunch. Nice to meet you, Jared."

Jared stared after her, his jaw hanging open. "Holy crap," was all he could repeat.

Nathan shook his head, putting a finger under his brother's chin. "You're drooling, little bro. Not to mention a married man. With a child."

Jared pushed his hand away. "Don't care. No law against looking. And, uh, wow. Who was that?"

"She works in Nathan's office, dear," volunteered Alexis helpfully. "Well, technically, I suppose she works for Travis. Isn't she lovely?"

Jared coughed. "Uh, yeah. Lovely, very lovely." To Nathan he whispered, "More like fucking hot. How do you keep your hands off all that lusciousness?"

Nathan gave a short, impatient shake of his head, silently imploring his brother to shut up. Jared got the hint quickly enough, but unfortunately Julia's unexpected appearance had started Alexis off again on singing the girl's praises.

"She's the sweetest little thing, too," cooed Alexis. "Nathan, dear, does she have a boyfriend? She's so beautiful I can't imagine that she doesn't."

"I'm sure she does, Mom, but I really don't know any details," he replied shortly.

Alexis laid a hand over Jared's. "Maybe you should introduce her to one of your teammates, darling. Do you know any nice men who'd like to meet her?"

Nathan spewed out the mouthful of Sangria he'd just swallowed, his eyes watering. Jared grinned, patting his brother on the back.

"Easy there, big bro. Nothing to get choked up over. As far as any nice men who'd like to meet Julia, I can probably think of at least twenty off the top of my head who'd love to do just that. Nathan, what do you think about Mitch Rivington?"

Nathan was sorely tempted to give his brother the finger. "I think he's a freaking manwhore who's had more women than he can remember," he retorted. "Not a good choice."

"You're right. Brandon Solomon is a much better choice. Think I could get a photo of Julia so I can text it to him?"

Nathan bared his teeth at Jared, knowing instinctively that his brother sensed his attraction to Julia and was jerking him around big time. "Drop it, okay? I'm sure she can get a guy whenever she wants without our interference."

Thankfully the subject of Julia was dropped for the duration of their lunch. Jared had to attend some team press conference afterwards while his parents were going shopping at Union Square, allowing Nathan several hours to get caught up at work. With his family in town, he'd been away from the office more than usual this week and was behind on several projects.

As timing would have it, Julia arrived back at the office at precisely the same time he did, resulting in an awkward elevator ride. In a casual attempt to lessen the tension, he asked "Enjoy your lunch?"

She seemed surprised that he was even speaking to her, but nodded. "It was good, thanks. And yours?"

"Awesome. It's always good when my family visits." He hesitated before inquiring casually, "How was your date yesterday?"

She blinked. "My date?"

"With Todd."

She frowned. "You seem awfully obsessed with him. Why do you even remember his name?"

Nathan shrugged. "I don't know. I glanced at his business card and the name just stuck with me. So how was it?"

"Why do you want to know?" She sounded annoyed. "Frankly, I'm not comfortable discussing it with you."

"Fine," he said brusquely. "Date whoever the hell you want."

Julia glared at him. "Now, that sounds like a great idea. I think I will. Not that I need your permission, of course."

The elevator stopped on their floor, and she flounced off without a backwards glance. Nathan watched as she walked away, mentally calling himself ten kinds of an idiot for putting the idea in her head.

✳✳✳✳✳

The balmy day had given way to a much cooler evening, but Nathan and Jared didn't seem to mind as they sat outside on the balcony of the condo. Their parents had already turned in for the night, and Jared was getting ready to head back to the team hotel once he finished his beer.

"So, you seemed awfully touchy today when I was mentioning guys to introduce to that girl," drawled Jared. "Any particular reason?"

Nathan tried to seem as nonchalant as possible. "Mom seems obsessed with her for some reason. I was just trying to steer the conversation away from her."

Jared took a swig of his beer. "Bullshit. I can read you like a book. You didn't like the idea of me introducing her to my whoring buddies because you want her for yourself."

"Now you're the one spouting bullshit. Don't forget I'm engaged."

Jared gave a hoot. "Hell, I'm happily married and have a baby at home. Doesn't mean I can't appreciate the finest piece of booty I've ever seen. You're only engaged, bro, plus you get to check out that smokin' hot chick every day. Don't know how you've managed to hold out this long."

Nathan hesitated. What had happened between him and Julia in New York had remained a deep, dark secret between the two of them so far. But he'd longed to unload the guilt he'd felt for long months now, and he trusted Jared more than anyone else.

"Can I tell you something?" he began. "Something you have to abso-fucking-lutely swear is only and always just between us?"

Jared grinned. "Oh, this sounds like it's gonna be juicy."

"I'm serious, Jare. This is something big. It's been bothering me for months now, and I haven't had anybody I could talk to about it. Please."

Jared instantly sobered. "Okay, sorry. Yes, you know I won't tell anyone. Even Brooke. You can trust me, bro. Always."

"All right, then." He took a deep breath. "I first met Julia back in September. In New York. I was attending a conference and she was living there at the time." He ran a hand over his face. "And so help me God, I'm pretty sure I fell in love with her the minute I saw her face."

Jared's light blue eyes, so similar to his own, widened. "Shit, not the L word. That's pretty deep, Nate. So what happened exactly?"

Nathan related the series of events – seeing Julia twice before finally asking her out for a drink. He skimmed over the more intimate details of their night together, but Jared certainly got the picture.

"So let's see if I've got all this. You see this woman a couple of times, develop some sort of fixation with her, finally ask her to have a drink with you, fuck her like an animal, and then say the next morning, 'Sorry, babe, gotta run back to my fiancée now?' That's kinda harsh, Nate, especially for a nice guy like you. Now, my buddy Mitch I can totally see doing some douchebag thing like that, but you – what the fuck, bro?" asked Jared in disbelief.

Nathan hunched forward, his elbows on his knees, hands messing his hair. "I know, I know. I should have got the award for Asshole of the Year for what I did. Hey, I've had plenty of one-night stands before, but I never felt guilty about any of them. Not like this. And on both sides of the coin, too. I mean, of course I feel like a total shit for cheating on Cameron, but I really, really feel like a prick for what I did to Julia."

"So why the hell after what you did to her would she willingly move out here to work in your office? Oh, shit, she isn't like one of those crazy ass stalker chicks, is she? I mean, she seemed perfectly normal."

"She isn't a stalker. And she didn't follow me out here. This is how fucked up the whole thing is – can you believe it was a complete one hundred percent bad, bad coincidence? First that she's an interior designer, second that she already knew Travis? Both of us almost passed out when we saw each other again in January."

"Maybe it's like – what do they call it – serendipity?"

Nathan frowned. "Like I know what the hell that means. I call it a little black storm cloud following me around."

Jared shook his head. "No, no. Didn't you ever see that movie with John Cusack? I'm pretty sure it was even set in New York. He meets this hot chick but they're both involved with other people and go their separate ways only to meet up again by accident. In fact," he typed something into his phone and waited for the screen to load, "according to good old Wikipedia, serendipity means a happy accident. That's what it was when the two of you met again like that."

"Yeah, well, the accident part I'll buy. Not so sure about the happy part," Nathan grimaced. "My life has been a daily hell since she's been in San Francisco."

Jared frowned. "Thought you said she wasn't in stalker mode. Or is she just pissed off and making your life miserable? She seemed so sweet, though."

Nathan groaned. "She is. And no, it isn't anything she's said or done. In fact, she's been a total pro about this whole fuckfest. What I meant was that it's been hell for me to see her every day because she's so fucking gorgeous all I can think about is jumping her bones."

"Oh." Jared waved a hand in the air. "Well, that's totally understandable. Hell, I have a hot wife at home who'd castrate me if I even thought of cheating. That doesn't mean she can stop what goes through my brain, and if someone as fine as Julia worked with me, I'd spend half of each day fantasizing about different ways to bang her."

"Yeah, but you don't have the extra baggage of knowing *exactly* what it's like to bang her. Every time I see her all I can think about is that night in New York. And then I have to feel guilty all over again. Thus the daily hell."

Jared finished his beer and set the bottle on the ground. "Stupid question here but – you haven't told Cameron about this, I assume?"

Nathan's jaw dropped. "Do I look like a guy who wants to walk around without testicles? Of course not. Jesus, the first time she met Julia I thought I was going to puke or faint. Both. Fortunately, Julia's been cool about it, not giving anything away. Even when Cam bitch slapped her."

Jared stared. "Wait a sec. I think I need another beer for this one. I'll sleep it off in time for the game tomorrow." He reached into the cardboard six- pack they'd brought outside with them and popped the top on another bottle, taking a long swig. "Okay, now tell me about the cat fight. Damn, I can't believe all of this has been going on and you never said a word. And here I thought your life was boring as hell."

"I wish. And there wasn't a cat fight. It was pretty much one-sided. We were all at a client dinner. Cam was having a hissy fit because Julia looked super hot, confronted her in the ladies room, accused her of sleeping with me, and walloped her. She's lucky Julia didn't press charges."

"Holy fuck." Jared took another drink. "Not that I don't understand why Cameron might be jealous of your hot little lover, but to actually hit her?"

Nathan shrugged. "Cam was pretty tanked, not that getting drunk is an excuse. And Julia isn't my lover, okay? It was that one night only."

"Why'd you do it, Nate? I mean, weren't you already engaged back in September, even unofficially?"

"I was. As for why – I ask myself that a lot. Part of it was I'd just had a fight with Cam on the phone and I was royally pissed off. And I'd probably put away about four glasses of Macallan by then so I wasn't thinking with a totally clear head. But mostly," he sighed, "I just fucking wanted her. Call me a selfish SOB – I have plenty of times – but I couldn't stop thinking about her. It wasn't just the pretty face and the wet dream body. When I looked at her there was just – something."

Jared studied the label on his beer bottle. "So what happens now?"

"What do you mean?" asked Nathan warily. "Nothing. We go on like it never happened. Cameron and I are getting married next February. That part has never been in question."

"What about Julia?"

"What about her? For all I know, she's out fucking some new boyfriend right about now. She told me once when I was being a real prick to her that she could walk into any bar or restaurant and have a new guy in a matter of minutes. And she's right. I've seen the way total strangers check her out just walking down the street. Most guys would kneel in front of her and kiss her feet in order to have coffee with her."

"And you're okay with that?"

Nathan grabbed another beer. "Fuck no. But I don't really have a choice in the matter, do I? She isn't mine, never was, and I don't have any rights at all to her. Seeing her every day, feeling the urge to back her up against the wall and drill her till she can't walk, but knowing I can't even hold her hand – that's my hell, Jare, my punishment for being a lying, cheating bastard."

"You should tell Cameron it's over. Obviously, it wasn't meant to be with you two, not if you've fallen so hard for someone else."

"No." Nathan was adamant. "I am not going to be that guy, okay? It's not Cam's fault that I was weak, that I was a selfish prick. She and I have a good thing going, and will have a good marriage. So what if it isn't fantasy stuff? I mean, once you get married all the romance fades away anyway, doesn't it?"

"Not necessarily. It sure hasn't for me and Brooke. And that's a really shitty attitude, Nate. To enter into something like marriage with the thought that you're just going to be good buddies with your wife? If you're already feeling that way, you should just do both of you a favor and end it. How are you going to be happy – and make her happy – when you're in love with someone else?"

"I'll make it work," Nathan insisted stubbornly. "Mind over matter, that sort of crap. That's just the way it has to be. I'm not going to be the dickwad who breaks his engagement to the woman who's done nothing to deserve that sort of treatment just because his cock twitches every time he sees some other woman. I really don't think I could live with myself, provided I could ever have big enough balls to actually do it."

Jared smirked. "Yeah, if Cameron slapped Julia just for looking too pretty, I can't even imagine what she'd do to you for breaking the engagement. Didn't you tell me once that her father insists she keep a loaded gun in her condo?" He glanced at his phone, noting the time. "Hell, I really do have to go now. Thanks for dinner and the brews. You've got the tickets for the game tomorrow night?"

Nathan nodded. "Club level passes, parking permits, the works. You know how to take care of your loved ones, bro."

The brothers stood and exchanged a hug before walking through the living room to the front door.

"Hey, thanks for listening to me, Jare. You don't know how hard it's been to keep all that bottled up for so many months. I appreciate having you to lean on."

Jared patted his older brother on the shoulder. "No problem, Nate. Call me anytime you need to talk. My lips are sealed. But you gotta answer one question I've been dying to ask since meeting Julia yesterday."

Nathan eyed him warily. "What's that?"

Jared grinned wickedly. "Her tits. Are they real?"

Nathan couldn't help returning the grin. "Well, to quote one of our favorite *Seinfeld* lines of all time – 'they're real and they're spectacular'."

"That's what I thought. Then you're more of an idiot than I imagined to walk away from a rack like that. Maybe I should set her up with Brandon after all. He loves big tits."

Nathan wrenched the door open and shoved Jared out. "Get lost. And forget about it. She doesn't need to be fixed up, especially not with your slutty guy friends."

"Sounds like sour grapes to me, Nate."

Chapter Twelve

May

Angela perused the half dozen dresses carefully arranged on Julia's bed, tapping one finger against her mouth. "You know what the problem is, Jules? You don't have enough clothes. I think we should take a shopping trip to Neiman Marcus."

Julia tossed a throw pillow at her friend. "You aren't helping. I invited you over to help me pick out a dress. Well, and to try and feed you as well. But mostly for the dress."

"I'm not hungry." Angela took a sip of her red wine. "And don't give me that look. It reminds me – not in a good way – of my mother. Not that any reminders of my mom are good ones."

Julia pointed a finger at Angela. "One way or the other you are going to eat something before you leave here tonight. What have you eaten today – like, a Power Bar and a banana or something? After running, oh, fifteen miles or so?"

Angela shrugged. "Yes to the bar, no to the banana. And it was a twenty mile run, thank you very much. Stop trying to force me to eat, Jules. I'll eat when I'm hungry, okay?"

Julia frowned as she studied the tall, graceful form of the woman she'd known since fourth grade. Angela DelCarlo had actually been more Lauren's friend, but she'd been close to Julia as well. Angela had always been slender and willowy, but ever since a disastrous break-up two years ago, she'd lost so much weight that she looked waifish. She was at least twenty pounds lighter then she'd been in college, where she had played volleyball while at Stanford. Lauren thought Angela was scary-skinny, worried that she had an eating disorder, and vowed to do some real damage to the controlling prick who'd destroyed her during their tumultuous year together. Julia just wanted her to eat a sandwich once a day. Oh, and help her pick out a smashing dress for the Design Awards dinner next weekend.

"Okay, here's what I'm narrowing it down to – these three. The Alexander McQueen blush corset dress, the Dolce and Gabbana black lace, and the Dina bar El blue satin halter. What do you think?" prodded Julia.

"Hmm." Angela studied the three dresses carefully. It was hard to believe, given that Angela's normal attire outside of the office these days consisted of workout gear or sweats, but the girl did have a good eye for fashion. Once upon a time she had been a stunning beauty with a figure most models would envy. Now she looked like a strong wind would blow her away, and hadn't smiled for what seemed like forever.

"Not the McQueen. The color is too pale for you, and the style is a bit girlish in spite of the corset top." Angela set that dress aside. "The bar El is gorgeous, amazing color on you, Jules. But the Dolce screams sex. If you curl your hair, do a smoky eye and red – no, burgundy lips – every guy in the room will want to fuck you if you wear that dress."

Julia flushed. "I'm really not sure that's my intent, honey. I just want to make sure I upstage that bitch Cameron."

Angela smirked. "Well, you could wear your rattiest yoga pants and a baggy T-shirt and do that from what you've told me."

"Impossible. I don't have anything in my entire wardrobe you could call ratty. And I never wear baggy clothes. Now that we've got the dress, let's pick the shoes."

They studied the neatly arranged shelves of shoes, sorted by color, until Angela pointed to a particular pair. "These. Absolutely this pair."

Julia grinned. "Also D & G. Good eye, Angie." The sky-high black pumps were made of tulle and suede, with a peep toe, a sultry ankle strap, and a tantalizing little rosette detail on the forefoot.

Angela sighed. "I wish I wore a size six shoe. It's hard to find cute ones in ten and a half. I have to special order my running shoes."

"Yes, but I have to hem almost every single dress and skirt because I'm too short. So we all have our little fashion dilemmas. Now, since you've been so awesome in helping me pick out a killer outfit, let me feed you, okay?"

Angela rolled her eyes. "Are we still on that? Fine, tempt me with something really yummy and I might eat a few bites."

Julia pumped her fist in triumph. "Honey, everything that comes out of my kitchen is yummy. Come on, let's tempt those dormant taste buds of yours."

Angela drank another glass of wine while Julia whipped up a tomato and cheese tart, salad nicoise, and crème Brule.

"So how did cocktails with that guy turn out the other night?"

Julia shrugged as she mixed up the salad dressing. "About how I figured they would. Todd's a nice enough guy – and very good looking – but he's got player written all over him. Plus, his very favorite topic of conversation is Todd, more Todd, and, oh yes, still more Todd."

"So he struck out then, huh?"

"I didn't say that." Julia smiled mischievously. "He's taking me to the Design Awards dinner on Saturday." At Angela's look of disapproval, she defended herself by saying, "Hey, I needed a date. And he needed to be some real serious man candy."

"Let me guess. So you can piss off Cameron."

"No." Julia shook her head. "She'll probably be all too happy to see me with a good-looking guy, figuring I wouldn't be interested in Nathan anymore. *He's* the one I want to piss off."

"Good for you, sweetie." Angela toasted her. "Show that bastard you don't give a crap about him any longer, that you've moved on."

"That's the general idea."

During a drunken girls night-in about a month ago, Julia had tearfully confessed everything to Angela about what had happened in New York. It had been a comfort to finally have it all out in the open and be able to discuss the whole episode with someone. She had only told Lauren some sketchy details, and had sworn Angela up and down not to breathe another word to her sister, for Julia wouldn't put it past her twin to actually confront Nathan and give him hell – or even a few bruises. Julia was quite certain that was why Angela had never told them the name of the guy who had wrecked her so badly.

During dinner, which Angela actually ate more than a few bites of, they talked mostly about work, Angela's marathon training, and Julia's yoga classes. The one thing they didn't discuss – by silent mutual agreement – was their equally fucked up love lives. Angela hadn't dated – hell, had barely left her flat, in fact, except for work and running – since her soul-wrenching breakup, and showed absolutely no interest in men at all, unless they were wealthy clients who wanted to buy a mutual fund or annuity. Julia was interested in men but didn't trust her judgment these days, since her last two relationships had pretty much imploded.

"How do you shut it off?"

Angela glanced up in surprise from her crème Brule, which she had actually finished, at Julia's sad, slightly drunk question. She knew exactly what her friend meant.

"The hurt? The betrayal? The heartache?" At Julia's nod, she licked her spoon. "By shutting down everything. I just don't feel anything anymore. It's the only way I've been able to deal. It was either that or just be drunk all the time."

While Julia was getting ready for bed later that evening, Angela's pragmatic words came back to her, and she knew she didn't want to live that way. Unlike her friend, Julia wanted to feel, to enjoy life, and to be in a happy relationship. That Angela had been severely damaged was both obvious and tragic, and Julia vowed she'd never let a man have that much power over her.

It was good, therefore, she told herself firmly as she tried to fall asleep, that she was bringing Todd as her date next weekend. The time had come for her to move on and forget about Nathan. Oh, he might desire her but he wasn't going to act upon that fact. And he certainly wasn't going to end his engagement for – what for him, at least – was obviously just a bad case of lust. It was well past the time that she wrote Nathan Atwood off as a closed chapter in her life and started living again. And next Saturday night was going to be the perfect launching off point.

✳✳✳✳✳

Nathan let himself into Cameron's condo while the driver waited outside. He'd warned the driver that they might be a few minutes, and had received a knowing chuckle in response, with the driver lamenting the fact that his wife was always at least half an hour late for everything.

It had been Cameron's idea almost a year ago to exchange keys to each other's place. He'd been a little reluctant at first to hand over a key to his condo, but had relented after she'd persisted. It wasn't that he didn't like her having the key, or minded her being in his condo if he wasn't there. But he had always been something of a private person, liking his own space, and his two-bedroom condo wasn't exactly spacious. For whatever reason, he always felt a little hemmed in when Cam stayed over, though that likely was due to the fact that she was a huge slob. Evidence of her untidiness was apparent around her condo as he walked into the expansive living/dining area.

There were newspapers, books and files piled haphazardly on the coffee, entry and dining tables. Shoes, handbags, and coats were strewn around without a care. He knew if he walked into the kitchen there would be dirty dishes piled in the sink, and half-empty coffee mugs and takeout containers littering the counters.

Nathan shuddered as he imagined the utter chaos of her bedroom and bathroom, with clothing, shoes and accessories flung every which way in the bedroom, and cosmetics, hair products, wet towels and dirty laundry in complete disarray in the bath.

Fortunately for Cameron, she had a cleaning lady who came in once a week, and Nathan only hoped the poor woman was paid a handsome salary because she would sure as hell earn it cleaning this place. He couldn't stand living or working in such a mess, one of the reasons he didn't especially enjoy having Cameron stay over at his place very often. She had long ago started keeping some clothing and toiletries at his condo, a few too many for his preference, while he kept a bare minimum of stuff here at her place. Every time she stayed over at his home, there would be a huge mess to tidy up the next day, despite his frequent pleas to her to pick up. Cameron usually laughed it off, making fun of herself as a hopeless slob, and claiming that she was far too busy to pick up after herself on a regular basis.

It was yet another serious issue they were going to have to resolve very soon, and certainly before they began looking for somewhere else to live. Neither of their current places was large enough for both of them, especially given the complete and utter disaster that was Cameron's closets. Both bedrooms at her place were spilling over with all of her shit, and there was no organization to either closet whatsoever. Nathan wouldn't even be able to store a single pair of shoes in either one. That they needed a larger place was obvious, but the real dilemma was exactly where that place should be.

His own place in the south of Market area was three blocks from his office, and as a result he walked there most days. Cameron, on the other hand, lived high atop Nob Hill in the multi-million dollar unit her parents had purchased for her ten years ago, while her gallery was on Union Street. She either drove or took taxis to and from work every day. Understandably, both of them wanted to live as close as possible to their jobs, though Nathan at least was willing to compromise and find someplace halfway between. Cameron, however, was being stubborn and so far had only been willing to consider properties within a couple of miles of her gallery.

And Nathan hadn't even begun to broach the topic of his Tiburon property with her, knowing the timing really wasn't good right now. Three years ago, during a downturn in the real estate market, he'd bought a vacant lot with amazing waterfront views in the affluent Marin County community. He planned one day – hopefully soon – to finish designing and then building his dream home and living there full time. The weather was great, the community about as safe as possible, the schools highly rated for their future children. But he wasn't convinced that he'd ever be able to persuade Cameron to live there, devoted city girl that she was.

'One thing at a time,' he told himself. 'Let's find a place to live in the city first."

When Cameron didn't emerge from her bedroom a couple of minutes after he arrived, he called out to her, "Hey, are you almost ready? The driver is waiting downstairs for us."

He heard doors being slammed, and other commotion coming from the direction of her bedroom. "Oh, hey, babe. Didn't hear you come in," called Cameron. "Yeah, I'll be out in a few. Sorry, running a little behind schedule."

"As usual," he muttered under his breath. Cam's perpetual tardiness drove him nuts, and it went hand in hand with her sloppiness and general lack of organizational skills.

"Try to hurry, okay?" he admonished. "I'd like to get there before the cocktail hour is over this time."

"Hah, ha, very funny!" she retorted. "I'm working on it, babe! Be patient."

His comment hadn't been an exaggeration, since they had arrived at last year's Design Awards banquet just as people were sitting down to dinner. He had vowed that wouldn't happen this year, and had even hired the town car to pick them up and drop them off so he wouldn't have to hassle with parking and the extra time that would take. The hired car would also allow him to relax and have a few drinks without having to worry about driving home safely.

After nearly a fifteen minute wait, Cameron finally emerged from the bedroom, and he could only stare at her in mingled surprise and a feeling close to horror.

'Holy shit," he mumbled under his breath.

For the Cameron standing proudly before him, hand on one cocked hip, bore little resemblance to the classy, somewhat conservatively dressed woman he'd dated for over two years. She'd obviously been aiming for the total bombshell effect tonight, but somehow something had gone horribly wrong.

The most glaring change to her appearance was the long hair extensions that fell halfway down her back. They were stick straight, very blonde, and so obviously fake that she looked like she was wearing a bad wig.

The second, and almost equally glaring change, was the deep gold spray tan. Even her heavily made-up face – with the longest, thickest false eyelashes he'd ever seen up close – was darkly bronzed. Her lips looked fuller and poutier, her lipstick a screaming shade of crimson that matched the color on her long fingernails and the toenails that peeked out of sky high strappy gold shoes.

And a great deal of that fake-tanned skin was exposed by the short, tight, strapless red sequined dress she wore. Nathan's eyes widened at the display of her cleavage over the low-cut top, and he wondered what sort of miracle bra she'd found to give her small A cup boobs the illusion of being C's. The hem of the dress ended well up on the thigh, baring most of her long, skinny legs. Cameron typically never wore anything that bared so much of her legs and arms because of their extreme slenderness, but for some reason it was all on full display tonight.

She grinned as he continued to stare at her. "Surprised? I've spent something like four days getting ready for this dinner tonight, but I'd say it was well worth it, wouldn't you?"

Nathan gave himself a mental shake, choosing his words carefully. "I barely recognized you. You look, um, so different."

Cameron laughed and strode over to him, looping her arms around his neck and giving him a long, deep kiss that he accepted more than returned. Thankfully, she didn't seem to notice his lack of response. "But don't worry," she murmured in his ear. "I waxed two days ago so it won't interfere with our fun tonight." She tugged at his earlobe with her teeth while sliding her palm to his crotch, stroking his non-existent erection. "Just so you know, I'm very, very horny. Hope you're in the mood for some loud, raunchy fucking."

Nathan was somewhat guiltily aware that he'd never felt less like having sex than he did right now. Not only did Cameron's startling appearance repulse him, but there were a variety of scents clinging to her that were all co-mingling and producing a rather nauseating result – her heavy, musky perfume, the spray-on tan solution, some sort of hair gunk – perhaps whatever had been used to attach those ridiculous extensions.

When she realized after long seconds of rubbing his crotch that he didn't have an erection, she frowned slightly and stepped back. "Everything okay?"

"Yes, just fine. But we should really get going. Do you have a coat?"

She giggled and ran her hands down the miniscule expanse of her dress. "Nope, what you see is what you get. It's a nice night, and we have the car to take us both ways. I wouldn't think you'd want me to cover all this up, babe."

He gave her a forced smile. "You're right. Come on, then. Careful in those shoes, you don't usually wear such high heels."

He didn't mention that with the towering stilettos Cameron was now a bit taller than he was. He also didn't dare mention that instead of looking like the sexy siren she undoubtedly believed herself to be that she more closely resembled a high class hooker. It was all just a little too much, especially the short, tight dress that was rather inappropriate for the awards dinner venue. But he knew if he even hinted at any of this that Cameron would be hurt or angry or both, and that his evening would be ruined before it even began.

So he kept his opinions to himself as he helped her inside the back seat of the town car. Her dress rode even further up her thighs, exposing her all the way to the crotch where he could see her red lace thong peeking out. He'd never really had the guts to tell her that he actually didn't like it when she got one of her Brazilian waxes. He knew a lot of guys preferred it when their women waxed off all their pubic hair, but he was just the opposite. He was fairly certain the main reason Cameron waxed regularly was so he wouldn't suspect she wasn't a natural blonde, something he had been well aware of since meeting her.

She seemed especially amorous tonight, sitting so close beside him she was practically in his lap. She continued to run her hand up and down the length of his thigh, her fingers teasingly brushing against his crotch. With the other hand she pressed his arm against her small breast. Nathan felt guilty again, knowing that between their hectic work schedules and his own odd ennui lately, that it had been more than two weeks since they'd slept together. And that had been a quick, hurried encounter that he'd been half afraid he wouldn't even be able to finish given his lack of arousal.

"I am *sooo* looking forward to tonight," she whispered sensuously in his ear. "Maybe we can cut out of the dinner a little early to get started on the night's real festivities." She cupped his crotch, fondling him through his trousers. "Unless you want to have a quickie right now," she suggested naughtily.

Nathan was uncomfortably aware that he wasn't even the least bit hard, and was desperately trying to think up a reason why when he was saved by the trilling of Cameron's cell phone. She grabbed it out of her bag somewhat impatiently, but her eyes lit up when she saw who the caller was.

"Damn. Sorry, babe, this is an artist I've been trying to get a hold of for a week now. I need to take this."

He was relieved when she moved slightly away from him to take the call, and even more so when the call didn't end until the driver pulled up outside of the hotel. The pre-dinner cocktail party was in full swing when they arrived, though Nathan was relieved to see they still had a half hour or so until dinner. In addition to his co-workers and staff present tonight, there were bound to be several friends and acquaintances he knew. After ordering his usual scotch on the rocks and a dirty martini for Cameron, he was tapped on the shoulder. Spinning around, he grinned to see Ryan Latimer standing there, accompanied by his very pregnant wife Sophie.

The two men exchanged a quick hug, and Nathan bent to kiss Sophie's cheek while Ryan did the same to Cameron. He and Ryan had been classmates at Berkeley, and kept in frequent touch despite the fact that Ryan worked for one of Atwood Headley's chief competitors.

"Awesome to see you, buddy," greeted Ryan. "I figured you'd be here seeing as you and your group are up for three awards tonight. Again."

Nathan smirked. "What can I say? It's been another good year. But great to see both of you, too. Baby's due when – two months?"

Sophie, a pretty brunette of medium height, nodded. "Ten weeks, to be exact. If I last that long. It's getting a little uncomfortable to waddle around these days."

Ryan grinned and pressed a kiss to his wife's head. "Don't listen to her. She's doing great. But let's have a look at this gorgeous thing next to you." He let out a low wolf whistle as he regarded Cameron. "Almost didn't recognize you, Cam. You're looking hot, girl."

Cameron visibly preened at the compliment, the kind that Nathan hadn't been able to bring himself to give her. "Thanks, hon. Thought I'd try a new look. Spice things up a bit, you know?"

As the Latimers continued to compliment Cameron on her new look, Nathan wondered if they were being sincere or just polite. He'd seen the startled look on both of their faces when they'd first seen Cameron, especially Sophie's. In fact, Cameron seemed to be getting quite a few looks, from both men and women, and Nathan was starting to feel a little self-conscious with her hanging all over him. She was by far the most scantily clad woman here so far, her attire much more suited for a dance club than a semi-formal dinner.

They walked around the room, greeting several of his co-workers including Eric, Jake, and Brent, all of whom exhibited equal surprise at the sight of the new Cameron. From across the room he caught Travis' eye, and his partner was staring at Cameron in frank disbelief. Travis bent to whisper something in Anton's ear, and the shorter man looked over at Nathan and Cameron, only to gape at them slack jawed. Nathan quickly hustled Cameron out of their range of vision, not wanting any sort of confrontation tonight.

With that goal in mind, he'd given Travis very strict instructions not to sit at the same table with him and Cameron. Travis had assured him that he had requested a separate table just for his staff, which had silently answered another of Nathan's requests – to keep Cameron and Julia far apart.

He assumed she was here tonight, though in this crowded, tightly packed room it was difficult to find anyone, and he certainly wasn't going out of his way to locate her. The further apart he could keep the two women the better. So far Cameron seemed to be having a great time tonight, chatting and laughing with everyone they came in contact with. It was a major change from the tense, uncomfortable atmosphere at the Taverna Francesca fiasco a couple of months ago.

He'd just handed Cameron a second martini and was about to take a sip from his re-filled glass of scotch when yet another old friend approached to shake his hand. He and Travis had worked with Will Dunleavy at their former firm. Will had moved on to a smaller firm, but he kept in regular contact with Nathan. The last time he'd actually seen Will, though, had been last year at this very same function.

"How the hell are you, man?" greeted Will. "Can't believe we haven't seen each other in a whole fucking year. Where does the time go?"

Nathan shook his head. "Tell me about it. I never seem to have a free minute these days."

"I haven't even congratulated you on your engagement," bemoaned Will. "Saw the news on your Facebook page. Cameron's a great girl. I hope the two of you will be real happy. Where is the beautiful bride-to-be anyway?"

Nathan spied her a short distance away chatting up the wife of yet another Berkeley classmate of his, and pointed her out to Will. "What about you, William?" he asked, jokingly using his full name. "Surely you're not here solo tonight?"

Will shrugged. "'Fraid so, my man. I was seeing someone for a few months but we just split up a couple of weeks ago. I haven't been in the mood to start trolling around for a replacement. You know, it gets kind of old after awhile."

"Yeah, I know exactly what you mean," agreed Nathan with a grimace. "That's one of the main reasons I wanted to get married. Playing the field is great for about ten years, and then it all gets to be a big game you grow tired of."

"I hear you." Will glanced across the room, his smile deepening. "Oh, hey, there's old Travis. I see he and his little dude are still together. What's his name again?"

"Anton. And yes, they just celebrated their fourth anniversary. It's kind of sad that Travis has been in a longer-term relationship than either of us."

Will chuckled. "How about that." Then his jaw dropped and he let out a long, low whistle. "But who the hell is that standing next to the happy couple? Goddamn, that is the hottest babe I've ever seen in my life. How the fuck does Travis know someone like that?"

Nathan knew who Will was drooling over even before he turned and saw Julia for the first time that evening. "Fuck me," he muttered under his breath, his heart pounding furiously as he saw how gorgeous she looked tonight. Gorgeous, and sinfully, erotically sexy.

He'd never seen her looking quite like this – in full-out femme fatale mode. And while Cameron's own attempts to look like a sultry siren had failed rather miserably, Julia had no such problem. She looked like – sex.

She wore a black dress with a ruffled hem and a V-neckline trimmed in black lace that showcased her spectacular tits. Nathan quickly bolted down the last of his scotch as his gaze remained fixed on the generous amount of cleavage she was displaying tonight, and the erection that he hadn't been able to summon up earlier was at instant and full attention now. She'd left all that glorious hair loose, except for a few curls she'd piled messily on top of her head. She was wearing more makeup than usual - her eyes darkly shadowed and lined, her pillowy lips shiny with dark red gloss. She was wearing those sheer black stockings that were the bane of his existence, and the sexiest shoes he'd ever seen – high, high heels, ankle straps, and a bow on the forefoot.

She was so delicious, so arousing, that he wanted to fling himself at her feet and beg for whatever small attention she might be generous enough to bestow upon him. He saw now how many other covetous male glances were being directed her way, staring at her face, her mouth, her breasts, her legs. And Nathan longed to yell out to all of them to stop looking at her because she was his. He wanted to stride over and cover her up with his black suit jacket so that no one else could admire and lust after her gorgeous tits.

Will was nudging him frantically. "So spill the beans. Who is that beautiful creature? And how can I get an introduction?"

Nathan motioned a passing waiter to bring him another scotch before answering Will. "Her name is Julia McKinnon and she's one of Travis' designers. As for an intro, buddy, you'll have to finagle that yourself. I, um, stay out of my employees' personal lives."

"Well, probably doesn't matter anyway. That guy she's with sure as hell doesn't seem like he wants to share. And as much of a stud as I am, I've got to admit I'm not in his league."

Nathan felt the rage begin to build rapidly, like water about to boil over, as he belatedly noticed the man glued to Julia's side. She'd brought a date – a fucking *date* – and what made matters so much worse was that the man with her tonight was Todd Bryant. Nathan had to acknowledge – reluctantly – that the fucker was even better looking than his Linkedin photo and about two inches taller than himself. They did look awfully good together – Todd tall and darkly handsome, Julia petite and fair and lovely.

Nathan snatched his third glass of Macallan from the waiter and downed half of it at once, his gut clenching unpleasantly as he watched Todd slide an arm around Julia's waist, hugging her close to his side. She looked relaxed and happy, daintily sipping on a flute of champagne.

'Motherfucker!' he cursed under his breath. 'Champagne.' Julia was drinking champagne. What was it she'd said at the Taverna dinner – 'I only drink champagne when I want to be seduced.' She was planning on letting this suave, smooth talker with the gel-spiked black hair seduce her tonight. Shit, for all he knew they'd already fucked, multiple times. He watched the way Todd's gaze dropped to Julia's cleavage, and he wanted to run over and slam his fist in the prick's gut.

The call to dinner came then, but his relief was short-lived for the table that Julia and her overly-amorous escort sat at was across from his own, giving him a direct line of view.

Despite the lively conversation at his table – where three of the other architects and their guests sat along with him and Cameron – Nathan grew increasingly silent and terse as the evening wore on. He polished off his fourth glass of scotch before starting on the Cabernet Sauvignon. He knew he was getting quietly, steadily drunk, barely touching his food, but it was the only way he knew how to cope with seeing the woman he so desperately desired being continually pawed by another man.

Nathan had to temper down his rage as he watched Todd touch Julia on the arm, the shoulder, the nape of her neck. He wanted to throw wine in the asshole's face when Todd ran his fingers through a lock of Julia's silky hair. Todd's gaze seemed frozen on her breasts, and to Nathan it appeared that her neckline revealed more and more full, creamy flesh as the evening wore on. He was hard and aching, his balls throbbing with the need for release, but he only wanted Julia and it seemed like she was now completely off limits to him.

She looked up once and caught his burning gaze upon her, giving a little gasp. She worried her bottom lip uncertainly before looking away. Fortunately, Cameron was too busy being in her element as the center of attention and didn't notice his preoccupation with the next table over. It would have only taken one time for her to notice the way he was staring at Julia, most certainly with a combination of undisguised lust and barely controlled rage, and she would have gone crazy.

When the awards ceremony started while dessert was still being served, he kept his fingers crossed that he wouldn't win any awards that would require him to walk up to the stage and make an acceptance speech. At this point he wasn't sure his legs would be steady enough, and he was damned certain his brain was far too addled with booze to utter a coherent sentence.

He wasn't nominated for any individual awards this year but the firm as a group was. In addition, both Travis and Eric were up for individual honors. The firm wound up losing to another group, but Travis and Eric did win, and Nathan joined in the rowdy applause coming from the tables occupied by the staff.

The evening continued after the awards presentation with dancing. The bar also remained open, and Nathan watched grimly as Todd escorted Julia there, walking right past his table without glancing at him or saying a word.

Cameron noticed them as they passed and frowned. "I didn't realize she was here tonight." She sniffed. "At least she brought a man of her own so she doesn't have to pant after mine."

He finished off his wine, having lost count of how many glasses he'd consumed. "Don't start, okay? It's been a nice evening so far, don't ruin it."

"Yeah, a nice evening where you haven't said a word, and you've been pounding back the drinks all night. What has you so pissed off anyway?" she hissed.

"I'm not pissed off."

"Fine," she challenged. "Then dance with me. Come on."

Nathan gave a slight groan but allowed Cameron to pull him to his feet – a bit shakily – and propel him to the dance floor. Fortunately, it was a slow dance so he didn't have to do much more than guide her around in circles. The feel of her body pressed up closely to his wasn't the least bit arousing, and in fact he found her clinginess tonight annoying. He was relieved when the song ended, to be replaced by a fast song currently popular on the charts.

"I'm going to sit this one out, okay?" he told her. "Maybe get some coffee."

She looked annoyed but merely gave a shrug as she sauntered off to join in the dance with a group of other wives and girlfriends. Soon there were nearly a dozen women all gathered in a tight group shaking and shimmying to the music. Grateful to escape, Nathan started making his way to the bar, hoping they had a hot pot of coffee ready. He was really starting to feel the effects of too much alcohol, his head beginning to pound and his gait unsteady.

But then he saw Julia leaving the banquet room alone, and he changed his mind about the coffee.

✳✳✳✳✳

Julia escaped into the quiet sanctuary of the ladies room gratefully. She really needed to get away from Todd and his overly eager hands for a few minutes. It had been a huge mistake to invite him along as her date tonight. She'd known that the minute he had picked her up at her flat, sweeping her into an amorous embrace and a demanding kiss. He'd suggested having a quickie before going to the dinner, and even blowing the dinner off altogether. He had been a bit pissy when she had gently but firmly refused both ideas and she wasn't looking forward to the end of the evening when she was going to refuse him again. In fact, she already knew she wouldn't be seeing him again after tonight.

Oh, he'd been charming enough, maybe a little too much considering how touchy-feely the guy was. It seemed that his overeager hands were everywhere, and not just on places like her arm or shoulder. Three times now his hand had been sliding up her thigh, even under her dress, and she'd had to remove it a little more firmly each time. And she was cursing herself for wearing the Dolce & Gabbana, given the way Todd kept staring at the lavish display of her breasts in the low-cut dress. She swore she could practically feel his hot breath on her bare skin, and had felt his hand "accidentally" brush up against the side of her boob a couple of times.

And while there was no denying the guy was handsome – Julia had noticed all the roving female eyes directed his way – he made her skin crawl for some reason. Maybe it was the fact he wore too much cologne mingled with the scent of his hair gel, or that he talked incessantly about himself, no matter who tried to change the subject. And he was constantly checking his phone for messages or sending texts – in between talking about himself, of course. Julia was quite certain that the texts were to and from other women, a fact that didn't bother her in the least.

The guy was a player through and through, and under normal conditions she wouldn't have given someone like him the time of day. But it had been a necessary evil to bring a date tonight – and not just any date. Knowing that Nathan and Cameron would be in attendance, Julia supposed it was a matter of pride to show both of them that she had her own hot guy and didn't need to lust after Cameron's. She sure as hell hadn't wanted any sort of confrontation with Cameron, and bringing Todd along had pretty much guaranteed that wouldn't happen.

But, truth be told, she'd really wanted to make Nathan jealous, to make sure he really knew just how capable she was of getting a man. And, of course, to rub his nose in the reality of just what it was he'd rejected, to remind him quite blatantly of all that he was missing. While helping her get ready tonight Angela had assured her that she looked hot enough to sizzle to the touch, and Todd's jaw had dropped when he'd first seen her in the scintillating black dress. She had hoped rather snarkily that Nathan would be eating his heart out by the time the evening ended.

The tables had wound up being turned on her, however, when she saw how mouthwateringly sexy he looked tonight. Clad all in black – suit, shirt, silk tie – he looked like the devil in his most handsome and tempting form. His thick, dark brown hair had been expertly styled, and she'd longed to climb onto his lap, kiss him senseless, and run her hands through his locks. She'd been sneaking discreet little glances at him all though dinner and the awards, occasionally meeting his gaze. Fortunately, Cameron had been chatting with someone each time and hadn't witnessed their brief interactions.

Julia had been startled – more like shocked – when she'd seen Cameron for the first time tonight. The change in her appearance was astounding, but Julia privately didn't think it was in a good way. The very obvious hair extensions were too long and stick straight, and didn't suit Cameron's long, thin face at all. The short, tight dress was all wrong for her tall, slender body, for it emphasized just how skinny she was. And the killer heels – which Julia enviously recognized as Jimmy Choos – made Cameron an inch or two taller than Nathan.

Travis and Anton hadn't been anywhere near as kind with their opinions. After they'd stopped alternately staring in horrified disbelief, then laughing hysterically, the comments had really poured out.

"My God, she looks like a bad female impersonator," gasped Travis in between bouts of giggles. "I swear I know half a dozen trannies that are better looking and have more curves than her."

"Well, if her art gallery folds it's nice to know she's got another career to fall back on," smirked Anton. "One that involves a *lot* of falling on her back. Ooh, I've got to get a photo and Instagram it to Stephanie. The girl can add it to her Facebook album."

Todd, naturally, had been rather bemused at their cackling and commentary but Julia had told him this was how Travis and Anton usually behaved. That hadn't, however, stopped Anton from keeping the quips up all during dinner, albeit in whispered tones to either Julia or Travis.

"She's only tarted herself up, you know, to try and compete with you," Anton had murmured. "Oh, not that you look like a tart, baby girl. On the contrary, you look more fabulous than ever. But instead of looking sexy, Cameron just looks like a sad clown."

Julia finished tidying up her hair and makeup before tucking her lip gloss back inside her black satin clutch. As she exited the empty ladies room, she wondered what Nathan thought of his fiancée's dramatic new style. The few times she'd dared glance in his direction, he'd seemed silent and morose, but each time Cameron had been hanging all over him – clutching his arm, rubbing his neck, kissing his cheek. Julia's fingers had itched to go yank those ridiculous hair extensions from her scalp or to dunk her overly made-up face into her bowl of soup.

They said jealousy was a two-edged sword, and that was definitely the case tonight. While she had tried to make Nathan jealous, she herself was almost sick with the same emotion as she saw him with Cameron. Her ploy at bringing Todd along as her date hadn't worked out so well, for it didn't seem to be bothering Nathan in the least.

She hadn't walked more than a few yards from the ladies room on her way back to the banquet when a hand reached out and manacled itself around her upper arm. Julia gasped in surprise as she spun around to face a livid Nathan. He was unsmiling, his face slightly reddened, and she half-expected to see smoke curling out of the top of his head.

"Nathan, what in the world -"

She was cut off from the rest of her sentence when he began to walk in the opposite direction of the banquet room, propelling her along in his wake. He didn't say a word, but his anger was obvious and she had zero idea why he was so pissed off at her when they hadn't exchanged a single word all evening. She could smell the lingering traces of alcohol on his breath, and wondered how much he'd had to drink tonight. He didn't stop his progress until they reached the end of the hallway, and he yanked her inside an empty, darkened meeting room, slamming the door shut behind them.

"What are you do -" she began, only to be cut off again, this time by him shoving her up against a wall and kissing her with such force that she whimpered. He held her face between his hands, his tongue ravaging her mouth as he pressed his body against hers, pinning her in place and not permitting her to move away. Julia clutched handfuls of his suit jacket, not sure if she should be pushing him away or pulling him closer. He kept kissing her with those hungry, devouring kisses until her head began to spin and she thought she might faint from lack of oxygen. She began to push at his shoulders almost frantically, and finally tore her mouth away, gasping for air. Nathan rested his head on her shoulder, his mouth pressed against her throat, his breathing as ragged and uneven as her own. His body continued to press against hers, holding her firmly pinned with her back against the wall, and she squirmed to get loose.

"Nathan, we – we can't," she whispered faintly. "Please, we should get back. We'll – they'll start to wonder where we are."

"I don't give a shit," he muttered. "Unless you're in a hurry to get back to your new lover, that is."

Julia winced at the rage in his voice and tried to turn her head away. "Don't, Nathan."

He grasped her chin, forcing her to look at him. Even in the darkened room, with only the Exit lights lending a bit of illumination, she could see his light blue eyes glittering fiercely. "I'll bet he's real anxious to get you home so he can fuck you good and hard," he bit out. "The way he's been putting his filthy hands all over you, how he keeps staring at these beautiful tits." He ran a rough hand over her breast, squeezing it until she gasped. "Unless, of course, he's already fucked you. Has he, Julia? Have you let that asshole fuck you?"

She closed her eyes, trembling from the force of his anger. "No," she confessed breathlessly. "We haven't – done that yet."

Nathan's hand caressed her cheek. "But he wants to. Badly. I can tell you all the filthy, nasty things he's dying to do to you, baby. The first involves this pretty, sexy mouth of yours."

He tugged her lower lip with his teeth, sucking at it until she groaned, and then kissed her again with long, slow licks. His kisses were different from earlier, more sensual and arousing, more deliberate, and she began to make hungry little noises beneath the coaxing pressure of his mouth. He kissed her until she was whimpering, her lips feeling bruised beneath the demanding pressure of his mouth, his tongue ravishing her endlessly.

"He wants to kiss you just like this," he breathed in between those slow, seductive kisses. "To taste this delicious mouth with his tongue, lick these perfect lips, have you suck his fingers just like this." He slipped two fingers inside her mouth, groaning when her tongue flicked out to curl around them. "But that's only the beginning of what he wants you to do. He wants you to suck his cock, to wrap those pretty lips around him and blow him hard until he shoots his load down your throat, and watches you swallow every drop."

Julia whimpered at this deliberately dirty talk, finding it wickedly arousing. He kissed her again, a wet, open-mouthed kiss that took complete possession of her mouth, leaving her weak-kneed and shaking. She was so turned on that she couldn't speak, or think of anything but how much he was arousing her, how much she craved him to fuck her again.

He pressed his hot mouth against the side of her neck, running his tongue around her ear. "Next, he wants to mark you right here so that everyone will know you're his. So that no one else would dare to do any of these nasty things to you, because he's the only one who has that right."

She gave a little cry when he bit the tender skin, sucking hard enough to leave a mark. He followed this action by soothing the bite with his tongue, before tugging the lobe of her ear with his teeth.

His hand moved up and down her bare arms caressingly, toying with the lace-edged strap of her dress. He ran a finger over the high curves of her breasts before dipping into the space between them. Her breathing grew choppy as he deliberately aroused her, taunting her with his caresses. There was zero doubt that he was the one in complete control right now, and she could only stare at him mesmerized and let him do whatever he wanted.

"And of course, what he really wants is to see these beautiful breasts." Slowly he slid the strap of her dress off one shoulder, revealing the full globe of her breast encased in a low-cut black lace bra. "Every man in that room tonight wants to see these big, gorgeous tits." He slipped his palm beneath the lacy bra cup, squeezing the bare, warm flesh of her breast.

"Nathan." His name escaped her lips with a moan as his fingers pinched her nipple and her head fell back limply against the wall.

"He wants to kiss them." He pressed hot, hungry kisses along the bared flesh of her upper breasts and into the deep cleavage between. "Suck and lick these pretty pink nipples." She gasped as he yanked the bra strap down her arm, causing her breast to pop out. "Make you scream his name and beg for more."

"Oh, God," she panted, threading her hands into his hair as he bent and took the nipple into his mouth, suckling her hard.

Without lifting his head from her swollen, achy breast, he yanked the strap of her dress and bra down the other side until both breasts were bared, her arms trapped in place. While continuing to lick and suck at one breast, he cupped the other in his hand, twisting the nipple between his fingers.

"Ohhh," she murmured in pleasure, feeling the wetness between her legs as he continued to lavish attention on her ultra-sensitive breasts. "God, that feels so good, Nathan."

"Shh." He lifted his head from her breast, placing a finger over her lips. "I haven't finished yet." He sunk to his knees in front of her, running his hands up and down her stockinged legs from ankle to knee.

"He'll want you to leave these shoes on because they're so damned hot. He's been thinking all night about fucking you while you're wearing these sexy shoes, with your legs wrapped around his neck." He toyed with the little bow on the instep before wrapping his fingers around her ankle. "And he'll be almost ready to blow his load when he feels how silky these stockings are, and sees up close how amazing your gorgeous legs look in them."

Julia groaned when he began to run his tongue along the back of her knee and up her thigh. He grasped the hem of her dress, and slowly began to roll it upwards, an inch or two at a time, until the fabric was bunched at her waist, baring her lower body to his hot, fevered gaze.

"Jesus, look at you." His voice was hoarse, barely audible as he slid his hand to the top of one silky black stocking, two of his fingers slipping inside to tease the soft flesh of her thigh.

"You look like a fucking wet dream come to life in this, baby," he said raggedly, tugging at the ultra short hem of her sheer black garter skirt. His roaming hands crept under the sexy little garment to cup her butt, half-bared by the high cut of her lacy black panties.

"Naughty, dirty girl, baring your ass like this," he scolded playfully."Naughty girls like you need to be spanked when they've been bad."

Julie cried out, startled, when his palm smacked one round buttock, then the other. She was so aroused, so desperately needy for his touch that her whole body was quivering now. She was so wet that she thought she'd go mad if he didn't touch her – there – and soon.

"Nathan, please. Oh, God, I need –" she broke off, unable to form the words.

"I know what you need, baby. And I'm going to give it to you real soon," he promised in a husky voice. "Now let me finish, hmm?"

He hooked his thumbs in the waistband of her panties, and pulled them slowly down her legs until they pooled at her feet and she stepped out of them. He picked them up, bringing them to his face, and inhaled deeply.

"Aw, hell, you smell so good, baby. And you got these pretty, sexy panties all wet. Mmm, I'll bet your pussy is real juicy by now. Let's find out, hmm?"

She let out a sigh of bliss when he ran his tongue through her slick folds. He licked her clit before sucking on it hard, drawing a long moan from her throat. And then he was thrusting two long fingers deep, deep inside of her while continuing to suck on her clit.

Julia was so aroused, so desperately needy, that the first orgasm came quickly, and she shuddered with the force of it, crying out weakly as her hands tangled in his hair. But Nathan gave her no respite, simply removing his fingers from her throbbing pussy and replacing them with his eager, hungry mouth. He licked her wet folds, sucking her labia between his lips while his thumb rubbed circles around her clit. It seemed like mere seconds before she was climaxing again, clutching his head to her as he continued to stimulate the super-sensitive flesh between her legs.

Nathan slid back up her body, holding her close as she shook, soothing her by stroking her hair and pressing kisses to her temple, her forehead. "He wants to do all that to you and more, baby," he whispered in a low, wicked voice. "To finger fuck that hot little cunt until you scream, and then lick up all the juice until you come again. And then he wants you to taste how delicious you are."

His lips were still shiny with her juices and she groaned when he kissed her savagely, bruising her mouth and letting her taste the salty muskiness. She was wild for him now, slipping her hands inside his jacket and pulling him close, rubbing her bare breasts against his shirt and loving the way the fabric abraded her flesh. She kissed him back with equal force, sucking on his tongue and biting his lip until he swore softly.

She could feel the heavy thudding of his heart against her breasts, hear how his breathing was labored and uneven. He was grinding himself against her as they kissed hungrily, unable to get close enough. She slid a hand down his chest, over his stomach, until her palm opened and cupped his rock hard erection through his pants.

He moaned, a sound that was a mix of pleasure and pain, and he fisted his hand in her hair, still kissing her, as she stroked the length of his cock. "Ah, Julia, sweetheart," he gasped. "Fuck, that feels so good. God, I'm going to explode in another minute. I want you so much, baby. Here, let me."

He unzipped his fly and released his cock, which she immediately took into her hand, stroking and pumping it. He put his hand on her wrist, stilling her motions. "No, stop, baby. I'm going to come in your hand if you do that. And that's not what's supposed to happen."

Nathan lifted one of her legs, wrapping it around his hip. Their eyes met in the semi-darkness, and she was almost afraid of the rawness of his expression.

"Because what he wants most of all," he drawled seductively, "is to ram his cock so deep inside of you, fuck you so hard and so good, that you won't be able to walk tomorrow. That's all he's been able to think about all night – fucking you just like this."

"Ohhh, God!"

"Ah, Christ!"

Their cries of passion were vocal and simultaneous, as he thrust inside of her in one swift, hard movement. Nathan stilled briefly, holding her leg wrapped firmly around his, as he buried his face in the side of her neck.

"Nothing has ever felt this good before," he uttered brokenly. "And it's never felt so right."

He started to move again, his thrusts slow and controlled at first, then increasing in force and speed as he pounded her against the wall. Julia was pinned between the wall and Nathan's hard body, and she whimpered in mingled arousal and fear, never having seen this aggressive, domineering side of him, as he didn't just fuck her but possess her. He rode her so hard that she saw stars, her head banging against the wall with each powerful thrust. Time and time again she felt herself on the very brink of orgasm, but she intentionally held back, wanting to prolong the bliss as long as possible. She clutched him to her, needing him so desperately that it brought tears to her eyes, her body starved for the lover she'd missed so badly. Greedily, she didn't want this to end, wanted him to go on fucking her for hours and hours, until she was raw and bruised. It would be worth it, she thought incoherently, willing to pay any price just to have him back inside of her like this.

He was breathing so hard she could barely understand the words he whispered to her, his voice guttural. "I'm going to come any second now, baby, fill you up with cum until I'm drained. Touch yourself, baby, come with me."

Gasping, Julia touched her clit, which was almost unbearably sensitive from her prior orgasms. But she obeyed his command, rubbing her fingers over and around the distended nub as he continued to fuck her like a madman, catapulting both of them over the edge to a screaming, shaking climax. Nathan called her name out over and over, like a chant, crushing her against him as he came, his mouth sucking her neck in another of those searing love bites. She tried to utter a cry, but only silence escaped her parted lips, too wrung out to make a noise.

When he finally lifted his head and pulled away to adjust his clothing, Julia's wobbly legs gave out and she slid down the wall, too weak to stand. She was too dazed and exhausted to care what she looked like at this moment – half-undressed and thoroughly fucked. She sat on the floor, her legs sprawled out like a broken doll's, her head lolling to one side.

Nathan squatted down beside her, grasping her chin in his hand and forcing her to look at him. He looked satisfied and almost smug, the side of his mouth curling up into a wicked half-smile.

"Your would-be lover might crave everything I just had," he told her quietly, "but he's going to know that I was there first. He's going to smell my scent all over your body, see where I left my mark on your skin, and hear my name on your lips. And if he still dares to fuck you, he'll feel my cum deep inside you."

She moaned softly at his words, closing her eyes, until he pressed a soft kiss to her lips. "God, don't let him touch you, Julia," he pleaded. "I know I don't have the right to ask but I'm asking anyway."

A single tear ran down her cheek as she opened her eyes and gazed at him. "And can you tell me you aren't going to touch Cameron tonight?" she whispered shakily. At his startled expression, she turned her head away. "Don't bother answering that. Just go now, Nathan. Please. I need to be alone."

"Baby -" he began, only to shake his head as he got to his feet. "Julia, I'm not going to leave you here, not like this. Come on, I'll walk you to the ladies room."

"No." She brushed away the hand he extended to her. "I want to be by myself for a few minutes. Leave me alone, Nathan."

She curled herself into a little ball, wrapping her arms around her bent knees and hiding her face. Silent sobs shook her body, but she refused to let him comfort her. Moments later, she heard the quiet click of the door as he left, and only then did she raise her head, tears streaming unchecked down her cheeks. Once again, Nathan had made her cry, and she mentally kicked herself for allowing him to have this affect on her.

He was her addiction, the forbidden temptation that she just couldn't leave alone, and he was slowly destroying her. The scariest part of that realization, though, was that she knew she didn't have the strength to kick the habit.

Chapter Thirteen

Nathan sat in his car for more than ten minutes before he finally summoned up the nerve to get out. And then he stood on the sidewalk for a couple more minutes, staring up at the building in front of him, double checking the information on his phone to make sure it was the right address.

Just as he was about to mount the stairs to the landing, a tall, dark-haired woman came running down the street at a faster pace than he had ever been capable of. She slowed as she approached the building Nathan was standing in front of, coming to a halt as she reached him.

She looked at him with a mixture of curiosity and suspicion. "Are you lost or something?"

Nathan took in her ultra-slender figure, clad in running shorts and a short-sleeved T-shirt, some type of hi-tech shoes on her feet. Her black hair was pulled back into a long ponytail, and her sweat-dampened face was free of makeup. She carried some sort of water bottle flask in one hand.

"No, I've got the right address, thanks," he replied, and began to walk up the stairs.

"Wait." He turned as she called out to him. "I know you aren't here to see me, so that just leaves Julia. And she isn't here right now."

Nathan stepped back onto the sidewalk, frowning. "Are you her roommate or something?"

"Neighbor, actually. I live in the upstairs flat. Angela Del Carlo. And you are?"

He stuck his hand out. "Nathan Atwood. I'm, uh, Julia's -"

"Yes, I know who you are," she said in a tone that indicated she wasn't at all impressed with this knowledge, giving him the briefest of handshakes. "What are you doing here?"

He cocked his head to one side, regarding her carefully. "Exactly what has Julia told you about me?"

Angela shrugged. "Pretty much all of it. She didn't mean to, but we got carried away with the tequila poppers one night. But don't worry, your little secret's safe with me. It's not like we know any of the same people."

He couldn't very well be annoyed with Julia at having confided in her neighbor when he'd spilled his guts to Jared. "I, uh, need to talk to her. Do you know when she'll be back?"

She checked her equally high-tech running watch. "It's ten a.m. now. Her yoga class ends at ten-thirty but she usually goes to coffee with people from her class or sometimes her teacher."

"Where's the yoga studio?"

Angela blinked. "Well, someone's anxious, aren't they? What's the matter – need to meet your fiancée afterwards?"

The dark-haired woman's snarkiness surprised him, for she seemed like a relatively quiet, passive person.

He flushed. "No, I don't, actually. I just really need to talk to Julia as soon as possible."

"Fine." She sighed in resignation. "The place is called SF Flow and it's about four blocks from here on Divisadero near Pine. Good luck finding a parking space."

"Yeah, that's the least of my worries. I'm more concerned with Julia clobbering me with a yoga mat or something. Or not speaking to me ever again."

Angela smirked. "Buy her a café au lait and a chocolate croissant and it might help. Food usually puts her in a good mood. God knows she's always trying to feed me."

Nathan privately thought he knew why that was, for Angela was at least ten to fifteen pounds lighter than she ought to be, her arms and legs like toothpicks. But he merely nodded and said, "Thanks for the tip. I'll try that."

"Sure. I'm not positive Julia will appreciate my telling you but what the hell. And, hey – Nathan?"

He paused by his BMW Roadster, about to open the door. "What is it?"

Angela's big brown eyes darkened and her expression was grim. "Don't fuck around with her, okay? In case you haven't figured it out yet, Julia's a real prize. And from what I've heard you sure as hell don't deserve her."

Grimly, he nodded. "You're right on that count. I'm the first to admit I've been a total prick to her, but that's going to change."

She began to ascend the stairs. "It had better. Otherwise, I'm going to call Julia's twin and tell her everything. And that's bad news for all of us."

Angela went inside before he could quiz her further, but decided he was better off not knowing more about this terror of a twin sister anyway.

He found the yoga studio easily enough, and lucked out getting a parking space just around the corner. It was a few minutes before ten-thirty as he waited outside the building, and he was glad he'd worn a sweater for the fog had rolled in this morning. He didn't expect Julia to be exactly thrilled to see him, not after the way he'd accosted, seduced and fucked her, only to leave the banquet with another woman. This was the third time he'd done something like this to her, and right now he was feeling like the lowest sort of life form. But he had to see her – to apologize, to make sure she was okay, to say God knew what else.

The trick was going to be in getting her to listen to him without flipping him off or calling him an asshole. Truth be told, he wouldn't blame her in the least for doing both.

✳✳✳✳✳

"Hang on a sec, Julia. I need to ask you something."

Julia paused in the doorway leading from the practice room into the reception area of the yoga studio, glancing back curiously at her teacher. "What's up, Sasha?"

Sasha put her hand on Julia's arm, a light touch that nonetheless conveyed the concern behind her words. "I just wanted to make sure you were okay. You seemed a little off your game today."

Julia sighed. "Yeah, I know. Not at my best for sure."

She'd fallen out of a handstand, wobbled on an arm balance posture that was usually easy for her, and had none of her normal high energy during class. Even in this very advanced, difficult class Julia was normally one of the top students, able to do nearly every pose that Sasha threw at them. She and her teacher had bonded almost instantly, from the time of Julia's first class, and occasionally hung out after class to have a cup of tea and talk.

Sasha shrugged. "We all have off days. And it is close to the full moon, you know, which can throw our balance off."

Julia knew that her teacher fully embraced the yogic lifestyle – not just the practice but also the diet and the beliefs – and being in touch with the moon phases was only a small part of that commitment.

"I'm a little tired, too, and maybe a bit hungover," confessed Julia. "I was at a banquet last night and didn't get home until late."

"That would do it. You should have a big glass of wheatgrass juice to help with the hangover. It's a wonderful energizer and detoxifier."

Julia thought privately that wheatgrass sounded completely nauseating but she wasn't about to insult Sasha with that opinion. "Okay, maybe I will."

"And I noticed you wincing a little, especially when you were in *hanumanasana.* Do you have a muscle strain?"

Julia did wince as she recalled the slight discomfort she'd experienced doing the full splits pose. "Um, no, just, er, sore. I, um, was —well, for lack of a better description, let's call it wallbanged last night. Guess I'm just a little tender this morning."

Sasha's light green eyes widened, and then she laughed behind her hand. "Well, I hope it was worth it. Sounds a bit kinky, but I'm all for a little kink every so often."

Julia flushed. "I can't believe I just told you that. You must think I'm shameless."

Sasha gave a rather undignified hoot. "For getting fucked against the wall? Sweetie, not much shocks me anymore. I grew up in a very bohemian household, so I'm generally pretty open-minded about most things."

"Well, thanks for checking on me. I promise to be back to normal by next class," vowed Julia.

"So, no more wallbanging for you?" joked Sasha.

Julia's mouth tightened. "Not with the same guy, anyway. I'm officially not speaking to him."

"Too bad. Any guy who can fuck you hard enough to make you walk funny must be pretty awesome in the sack." Sasha's eyes twinkled. "Or in this case, against the wall."

Julia rolled her eyes and gave her teacher a quick hug before leaving the practice room to retrieve her shoes, jacket, and mat bag. The reception area was already filling up with students for the next class, so she got ready to leave quickly.

Only to stop short upon leaving the studio when she saw who was waiting for her just outside, his tall, leanly muscled frame slouched against the side of the building.

It wasn't fair, she thought wildly, that she kept having these sorts of reactions to him. He looked so handsome, so yummy, that he ought to be illegal. He was casually dressed today – dark jeans, loafers, and a midnight blue V-neck sweater with a white shirt beneath it. His beautiful, thick hair was as well-styled as ever, his expression somber and unsmiling.

And then she remembered how desperate, how passionate he'd been last night, only to leave the banquet with Cameron, the woman he was going to marry next Valentine's Day. And given the way Cameron had been hanging over him all night, Julia wasn't naïve enough to believe she hadn't expected a rollicking fuck from Nathan. Had he gone from her arms right into Cameron's? She shuddered at the thought, refusing to torture herself with it.

Julia gazed at him for a moment longer before recalling her vow not to speak to him. Sliding her yoga mat bag over her shoulder, she started walking down the block away from him, silently fuming that he would just show up this way. What the hell gave him the nerve to think she would ever speak to him again after the way he'd treated her last night?

Not surprisingly, he caught up to her before she'd gone half a block, his voice low and pleading. "Julia, wait. Please. We need to talk and you know it. Stop."

Stubbornly, she kept on walking until he took hold of her arm, stilling her. She refused to look at him and tried unsuccessfully to pull her arm free.

"Let go of me, Nathan," she said quietly. "I don't want to talk to you."

"You don't have to talk, just listen. But can we go somewhere more private? Can I buy you a coffee? Please, Julia. I need to apologize, make sure you're okay, and I really don't want to do that here on the sidewalk."

She gave a small shrug. "I'm fine. You've apologized, Nothing left to say. Now let me go."

"No. Hey, I get that you're pissed off at me and I don't blame you. But please — it's just coffee, okay?"

Julia emitted a little huff. "Fine. There's a place on the next block."

"Is that where they serve the chocolate croissants?"

She blinked at him, wondering how in the world he would know about that, and then it dawned on her. "Angela. That rat. She told you where to find me. Nice to know I can count on my friends when I need them."

Nathan smirked. "If it's any consolation, she warned me to play nice. Threatened to tell your sister if I didn't."

Julia fought down a sense of panic at the very thought of Lauren ever figuring out that the bastard who dumped her back in New York was now her employer. "Well, that would be a very bad thing. My sister isn't known as the Queen of Confrontation for nothing. And she's coming for a visit next month so Angela needs to zip it."

"How does your neighbor know your sister so well?"

"We all grew up together in Carmel, went through school and all. Angela is actually more Lauren's friend than mine but we're still close. When she learned I was moving here she told me about the flat for lease below hers."

Nathan kept hold of her arm as they continued walking. "Your friend isn't exactly warm and sunny, is she?"

Julia's eyes flashed green fire. "She used to be, until some prick did a real number on her a couple of years ago. She was a total wreck for a long time – stopped eating, lost a ton of weight, wouldn't leave her flat except to go to work. Things haven't improved much, either."

"Why didn't she just sic your sister on the guy? Sounds like your twin is a force to be reckoned with."

"Because Angela won't tell us his name, and we never met him. Lauren and I think he had her wrapped up in some sort of borderline BDSM relationship where he controlled her entire life. Then when he dumped her she couldn't cope."

He shook his head. "That sounds pretty sick."

"Yeah, I wonder sometimes if she'll ever get back to normal. Here we are."

They scored a small table for two in a back corner of the coffeehouse, and Julia waited uncertainly while Nathan placed their order. She was conscious of not exactly looking her best – no makeup, pale from lack of sleep, her hair scraped back off her face into a long braid. At least her yoga clothes were as stylish as the rest of her wardrobe – fitted black Lululemon pants and a cute black and white graphic print tank with crisscross straps. Due to the foggy morning she had thrown a long, fitted black cardigan on over her outfit. And yoga class was just about the only time she ever wore flat shoes – black Keen Mary Janes.

Nathan returned with a tray bearing her café au lait and croissant, along with his own black coffee and toasted bagel. They ate and drank in silence for several minutes, Julia being very careful not to meet his eyes even though she could feel his gaze upon her. Then, he unexpectedly reached out and ran his fingers along the side of her neck, wincing when he saw the dark purple marks he'd put there the night before.

"Sorry about that," he said hesitantly. "I, uh, hope they don't hurt."

She shrugged his hand off. "I'll live. I must say, though, no one's given me a hickey since high school. At least I don't have to hide it from my parents this time."

Nathan smiled. "I'll bet you had a ton of boyfriends in high school. And with two of you, your parents probably went a little crazy."

"Not exactly. Lauren was a huge tomboy, and was more interested in sports than boys. She didn't really date until senior year, and my parents always knew she could take care of herself." Julia took a sip of her coffee. "My sister has studied martial arts since she was six years old. And not the tamer stuff like judo or tae kwon do. We're talking karate, kung fu, capoeira."

"Jesus." Nathan gulped. "No wonder everyone is terrified of her. What about you? Did you do martial arts as well?"

"God, no." She gave a little shudder. "Too violent for timid little me. I did ballet and gymnastics and then yoga when I was in high school. Besides, it was always important for Lauren and me to have our own separate identities and interests. Thank God my mom never believed in dressing us alike once we became toddlers."

He chewed a bite of bagel. "You didn't answer my question about boyfriends. Did you date a lot in high school?"

"One boyfriend for all four years of school. Plus almost two years of college. Sam and I were the classic high school sweethearts. At one point I was convinced we were going to get married and spend the rest of our lives together."

"So what happened?"

Julia gave him a sad little smile. "He wanted to move on, date other people. It was hard maintaining a relationship during college. I mean, we tried. One of the reasons I chose Cornell was because it was only a three hour drive from Penn State."

He frowned. "That's not really close. Why didn't he find a school closer to Cornell?"

"Because Penn State was the top school to recruit him. Sam played football there."

Nathan set his coffee cup down and stared at her in surprise. "Wait. Sam – Penn State. You're not talking about Sam Patterson, are you? The quarterback for the Arizona Cardinals?"

Julia nodded. "That's him. I'm guessing you know who he is?"

"Uh, yeah, he's only like one of the top-rated quarterbacks in the NFL today. Jesus, you dated him for what – six years?"

"About that, yes."

"Were you upset? I mean, when he told you he wanted to move on?"

She nodded. "I saw it coming, though. In our sophomore year of college, Sam was named the starting quarterback when someone else got injured. Suddenly he was way busier – more practices, press conferences, publicity. He told me he would get approached by people all the time who'd never known he existed before. Especially women."

"Hmm. And being – what – nineteen, twenty years old? Guess that's hard for a guy to resist too long, especially when his girl is three hours away."

"That was most of it. We'd probably started drifting apart a bit before then anyway. At least Sam had the decency to tell me before he started dating other people."

"Still, it must have been hard for you."

"Yeah." She studied her café au lait for long second. "I was more sad, I think, than upset. We'd been together for so long, been such a huge part of each other's lives. But we were able to remain good friends. I still keep in contact with him, and even saw him briefly at Christmas when he came to visit his parents."

"Were you able to move on?"

She blinked. "Eventually. But that didn't turn out so well. I seem to have atrocious taste and very bad luck with men."

Nathan flushed. "I'm guessing that's a ding on me."

"Not just you. I ought to have known better, going off with a complete stranger. But our ill-fated one night stand was nothing compared to the guy I was involved with after Sam." She scooped a dollop of foam from her mug and licked it off her fingers. "I was with him for almost two years and never knew he was married. With a small child."

He stared at her slack-jawed. "Shit. So when I told you I was engaged, you -"

"Felt cursed. Pissed off. Lied to. And royally screwed over once again. Hence the aforementioned bad luck. No, make that really, really shitty bad luck."

Nathan ran a hand over his face. "I'm so sorry, Julia. For everything. For lying to you in New York. For being a total jerk to you when you moved here. And for treating you so roughly last night. I worried about you all night long."

"Really?" she asked sarcastically. "That must have put a real damper on your evening with Cameron."

"What?" He gaped, astonished. "Hell, please tell me you do not think I took her home and fucked her after what happened. Even I'm not that big of a douchebag."

She stared at her plate, crumbling the last bit of her croissant into tiny pieces. "I have no idea what to think, Nathan. I mean, she is your fiancée, after all, and she seemed awfully amorous last night. Not to mention, it's obvious she went to a lot of trouble to look hot for you."

He gave a visible shudder. "It – wasn't exactly a good look for her. Instead of being turned on like I'm sure she intended it was just the opposite."

Julia held up a hand. "Okay. Stop right there. I really don't want to hear this. Speaking of which, I think you've apologized sufficiently. Can I go now?"

He placed a hand on her forearm as she began to rise. "Not yet, no. I'm not finished. Hell, I've barely begun. Look at me, Julia."

Reluctantly, she dragged her gaze up to his. "What?"

Nathan caressed her cheek with exquisite tenderness. "How could you possibly think I'd go to another woman after being with you? Believe me, baby, I had nothing left after that – nothing. Even if I had – God, I would have felt like a dirty manwhore being with someone else so soon afterwards."

She closed her eyes, fighting off tears. "Yeah, well, now you know how I felt. Twice now. Used, dirty, -"

"Hush." He placed two fingers over her lips. "God, don't say things like that. You are so far from being dirty or cheap, Julia. You are the finest, most beautiful thing I've ever seen."

Her voice choked on a sob. "Then why did you treat me like a whore last night? The way you talked to me, taking me up against the wall. You didn't even take your jacket off, for God's sake."

Nathan looked shocked at her words, the color draining from his face. "Oh, my God, baby. No, Julia, no. It wasn't like that. Listen to me." He gripped both of her hands urgently. "I was jealous, baby. So fucking out of my mind crazy jealous. I had to watch you all night long, looking so sexy, so hot that you almost set the room on fire. All I could think about was how much I needed to kiss you and touch you, especially wearing that goddamned dress that showed off every curve of your body."

She flushed at his words. "Nathan, don't -"

"Let me finish, because I'll be damned if I want you thinking I treated you like a whore. Nothing is further from the truth," he assured her.

"Go on," she said tiredly.

He interlaced his fingers with hers. "I wanted you so badly but couldn't do anything about it. Except to watch that bastard you brought along as your date touch you and stare at your tits. I kept getting more and more pissed off, and as a result kept drinking – a lot more than I normally do. And what made me even angrier was knowing I didn't have any right at all to be jealous – no right to *you* at all. But that only made things worse. "

Julia was silent for an uncomfortably long while, not at all sure how to respond. "You really don't have the right to be jealous, you know," she murmured. "You told me to date whoever I wanted. So I did."

"Yeah, and don't think I wasn't kicking myself all night long for having said that. Especially when I didn't mean it. I'm aware of what a selfish asshole I am, Julia. I can't offer you anything myself, and yet I don't want anyone else to have you, either. When I saw you with him – Todd – I just went off the deep end a little. The thought that he was going to be the one to take you home and fuck you instead of me – it was more than I could handle. All I could think about was having you first, spoiling you for him. I wanted you to be so thoroughly fucked that there was no possible way you'd let him touch you."

"Jesus." She stared at him in disbelief. "That's kind of sick, Nathan. And completely unreasonable. What am I supposed to do – live like a nun while you're engaged to someone else? In what universe is that fair?"

"I never said it was fair or reasonable." He looked chagrined. "I'm just telling you how I felt last night. I realize this whole situation is completely and utterly fucked up."

She shook her head. "I should have never taken this job. And when I realized you were my employer, I should have quit. We're fooling ourselves by thinking we can work together anymore. It's – this is too hard for me, Nathan."

"I know, baby. And I've made it even more difficult for you, haven't I? Telling you on the one hand that we have to be strictly professional with each other, keeping my distance from you, but still wanting you on the other hand, so much that I was like a psycho stalker last night." He squeezed her hand. "Please tell me I didn't hurt you. I know I was rough and you felt so tight."

"You didn't hurt me. I obviously enjoyed what we did. It – I haven't been with anyone else since you last September. And no, I didn't do anything with Todd last night, either. He was too busy fielding texts from other women."

"He's a loser. He doesn't even deserve to be in the same room with you." He brought her hand to his lips. "But then, neither do I. I hope – some of the things I said – the dirty talk -"

She gave him a small smile. "It's okay. You must know that it's a huge turn-on for me. Talking dirty didn't make me feel dirty, Nathan. It's what you did afterwards that made me feel like a whore."

"Going home with Cameron." At her nod, he exhaled deeply. "I know. She was furious, by the way. That I drank too much and wasn't in the mood for – uh, you know."

Julia turned her face away. "Yes, I get the picture. And I suppose I should say I'm sorry but I'm really, really not. The way you felt about Todd last night – imagine feeling that way all the time."

"It would fucking kill me to imagine you belonging to someone else," he whispered. "Julia – it's not the same with her, believe me. I don't feel - "

"No details, okay?" she interrupted harshly. "And no comparisons. And I hope like hell that I'm not going to get some sort of third party disease or infection from her. In case you forgot, you didn't use a condom last night."

"No, but I always use one with her." At Julia's quizzical expression he explained further. "Oh, she's on birth control – when she remembers to take it, that is. After the third time she forgot to take a pill, I decided I couldn't rely on her anymore and always use a condom no matter what." He gave her hand another squeeze. "I hope that helps to set your worries at ease. As well as know that you're the only woman I've ever been inside bare."

Julia felt her cheeks grow hot. "Um, should I be flattered at that knowledge?"

He chuckled. "I don't know about flattered, but it's certainly the truth. When I met you again that night in New York and knew we were really going to happen, I didn't want anything between us. You were perfect, we were perfect together."

She pulled her hand from his grasp and reached for her yoga bag. "Until the night was over and reality set in, that is. I need to go, Nathan. I can't talk about this anymore. It's too hard."

"I know, baby. I just needed to tell you how sorry I am and make sure you're okay."

Her eyes shimmered with tears. "But I'm not okay, don't you get it? I don't mean physically – I already told you that. But this is wrecking me emotionally, Nathan. It's why I have to find another job, not see you anymore. It breaks my heart every single day to see you and want you so much but know you belong to someone else. If this keeps up much longer, I'm going to be like Angela – a shell of her former self."

"Christ, what a mess." He buried his face in his hands. "I've managed to fuck up both of our lives, haven't I? Julia – don't leave your job. Please. We'll work something out. I – I've got some hard decisions to make. And soon."

"What sort of decisions?"

He picked an imaginary piece of lint from his sweater, avoiding her gaze. "I need to decide if staying with Cameron while I'm so obviously attracted to you is fairer to her than breaking off our engagement and hurting her."

"Well, you certainly can't ask her opinion on the matter, can you?" she asked bitterly. "And I'm sure you can guess my choice. Sorry, but you're on your own with this one."

"Yeah, I've pretty much figured that out already." He blew out a breath. "Just – have a little patience with me, okay? This isn't easy, Julia. One way or another somebody gets hurt. And that's the last thing I ever intended to happen."

"I'll try, Nathan. But don't make things harder for me in the interim, okay? In fact, unless it's about business, please leave me alone," she pleaded.

"Julia -"

She stood and picked up her mat bag. "I mean it. I've been in this sort of situation before, remember? I won't ever be the other woman again. So unless you're going to tell me your engagement is broken, it's strictly business from here on. Thanks for the coffee."

Slinging the bag over her shoulder, she strode out of the coffeehouse without a backwards glance.

Chapter Fourteen

June

"Nathan, do you have a moment? I'd like to speak with you privately."

Nathan glanced up in surprise at Ian's softly spoken request. "Of course. Should we adjourn to your office?"

"Yes, let's do that. This won't take long."

Nathan glanced across the large conference room table, noticing that Julia was deep in conversation with two of Ian's staff. Since they had arrived here for the meeting separately, it wouldn't be necessary for him to tell her to wait for a ride back.

It had been ten days since the awards banquet, and things had been strictly business between them since. In fact, they had seen very little of each other this past week and a half, and the few times they'd met had been stilted, brief, and uncomfortable.

And despite nightly debates with himself, he wasn't any closer to making a decision about the future of his engagement to Cameron. Each time he made up his mind to break things off with her so he could be with Julia, he would get a guilty conscience, telling himself that wasn't the right reason to end things. And then, each time he tried to think of what words he might use to actually break up with Cameron, a cold chill went through his entire body as he imagined how furious she would be and how she would react.

But then, on the flip side, he'd remember in all too vivid detail what it felt like to lick Julia's nipples, to thrust his fingers inside her hot, tight core, the bliss of coming hard after fucking her brains out. And the thought of never knowing those delights ever again left an empty feeling inside of him. In fact, in every possible way, Julia was probably the perfect woman for him. It went way beyond sex, too, though she was unquestionably the best he'd ever had by far. She was sweet and kind and gorgeous; she was in the same line of work and understood his business, especially since her own father was one of the greatest architects of modern day; she was neat and tidy and organized from the looks of her office. And, perhaps more important than anything else, his mother adored her. And when a guy's mom gave her unsolicited approval – well, he ought to read the writing on the wall and know that this girl was the one. It was just too damned bad that he was already committed to another girl.

Ian's office was massive and spacious, with its own small conference table and en suite bathroom. It was easily twice the size of Nathan's own office. But then, as successful as Nathan had become in recent years, he certainly wasn't in charge of several dozen exclusive five-star hotels and resorts, or a billionaire like Ian and his family members were.

"Please, sit." Ian waved a hand at the grouping of love seats and chairs arranged in a square around a low table. "This really won't take long. I hesitate to mention this at all, but I did feel you ought to be aware."

Nathan frowned as he took a seat. "Is there a problem with the hotel design? If so, we'll need to move fast since we break ground in a month."

"No, not at all. It's nothing to do with the hotel, all of that has long been settled. This is about Julia."

That startled him. "Julia? What about her?" A sudden disturbing thought entered his mind. "Are you thinking of asking her out? Is that what this is about?"

Ian gave a hoot of laughter, an oddly irreverent sound for someone who was always the refined, reserved gentleman. "No, that's not it, either, I assure you. Not that she isn't an extraordinarily beautiful woman who I'm certain would be a delightful companion. But I never mix business with pleasure. Besides, I'm well aware that the two of you are very attracted to each other. I wouldn't dream of interfering with that."

Nathan gaped at him. "Excuse me?"

Ian chuckled. "It isn't often that I can shock you, Nathan, but I see this is one of those rare occasions. Oh, I'm aware that you're engaged, but it's been obvious to me from the first time I saw the two of you together that there's something there."

Nathan fidgeted, suddenly ill at ease with this conversation. "As you've mentioned, she's a beautiful woman. I can appreciate that as much as the next man. But that doesn't mean there's anything between us. Any more than there is between you and Tessa."

Now it was Ian's turn to look startled. "Tessa? Good God, what made you think of her? She's a married woman and far, far too young for me in any event. *And* my employee, so off limits in every possible way."

"Sorry," apologized Nathan. "I didn't mean to suggest anything inappropriate. Julia is actually the one who's convinced you're attracted to Tessa."

Ian smiled wryly. "Well, I think Julia is a true romantic but in this case her imagination is getting the better of her. Tessa is a sweet, lovely girl and an exemplary employee but that's the extent of it. Now, what I wanted to tell you – in strictest confidence, of course – was that Julia has brought up the subject of working for the Gregson Group with me."

"What?" This time Nathan was truly shocked. "Was this recent?"

Ian nodded. "Very. Just a few days ago, in fact. She's sworn me to secrecy but I consider you a friend as well as a business partner, Nathan, so I thought I should tell you regardless."

Nathan frowned. "Technically, she works for Travis. I wonder why you haven't told him."

Ian rolled his eyes. "Because Mr. Headley is a known gossip and wouldn't keep it quiet. He'd very likely confront Julia about it, and I did promise her it would be kept a secret for now."

"So what did you tell her? About the possibility of a job, that is?"

Ian shrugged. "I kept it rather non-committal. Asked her what sort of job she might be interested in, given that we don't employ interior designers directly. Seems that she's always wanted to live in Paris, so she'd love to work at one of our hotels there in some capacity. I told her I'd see what I could find out. I haven't, however, made any such inquiries just yet. Not until I had the opportunity to discuss this with you first."

"I see. Well, I do appreciate the heads up, Ian. I'm rather surprised, though. I thought Julia liked her current position, and she's certainly doing a fantastic job."

Ian shook his head. "Well, of course she does, Nathan. It's quite obvious – to me, at least – that the real reason she's considering leaving has nothing to do with her job satisfaction and everything to do with an uncomfortable office environment."

Nathan sighed. "And you think this situation involves me?"

Ian gave him a wise smile. "Oh, I don't think, old chap. I know it does. Oh, she didn't say that, of course, even when I came out and asked her directly. But I consider myself quite a good judge of people, Nathan – you have to be in my position. And that girl is very much in love with you. That's why she's looking at other job options – because it's too difficult working in the same office with you while you're set to marry someone else."

"Please don't say anything to Travis about this," pleaded Nathan. "He'd have my head if he learned about this and thought I was the reason behind it."

"I won't say a word. But you also can't speak to Julia about it. Our conversation was in strictest confidence. If you don't want her to leave, you'll have to figure out a different way to keep her."

"Yeah." Nathan expelled a tense sigh. "Fresh out of ideas here. You got any?"

Ian held up his hands. "Far be it from me to give you that sort of advice. I'm a lifelong bachelor with one broken engagement along the way. I hope you'll forgive my frankness, Nathan. I certainly don't mean to butt into your personal business."

"I know you don't. And I do appreciate learning about this. Please tell me if there are any new developments."

"You have my word. Let's hope you can figure out a way to retain her. As much as I'd love to have her working for my company, I'd prefer to work with her as a designer for our hotels."

Nathan was still dumbstruck as he left Ian's office, both at the knowledge that Julia was actually taking steps to find another job, and at the revelation that Ian Gregson was quite aware that he was attracted to Julia. Apparently he hadn't been as discreet as he'd imagined, and he wondered in something of a panic who else might suspect – that nosy bastard Travis, the sardonic Courtney, his very observant PA Robyn, his own mother for God's sake.

He was still pondering how much damage control he might have to do as he was walking to the elevator, and stopped short to see Julia also there waiting for a car to arrive.

She looked as elegantly beautiful and alluring as ever today in a sleeveless pale blue crepe sheath dress that hugged all of her curves, and silver gray platform pumps. She'd wound all of her thick, abundant locks into a knot at her nape, a style that emphasized her perfect bone structure. Her lips – those lush, tempting lips – were shiny with pale pink gloss.

She glanced up at his approach but didn't smile. "On your way back to the office?"

"Yes. The meeting went well today, don't you think?"

Julia merely nodded as they stepped inside the elevator, pushing the button for the lobby. Nathan frowned as he in turn pushed the button for the garage level.

"Didn't you park in the garage?" he inquired.

"I don't own a car. I took a cab here."

He regarded her with surprise. "I didn't realize you don't have a car."

She shrugged. "Hardly anyone owns a car in Manhattan so when I moved out here I didn't have one. I've been procrastinating about buying one."

The elevator began its descent. "So how do you get around?"

"Bus. Taxi. Walking. Sometimes Angela gives me a lift or I borrow her car. When I go see my parents I rent a car for the weekend."

"So let me give you a ride back to the office then," he offered.

Julia shook her head. "I don't think that's a good idea. It's a nice day out, I might walk back."

"It's just a ride, Julia," he told her quietly. "And it's a long walk for you in those shoes. Let me give you a lift back."

"No, thank you. We shouldn't be alone together, even in a car."

He chuckled. "What's the matter? Afraid you can't keep your hands off of me?"

In the next instant he was startled when Julia grabbed his tie and yanked him towards her. Her green eyes were dark and intense as she stared up at him.

"That's exactly what I'm afraid of," she hissed. "You're wearing my favorite suit today. *And* my favorite cologne. All I could think about during that meeting was crawling under the table to where you were sitting, unzipping your pants, and giving you the best blowjob of your life. So you can see why being closed up in a car with me might not be a good idea."

He gulped, feeling his cock twitch with arousal at her deliberately provocative words. "Well, I'd say that was a matter of opinion. And I would have an extremely favorable opinion."

She let him go and stepped away. "Me, not so much. I told you what it would take, Nathan, and that hasn't changed."

The elevator stopped at the lobby level and she walked out without another word, leaving Nathan cursing softly as the doors closed after her, his balls aching.

✳✳✳✳✳

Lauren McKinnon was very aware of all the admiring – and curious – looks that she and her sister were receiving from passers-by as they lunched at an outdoor table. Unlike her far more reserved twin, however, she didn't always ignore or look away from her admirers but returned their stares boldly. If the man happened to be attractive, she might even grace him with a smile. And if he was super smokin' hot, she'd make it quite obvious that she was interested.

So far today there had been precious few who fell into the first category, and absolutely no one in the latter. It had been awhile – quite awhile – since she'd gotten horizontal with someone, and with her impending trip to Nepal it was likely going to be awhile longer. When she was on a job, she was usually all business and was extremely careful to protect herself in every way. She rarely travelled alone, especially to a more remote locale like Nepal, but there was no question of boinking one of her fellow crew members. She'd learned the hard way that business and pleasure didn't mix. Besides, she normally worked with the same crew on her assignments and they were all rather like family at this point. Fucking one of them now would just be weird.

But there were still a couple of nights left before she flew out on Saturday morning to the job site. Maybe she could talk her baby sister into going clubbing with her where she could find a willing and worthy partner for a night.

Lauren sighed as she took a sip of her wine. Knowing Julia's reticence with men, it was highly unlikely she knew of any hot clubs to check out. It was a possibility that Angela might, but given that she hadn't been on a date – or even left her flat on a Friday night – for two years, there were no guarantees.

She regarded the blond, almost pretty man in the navy Gucci suit across the table and wondered if Travis might know of any hot, swinging clubs that weren't gay hangouts. Lauren had her doubts about that one. His odd young assistant Courtney might have a better handle on it, but Lauren wasn't sure a hipster bar was what she had in mind, either.

One thing was for sure – wherever they wound up going tomorrow night,, she was dragging Julia and possibly Angela with her. Both her twin and their best friend needed some serious action and soon. Lauren had grown used to Angela's morose, almost catatonic state over the past couple of years, though she wasn't giving up hope on her just yet. Julia, on the other hand, certainly had some bug up her perky little ass. She'd been in a crappy mood since Lauren had arrived for a visit last Sunday, and Lauren was about ready to shake or slap her twin if she didn't snap out of it. Julia was being extremely closed-mouth about it, too, but Lauren was willing to bet there was a man involved somehow. It was almost impossible for the twins to hide anything from each other, even when they saw one another so infrequently these days. And if it was a man causing the usually sweet-tempered Julia to act like a hormonal bear, then she wasn't confiding in Lauren about it, which was very odd. And made the matter even more intriguing. There had to be a really good reason for Julia to keep a lid on the matter, and Lauren was determined to find out why.

The twins were both dressed appropriately for the warm, almost-summer day, though their styles were very different. Julia was in one of her usual high-fashion sheath dresses – this one of a luscious mint green with a crisscross neckline that showed a hint of cleavage. A wide cream satin sash emphasized her small waist. She wore those killer stilettos that Lauren cringed at the thought of wearing – these in a mint green with a peep toe. Julia's caramel colored curls fell long and loose down her back, her makeup flawless and glowing.

Lauren, by contrast, was far more casually attired in a white James Perse cotton tank top paired with a slim fitting black and white striped maxi skirt. She wore flat black strappy sandals and not a lick of makeup. Her own tresses – cut several inches shorter than her sister's – were bound back in a neat French braid.

Today was Thursday, nearing the end of Lauren's visit with her sister before flying off to Asia in a couple of days. Julia had cooked an incredible dinner the previous evening for Lauren, Travis and Anton – the four of them had gone through three bottles of wine – and now Travis was returning the favor by treating the twins to lunch at a tapas restaurant near his office. Lauren hadn't met Travis before this visit but was getting along famously with Julia's boss. He was a perfect foil for her own bold, sarcastic way of speaking, and seemed to thoroughly enjoy some of her more ribald comments and stories.

Travis' eyes twinkled as he gazed from one sister to the other. "I still can't get over how different the two of you are. Oh, not in looks, of course – you're identical from head to toe and everything in between." He gave a mock lascivious leer at both girls' generous bosoms. "But personality wise – it's rather startling."

Julia took a small sip of her wine and looked at her sister wryly. "You mean because I'm such a refined lady and Lauren's a bawdy tomboy?"

Lauren snickered. "Appearances can be deceiving, Travis. Julia can cuss like a sailor when it's called for, and drink like one, too."

"And you'd be surprised at how nicely Lauren cleans up," added Julia with a grin. "When you can pry her out of those baggy cargo pants and hiking boots, that is."

Travis laughed. "I'll bet the two of you together are really something when you're in the mood to have fun."

The girls exchanged a look that Travis didn't even try to interpret, guessing it was one of those weird twin-radar things. He was about to ask another question when he glanced at the entrance to the restaurant and waved at someone.

"Ah, good timing. There's Nathan, just finishing up lunch from the looks of it. You have to meet my business partner, Lauren."

Lauren, being extremely attuned to her twin's moods, immediately noticed the expression on Julia's face when the name Nathan was mentioned. It was a curious mixture of panic, annoyance, and fear. And that put Lauren on instant alert as she watched her sister's reaction to the seriously sexy man who was approaching their table.

Nathan Atwood wasn't Lauren's usual type – she didn't do guys in suits and ties – but there was no denying he was one of the handsomest, smokin' hot men she'd ever seen. She might not care for suits, but there was a whole lot to admire about the body inside of it. The glittering light blue eyes, thick dark brown hair, and sexy mouth weren't too bad, either.

The hottie grinned as he shook her hand. "So you're Lauren. I've heard a number of interesting things about you."

Lauren raised a brow. "Is that right? Well, knowing my sister she only told you the tamer stories."

Julia rolled her eyes at her twin. "That's because you don't tell me the wilder ones. You're afraid I can't handle them."

"Baby sister, I *know* you can't handle them."

Travis grinned up at Nathan. "Have a seat, mate. These two are very entertaining when they get going. Anton and I were practically rolling on the floor when we had dinner with them at Julia's last night."

Nathan glanced at Julia, and then both of them looked hurriedly away. But Lauren instantly felt the sizzling heat between the two, and suddenly several lights went on in her head at the same time, and the wheels began to spin in rapid motion.

"I can only stay a few minutes, I'm afraid," said Nathan as he pulled out a chair. "I have an appointment in less than an hour at the office."

Lauren held up the mostly empty bottle of wine. "Care for a glass?"

Nathan shook his head. "I'll pass, thanks."

"Suit yourself." Lauren poured the rest of the bottle into her glass. "I'm the only one who doesn't have to go back to work this afternoon, so I won't say no."

"Lauren's a photographer for National Geographic, Nate," explained Travis. "She's off to a photo shoot in Nepal in a couple of days."

"You're very young to have landed such a high-profile job," Nathan remarked.

Lauren grinned. "That's because I'm very good at what I do."

"Lauren won a couple of national photography contests while she was still at UCLA," explained Julia. "National Geographic sponsored one of the contests and they actively recruited her after graduation."

"Interesting. So everyone in your family is some sort of artist – your father the architect, your mother the painter, and the two of you in interior design and photography," commented Nathan.

"You're leaving out our aunt, who's a former fashion designer," added Lauren. "Aunt Maddy is the head buyer now at Bergdorf Goodman. She's the reason why baby sister here always looks so hot. I know for a fact you guys don't pay her enough to afford an Unger dress and Badgley Mishka shoes."

"She sends you nice stuff, too," retorted Julia, "but most of it gets shoved to the back of your closet. You'd rather grub around in stuff from the army surplus store."

"Hey, when you're lying in a muddy ditch trying to get the perfect shot of a herd of wild horses, you're not thinking of whether you're dressed in head to toe designer," Lauren shot back. "Besides, like you said earlier, Jules – I clean up real nice."

Travis grinned. "Do the two of you go out much together? I'll bet you get lots of attention."

Lauren hitched her head towards Julia. "Well, this one here isn't much of a party girl, but when she does let her hair down, the two of us have been known to get a little wild and crazy." She winked at Nathan, and grinned when she saw the look of alarm on his face.

'Oh, yeah,' thought Lauren triumphantly. 'There is definitely something going on here with pretty boy and baby sis. He *so* does not like the idea of Jules getting her bad girl on.'

"So, I've got to ask you this," said Travis with a naughty twinkle in his eye. "Anton and I were wondering about this after we left you two beauties last night. Has a guy ever approached both of you at the same time to suggest, uh -"

"A twin sandwich?" finished Lauren mischievously, watching in amusement as Nathan's jaw dropped and he looked horror-stricken. "Sure, that's happened before, hasn't it, Jules?"

Julia shook her head, her cheeks flushed, and she looked mortified. "I cannot believe you had the nerve to say something like that, Lauren. And in front of my bosses, no less."

"Pah." Lauren waved a hand in dismissal. "Like anything I could say would shock this one," indicating Travis. "You didn't hear some of the stories he and Anton were regaling me with last night while you were cooking dinner." She turned to Nathan and blinked at him flirtatiously. "And I'll bet the idea of two hot, sexy women at the same time isn't something you'd say no to. Am I right?"

Julia banged her head on the table while Travis laughed uncontrollably. Nathan just stared at Lauren in speechless shock, a deep red flush staining his cheeks.

"I, uh, I'm – er, engaged," he mumbled.

Now it was Lauren's turn to burst into laughter. "Oh, that's a good one. Honey, you might be engaged but you aren't dead. Unless – " she eyed him suspiciously, "you're engaged to a dude. Travis, does he bat for your team?"

Travis had tears streaming down his cheeks from laughing so hard. "No, he's straight," he managed to choke out.

"Ah." Lauren grinned saucily at Nathan "So if I got Jules drunk enough to agree, would you be interested in having a go at it?"

"Lauren, stop it." Julia's voice was firm and she sounded seriously pissed off. "I mean it. Your sense of humor is getting a little too twisted, and you're embarrassing me."

Lauren chucked her sister on the chin. "Relax, baby girl. I'm just having a little fun. Besides, it's not like you can really share a man the way you can clothes or makeup, can you?"

Julia's undoubtedly taut response was cut off by the ringing of her phone. She snatched it from her cream Gucci tote almost gratefully, as though she was desperate for an interruption.

"It's the fabric supplier I've been trying to reach since Monday," she told Travis. "Excuse me for a few minutes while I take this."

Lauren waited until her sister had walked around the side of the outdoor eating space, out of earshot, before turning to Nathan again. "So, maybe you can help a girl out here, handsome."

Nathan regarded her uncertainly. "I'm not sure I can handle one of you, much less two. And my fiancée really, really wouldn't understand."

She pinched his cheek teasingly. "Aren't you cute? No, it's not that, hot as it sounds. Before I leave for Nepal for three weeks, I need to let off some steam. My sister is too new to town, my best friend has decided to become a hermit — or a nun, I haven't figured out which — and Blondie here" indicating Travis "can only vouch for the gay bars. I'm hoping a hottie like you can tell me about a good club or two to hit tomorrow night for some action."

"Oh." Nathan seemed relieved that all she wanted were suggestions on where to go clubbing. "Sure. The two places I'd suggest are Level Two and Sapphire Sky. The DJ's and the drinks are about the best in town."

"Yeah, but what about the action?" quizzed Lauren. "Is a girl likely to get lucky at one of those places?"

Nathan coughed, clearly more than a little uncomfortable with this line of conversation. "Uh, yes, I would say so. I'd guess you would get very lucky at either place — if that's what you're looking for, that is."

Lauren finished off her wine before replying as nonchalantly as possible. "Oh, I'm not actually looking, no. I was really asking for Julia. She's been in a crabby mood this week, which means she desperately needs to get laid. Thanks for the suggestions, sweetie. I'm sure we'll find her a hot guy or two."

She was half afraid that Nathan was going to have a stroke – or scream – based on the murderous look on his face. Travis, meanwhile, couldn't stop chuckling, as though he fully shared Lauren's suspicions that there was something between Nathan and Julia.

Julia returned to the table at that moment, glancing at an amused Travis, a pissed-off Nathan, and a very satisfied Lauren, and frowned. "What's going on? Lauren, what outrageous thing did you say now?"

"Me?" Lauren asked innocently. "All I did was ask Nathan for a couple of ideas where we can have a fun girls night out tomorrow."

Nathan glowered at Lauren, getting to his feet. "I'm afraid I need to get back to the office. Enjoy the rest of your lunch."

Julia stared at his retreating form before turning to Lauren accusingly. "What the hell is going on? What have you done?"

"Just trying to start a little fire, baby sister," drawled Lauren. "Let's see if any sparks start to fly."

Chapter Fifteen

Nathan was not a happy camper as he elbowed his way through the noisy, crowded dance club. He remembered why he so infrequently patronized these places anymore, though as little as three or four years ago he'd spent many wild nights at clubs like this one. He'd grown tired of that scene, no longer interested in picking up different women and having casual, no-strings-attached sex with them. It was one of the reasons that he'd let himself be persuaded into a long-term relationship, and ultimately an engagement, with Cameron.

He continued to weave his way through the sea of bodies, completely ignoring the various women who called out suggestive comments to him, or looked him over seductively before offering up a carnal smile. It was still another reason he was glad his clubbing days were over.

He muscled his way over to the crowded bar, and was somehow able to order a Corona over the deafening noise of the music. Carefully avoiding eye contact with any of the women hanging around the bar, he began to scan the packed dance floor and surrounding tables for the person he'd come here specifically to see. He wasn't even sure if this was the club she would have wound up choosing. For all he knew, Julia and her troublesome twin were at Sapphire Sky instead. Or at a completely different club they had heard about. Or maybe Lauren had just been fucking with his head, and was lying about the whole girls' night out thing and finding a man for her sister to screw, and the twins were at home having pizza and watching chick flicks. No, there was no way Lauren would ever watch something as prissy as a chick flick, and he couldn't see Julia agreeing to the action or horror movie that would be more Lauren's style. So maybe they actually were out on the dance floor at this very moment, trolling for men, and that idea really, really pissed him off.

Nathan grimaced when he recalled Lauren's deliberately saucy words and impish smile yesterday. Somehow she knew about him and Julia, or at the very least suspected that there was something going on between them. He didn't think that Julia had told her sister that the man she'd been with in New York was actually her current employer, especially after having met Lauren for himself and seeing just how fearless she was about saying whatever came to her mind. But Lauren had definitely sniffed out something, and he was convinced that her comments about getting Julia laid had been very intentional, intended to piss him off and make him jealous.

And they had worked all too well, dammit. That he was here now in this noisy den of bedlam, and most likely on a wild goose chase, spoke volumes about his obsession with Julia. He'd been furious at the image Lauren had intentionally conjured up in his mind – that of Julia dancing with other guys until she found the one she wanted to go home with. Or even worse – letting Lauren get her tipsy enough to agree to the so-called "twin sandwich" with both gorgeous sisters heading out with one extremely lucky man.

He shuddered at that image, unable to picture sweet, refined Julia actively doing something that kinky. Lauren, on the other hand, he could definitely see in some type of three-way arrangement, though it was far more likely to be her and two men. And, he thought darkly, with both men tied up and blindfolded while Lauren brought out the whips and chains.

What his purpose in being here tonight wasn't precisely clear to Nathan. On a typical Friday night he'd be out somewhere with Cameron, but she happened to be away this particular weekend at her annual getaway with her college girlfriends. She'd flown out to Las Vegas this morning and wouldn't be back until Sunday night, so he was pretty much on his own right now. He'd started the evening by getting Chinese takeout and settling in to watch a baseball game. But, as the evening had worn on, he'd kept replaying that little scene with that vixen Lauren from yesterday, and all he could think about was Julia dirty dancing with some sleazeball, someone who'd be all too happy to take her home and fuck her senseless. Before he knew it, he was in the garage of his condo building and getting behind the wheel of his BMW Roadster.

He'd guessed that Lauren would choose Level Two since it was overall a classier, more upscale place than Sapphire Sky. Not that the tough-talking Lauren would have minded the latter's slightly earthier atmosphere, but Julia would have been more at ease with Level Two's environment.

But now, after searching the dance floor and the surrounding tables for close to a half hour, Nathan was ready to give up and move on to the next place. He had just set his empty beer bottle on the bar when he happened to glance up and recognize the tall, uber-slender woman ordering a drink to his left.

Angela. Julia's neighbor and evidently close friend to both of the sisters. The raven-haired girl looked less than happy to be here, and Nathan watched as the bartender poured her a hefty portion of Absolut Citron over ice.

"That stuff isn't exactly lemonade, you know," he drawled as he stepped closer to her.

Angela glanced up at him in surprise, and then smirked as she took a healthy swallow of her vodka. "Yeah, that's sort of the idea." She set her drink down on the bar, eyeing him suspiciously. "What are you doing here anyway? No fiancée tonight?"

He shrugged. "Free country. Why shouldn't I be here having a drink?"

"Alone? And very coincidentally in the same club that Lauren, Julia and I are at?' asked Angela sarcastically. "Seems to me like you're stalking one of us."

"Where is she?" His question was brusque, almost angry.

"Why do you want to know? I warned you last time not to fuck with her, and ever since that day she's been in the lousiest mood I've ever seen her in. And I've known her since we were eight years old."

Nathan was a bit taken aback by the steely glint in Angela's dark eyes, and the threatening tone of her voice, but he wasn't ready to back down. "This is between Julia and me. Stay out of it, okay? And just tell me where she is."

Angela sighed. "Fine. She's out there dancing. Good luck finding her. Asshole."

Without a backwards glance, she took her drink and walked off before he could stop her, and he cursed viciously. With no other options remaining, he braced himself and made his way to the dance floor, impatiently brushing off the assorted female – and male – hands that reached out as he pushed himself through the frantic throng. He felt more than a little claustrophobic at the sheer number of dancing, writhing bodies crammed onto the floor, and his head started to pound from the rhythmic bass beating through the speakers. He was close to screaming in frustration when all of a sudden he saw her. Or rather, them.

The twins were putting on quite a show as they danced together, shimmying and shaking, and drawing all sorts of attention. Lauren wore skintight, low-rise jeans, baring a shooting star tattoo at the small of her back, and a jeweled bra top that bared an awful lot of her tits. From first glance, she was every bit as well endowed as her sister and didn't seem in the least bit shy about flaunting her assets. She'd traded her flat sandals for sky high black stilettos, had curled her hair, and was even wearing makeup.

The saucy comment she'd made yesterday about "cleaning up nice" had definitely been spot on.

But it was Julia whose appearance caused him to gape and stare in disbelief. Whereas at the design awards dinner she'd gone all femme fatale, tonight she was hot chick. She wore a cream lace bustier top that exposed half her breasts, and a very short, black flared skirt that bared a lot of leg. Somehow she was able to dance wearing a pair of gold strappy sandals with a towering heel.

And dance she did. Nathan's eyes almost bulged out of their sockets as he watched her bump and grind against Lauren, before spinning away to shake her pert little ass while raising her arms above her head. A dozen or more pair of male eyes were glued to the round, half-bare globes of her tits as they jiggled and bounced before traveling down the length of her slim, toned legs.

A tall, leanly built guy with shaggy dark blond hair and stubble danced over to Julia, sliding a hand to her hip and grinding himself against her. She laughed at something he said, and rested her palms on his shoulders as they danced together – if one could call the suggestive movements of their bodies dancing.

Nathan saw red as he continued to watch Julia dance in a deliberately provocative manner, and started moving towards her, like he was stalking his prey. When he reached her, he grabbed her from behind by the hips, jerking her back against him, which elicited a squeal of surprise that he could still hear above the din of the music. She turned her head and gazed at him over her shoulder, her eyes going wide with surprise to realize he was somehow here.

He growled at the grungy-looking guy she'd been dancing with. "Get lost. She's already spoken for."

The blond guy looked more than a little wasted, and in no shape to argue, so he merely grinned and ambled over to try his luck with Lauren instead. She gave him a 'don't fuck with me' glare, and he sheepishly slinked away to find a more agreeable partner.

Nathan wrapped his arms around Julia's waist, holding her tight against his chest, and murmured in her ear, "If you needed to get fucked that badly, all you had to do was give me a call."

She gasped. "As if! And what are you doing here anyway? I know Angela didn't rat me out this time."

He began to roll his hips against her ass, bending slightly at the knees and moving her with him to the beat of the music. One hand splayed over her belly while he moved the other hand up and down the side of her hip. "Making sure nobody else gets any of this prime little ass," he breathed into her ear. He licked a hot trail from her earlobe down the side of her neck, smiling with satisfaction when he heard her gasp.

Julia leaned back into his chest, her arms sliding behind his head to clasp at the back of his neck. She gave a little "mmm" of pleasure as he ground his rock hard erection against her butt. "How are you going to make sure of that?" she asked in a husky voice. "I wasn't aware you'd put a claim on me."

Nathan worked his hand beneath her short skirt, his actions hidden by the darkly lit room and the way their bodies were plastered against each other. He groaned as he encountered the bare cheeks of her ass, realizing she wore only a tiny thong beneath that almost indecently short skirt. He gave her a playful pinch on one bare cheek. "I'm claiming you now," he hissed. "You're mine, Julia. You have been since New York and you and I both know it. No one else gets to touch you or kiss you. And they sure as hell don't get to take you home and fuck you. This belongs to me."

Her body bucked against his as he parted the crotch of her thong and slid two fingers deep inside her wet slit. Her head fell back against his shoulder as he slowly withdrew his fingers, only to inch them back inside of her.

"Oh, God," she moaned, as he continued to stimulate her, her pussy growing wetter with each slow, deliberate thrust of his fingers, and his cock growing harder with each little sound she made. He rubbed himself back and forth along the cleft of her ass, simulating the action he really craved - being buried deep inside her tight, wet cunt, fucking her so hard that she'd see stars.

"Shall I make you come right here on the dance floor?" he murmured in her ear. "Right here in front of all these people? Do you want to be a dirty girl, baby, and let all of them watch you when you get off?"

His thumb flicked over her clit, causing her to grind her butt against his huge erection. Her eyes were closed and her plump, glossy lips were open in a round 'O'.

"You naughty girl, letting me finger fuck you here in public," he breathed, loving the whimpers escaping from her throat. "You're a bad, bad girl, Julia. I think instead of an orgasm I should give you a spanking."

He withdrew his fingers from her soaking wet cunt, giving her butt another pinch, and then licked her juices from his fingers. "Mmm, you might be a bad girl, baby, but you taste real good. You taste like sin," he growled. "And I want to eat you up."

She turned in his arms, her hands still locked around his neck, and pressed herself up against his body. Nathan could feel the imprint of her round, half-naked breasts against his thin white cotton shirt, and smell the scent of her arousal as she half-danced, half-dry humped his throbbing cock.

"Kiss me," she begged, and his mouth was on hers instantly, ravaging her with his tongue and lips, eating her up. He was dimly aware of the sound of cat calls and whistles coming from other couples on the dance floor, but he was well beyond the point of giving a shit. All he could think of was how good it felt – how right – to have Julia in his arms again.

He broke the kiss to whisper urgently in her ear. "I need to fuck you immediately. Do you want to come to my condo?"

Julia stiffened in his arms. "Has she been there with you?"

Nathan knew she meant Cameron and answered honestly. "Yes. Not often, but yes."

"Then we'll go to my place. Lauren can crash with Angela tonight. Let's go tell her."

Lauren was dancing with not one but two attractive men a short distance away, one pressed up against her back, holding her swaying hips, while the other faced her as she wound her arms around his neck. When she noticed her sister wrapped up in Nathan's arms, she grinned and sidled up next to Julia, completely ignoring her two eager dance partners.

"Hey, look who showed up!" she said cheerfully. "I'd ask if you were having a good time, Nathan, but I'd say that's pretty obvious."

Nathan longed to flip her off, but didn't think Julia would appreciate the gesture. He was also half-afraid that Lauren would either dislocate the offending finger or break it in two.

Julia whispered something in her sister's ear, drawing a wide grin from Lauren and an enthusiastic nod, not to mention the knowing wink she sent Nathan's way.

"Let's go," Julia said to Nathan. "It's all set. We'll have my place to ourselves."

He hugged her close against him, dipping his head for a long, drugging kiss as they half-walked, half-stumbled to the front entrance of the club. As they waited for the valet to bring his car around, he kept her wrapped in his arms, his head resting on top of hers, his hand caressing her back. She snuggled her face against his chest, pressing her lips to the bare skin she'd exposed by undoing the top two buttons of his shirt.

"Mmm, you taste so good," she whispered. "And you smell even better. I love the way you smell, Nathan. And I really, really want you naked right now so I can lick every inch of your body. Especially this."

Sweat broke out on his brow as her small hand worked its way discreetly between their closely meshed bodies to palm his crotch. "Oh, fuck," he said harshly, through tightly gritted teeth.

Naughtily, she nipped at his earlobe. "Exactly what I was thinking. Great minds think alike, don't they? What car did you drive tonight?"

Nathan groaned into her hair as she kept stroking his cock, aware that they were drawing the interested stares of other couples waiting for their cars. "The BMW. Why do you ask?"

She blew in his ear. "Too bad. I was hoping you'd brought the Lexus so we could slip into the back seat and find somewhere to park. I'm not sure I can wait until we reach my place to have you inside me."

"Shit." He was so hard he was afraid he was going to bust the crotch of his jeans. "Don't say things like that to me, baby, when you know I can't do anything about it."

"It's your fault." Her voice was breathy, sexy. "You're the one who started grinding this big cock against my ass. I'm so wet right now I'll probably leave a stain on your car seat."

His fingers bit so hard into the sides of her hips that she whimpered. "Christ, Julia. Stop saying those sorts of things, or we're both going to see if fucking in a two-seater is really possible. Now be a good girl or I swear I'll spank you in front of all these people."

She removed her hand from his crotch. "Ooh, you bad man. Now you've only made me wetter. I hope you're prepared to lick me dry."

Nathan growled, swiping his thumb across her plush lips. "Baby, I'm going to lick your entire body from head to toe, and especially that sweet, juicy cunt. Now behave. I won't be able to get inside the car with this hard-on you've given me."

She pouted prettily, but slowly stepped back a bit from him. "Okay, I promise I'll be good."

He grinned lasciviously. "Well, I already know that."

The valet roared up in his BMW at that moment, and he was grateful that his raging erection had subsided just enough to be decent. He handed Julia into the low slung car, hissing as her skirt hitched up almost to her crotch, while at the same time her tits nearly spilled out of the tight, low cut bustier.

"You'd better plan on spending all weekend in bed, baby," he muttered low enough for only her to hear. "Because you're going to get fucked so hard and so often you won't be able to walk."

Her green eyes sparkled with mischief. "Is that a promise?"

He bent low and kissed her wetly on the lips. "Honey, that's a guarantee."

Nathan wasn't sure how he managed to drive them safely to Julia's flat, with her teasing hands all over his body – caressing his thigh, his arm, his cheek. She kept reaching over to press kisses along his jaw, his ear, the base of his throat. He groaned when she skimmed her fingers over his massive erection, only to retreat in the very next moment.

At a red light, he glanced over at her and she grinned impishly, tracing her fingers over his lips, and then gasping when he held onto her wrist and sucked her fingers into his mouth.

"You know, two can play at this little game," he cautioned.

Julia feigned innocence even as her other hand slid between his legs and cupped his balls. "I don't have any idea what you mean."

The light turned green, and he had to let go of her hand in order to shift gears. Once in gear, he slid his hand to her bare leg and then up and under her skirt to her drenched crotch.

"Damn, you weren't kidding, were you?" he breathed. He pushed the fabric of her thong aside, and slipped two fingers inside her slit. "Jesus, you're so delicious, Julia. I can't wait to eat you out. Let me have a little taste to hold me over."

She groaned as his fingers gathered up her juices, then withdrew so he could lick them off. "Mmm, you taste so sweet, baby. I think you should have a taste, too."

"Ohh," she gasped as his fingers slid back inside her dripping cunt, gathering more of the creamy fluid. Then he slipped his fingers inside her mouth, urging her to suck them. Her tongue fluttered against his fingers before sucking them hard.

"I can't wait to have your cock in my mouth instead," she breathed raggedly as he withdrew his fingers.

Nathan ran his finger over her lips, then down her throat to the tops of her breasts. "That's because you're such a naughty girl," he scolded. "You're really asking for a spanking tonight."

She gasped as he slid his hand inside the shallow cup of her bustier and pinched her nipple. "You've been making an awful lot of threats tonight – spanking me, eating me, fucking me. Sure you're going to be able to deliver, sweetie?"

He grinned. "Oh, honey, you have no idea. How far to your place?"

"Two more blocks. Park in the driveway. Angela's car is in the garage since we took a cab tonight."

"That's a relief. You neighbor was belting back the vodka pretty seriously when I saw her. I'd hate to think of her getting behind the wheel." His palm opened up to cup her full, swollen breast, eliciting another groan from her throat. "Which reminds me - I've got to know that you aren't drunk, Julia. I want to be sure you're fully aware of what we're doing right now."

She closed her eyes as he tweaked her nipple. "What you're doing right now is making me even wetter," she whispered raggedly. "And no, I'm not drunk. A little tipsy, maybe, but not so much that I can't remember stuff like the capital of North Dakota. Or count to fifty in French. Or the lyrics to - "

"I get it," he interrupted. "And we've arrived. Thank Christ. Get your keys out, baby, and hurry. Otherwise I'll throw you over my shoulder and carry you."

They got out of the car swiftly, Julia fishing her house keys out of her small clutch while Nathan locked the BMW and engaged the alarm. He grabbed her hand and pulled her up the stairs, uncaring about the towering heels she wore or if she stumbled here and there.

She'd barely opened the door and flicked on the light when he swooped her up into his arms and muttered, "Where's your bedroom?"

She looped her arms around his neck and joked, "What? The wall isn't good enough?"

He gave her a hard swat on the ass, causing her to squeal in surprise. "Baby, unless the walls in this place are made of reinforced steel they wouldn't be strong enough to hold up for as hard as I'm going to fuck you."

He found the darkened bedroom by process of elimination, and tossed her on the bed. He made quick work of his clothing but shook his head when she began to undress.

"Leave everything on. I need to fuck you just like this, baby. With that short little skirt almost baring your sweet ass cheeks and your tits half out of that sorry excuse for a top. You're never wearing that outfit in public again, by the way."

Julia's gasp of protest was abruptly cut off as he eased himself onto the bed, and took her mouth in a blistering kiss. His hands slid up beneath her flared skirt, fisting the flimsy fabric of her silky thong before tearing it off her body almost savagely. With one aggressive surge, he was deep inside her, his hugely engorged cock battering against the tip of her womb.

She cried out in shock at his sudden and demanding intrusion, her palms braced against his shoulder. "Ah, God, Nathan. I don't think - "

He braceleted her wrists and drew them over her head, holding her down. "Don't think, baby. Just feel. Feel how much I want you. I can feel your tight little cunt grasping my cock like a fist. A hot, wet fist."

"It's too much," she whimpered. "You're too big. I can't take _"

"You can take it. You know you want it. Now let me fuck you, Julia."

He groaned loudly as he withdrew from her, nearly to the throbbing tip of his cock, only to surge back inside of her, burying himself to the balls. He repeated his actions, over and over, picking up the tempo with each hard thrust until he was driving into her relentlessly. Julia's whimpers quickly evolved into gasps of pleasure as her body opened to his willingly.

He lifted her legs one at a time to wrap around his hips, giving him a deeper angle to penetrate her. The position heightened the unbelievably intense sensations as he fucked her hard, pounding into her without pause. He needed to come urgently, but also wanted to prolong the ecstasy as long as possible. And Julia hadn't come yet, though from the erotic little sounds coming from her throat he could tell she was close.

Nathan yanked the strap of her top down, baring one full, round breast. He pinched the nipple, twisting it between thumb and forefinger, and he smiled with satisfaction to see how her mouth fell open in a soundless gasp of pleasure. Knowing that she liked his dirty talk and found it arousing, he yanked the other strap down and bent to lick the nipple as her breast popped out, murmuring,

"Look at these beautiful tits. Mmm, did you want every man in that club tonight to look at these big tits and wish they were the ones who got to see them like this?"

Julia cried out as he bent his head and bit a nipple, only to soothe the bite with long, lavish licks. "N-nno. I-I just liked the top."

Nathan circled his hips, thrusting into her from a different angle, his hand cupping one swollen breast. "Well, they all liked it, too, baby. They liked how these pretty tits looked like they were going to spill out at any minute." Without warning, he gave her a hard smack on the ass, eliciting a loud gasp of surprise. "You're such a dirty girl, showing off your breasts like that. Were you hoping to meet some filthy bastard who'd take you home and screw your brains out? Fuck you hard like I'm doing now?"

She whimpered, her head thrashing wildly against the pillow as he continued to pound into her fiercely. "No, no. I only wanted you, Nathan. No one else."

"Damned right, baby. You're mine and don't forget it." He fondled one breast. "I'm the only who gets to touch these. And this." His thumb circled the hard, swollen button of her clit. "And I'm the only one who gets to make you come."

"Yes, yes," she sobbed, the tears starting to trickle down her flushed cheeks. "Oh, God, yes, Nathan. It feels so good, I'm so close. Ah, yes!"

He felt the walls of her cunt contract around him, squeezing his dick like a vise as she cried out, calling his name like a prayer. It was all he needed to plunge over the edge, his body driving hers further into the thick mattress as he came hard, his head thrown back as a cry rose from deep in his throat and echoed off the walls.

Completely spent, he collapsed on top of her, her legs still wrapped around his hips. She threaded her hands into his damp hair, holding his head to her breasts. He felt the sweet, light kisses she pressed to his temples, the top of his head, his cheek. It took awhile for his breathing to slowly return to normal, with Julia stroking his back and shoulders comfortingly.

Then she cupped his face in her hands and lifted his head until their eyes met. Even in the darkened room he could see the shimmer of tears in her eyes, but she was smiling.

"Just so you know," she whispered, "I'm not letting you go this time. You belong to me – only me – and its way past time for you to admit it."

Nathan groaned and captured her lips in a long, thorough kiss. She wound her arms around his neck, pulling him closer, as though she were afraid he'd disappear if she let go.

"I'm not going anywhere, baby," he murmured in her ear. "I'm so crazy in love with you, Julia. I'm just sorry it took me so long to come out and admit it."

She squealed in delight, scrambling from beneath him to climb onto his chest and fling her arms around his torso. "Oh, God, I love you, too, Nathan. I never, ever, thought I'd hear you say those words to me."

He pushed her damp, tangled hair from her cheek and kissed her forehead. "I think I fell a little in love with you that first time I saw you in New York. You had that sexy white dress on and some kind of purple shoes and you looked both cool and hot at the same time." He frowned. "Does that even make sense?"

Julia giggled. "Oddly enough, yes. And those shoes aren't purple. Those are my mauve Gucci's. Now, speaking of clothes and shoes, is it okay for me to get undressed now?"

He grinned. "Yes. As long as I get to undress you."

She slid onto her side facing away from him as he unzipped the little skirt and slid it down her legs. He unfastened her gold sandals, letting each one fall unheeded to the floor. Julia shivered as he ran his hands up the back of her thighs, cupping the bare, rounded cheeks of her ass.

"Guess I owe you a pair of underwear, huh?" he murmured in her ear. "Though that flimsy piece of fabric you were wearing doesn't really qualify as underwear in my book."

She groaned as he caressed the soft flesh of her buttocks. "It was La Perla, you horny bastard. That was $55 you tore off my body."

Nathan shook his head in disbelief. "For that tiny thing? Baby, you got ripped off big time. But I'm more than happy to replace it. Just as long as I get to see you model it for me."

She twisted her head around to steal a kiss. "Deal. Now, why don't you finish undressing me? You've still got promises to keep, mister."

He fumbled briefly with the back hooks of her top, and then made quick work in divesting her of it. She gasped as his hands slid around to cup her breasts, and his lips caressed her throat. "And what promises might those be, my sweet?"

Julia's breath grew labored as he tweaked her nipples, and his tongue traced her ear. "You, ah, promised to – oh, God – fuck, spank and eat me. And – ah, that's so good – you, ah, haven't completed that list just yet."

He flipped her over onto her back and loomed over her, sliding a hand over her quivering belly. "Well, far be it from me not to fulfill my promises. Though I really think you need another spanking, baby. You were a bad, bad girl tonight."

She opened her legs as his fingers tickled her pubic hair. "Mmm, but I made all that up to you. If anything, I think I've earned another fucking."

Nathan slipped two fingers deep inside her soaking wet slit. "But you're so wet it's going to take me a really long time to lick you dry. And then you'll get all turned on again and get even wetter."

Julia's head thrashed back and forth on the pillow as he added a third finger, plunging them in and out of her in a quickening rhythm. "I'm always wet for you, Nathan," she said huskily. "Every time I'm near you all I can think about is your big cock fucking me hard and I get wet."

"Jesus." He kissed a path down between her heaving breasts to her navel. "You're such a hot little thing, Julia. And every time I see you I get hard. Especially with those sexy dresses and high heels you wear. Do you dress that way just to tease me?"

She thrust her hips up at him as he nuzzled her pubic hair. "Just wanted to make sure you knew what you were missing, sweetie."

He growled. "You *are* going to get another spanking just for that. But first."

She threaded her hands in his hair, stopping him just as he was about to suck her clit. "Nathan, wait. I should wash first. I'm all sticky."

"I don't care. I want to see how you and I taste together. My cum and your juices. I'll bet it's delicious."

"Ah, God," she cried as his tongue stabbed inside her hot, wet core. Her flesh was already super-sensitized from the hard fucking he'd given her, and she quivered with each long, deliberate lick of his tongue. He licked the inside of her thighs, cleaning away the sticky traces of his semen, before nuzzling his face into the wet folds of her labia. He drew her already tender clit between his lips, sucking it hard, and she fell apart with another wrenching climax. But he was relentless, his tongue lapping at her again while her body still shook.

She slid her hands into his hair, tugging his head up. "No more," she whispered. "It's too much."

He held her still by the hips. "One more. Let me make you come one more time, baby. Then I need to fuck you again. I feel like I could fuck you all night long. That's how hard I am right now."

She groaned and acquiesced as his head dropped between her legs again. This time he alternated between licking her and fucking her with his fingers, between sucking on her clit and circling it over and over with his thumb. She was so wet her juices were running down the inside of her thighs, and he couldn't lick them up fast enough. When she came again, her body bucked up off the mattress, and the cries that escaped her throat were weak and almost plaintive.

But Nathan was relentless, too aroused and needy to let her recover, and he pulled and pushed her limp body until she was on all fours. Julia gasped as he plunged into her from behind, mounting her, and then fucking her savagely. He banded an arm around her torso, pulling her upright to intensify the angle of his deep thrusts, while he bit down on the tender flesh of her neck, marking her. Her breathing was labored, escaping from her throat in frantic little gasps, as though she couldn't draw in enough air. His balls were so full and swollen they ached with the need for release, but it felt too good to be inside of her to stop. He'd never, ever, been this aroused, this excited, and knew that only Julia would ever be able to turn him on this way.

He felt her tight little cunt begin to convulse around his cock, squeezing him like a noose as she came, her head falling back helplessly against his shoulder. She was so wrung out she could only pant, no sound escaping her throat. Only then did he allow himself to come, and it felt like the longest, hardest orgasm of his life, his cock continuing to spurt out cum long after he'd figured he was sucked dry.

It took him for what seemed like forever to gradually start to recover, and when he did he instantly felt Julia shaking in his arms. He lowered her gently to the mattress before curling up next to her, wrapping her in his arms.

Clearly exhausted, she barely had the strength to press a sweet kiss to his mouth and whisper, "I love you, Nathan," before nuzzling her face into his chest and falling fast asleep.

He realized belatedly that he, too, was completely spent, and only had time to pull the duvet up over them before joining her in a deep sleep.

✳✳✳✳✳

Nathan woke slowly, reluctant to open his eyes, and felt a lazy, indescribable sense of contentment. It was already light outside, though a quick glance at an unfamiliar bedside clock showed it to be just past six a.m. Then he turned to face the warm, curvy little body snuggled up against him, and he smiled in utter joy.

He didn't know how many times over the past eight months that he'd dreamed of this very moment – waking up again with Julia next to him in bed. He'd felt more than a little guilty after many of those dreams, especially when it had actually been Cameron next to him in bed. But this morning it was really Julia, the woman he now knew he was completely in love with, the one he was meant to be with.

The fact that he was still engaged to Cameron was one that weighed heavy on his mind, and he knew with a sense of dread he was going to have to deal with the situation very, very soon. But since he wasn't about to break things off with her over the phone or via email, he was going to have to wait until at least tomorrow night to speak to her in person. Until then, he was going to try like hell not to think about what he had to do, and instead enjoy the rest of the weekend with Julia.

Feeling in urgent need of the bathroom, he slipped out of the big, comfy bed gingerly, careful not to wake his sleeping beauty. He snagged his dark blue briefs en route, for the bathroom was not en suite but just outside in the hallway. After taking care of his needs, he padded barefoot into the kitchen to grab a glass of water.

He hadn't had time – or cared very much – last night to even notice his surroundings. He'd been in far too much of a hurry to take Julia to bed and keep her there, and everything else had faded into insignificance. This morning, though, he took in the warm, charming décor of Julia's living space, liking all of the color and the sophisticated but still homey touches. He recognized one of the paintings as a Benoit, and guessed that the framed photographs from various locales around the globe had been taken by Lauren.

Even the small, cozy kitchen was charming, with little touches like the bright yellow tea kettle, colorful assortment of hand painted ceramic coffee mugs, and a blue glass vase filled with cheerful yellow sunflowers. He instantly felt like he was at home, in a way he'd never done at Cameron's ultra-modern condo or even at his own place that he'd decorated sparsely, with few personal touches.

Without warning, the front door to the flat opened, and Lauren strode in before he could escape back to the bedroom. He was glad he'd at least had the foresight to pull his underwear back on instead of facing Julia's sister bareassed naked. He was doubly glad of this when he saw the knowing smirk on Lauren's face.

"Well, fancy seeing you here this fine morning, Mr. Atwood," she joked. "And looking mighty fine, I might add."

He flushed uncomfortably as she openly ogled his bare chest, and was grateful the high kitchen counter hid his lower body from view. "Hello, Lauren. Get lucky last night?"

She laughed. "Not as lucky as you, apparently. Actually, I spent the night upstairs at Angela's. Not for lack of opportunity, mind you."

"I would imagine you rarely have a lack of willing partners. Your sister told me once that she could pretty much have any guy she wanted. Being identical twins, I'm guessing it's the same for you."

Lauren grinned. "Julia said that? She must have been pissed off at you for some reason because she hardly ever brags about our mutual hotness. And despite what she might have told you, she typically ignores most men. Except for you, apparently. Twice now."

Nathan frowned. "What does that mean?"

"Oh, sweetie, it was pretty obvious at lunch the other day that you and baby sister had it bad for each other. She never told me the name of the guy who fucked and forgot her in New York last fall, but she did describe what you looked like. I just put two and two together." Her smile disappeared as she added, "And damned lucky for you that you've finally wised up and realized what it is you've got in her. You *are* going to break things off with your fiancée, aren't you?"

The fierce look on Lauren's face scared the shit out of him, and he was glad he was able to reply truthfully. "Yes. I'm guessing I pretty much made that decision before chasing after you wild women last night. I'd promised Julia that I wouldn't bother her again unless it was for real this time."

"Good to hear. Now I don't have to kick your ass. Which I'm very capable of doing, by the way."

"Yeah, so I've heard," he gulped.

"Lauren, are you threatening my boyfriend?" asked an indignant Julia.

Nathan glanced over at her gratefully as she stood poised in the doorway between the hall and the living room. She looked magnificent this morning, her cheeks rosily flushed, her lush mouth still swollen from his ravaging kisses, her hair falling in tumbled waves down her back. She'd wrapped a robe of pale apricot satin trimmed in ivory lace around her curvy body, and all he wanted was to carry her back to her warm, comfy bed and treat her to a lazy good morning fuck.

As Julia walked into the living room, Lauren threw an arm around her sister's shoulders, giving her a little hug. "Nope. Just wondering what took him so long to figure things out. I should have visited months ago."

Julia raised a brow to her twin. "Oh, so you're taking credit for this, are you?"

"Of course I am. Nathan here just needed a little push. Nothing like the fear your girl is going to shag some guy she picks up in a bar to spur you into action."

Nathan knew he should have been royally pissed off, but could only chuckle helplessly. "I guess I ought to be thanking you then, hmm?"

Lauren smirked. "Well, that goes without saying. You can also buy me a really expensive dinner when I get back from Nepal to show your gratitude. Speaking of which, I need to grab my stuff. My cab will be here in a few minutes."

Julia frowned. "I thought Angela was going to drive you to the airport."

Lauren grimaced. "She's not in any shape to drive right now. Better to let her sleep it off. Now, give your big sis a hug. I'll email you from Kathmandu."

The twins shared an affectionate hug, Julia cautioning her sister to be careful, and Lauren carelessly brushing off her concern.

Lauren waved at Nathan. "I'd hug you goodbye, too, sweetie, but I don't think Jules would like that very much, given your – er, lack of attire. So just make sure you treat her like a queen or I'll be using you for my next kung-fu practice."

Dressed in tight jeans, Ugg boots, and a leather jacket, her hair in a ponytail, Lauren grabbed her bags and headed out just as her cab tooted its horn. Only then did Nathan venture out from behind the kitchen counter, and instantly sweep Julia into his arms.

"Is she always like that?"

Julia grinned. "You mean my shy, sweet and submissive twin?"

Nathan made a rude noise. "None of those words would ever be attributed to your sister. More like ballbreaking, fearless, and terrifying. I assume she takes after your father?"

"Some. But truth be told Dad is kind of scared of her, too. Lauren is just – formidable. She has to be, you know, to succeed at her profession."

"The way she acts one would think her profession is an assassin, not a photographer," he muttered darkly. "Christ, I feel sorry for any guy crazy enough to make a pass at her. She's probably into tying them up or something."

Julia giggled. "Now you're just being silly." She wrapped her arms around his waist and nuzzled her face against his bare chest. He let out a low groan when she flicked her tongue over his nipple, and slipped her hand beneath the back of his briefs to cup his ass.

"I never did get to give you a good morning kiss," he murmured, threading his hands into her hair. "You looked so peaceful, so happy, that I couldn't bear to wake you up."

She sighed with pleasure as his lips trailed a path from her temple to her cheek to the corner of her mouth. "You should have woken me. From now on, every morning that we're together, I want you to wake me with a kiss."

"Your wish is my command, baby." He claimed her mouth in a lazy, lingering kiss, his tongue making slow, thorough sweeps through her mouth. Julia slid her hands up his bare back, caressing his skin, and causing a shiver of arousal to pass through his entire body.

She gasped when his hands slid up her waist to cup her breasts through the slippery satin of her robe. Her nipples were already hard as he flicked his thumbs over them. Still kissing her, Nathan deftly untied the sash, parting the robe, and revealing the lush curves of her naked body to his hot gaze.

He fondled the swollen mounds of her breasts, loving the way she whimpered in arousal. He bent his head to tug a nipple into his mouth, sucking her hard, as his other hand slid to her bare buttocks. He held her in place as he ground his erection against her mound, only the thin fabric of his briefs separating them.

"Christ, what you do to me," he rasped. "You've got me ready to explode already."

Before he could stop her, she dropped to her knees and pulled his briefs down over his hips, taking his cock in her hands. Nathan's eyes shut, his head falling back as he groaned in ecstasy as her small, soft hands stroked him. Julia ran her tongue up and down his rigid cock, flicking the slit at the broad crown, and sucking the pearly bead of pre-cum.

Her hand fisted him, squeezing him. "This is mine," she declared fiercely, mimicking his own possessive words from last night. "From now on I'm the only one who gets to touch this, lick this, suck this." She pumped him slowly. "I'm the only one who gets to have this big cock fuck me." She reached back to cup his swollen, aching balls. "These are mine, too. Got all that, lover?"

He gave a feeble laugh, too aroused and needy to marvel at how fierce and possessive his previously ladylike and reserved Julia was acting. And then he couldn't think at all as she took his throbbing erection deep into her eager mouth.

"Oh, baby, that's so good," he grunted. "So fucking good. That's it, my sweet Julia. Ah, you suck me so good with that delicious mouth."

He held her head, guiding her mouth up and down, thrusting a little deeper into her with each movement. He was close, so close to losing it, to shooting his load off down her throat. He was lost in the sweet, hungry way she devoured him, the way her lips and tongue kept bringing him to the edge, the feel of her hand fondling his balls.

But just when he was almost ready to blow, he pulled out of her mouth, and urged her to her feet. He sat on one of the barstools near her kitchen counter and pulled her between his legs.

"Ride me, baby," he muttered. "I want us to come together. Are you wet?"

In answer, she straddled his lap, lifting her hips high enough to impale herself on his cock in one swift, sudden movement. She was wet and hot, and took him deep inside her body, all the way to the root. She cried out with the intrusion but made no move to dislodge him.

Nathan grit his teeth and gripped her hips. "Jesus, baby. Give a man some warning next time. Am I hurting you?"

She twined her arms around his neck and began to bounce up and down on his rigid cock. "God, no," she breathed. "You feel so good, Nathan. I was so wet from sucking your cock, so needy. But I wanted you to come in my mouth."

He licked her nipple, her engorged breasts nearly at the level of his mouth. "Tough. I didn't get to give you a good morning fuck in bed. So I'm giving it to you now."

His hands at her hips moved her in conjunction with his thrusts, her thighs wrapped around his, his cock buried to the balls inside of her pussy. She was already so wet and aroused that it only took a few hard thrusts and the merest flick of his thumb on her clit to set off her climax. Nathan finally let himself find release, his mouth clamping down on her breast as he came long and hard.

They half-walked, half-stumbled into her bathroom where he turned on the shower taps while she grabbed towels for them. Then they were in the shower, under the hot, steamy water, washing each other, their wet, soapy hands caressing bare flesh. Julia pulled his head down to her, kissing him open-mouthed and rubbing her breasts against his chest.

"Hmm, greedy girl," he scolded, his hands cupping her bare ass as he ground himself against her. "You're not trying to get me hard again, are you?"

Julia's hand captured his rapidly hardening dick. "I think we're already beyond trying, lover," she snickered. "Are you always this horny first thing in the morning?"

He gave her a hard swat on the ass, which only caused her to stroke his cock more aggressively. "Only with you, baby," he hissed into her ear. "You'd think it had been ten days since I last came, instead of ten minutes. I should be wrung dry now – coming three times in about eight hours – but you've got me hard again. I think you're a witch. Or a devil."

She nipped his earlobe as she pumped his cock. "And I think you're a stud." She slid her hand back to squeeze his testicles, making him groan. "*My* stud. You love me so good, baby. I've never come so easily or so hard before. Only with you."

Nathan slipped two fingers deep inside her cunt, fucking her as she continued to stroke his penis. As he felt himself drawing ever closer to release, he added a third finger and flicked the hard bud of her clit with his thumb. He felt her convulse around his fingers, heard the ragged sounds of her breath, and he couldn't hold back a second longer. He came in her hand almost violently, spilling himself until his body finally stopped shuddering in release.

He groaned as he felt Julia's small, soapy hands on his still semi-hard cock, her voice whispering wickedly, "Mmm, just when we'd gotten you all nice and clean you got dirty again. Guess we'll have to start all over, baby."

Chapter Sixteen

Nathan closed his eyes in ecstasy, licking his lips and giving a little groan. "My God, woman. Not only are you drop dead gorgeous and an insatiable dynamo in bed, but you're also the most amazing cook. I can't believe you just whipped that meal up so fast."

Julia grinned. "Want another mimosa?" She held up the nearly empty bottle of champagne.

He patted his washboard flat abs. "No thanks, baby. I couldn't eat or drink one more thing." His light blue eyes twinkled wickedly. "Well, unless that thing was a sexy, green-eyed siren with long hair and big - "

She laid her index finger over his lips. "I get it. And as yummy as that sounds I need a little time to recover, stud. You weren't kidding last night when you told me I wouldn't be able to walk today. I'm a little wobbly."

He smirked. "Guess I'll just have to carry you, then. Not to mention help you with the dishes."

She squeezed his hand. "I love a domesticated man. I'll wash, you dry."

After their sensual shower, they'd tumbled back into her bed and fallen asleep for a couple of hours. This time Nathan had woken her with the slow, lazy fuck he'd promised her earlier – light, teasing kisses, gentle caresses, tender lovemaking. It had been so sweet, so beautiful, that she'd had tears in her eyes as she'd climaxed. He had kissed them away, telling her that he never wanted to make her cry again, and she'd replied that they had been tears of happiness.

Julia had quickly put together a breakfast of French toast, bacon, sliced fruit, French pressed coffee, and the mimosas. They had eaten heartily, both of them wrung out from their numerous and very physical bouts of sex, and needing the nourishment badly.

"Do you have plans for this weekend?"

She shook her head at his question. "After spending most of this past week entertaining Lauren, I'm ready for a peaceful weekend."

"Me, too. And I want to spend it with you."

Julia bit her lower lip worriedly. "You know, we haven't discussed the elephant in the room. Namely your fiancée."

He sighed heavily, thrusting a hand through his hair. "I know."

"Aren't you supposed to see her sometime this weekend? I'm a little surprised you weren't with her last night."

"Cameron's in Vegas for the weekend with some of her college friends. I'm supposed to pick her up at the airport tomorrow night. That gives me about thirty six hours to work up the nerve to end things with her."

Julia slid onto his lap, wrapping her arms around his neck and resting her head against his. "Oh, Nathan, I'm sorry. I know that's going to be hell for you. I wish there was something I could do to make it easier."

He slid his arms around her waist, burying his face between her breasts. She was wearing the apricot satin robe she'd had on earlier, and he loved the feel of the smooth fabric as he ran his hand up and down her hip.

"You make everything better just by being here. And I haven't quite figured out what to say to her. I know whatever I say isn't going to make it any less painful, and that it's going to be ugly and nasty no matter what."

She pressed a kiss to his forehead. "You probably shouldn't tell her about us. Break off the engagement for some other reason. She'll probably be a little less likely to freak out that way."

Nathan frowned. "If I do that, we're going to have to be discreet about our relationship for awhile."

Julia smiled naughtily. "You mean like keeping you all to myself? Like we're having some sort of sexy, illicit affair? Hmm, I'd have to think about that."

He nipped her earlobe. "Brat. But I'm being serious here, baby. We will need to keep things private for a little while. If you're serious about what you said, that is."

"I am. Don't get me wrong. There's nothing I want more than to announce to everyone that you're my man now, and that we're crazy in love with each other. But I'm trying real hard to be sensitive about Cameron's feelings. And to make things a little easier for you."

Nathan gave her a lingering kiss. "I appreciate that. Not sure how much it will help, and to be frank I'm guessing Cameron is going to suspect something amiss anyway. But if we can try and be a little discreet for a couple of months at least we won't be rubbing her face in it."

"Agreed. You realize, of course, that means spending a whole lot of time indoors. Alone. Wonder what we'll be able to do to pass the time."

She gasped as he cupped her breast through the satin robe, his thumb flicking over the nipple. He grinned. "I've got lots and lots of ideas, baby. Want to hear some of them?"

Julia clutched his head to her breasts as he spread the robe apart and began to lick her nipple. "Actually," she panted, "I want to hear all of them."

It was early afternoon before they finally left her flat. Nathan was still wearing last night's jeans and shirt, which was the primary reason they headed out towards his condo first. The sun was shining warmly, allowing Julia to have chosen a black and white batik printed sundress and black wedge sandals.

Nathan picked up her hand and brought it to his lips. "Even when you're casually dressed, you still look like a million bucks."

"Glad you like it."

He released her hand as he shifted gears in the BMW. "I'm still a little speechless about that closet of yours. Someday very soon you're going to put on a private fashion show for me, especially all that sexy lingerie. I'm going to be imagining you in that sheer black lacy thing I pointed out to you all day. What did you call it?"

"It's a chemise slip. Worn with a matching thong. And stockings, since it has attached garters."

Nathan groaned. "Enough. I'm trying to let you rest up in time for tonight. I'm already breaking my promise about keeping you in bed all weekend."

"But I have to feed you, honey. You'll need your strength for tonight." Julia ran a finger teasingly over his lips.

Besides stopping by his condo for clean clothes and toiletries, they were also hitting a supermarket to stock up on supplies. Julia had promised to cook him an incredible dinner, despite his repeated offers to take her out somewhere. She'd told him she liked pampering him, taking care of him, and sensed that he wasn't used to such treatment from Cameron.

His condo was about what she'd expected – a clean, modern, open space, though with less square footage then she would have guessed. It was comfortably if sparsely furnished, but she immediately picked up on the various personal touches he'd included – paintings, family photos, books and mementoes.

"So, does the decorator approve of my humble digs?"

She smiled. "Not so humble. I have an idea of what these places sell for, and you have one of the better views. But to answer your question, it's got a relaxed feel but could use some more color and a few more pieces." She bumped shoulders with him. "I could give you a discount on my services."

Nathan laughed, slipping his arms around her waist and pulling her in close. "Your boss – or at least his partner – might have something to say on that subject. Besides, I'm not sure how much time and effort I want to put into this place. I never intended it to be my main residence."

She looked at him curiously. "You have another home?"

"I own a waterfront lot across the bay in Tiburon. One of these days it will have the house of my dreams built on it. If I can ever get the design just right, that is. I must have drawn up at least six different versions so far, none of which felt exactly right."

Julia fiddled with a button on his shirt. "I'd love to see this lot sometime. I have a weakness for waterfront property, given that I grew up in an oceanfront house."

"Deal. In fact, maybe we'll take a drive over the bridge tomorrow to see it. After we have a fantastic champagne brunch at a very romantic restaurant. You are *not* going to cook for me all weekend."

She nipped at his bottom lip. "Sounds great to me, honey. Now, show me the rest of your place."

She loved the size and space of his kitchen, and sighed over the high end stainless steel appliances, especially the five burner stove. The smallish spare bedroom and guest bathroom got a quick onceover, and then she paused at the doorway to the master bedroom.

Julia looked uncertainly at the king-sized platform bed, neatly made up and covered with a plain graphite gray duvet. "Am I being unreasonable to not want to sleep in that bed?" she asked quietly. "Knowing that Cameron – and likely other women – have already been there?"

He rested his hands on her shoulders, pressing his body against her back. "No, not at all, baby. I understand exactly how you feel. I've tried real hard not to think about who else might have shared your bed."

She leaned back into him. "That didn't bother you last night?"

"I made myself block it out. I wanted you too damned bad to care."

She reached back and patted his cheek. "Well, no need to block anything out, honey. You're the only man who's ever slept in that bed. I bought it when I moved out here. My teeny tiny apartment in Manhattan would never have fit a bed that size."

He slid his hands down her arms and kissed the side of her neck. "Maybe I'll just buy a new bed. It would be worth it to have you stay over with me sometimes."

"Hmm, I think I could live with that. Though shopping for a new bed with you could be dangerous."

Nathan chuckled. "Baby, I'm always feeling a little bit in danger when you're around. Danger of being tempted to do lots and lots of dirty things."

"Tsk, tsk. My mother always warned me to stay away from bad boys like you. Good thing I rarely listened to her."

✴✴✴✴✴

"Have I told you how glad I am you wore that dress and those shoes today?"

Julia smiled across the table at her handsome, charming lover and took a small sip of her Bellini. "Hmm, I think this might be the third – no, make that the fourth time. But it's okay. I'm just glad you recognized it."

Nathan's glittering light blue gaze travelled slowly over the white Lanvin dress down to the mauve platform stilettos on her feet. "Not recognize the outfit you were wearing the first time I saw you? Baby, that particular dress has been featured in any number of my fantasies about you. Though not nearly as many as the pink dress. You'll have to wear that one again for me very soon."

She felt her cheeks flush at his intense regard. "Apparently with a different pair of panties, since that particular pair went missing."

"Ah, not true." He grinned at her devilishly. "Those very pretty pink lace panties are safely stashed away. For my eyes only."

She gasped. "You found my panties and kept them? That's – well, sort of pervy, Nathan."

He drew her hand to his lips. "I found them in the room after you left that morning and couldn't stand the thought of not taking them with me. They were a reminder of the most incredible night of my life." He ran the back of her hand against his now smoothly shaven cheek. "I thought about you all the time. Mentally kicked myself for what I'd done. And came real close at least four times to booking a plane ticket to New York and trying to find you again."

His confession touched her. "Really?"

"Yeah. One time I had the flight all ready to book on Orbitz, and was about to hit the confirm button when I chickened out. And then the more time that passed I figured you'd moved on and forgotten about me. Or that the odds of finding you again were pretty weak."

Julia traced her index finger over his lips. "But we wound up finding each other anyway. Guess it was fate."

"My brother called it serendipity."

She frowned "You told your brother about me? About us?"

He nodded. "Yeah. It was during his visit back in April, the same time you met him and my parents. The guilt had been weighing on me for months and I knew I could trust Jared not to say anything. So I unloaded on him one night over beers. Not, uh, anything too intimate, of course. Though he did ask if your boobs were real."

Julia gasped. "Well, that's rather rude. And he's a married man."

Nathan rolled his eyes. "Married but not dead. Besides, he also told me I should end things with Cameron and be with you since it was pretty obvious I was crazy about you."

She grinned. "Okay. I'll forgive him for the comment about my boobs. How do you think your parents will react to the news?"

"Considering my mom has a massive girl crush on you, I think they'll be thrilled. She asks me about you all the time, you know."

"Your mom is a sweetheart. So they won't resent me?"

He gave a little scoff. "Hardly. They weren't exactly close to Cameron. She's so attached to her own parents that it's been hard for her to bond with mine. But I can already tell it won't be the same with you."

"You're right. I really like your family, at least from the little time I've spent with them. Though it's going to take me awhile to forget about the boob comment from Jared."

"Baby, that's just guy stuff," he assured her. "Besides, you can't blame Jared. I mean, look at you. I'm not sure how I'm managing to keep my hands off you right now. If you were sitting next to me, and not on the other side of this damned table, I'd already know if you had on panties or a thong."

Julia smiled saucily. "Who said I'm wearing underwear?"

Nathan growled. "Okay, you are *so* getting a spanking when we get back to your flat."

As they lingered over a lazy brunch on the terrace of the ultra-romantic restaurant in Sausalito overlooking San Francisco Bay, Julia thought she'd never been so happy in her life. She and Nathan had already crammed so many memories into the past thirty-six hours that her head was spinning. She'd cooked him a really fabulous dinner last night – steak au poivre with mushrooms, a crisp wedge salad, tiny, buttery potatoes, and an almost sinfully rich chocolate torte. They'd fed each other bites of food, shared a bottle of expensive Cabernet, and cuddled over post-dinner cappuccinos.

And then he'd spent the rest of the night rocking her world again with his hungry, demanding lovemaking. He'd wrung several more stunning orgasms out of her – using his fingers, his mouth, his cock. He had alternated between teasing, almost playful sex to fierce, pounding fucking to slow, gentle lovemaking. She'd fallen into an exhausted slumber, completely wiped out, only to be woken in the middle of the night by his persuasive kisses and caresses for another mind-blowing session. And then it had been her turn to wake him just before daybreak by sucking his cock with slow, long pulls and deliciously arousing licks. Nathan had cried out his love for her as he'd come in her mouth, calling her his darling girl, his sweet temptress.

She'd quite intentionally chosen the white dress after learning he'd thought of her wearing it so often. And the look on his face when she'd walked out into her living room earlier this morning had been thrilling. As had the deep, scorching kiss he'd given her.

He'd taken her to this fabulous restaurant in Sausalito for a leisurely brunch, and they had sipped Bellinis, held hands, and exchanged kisses like the bedazzled lovers they were. Julia had noticed several other couples glancing their way – some with envy on their faces, others with indulgent smiles.

"We make a very attractive couple, if I do say so myself," she told him impishly.

He laughed. "After watching the way you've mastered the art of the brush-off, I still can't believe that I'm the lucky guy who finally managed to snag you."

She entwined her fingers with his. "I'm the lucky one. I love you, Nathan."

He kissed her hand. "And I love you, Julia. More than I can say. Now, let's finish up here so I can show you the future location of my dream home."

The spacious waterfront lot that Nathan owned in Tiburon was sandwiched between two sprawling, custom built homes. Holding hands, they walked the expanse of the lot, with Julia admiring the spectacular view.

"Did you keep the designs you made?"

"Most of them. I'm close, you know, but there's just something missing," he told her. "I'll let you have a look at them soon. Maybe you'll have some ideas."

"Well, I'm no architect, but I am the daughter of one so I understand the process. I'd love to look at your ideas, give you my opinion."

They lingered at the lot awhile longer before heading back to her flat. Julia knew that the time was drawing closer to when Nathan had to pick Cameron up from the airport, and his growing tension was becoming obvious. She stroked his arms comfortingly.

"It'll be okay, baby, "she assured him. "I know it's tough, but you're doing the right thing."

He pulled her onto his lap as they snuggled on her comfy sofa, burying his face in her hair. "I know. I've known for some time now that the only reason we're still engaged is because I'm afraid of hurting her. But I also know things could never work between us when I'm so in love with someone else – namely you."

She pressed a kiss to his temple, wrapping her arms around his neck. "Were you really in love with her? I mean, I guess you must have been to actually ask her to marry you."

Nathan chuckled. "I think she was the one who asked me to marry her in all honesty. We were at a wedding for one of my old college friends. I'd been drinking enough to feel a nice mellow buzz and having a really great time with all my buddies. Cameron caught the bouquet and then said something to me like 'now you have to marry me' and I just sort of agreed. Next thing I know everyone in her family and circle of friends hears that we're engaged and it became increasingly awkward to back out."

"How long had you been engaged when I first met you?"

"Not long at all. A few weeks at most. Obviously I was already having doubts, even that early into the engagement. And the way I felt the first time I saw you – not to mention what happened after that – should have set all sorts of alarms off."

Julia gave him a playful punch on the arm. "Yes, it certainly should have, you louse. Instead you broke my heart and left me swearing off men for the rest of my life."

"Not to mention leaving you there in New York in harm's way of that fucker who hurt you," he gritted out. "I still think your sister and I should pay that creep a visit. She can be my back-up. Or she can wail on your old boss instead."

She smiled. "Forget about it. I pretty much have. Especially since I hear that Vanessa's business has almost completely dried up. I got an email from Gerard a couple of weeks ago, and he thinks the bitch will be out of business by the fall. Just desserts, you know."

"It doesn't matter. I should have been there to protect you, defend you. I at least should have flown back there to beat the shit out of that creep."

"Don't, Nathan." She nestled her chin into the crook of his shoulder. "I just want to forget about it, okay? As well as how awful I felt during those months after you left. Being with you like this – I've healed a lot this weekend."

"Baby." He kissed her deeply, his tongue licking into her mouth and devouring her. She groaned as his hands were seemingly everywhere at once – cupping her breasts, skimming down the sides of her hips, caressing her ass. Deftly, he unzipped her dress, pushing the bodice off her shoulders to her waist.

He gazed hungrily at her breasts as they spilled out of her lacy white bra trimmed with lavender ribbon. "Beautiful," he whispered, sliding his hands up to fondle them, his thumbs rasping over the nipples. Julia clutched his dark head to her chest as he kissed the full upper curves of her boobs. Swiftly, he pulled one strap off her shoulder, causing one round globe to pop out of its lacy cup.

"I will never get enough of these tits," he murmured, and then tugged the nipple between his teeth before suckling it into his mouth.

Within seconds he'd stripped her naked except for her high heels, and freed his fully engorged cock. She straddled his lap, stroking his erection while he cupped her breasts and licked her nipples. Julia gasped as he thrust two fingers inside of her, where she was already wet and ready.

"God, I love how you're always wet for me, baby," he moaned. "You're so hot, so delicious."

She licked the side of his neck. "Only for you, lover. Now, you have too many clothes on. I feel like your slave girl, naked on your lap while you're fully clothed."

"Hmm, that sounds very dirty. And very, very hot," he breathed, tweaking her nipples. "I like the idea of you being my slave girl. Maybe I should bind you to the bed, blindfold you, and have you completely at my mercy."

She unbuttoned his pale blue shirt slowly, her lips following her progress. "That sounds really naughty." She ran her tongue down the middle of his chest. "And really hot. When are you going to do it?"

Nathan chuckled. "You are such a bad little girl. One day very soon I'll surprise you. Until then I want this tight little cunt riding my cock."

She rubbed her breasts against his chest, and bit his earlobe. "Only if you get naked first. Then I'll fuck your brains out."

He hurried out of his clothes in record time, and then let out a long groan as she impaled herself on his throbbing dick.

Chapter Seventeen

Cameron sensed something was wrong the moment she saw Nathan waiting for her at the end of the airport concourse. The smile he gave her in greeting looked forced, and there was a definite strain to his features.

Her suspicions only increased when he gave her an almost impersonal peck on the cheek instead of a welcoming kiss on the lips, and asked her in a monotone voice, "How was your flight?"

She linked arms with him, sidling up against his body, needing to feel physical contact with him. He didn't actually pull away, but he was definitely not making any effort to get closer to her, either.

"The flight was fine. The weekend was a blast. You got my texts, didn't you?"

Nathan nodded. "Yes, I did. Sorry I didn't get a chance to reply to most of them. How was the show last night?"

Cameron kept up a lively conversation while they waited for her luggage and during the drive to her condo, aware that it was largely one-sided. Nathan made only brief, polite comments from time to time but was otherwise silent and most definitely preoccupied. She had a very unsettling feeling but was reluctant to come right out and ask him what was wrong, for she feared she wasn't going to like the answer.

When they reached her condo, Nathan carried her suitcase upstairs as well as a large paper shopping bag that she knew she hadn't brought with her from Las Vegas. She frowned as he set it down beside her suitcase.

"That's not mine," she told him. "Why did you bring that inside?"

Nathan looked solemn. "Because it has all the things you had at my condo inside it. I'll get the stuff I have here before I leave."

Cameron felt like she'd taken a right hook to the jaw. Her legs felt wobbly all of a sudden, and she quickly sank into a chair. "What? Wh-why would you do that? Nathan – what the hell is going on?"

His voice was gentle. "Cam, I'm so sorry, but I can't marry you. I've been giving it a lot of thought for awhile now, and I know that it would be a mistake." He paused when she didn't answer him, when she *couldn't* answer him, for she was speechless with shock. "I'm sure this comes as a shock, and I'm guessing you're pretty pissed off right now, which I totally get."

"Jesus, Nate," was all she could rasp. "This was the very last thing I expected. I mean, if you weren't ready to get married you should have said so. Like before I started making wedding plans. But, okay, let's ease off for awhile, put the plans on hold."

He ran a hand over his face. "You don't get it, Cam. It's not just that the engagement is off. You and I – it's over. For good."

She fought down a rising sense of panic, shaking her head. "No. No, I don't accept that. I am not going to go through this again. This was supposed to be the real thing, Nate, the one that finally worked out. How in the world can you do this to me after what I've been through? You can't do this, Nate."

She got up and started pacing almost frantically around her living/dining space, shaking her head, and wrapping her arms around her waist.

"Cam, calm down, okay?" he said soothingly. "Christ, I know this is unexpected and I wish like hell I could make it right for you."

Cameron stopped in front of him, and threw her arms around his neck, pressing close against him. "Then do it. Don't leave me, Nate. God, I love you so much. You're breaking my heart here. Please, give me another chance."

Gently, he tried to disengage her arms and step away from her. "Cameron, no. I'm sorry, but it's over. I've thought about this for weeks, and it's just not the right thing for me. For us. I'm never going to be the man you deserve, the one who can make you happy."

The tears started falling down her cheeks and she choked on a sob. "But why? I don't understand. What happened to change things? Was it something I said or did? Can't we talk this out, fix whatever is wrong? God, give me a chance here!"

"It's nothing you did or said, Cam," he assured her. "But I should have never agreed to this engagement, not when I didn't feel completely right about it. And I've tried to make it work but things are over. I know I'm being a complete bastard to break up with you this way, but I'd be a worse asshole to stay with you for the wrong reasons."

Cameron glared at him through tear-filled eyes. "You *are* a bastard, no question there. How *could* you, Nate? My God, I'm going to be a fucking laughingstock again – the girl with three broken engagements. You have no idea how humiliating this is going to be for me. I'm thirty-five fucking years old, Nate! Who the hell is going to want to marry me now?"

He winced as her voice grew louder and louder. "Cameron, that's ridiculous. What difference does your age make? You're a beautiful, accomplished woman and you *will* meet the right man. I'm sorry but I'm not him."

She thrust her hands through her hair, which was back to being chin-length after having the extensions removed. "How am I going to tell my parents? God, my mother is going to be furious. And I just left all my girlfriends in Vegas after talking about wedding plans all weekend. They're planning on giving me a bridal shower, and a bachelorette party. Now I have to tell them to forget it. Jesus, how humiliating!"

"Again, I'm desperately sorry," he told her gently. "But none of those things are valid enough reasons to stay together when one of us isn't committed to making it work."

"You know, now that I think of it, you've been distant for awhile now," she said slowly, a niggling suspicion beginning to form in her mind. "For several months, in fact. Have you been having doubts all that time?"

Nathan shrugged. "I can't say for certain when they began but it's been awhile."

Cameron pointed a finger at him accusingly. "*I* think you started having doubts when that little whore began working in your office. And the more I think about it, I'm fairly sure you're breaking up with me because you're involved with her. How long have you been fucking Julia?"

The startled expression on his face was a dead giveaway, and now Cameron knew the real truth, despite his initial attempt to deny it. "Cam, that's not why I'm breaking up with you," he began. "It's just not -"

"Have you fucked her or not?" she screamed. "Just answer me."

Nathan hesitated but finally gave a brief nod. "Yes."

She slapped him as hard as she could, with all the anger and hurt and humiliation she was feeling at the moment. "You bastard," she hissed. "You filthy, lying, cocksucking bastard! How could you cheat on me – and with that bitch? How long has it been going on?"

He rubbed the visibly reddened mark on his cheek gingerly, and it gave her some perverse sense of satisfaction to know she'd hurt him as he had hurt her. When he didn't answer her, she gave him a hard shove.

"Answer me, you sonofabitch!" she demanded. "How long have you been fucking that whore?"

"Not long," he replied quietly. "We never meant for this to happen, Cam. Never meant for you to get hurt."

"Well, you should have thought about that before you fell into bed with her," she spat. "You could have at least ended things with me before you fucked her. I never would have thought you to be such a heartless bastard, Nate."

"Cameron, you need to know that I would have ended things between us soon anyway, whether Julia was in the picture or not," he told her in a gentle but firm voice. "So don't blame her for this."

Cameron fought to control the rage that blazed through her. "Don't blame her? My God, who else am I supposed to blame? If she hadn't come to town and thrown herself at you, none of this would be happening. *All* of this is her fault and she's going to pay for it."

"No. Leave her out of this. I get that you're pissed off and that's to be expected. But take your anger out on me, not Julia."

"Fuck your precious little Julia!" she screeched. "She's probably been panting after you since her first day on the job – shoving those big tits and wiggling that ass in those tight dresses in your face every day. What a slut she is, going after someone else's fiancé. Doesn't she have any shame?"

"It wasn't like that," he told her solemnly. "Neither of us wanted this to happen this way. We wanted to do the right thing."

"Then why didn't you?" she yelled. "Why couldn't you keep your dick in your pants?"

"Because I'm in love with her."

Cameron stared at him in horror then shook her head. "No, you can't be. Goddammit, Nate, that can't be true. You just want to fuck her, that's all. Once you get tired of her, you'll see what a mistake you're making, what you're throwing away. Or she'll get tired of you and dump you, move on to someone else. Then you'll come running back to me, begging me to take you back. That's exactly how it's going to happen."

"No, Cam. I'm sorry, but you can't think that way," he said firmly. "I'm not coming back to you. And despite what you think of Julia, she didn't pursue me. It just – happened. I'm going to get my things now, and then I think I should go."

She could almost taste the combined flavor of bitterness and desperation rising in her gorge, and she clamped a hand around his arm. "No, no. Please don't go, Nate. Don't end this. I love you so much. God, I'll do whatever you want as long as you don't leave me."

Gently, Nathan removed her hand from his arm. "Cam, stop this. You're just getting yourself more upset. I'll be right out and then I'm going to go."

"Nathan -" her voice drifted off as he strode resolutely down the hallway towards her bedroom, where he kept a few of his things. In the brief time he was gone, Cameron's anger reached the boiling point as she paced furiously around the room. She grabbed a bottle of vodka from her bar, and poured herself a shot, bolting it down in one swallow.

She was on her fifth shot when he emerged, carrying another paper shopping bag. He looked expectantly contrite, sympathy in his eyes, and for some reason that infuriated her even more. The last thing she wanted was his fucking pity.

"So this is it," she stated bitterly. "You're just taking your stuff and walking out. I never would have pegged you as such a heartless, unfeeling bastard, Nate."

He paused with his hand on the doorknob. "I wish there was something I could say to make all of this easier. But I know I can't, so I'm just going to leave. Good-bye, Cam."

As the door shut behind him, she tossed back another shot of vodka. Then, finding the bottle empty, she hurled it against the far wall, cursing vividly as it shattered.

"This isn't over, Nate," she hissed. "You and your little whore are really going to regret screwing me over like this. Someone needs to pay for humiliating me."

※※※※※

Julia hurried to open the door at the sound of Nathan's knock. He'd sounded awful when he had called her a few minutes earlier, and had gratefully accepted her invitation to spend the night.

Neither of them spoke as he walked inside, and Julia simply wound her arms around his waist, resting her face against his chest.

"I love you, Nathan."

Without a word, he bent and picked her up, carrying her into her bedroom. He laid her down gently before crawling up beside her, wrapping her in his embrace.

"I love you, too," he whispered into her hair. "Just let me hold you for awhile, okay?"

In answer, she snuggled more closely against him, entwining her legs with his. They were silent for several minutes, and Julia thought perhaps he might have fallen asleep.

"She knows about us. And I couldn't lie."

Startled, she propped herself up on an elbow and stared down at him. "How could she possibly know?"

"She's been suspicious for quite awhile, apparently. When I told her it was over between us, she couldn't let it rest and kept pushing for reasons. Guess I'm a terrible actor because she must have seen the truth in my face."

Julia caressed his cheek. "Speaking of your face, it looks like she got you pretty good. Let me get some ice for that bruise."

"It's okay, baby. It doesn't hurt, and I'm guessing it'll fade by morning. Nothing I didn't deserve."

She kissed the corner of his mouth gently. "I'm sorry."

He pulled her head down for a longer, lingering kiss. "It was worth it. And it needed to happen. We had good intentions in not telling her about us, but it's actually a relief that the truth is out. Now we don't have to hide."

Julia pouted and pushed his shoulders to the mattress before straddling him. "Aw, and I was looking forward to having this secret, dirty little fling with you."

Grinning, he untied the sash of her robe, pushing it from her shoulders. 'Well, I want this to be much, much more than just a fling. But no reason it can't be dirty." He flicked her nipple through the cream lace bodice of her short nightgown.

She groaned as he slipped the thin strap off her shoulder, baring one swollen breast. "Mmm, I was always a nice girl until I met you. Now all I want is to do lots of nasty things with you."

"You mean like this?" He suckled one erect nipple into his mouth, baring her other breast at the same time.

She clutched his head closer as he feasted on her aching breasts. "God, yes, exactly like that."

✳✳✳✳✳

"Hey, you got a few minutes?"

Travis looked up from the designs spread over most of his desk, and rolled his eyes in exasperation at Nathan, who had already strolled inside his office.

"No, not really, but that's never held you back before. What's on your mind, Nate?" he asked in resignation.

His business partner was grinning stupidly from ear to ear, and Travis cocked his head with sudden interest. Nathan hadn't been in a good mood like this one appeared to be in a very long time – weeks, perhaps even months.

"I just have some news to share with you. I thought under the circumstances that you should be one of the first to know." Nathan took a seat in front of the desk.

Travis leaned back in his chair. "From that dopey grin on your face, I'm guessing its good news. I'm also guessing it's not necessarily business related."

"Right on both counts. And I really shouldn't be grinning about this but Cameron and I are over. I broke things off with her last night."

Now Travis was the one who was grinning. "Well, halle-fucking-lujah! It's about time you did something about that. I mean, no offense, but I really did not know what you saw in that woman. How did she take the news?"

Nathan grimaced, rubbing a spot on his cheek that Travis now noticed was slightly reddened and bruised. "Uh, not well. I'm lucky I got off with one good slap. She may be skinny but damn she's strong. Overall I'd say she's mighty pissed off and upset, and that I haven't heard the last of her. Especially given the circumstances behind our breakup."

Travis rose and opened a cabinet door in his credenza, drawing out two crystal tumblers and a bottle of very expensive single malt Scotch. He poured them both a drink and handed Nathan a glass. They clinked glasses and bolted down the contents.

Travis screwed up his face in distaste. "I still don't know how you stand that shit. I keep that here mostly for clients, but give me a good martini or expensive Chardonnay any day over that stuff."

Nathan's grin returned. "And you're bolting it down at only nine-thirty in the morning, too. What a badass you are at times, Travis."

"Hey, getting that bitch out of your life is something worth drinking about. So now, spill. What are these aforementioned circumstances?"

Nathan set his glass down. "Understand that I would have broken things off at some point with Cameron anyway, okay? And I know you won't call me a bastard for this like a lot of people probably will. But there's someone else. And I wasn't going to tell Cam about her initially, but she's too sharp and guessed the truth. Naturally, her knowing that made things ten times worse."

Travis smiled knowingly. "Yes, I would imagine that Cameron was seriously pissed off to learn you were breaking off your engagement so that you could be with Julia." He chuckled at the look of astonishment on his partner's face. "You honestly think I didn't know how you felt about her? Christ, you can be awfully dense at times, Nate. I think I knew before you did."

Nathan shook his head. "Not possible. Because what you don't know is that I met Julia months before she started working here, when she was still living in New York. It was when I attended the convention last September."

Travis stared for a moment, and then grinned. "I knew it. I knew when the two of you met here in my office that there was something going on. I assume when you say you quote unquote 'met' her in New York, that - "

"We hooked up. Oh, yeah, big time. Mind-blowing, incredible sex, nothing else can even begin to compare."

Travis held up a hand. "Okay, no details. I have to work with both of you, remember? So let me get this straight. You met her in September. Weren't you already engaged to Cameron by then?"

Nathan had the good grace to look guilty. "That's the really bad part of this. I was a shit to Cameron for cheating, and an even bigger one to Julia for not being honest with her."

Travis frowned. "So what a hell of a coincidence – you being my business partner. I'm kind of amazed that she would have even applied for this job knowing she'd have to see you every day."

"Uh." Nathan looked chagrined. "She actually had no idea I worked here. We, um, didn't get around to exchanging last names at the time. Or cities of residence. Or professions. The fact that Julia already knew you and wound up in San Francisco was way more than a coincidence."

"Serendipity." The word popped into Travis' head automatically.

Nathan gazed at him curiously. "Weird. Jared said exactly the same thing. How come I never heard that word before – or knew what it meant – and now two people have both used it to describe this situation with me and Julia."

"Because you're a moron. But I'm glad to see that your taste in women has improved by leaps and bounds." Travis' tone grew serious. "I trust you're going to treat my girl like an absolute queen from here on end."

Nathan's grin stretched from ear to ear. "Like a fairytale princess. When I first met her I told her she was as beautiful as a princess in a storybook."

"Oh, brother. And she actually fell for a dorky line like that?"

"Hook, line and sinker." A smile played about Nathan's lips. "And I fell for her like a ton of bricks. Now, I'm fresh out of clichés and I have a client coming in soon, but I wanted you to know in case any office gossip starts floating your way. But Julia and I plan on being discreet about this, especially for the next few weeks."

"Ah, so I won't see the two of you locked in a passionate embrace in the lunchroom?"

"Hmm, don't tempt me. It's been hell these past few months having to keep my hands off of her. But I'll try to be professional about it here at the office."

"Well, where the hell's the fun in that?" said Travis indignantly. "Office sex is supposed to be naughty. So I wouldn't hold it against you if you wanted to do the horizontal tango with Julia in your office."

"Yeah, well, she might have something to say about that. But I'll tell her we have your blessing."

"In more ways than one, Nate. She's the right girl for you, perfect in fact. Can I tell Anton? He's such a romantic, he once told me he thought you and Julia would have made beautiful babies together."

Nathan had a horrified look on his face. "God, it's way too soon to think about babies. Tell Anton to keep those sorts of happy thoughts to himself for awhile. Julia and I are technically still getting to know each other at this point."

"Oh, sounds like you're very well acquainted in certain ways. And if the sex is hot, then everything else just falls into place. I've seen the way you two look at each other when you think no one notices. I'm guessing your bed sheets are burning up."

Nathan winked. "That's a pretty safe bet. Thanks for the drink. And the support."

"Don't forget to treat my girl like a queen. And let's all get together for dinner soon."

"It's a date."

Travis chuckled to himself as Nathan left. 'I knew it. I just knew there was something between those two,' he thought merrily. 'Maybe I am psychic after all.'

Chapter Eighteen

Nathan couldn't remember the last time he'd been in such a fantastic mood. Of course, the day had gotten off to an amazing start by waking up in Julia's bed with him spooned up against her warm, curvy little body. Since she had really wanted to go to her yoga class at six a.m., he'd restrained himself from sliding inside of her and waking her with a slow, sleepy fuck. He had dropped her off at her class, and then gone for a brisk run, returning in time to drive her back to her flat. This time he hadn't been able to resist her, and they'd taken a hot, steamy shower together. He'd been hard as a pistol within seconds of soaping up her wet, naked flesh, and had taken her right there in the shower, her breasts pressed up against the tiled wall while he fucked her from behind. He could easily see himself starting his day off in a similarly pleasant manner from here on end.

She'd fed him coffee, juice and granola parfaits, and then he'd thoroughly enjoyed watching her get dressed. Nathan had been instantly hard again as she'd shimmied into a bra and panty set of nude lace and silk, then rolled on sheer, thigh-high stockings.

Sweat had broken out on his brow. "Jesus, baby, do you have any idea of how fucking hot you look right now? You're like every centerfold and lingerie model rolled into one irresistible package. You'd better put that dress on quickly or you're going to get fucked again."

Julia had winked at him. "Promises, promises. Hmm, not sure this is the right dress, though. I think I should try on five or six others to be sure."

He'd growled. "Put the fucking dress on now or I'm going to drill you into that wall."

She had laughed and obediently put her dress on, though that had given him scant relief. Her dress was also nude colored, with fitted panels in front, and a low, square neckline. The fabric clung lovingly to her hips and ass, and offered a tantalizing glimpse of cleavage. He had groaned when she bent down to fasten the ankle straps of her gold metallic platform sandals, for the action had given him a tempting view of her lush breasts.

"Christ, I don't know how I'm going to get any work done today," he'd complained. "All I'm going to be able to think about is what's underneath that sexy dress. And fair warning, baby – don't you dare bend over like that in front of anyone but me. No one else gets to see those tits, understand?"

Julia had smiled at him teasingly. "My, someone has become very possessive as of late, hasn't he?"

He'd pulled her into a tight embrace, nuzzling the side of her neck and smelling her intoxicating perfume. "I told you Friday night, baby. I'm claiming you."

On the drive to work they had agreed to tell only a few people that they were now together – Travis, Robyn, Lauren, Angela, and Nathan's parents. Everyone else – including Julia's parents who didn't even know about her past with Nathan – would find out as time went by. It was a relief to Nathan that Cameron knew the truth, but he still didn't want to flaunt his relationship with Julia in her face. He and Cameron had quite a few mutual friends, and word of their broken engagement would certainly spread quickly. He was more than content to let her break the news first, though he suspected she was in no hurry to tell people. And he wasn't in any hurry to deal with the fallout that was sure to occur. But if a few friends got pissed off at him and gave him the cold shoulder for breaking up with Cameron, it would still be worth it in order to have Julia in his life.

Travis's reaction had been expected, and Nathan was grateful for his unequivocal support. Robyn, too, had beamed at the news, and he sensed his PA had never been much of a Cameron fan.

"Julia's the loveliest, sweetest girl," gushed Robyn. "Always so kind to me, and such a lady. Your mother absolutely adores her, you know."

Nathan had nodded wryly. "Yes, I'm well aware. She was asking me about her just last week."

"I probably shouldn't tell you this, but what the hell – seems like a good time to tell a few secrets," snickered Robyn. "Your mother told me she wished Julia was the one you were engaged to instead of Cameron. Looks like she's going to get her wish."

Nathan had held up a hand. "Whoa. First, Travis mentions babies and now you're talking engagement. Give us some time to just kind of hang out, get to know each other, enjoy things, hmm?"

"Fine. But if you let this one get away, you're an idiot. And I might quit," she threatened mockingly.

He shook his head. "Not a chance in hell of either of those things happening. But all in good time with Julia, okay?"

He'd been too busy the rest of the morning to call his parents, and the more he thought about it the more he wanted Julia with him – on speakerphone – when he told them.

Unfortunately, he'd had a lunch meeting with clients that he couldn't re-schedule, so it was mid-afternoon before he saw Julia again. She, too, had been in a meeting and was just finishing up with her clients in the small conference room when he happened to walk by. The clients were an older couple – late fifties, perhaps early sixties – and judging by their well-groomed, well-dressed appearances, quite well-to-do.

Julia looked extremely pleased to see him and introduced her clients. "Burt – Diana – let me introduce you to the co-owner of our firm – Nathan Atwood. He heads the architectural division. Nathan – these are our clients, Burt and Diana Newton."

Nathan shook hands with the couple. "A pleasure to meet you both. I trust your meeting with Ms. McKinnon went well?"

"Oh, goodness, yes," gushed Diana. "What fabulous ideas she has for our place. Burt and I just moved to the city from Hillsborough, and none of our furniture really fits into our new space."

"Downsizing," explained Burt. "We had an eight thousand square foot mansion, but with our kids all grown up and scattered across the country it was way too big for us. We always wanted to live in the big city so now we're in a condo on Russian Hill."

"Well, San Francisco is an exciting place to live, and I'm happy you chose our firm to help you realize your dream. And equally happy that Ms. McKinnon has been able to give you some design ideas." He fished a business card from his jacket pocket and handed it to Diana. "Please, if I can be of any assistance, don't hesitate to call me."

The Newtons exchanged a look and nodded as Diana took the card. "Thank you, Nathan," she beamed. "Once we get settled into our new home, we might be looking to remodel a vacation home we also own near Lake Tahoe. I assume you handle that type of project?"

"Absolutely. I'd be delighted to assist you with that if and when the time comes. A pleasure to meet both of you." Then he added to Julia, "Could you stop by my office for a moment when you're finished? I have a small matter to discuss."

Julia gave him a secretive little smile. "Of course. I'll be there shortly."

She was true to her word, hovering in the doorway of his office five minutes later. "You wanted to see me – sir?" she asked saucily.

He grinned and beckoned her in, relieved to see that Robyn wasn't at her desk. "I did. Come in and shut the door."

The second the door shut he was on her, sweeping her into an embrace and lifting her feet off the floor. She squealed in surprise, her hands gripping his biceps until he set her down.

"I missed you," he murmured huskily, his lips tracing a hot path down the side of her throat. "It's been hours since I've seen you. And even longer since I fucked you."

She traced her fingers along the buttons of his shirt. "You're insatiable, aren't you? How many orgasms have you had in the past seventy-two hours?"

His lips trailed across her shoulder blades to the upper curves of her breasts. "Too many to count, but not nearly enough to satisfy me." His hand slid down her back to cup the luscious curves of her butt, and held her still as he slowly ground his rapidly hardening erection against her cleft. "It's your fault, baby. All I've been able to think about all day is how you look in this sexy dress, and the even sexier little bits you've got on underneath."

She gave a little sound of pleasure as his thumb brushed over her nipple. "Ah, God, that feels so good."

Nathan ran a hand up and down the side of her hip. "As gorgeous as you look in this dress, I wish like hell it wasn't so tight. It makes it that much harder to pull up the skirt so I can fuck you."

She nibbled on his earlobe. "I am not letting you fuck me here in your office. *So* inappropriate."

"It's okay. We have Travis' permission." He laughingly told her what Travis had said earlier that day.

Julia's mouth dropped open. "That pervert. I'll bet he'd get off on eavesdropping, too. Or even watching."

He threaded his hands into her hair, holding her head still as he kissed her long and deep and wet. "Mmm, does that idea turn you on? Do you like the idea of other people watching you get fucked?"

She moaned as he slid a hand to her crotch and rubbed her ultra-sensitive flesh through the fabric of her dress. "Oh, God, that feels so good. But, no, I only want your eyes on me. I mean, kissing and stuff is fine in public to a degree, but I don't really go for heavy PDA."

He moved his hand and simply held her against him. "Good. I know some guys get off on voyeurism but I want you all to myself. I don't even like anybody seeing these beautiful tits, much less watching me fuck you. It was driving me crazy just seeing the way that dirty old man was looking at you."

"What?" She lifted her head from his shoulder and stared at him. "Who are you talking about?"

"Your new client. Burt. Oh, he was trying like hell to be discreet, especially since the missus was right there, but he was definitely sneaking peeks at these beauties." He trailed a finger over the swell of her breasts.

Julia flushed. "Come on, that's not true. I mean, he's older than my dad, for God's sake. That's just – eww – ten kinds of creepy."

"I agree. But the dude is old, not dead, and he's still a man so therefore he's going to admire the goods."

She grimaced. "Great. Next time I meet them I'll be sure to wear something less revealing."

"Yeah, well, I've seen your closet. There isn't much in there that isn't revealing in one way or another. And as many clothes as you have, I might have to make a few additions to your wardrobe."

"Like what?" she asked, frowning.

He gave her a playful swat on the ass. "Like some fuller skirts so it's easier to pull them up and bare this sweet little butt." He squeezed on round cheek. "One day soon I'm going to have you in here. Bend you over that sofa there, pull your dress up, and mount you. Fuck you until you're raw and shaking, until you can't walk a straight line."

"Stop," she pleaded. "You're making me so horny I can't bear it. And my panties are already soaked."

"Really?" He grinned naughtily. "Well, I have an extra pair around here somewhere."

Aware of her gaze on him, he pulled out the file drawer and fished around until he found the infamous pair of pink lace underwear. He twirled them around on his finger.

"These look familiar?"

Julia laughed. "I can't believe you've kept them all this time. Did you used to take them out and stare at them or something?"

Nathan was suddenly serious. "Actually, yes. Not often – I used to have to fight the urge all the time. But sometimes I just couldn't resist and I'd have to touch them. I know I sound like a total pervert, but they were the only thing I had of yours."

"I guess it's sort of romantic – in a pervy sort of way," she admitted.

"So do you want them or not?"

"You mean to change into now?" She shook her head. "I kind of like the idea of having wet panties for the rest of the day. It makes the anticipation that much hotter."

"Exactly what are you anticipating, baby?"

She paused with her hand on the doorknob. "That you're going to eat me out, and then lick up all the juice running down my legs right now. For starters."

He closed his eyes, his erection growing to painful, throbbing proportions. "Jesus, baby. You're damned right that's just for starters. I'm glad I had a big lunch. I've got a feeling I'll be burning off a lot of calories tonight."

She slipped her index finger into her mouth, sucking it before running it over her bottom lip. "You'd better have an afternoon snack, too. You've made me really, really horny." She blew him a kiss. "Love you, baby."

He sank down helplessly into his chair as she sashayed out of his office, mentally calculating how many hours it would be until he could be inside of her again.

$$*****$$

Julia glanced around the interior of the restaurant uncertainly, before looking back at Nathan. "Are you sure we ought to be here? I know for a fact that several people from the office eat here all the time."

'Here' was a bar and grill just around the corner from the office that served comfort food, but was usually frequented by their co-workers more for the drinks. It was the establishment of choice in the office for celebratory birthdays, promotions, snagging big projects, etc.

Nathan shrugged, seeming completely unconcerned with that fact. "So what? Baby, the news that we're together is bound to get around eventually. Your boss is the worst secret keeper I've ever met, so I'm amazed he hasn't told everyone in the office already." He reached across the table and captured her hand. "Besides, I want everyone to know we're together. I've had to hide my feelings for you for too long, Julia. Right now I'm about ready to shout at the top of my lungs that I'm crazy in love with you."

She couldn't help the warm, tingly feeling that rippled through her whole being at his earnestly spoken words. "Love you too, honey." She took a sip of her water. "By the way, I got an email from Lauren earlier today. She said to tell you you're welcomed, and that you still owe her a really expensive dinner."

He grinned. "That I do. When is your terrorizing twin due back stateside?"

"In about ten days. Why do you ask?"

"Will she be hanging around awhile or heading back to her home? Where exactly does she live anyway?"

"Lauren lives in a cabin in Big Sur," she told him. "A cabin that my father built by himself and where he was living when he met our mother. He was really just getting started as an architect, and Mom was spending her first summer after college on the coast to find inspiration for her paintings."

"I take it she found that and more."

Julia nodded. "Love at first sight they tell me. They were living together in that cabin before the summer was half over, and the rest is history. But they kept the cabin even after Dad built the house in Carmel, and Lauren always talked about living there someday."

"But not you?"

She gave a small shudder. "No. I mean, its beautiful there and a great little getaway. But I always loved my visits to New York to see my grandparents and Aunt Maddy. From the time I was a little girl I always wanted to live in or at least near a big city."

He kissed her hand. "I'll take you back to New York one day soon. Book a room at the Plaza. And be there when you wake up the next morning."

"I'd like that." She caressed his cheek. "And I'd love for you to meet my aunt, too."

"Not to mention your parents. Have you told them about me yet?"

"Yes. Not the part that we met in New York, or that you just broke off your engagement," she added. "As far as I'm concerned, they don't need to know any of that. All they need to know is that I've met the man of my dreams, and that I'm insanely in love with him."

"Ditto. And speaking of parents, I understand my mother called you again. How many times does this make?"

Julia smiled, not the least bit annoyed that Alexis had phoned her several times over the last ten days. She and Nathan had called his parents together and told them the news. As expected, Alexis in particular had been over the moon, and had insisted on getting Julia's phone number.

"Not really that many. This morning's call was four times, I think. She called to officially invite me to Thanksgiving."

"Christ, that's over four months from now," he replied in exasperation. "Let me know if she calls too often, okay? She can be a bit of a pest. And speaking of calling - that reminds me. Give me your phone for a minute, baby."

Puzzled, she took her phone from her brown leather satchel and handed it to him, then watched as he started scrolling and typing. "What are you doing?"

Nathan's mouth tightened. "I went ahead this morning and changed both my cell and home numbers. I want you to be the first to have them."

"Why did you have to change them? Oh. Has it really gotten that bad?" she asked in concern.

Within forty eight hours of their breakup, Cameron had begun calling, texting, and emailing Nathan incessantly. At first the tone of her messages had been needy, pleading, begging him to reconcile and take her back. Then they had gradually become angry, insulting and borderline threatening. That was when Nathan had changed the locks on his condo, having neglected to get his keys back from Cameron. He'd blocked her email address and deleted her from his list of friends on Facebook. But he hadn't been able to block her phone calls so changing his numbers had been a last resort.

"Yeah, it was getting to be a pain. Giving everyone my new numbers is also going to be a huge pain but it'll be worth it. I've already told Reception to put Cameron's calls directly to voice mail. And Travis and I have already discussed the idea of hiring a temporary security guard for the reception area if necessary."

A shiver ran up Julia's spine. "God, Nathan. Do you really think it's going to get that bad?"

"I hope not. But some of her texts and emails were getting pretty nasty. And if she can't get through to me any other way, it's certainly a possibility that she'll drop by unannounced and try to make a scene. Thank God she doesn't have your contact info or knows where you live."

Julia chewed nervously on her bottom lip. "Um, now that you mention it, I've had several hang-ups on my work phone lately. No real pattern to them and no voice on the other end. It may just be a coincidence."

"Bullshit. It's Cameron, no doubt about it. I'll tell Reception no calls from her numbers to you, either. I'm not going to let her harass you, baby. Let me know if you get anymore of those calls."

"Okay. But I'm sure it will all die down soon. You can't expect her not to be angry and hurt."

Their food arrived and Julia used the opportunity to change the subject. "Why did you ask me earlier when Lauren was due home?"

"I promised Travis that we'd get together soon with him and Anton. Just thought it might be amusing to have your sister there, too. This time hopefully she won't be deliberately trying to piss me off."

She giggled. "I guess she was trying to get a reaction out of you. I mean, you should have seen the look on your face when she talked about this so-called twin sandwich."

"I'll get her for that one someday," he vowed darkly. "Jesus, please tell me you have never, ever considered - "

"God, no!" she exclaimed. "And in spite of Lauren's smart mouth I really can't see her being serious about it either. Now, there is a real possibility, however, that she's had two guys at once. She's, uh, pretty feisty."

"Yeah, I hadn't noticed," he said sarcastically. "And just on the off chance you've got that on your wish list, forget it. I won't share you with anyone."

"Same here. Honey, you're all the man I need, and I can barely walk most mornings after a night in bed with you. Sasha told me this morning that you're ruining my yoga practice because my legs keep shaking in class."

Nathan's face flushed. "Shit. Sorry, baby. I know I need to be gentler with you. You just make me forget myself at times, and I feel like an animal. I'll try to control myself."

She reached across the table and grasped his hand. "Don't you dare," she whispered. "I love how you lose control, how fierce you are. How often you can make me come, and how hard. Sasha was just teasing me. Frankly, I think she's a little jealous that she isn't getting done as hard as I am."

"Christ, Julia." His eyes widened. "Sometimes I can't believe some of the smut that comes out of that pretty mouth. For such a refined lady you can be a real dirty girl at times."

She brought his hand to her mouth and sucked his index finger between her lips. "You've corrupted me. And I love it."

He ran that same finger over and around her lips. "I'm going to corrupt you some more tonight. And make damned sure your legs are shaking like a leaf tomorrow morning."

She bit down on his finger. "I'll hold you to that vow, lover. And just to make sure your animal instincts are fully aroused, picture this – I'm wearing a leopard print bra and panties today."

His gaze raked over her chocolate brown silk tank top and slim-fitting pencil skirt of palest taupe. "You devil," he muttered. "You know that's all I'll be able to think about this afternoon. And I have a client meeting, a conference call, and some designs to work on."

Julia forked a bit of her Cobb salad and chewed it slowly, a smile teasing at the corner of her mouth. "Just a little something to inspire you, honey. Help you make it through your busy afternoon."

"I'll tell you what would help get me through the afternoon," he told her in a dangerous voice. "You on your knees in front of my chair, that dirty mouth of yours doing very dirty things."

She grinned. "Ooh, sounds like fun. What time should I stop by?"

Nathan laughed. "As tempting as that sounds, I really do have a busy schedule today. But one day very, very soon you can stop by and surprise me."

"I'll look forward to it."

They were just finishing up their meal when Jake, Brent and their summer intern sauntered into the restaurant. Julia immediately avoided eye contact, but Nathan had no such qualms and waved the trio over. Much to her chagrin, he also reached over and took hold of her hand, giving her a warm smile, and an almost imperceptible shake of his head.

"Hey, look who's here," said Jake in greeting. "And looking very cozy, I might add. Something the two of you want to share with us?"

Julia opened her mouth to protest, but Nathan beat her to it, drawing her hand to lips.

"Absolutely," he replied. "I'm no longer engaged which makes Julia and I officially a couple."

Jake's mouth fell open in surprise, and Brent just stared dumbly while the intern hung back politely. Jake recovered quickly and chuckled, patting Nathan on the back.

"You sly devil," he laughed playfully. "I should have known you had your eye on this gorgeous thing. You're a lucky bastard." Jake winked at Julia. "And you've broken my heart, beautiful girl. But the two of you do look awfully good together."

Brent merely shook Nathan's hand and offered up his congratulations before the trio headed off to their table.

Julia shook her head in exasperation. "Now you've done it. Not only is Jake the biggest flirt in the office, he's also the biggest gossip, ten times worse than Travis, hard as that is to believe. The entire office will know before closing time."

Nathan grinned. "That bother you?"

"Not if it doesn't bother you. Which apparently it doesn't or you wouldn't have told the town crier about it."

"Well, let's really give him something to talk about then," he murmured, sliding his hand to the nape of her neck and pulling her close for a slow, open-mouthed kiss. She was panting by the time he released her, her cheeks burning and rather uncomfortably aware of all the interested stares directed their way.

"Was that too much PDA for you?" he asked teasingly.

She arched a brow at him. "I think if we keep that up we might get kicked out of here."

"Just for kissing?"

Deliberately, she slid her hand under the table and up his thigh. "No. For the hand job I'm going to give you in about thirty seconds."

Nathan gulped, and then quickly signaled their waiter for the check.

Chapter Nineteen

August

"Do you have a minute?"

Nathan glanced up at the sound of Julia's voice from his office doorway and grinned. "For you, baby, always. Come on in."

His eyes raked over her admiringly as she closed the door and walked across the polished wood floor to his desk. The heels of her navy stilettos clicked with each slow, deliberate step and her curvy hips swayed within the confines of her slim fitting navy pencil skirt. She wore a cap-sleeved pleated blouse in a sheer blue-gray fabric, and he could see glimpses of some sort of lacy lingerie through it.

He had missed seeing her get dressed this morning because he'd had to be in the office for an early conference call. Normally it was one of the highlights of his day – reclining on her bed and watching her get ready for work – putting on her lingerie and stockings, zipping up her dress, stepping into her shoes – always high heels. It was the sweetest sort of torture, for all he could think about the whole time was ripping off whatever she'd just put on, tumbling her to the bed or pushing her up against the wall, and fucking her silly. But since their mornings were usually rushed, he had to force himself to keep his distance. Especially since they had already had sex at least once that morning – either upon waking or during the shower they shared after their workouts.

And, of course, there was always the undressing to look forward to once their work day was over. Tonight he would be very eager to see what sort of lacy confection she had on beneath that sheer blouse.

"So what do I owe this pleasant little visit to? You know we have to leave for the Gregson meeting in about an hour?" he reminded her.

She nodded, a slow smile crossing her radiant face. "That's why I'm here, actually. I wanted to ask your opinion on a particular color."

Nathan knit his brow. "I thought we had all of the color palettes settled awhile ago."

Julia fiddled with the top button of her blouse. "Oh, the color in question isn't for something with the hotel. It's this."

His eyes widened as she deftly unfastened the buttons on her blouse before spreading the two sides wide. His curiosity about her choice of undergarments was satisfied, and his tongue left hanging out as he gazed hungrily at the sight of her breasts plumped up to even more generous proportions by the strapless satin and lace bustier.

He swallowed with some difficulty. "Uh, what, uh, was the question?"

She smiled saucily, running a finger over the lace edged cups of the bustier. "Well, I wanted your opinion on the exact color of this thing. The website where I ordered it said it was periwinkle blue. But I think it's more of a powder blue. What do you think?"

Sweat popped out by his temples as he watched her slide her hands to the undersides of her breasts, cupping them. "I'd actually call it cockteasing blue," he croaked. "Come here and let me have a closer look to be sure."

Obediently, Julia walked around the side of his desk, kneeling in front of him. She gasped when his hands cupped her breasts, his thumbs brushing over the tight nipples. She slid her hand up the hard muscles of his thigh to his crotch, and a low groan escaped his throat as she trailed her fingertips lightly, teasingly, along his fully erect cock.

"I think you're right," she whispered. "It is cockteasing blue. Here, let me, honey."

Nathan couldn't resist as she slowly unzipped his trousers and drew out the hard, throbbing length of his penis. His head fell back against his leather desk chair as she stroked him with her soft, warm hands. Already aroused nearly to the breaking point, he slipped his hands beneath the sexy bustier to find her lush, full breasts.

"Mmm, that feels so good," she murmured. "But this is about making you feel good, lover. Sit back now and let me take care of you."

It was all he could do to stifle the groan of pleasure that rose up in his throat as she bent her head and sucked him deep into her wet, eager mouth. His breathing grew harsh, his hips bucking in rhythm with the sweet, hungry pull of her mouth.

"Oh, God, baby, that's so good," he hissed. "You suck me so deep, Julia. I love fucking that sexy mouth of yours."

Nathan was mindless with the pleasure she was bestowing on him – her hand pumping the root of his cock and fondling his swollen balls while her mouth worked the head up and down. His hand went to the back of her head, urging her to take him deeper, and he felt himself growing ever closer to his release.

"Fuck," he growled in a long, low voice as he came hard, spurting his load into her welcoming mouth. She licked him clean before tucking his semi-hard cock back into his trousers and zipping him up. Then, her blouse still unbuttoned, she stood up only to straddle his lap. Her snug-fitting skirt hitched up her thighs, exposing the silky stockings clipped to the garters attached to the bustier.

His hands slid to her ass, half-bared by skimpy silk panties the same color as the bustier. "So was there a special reason for this extremely pleasant visit, or were you just feeling generous?"

She smirked, leaning forward until her breasts pressed against his chest. "I love sucking your cock," she whispered. "Love the way you look and the sounds you make when you come. Love how hard you come in my mouth, like you're going to blow the back of my head off."

He slid his hands up her silk-covered things, tugging at the frilly garters teasingly. "Mmm, well, you won't hear me complaining anytime you feel the urge to give me a BJ. Practice makes perfect after all."

"Greedy man." She licked a circle around his ear. "But to answer your question – yes, I did have an ulterior motive." She slid her hands to his cheeks and looked him in the eye. "In a little while we'll be at the Gregson meeting, and that bitch Morgan will try to flirt with you, and shove those fake tits in your face." She traced along the seam of his lips with her tongue. "So when she tries, the only thing I want you to think about is how amazing my boobs look in this bustier, and how awesome it felt having my mouth fucking your cock. Got all that, lover?"

He chuckled, his hands squeezing her breasts. "Baby, that pathetic, dried-up old hag can't begin to hold a candle to you in any way. You're the only woman I ever notice. But I will definitely keep the delightful mental pictures you just described fresh in my mind."

She playfully nipped his chin. "Good." She stood up gracefully and began to button her blouse, much to his regret. When she had walked to the other side of his desk she winked at him. "And just in case you need more inspiration, my panties are soaking wet. I'll see you when we leave for the meeting."

She blew him a teasing kiss and walked out of his office, giving her pert little ass a shake. Nathan didn't know whether to growl, laugh, or yank her back inside and give that same butt a good spanking.

As the meeting with the Gregson group came to an end, Nathan was aware of several things at once. Across the table, Morgan was pouting and in a snit because he'd virtually ignored her for the past ninety minutes. To his left, Julia was smiling and practically glowing, and he wasn't sure if it was because Morgan was pissed off or because they had been sneaking naughty little feels back and forth beneath the table during the meeting. And to his right, he was extremely aware of the knowing, interested glances Ian had been sending his way.

He wasn't the least bit surprised, therefore, when Ian discreetly ushered him into his private office when the meeting adjourned. The Brit was smiling broadly.

"I'm going to assume from the recent phone call I had from Julia, and how cozy the two of you seem, that you're officially a couple now?" he asked.

Nathan couldn't help the answering grin he gave his client – and friend. "We are, yes. For several weeks now. Though my little minx didn't mention that she'd called you."

Ian shrugged dismissively. "It was quite brief, and basically to thank me for my time, but that she was now quite content with her present job. I thought perhaps it might have something to do with you, and then when I saw the pair of you together today I knew immediately. Congratulations, Nathan. She's a beautiful woman, and you're a very lucky man."

"Don't I know it. Julia is – remarkable. And I've never been so happy. We should all have dinner together sometime," added Nathan. "Are you seeing anyone right now?"

Ian hesitated before shaking his head. "No, I'm still a stuffy old bachelor, my friend. Perhaps Julia has a twin she could introduce me to."

Nathan sputtered at Ian's lighthearted joke. "Uh, actually she does. But since you're my best client, I'll do you a huge favor and *not* introduce you to the very intimidating Ms. Lauren McKinnon. You'll thank me for it, Ian."

Ian regarded him quizzically. "Now I'm intrigued."

"Tell you what. Lauren is due to visit again next month, and Julia is planning a small dinner party. If you're still feeling brave, you should join us."

"Perhaps I will, if it's all right with Julia. After all, life's too short not to live on the edge occasionally, right?"

Nathan shook his head. "Hold that thought."

Chapter Twenty

Labor Day Weekend

The weather had been foggy and cool when they'd left San Francisco mid-morning, but had quickly turned warm and sunny about twenty miles south of town. Once they reached the Central Coast, Nathan lowered the top on his BMW so they could enjoy the warm late summer sun.

Julia sighed in contentment, her long hair blowing in the breeze. "I hope the weather is this nice in Santa Barbara. It'll be such a welcome change from all the fog we've been having."

Nathan snagged her hand and brought it to his lips, his tongue flicking over her knuckles. "It's supposed to be warm and sunny all weekend, baby. Don't you know I arranged for it?"

She returned his impish smile. "How sweet you are. But you have ulterior motives, lover boy. You just want it to be warm so I can wear a bikini."

"Can you blame me? I mean, you did look at yourself in the mirror when you modeled it for me, didn't you? Your tits look twice as big in that top. You are *not*," he added sternly, "leaving my side when you wear that itty bitty excuse for a bathing suit."

"Hmm, and here I was planning on parading through the hotel lobby wearing just the bikini and my favorite pair of Louboutins," she teased.

He bit her finger, eliciting a yelp. "I wasn't planning on spanking you this weekend," he threatened darkly," but I'm sure I can fit it into my schedule. Behave yourself, minx."

She smiled, sliding her abused finger inside his mouth and murmuring in approval when he sucked it. "I'll try. But every time I'm with you I feel this urge to be a very bad girl."

He ran his tongue over her finger. "Behind closed doors, baby, you can be as bad as you want to be."

"Then I guess we should lock ourselves in our room this weekend, hmm?"

Nathan laughed in agreement, and Julia noticed that he sped up by several miles an hour, apparently in a sudden hurry to reach their destination.

They were spending the three-day weekend at the luxurious Gregson resort hotel on the coast in Santa Barbara. It had been Ian's idea, offering them the use of the owner's suite en gratis, and they had eagerly accepted his very generous offer. It was a relief to get away, for it had been an extremely busy, hectic summer at the office, especially since all of the plans for the Gregson hotel in Napa had to be finalized by the end of September. Since officially becoming a couple over two months ago, this was the first chance they'd had to get away for a weekend.

They were together almost constantly, though, taking turns spending the night at each other's place. Nathan had followed through on his vow to buy a new bed for his master bedroom, and Julia had been all too happy to help him break it in. She now had a sizeable number of clothes and shoes at his condo, while he had several suits and other clothing hanging in her closet. Since both of them were neat freaks, they had been pleased at the other's tidiness and never argued about picking up after themselves. They had begun discussing the idea of finding a bigger place where they could live together, with Nathan joking that they'd need a third bedroom just for her wardrobe. He had also pulled out the various design plans he'd drawn up for his place in Tiburon, though Julia had agreed that none of them were exactly right. Unfortunately, he'd been too busy to do any additional work on the house plans, so he was no closer to getting his dream home built.

The weather was indeed warm and sunny when they pulled up to the entrance of the resort mid-afternoon. A valet took charge of Nathan's car, while a bellhop quickly unloaded their baggage onto a cart. Check-in was accomplished quickly and smoothly, and the front desk clerk who assisted them was exceptionally gracious. Julia was certain that he treated them with extra care because they were staying in the owners suite and quite obviously some sort of VIPs. She sent silent thanks to Ian once again for his generosity.

The suite was spectacular — far larger than either her flat or Nathan's condo — and almost overwhelmingly opulent. There was a spacious living room, separate dining room, full kitchen, and a huge bedroom with a fabulous en suite bathroom. The carpet was thick and plush, while the terrazzo floor in the bathroom was smooth and cool. Everything was first class and top of the line, from the furnishings to the artwork to the linens. There were two enormous flat-paneled, state of the art televisions with surround sound, one each in the living room and bedroom, and a very sophisticated stereo system. The kitchen was outfitted with high end appliances and gadgets, and Julia could only imagine the incredible meals she could create there. But Nathan had forbidden her from cooking this weekend, insisting on her being totally pampered and catered to.

The suite also boasted its own spacious outdoor patio complete with fire pit, hot tub, and small, private infinity pool. The outdoor space was completely private, and Julia impishly imagined the two of them sunning and sunbathing in the nude.

She glanced at the pool and then at Nathan, and they grinned at each other knowingly.

"You bad girl," he whispered in her ear, careful that the private concierge who was showing them around the suite couldn't overhear. "Always thinking of ways to be naughty."

She slid her palm to his chest, leaning in to nip at his bottom lip. "You must be rubbing off on me, you bad boy."

He pressed a soft kiss to her temple. "I'd like you to rub something right about now. It's been a whole seven hours since I fucked you last."

Her cheeks grew hot and she whispered urgently, "Behave, Nathan. At least until Stuart leaves."

He murmured back, "I haven't paid attention to one fucking thing he's said, have you?"

She giggled. "Some of it. Now, be nice. Please?"

He humored her by sliding an arm around her waist, and politely listening to the rest of what Stuart the concierge had to tell them about the suite and its many amenities.

"A complimentary wine and cheese cart will be delivered at five-thirty," Stuart told them in his crisp British accent. "As for breakfast, you may have that brought in anytime tomorrow morning. Just give us a mere fifteen minutes notice and we'll deliver it to you."

He went on about all the spa services, the top-notch fitness center and various exercise classes, the tennis courts and beach access. Nathan assured him that all of their questions had been answered more than adequately, and after thanking Nathan for the generous tip Stuart was thankfully gone.

"Christ, I thought he'd never leave," complained Nathan, jerking Julia into his arms. "Come here and kiss me, baby."

Her giggles were swiftly suppressed by the hungry pressure of his mouth on hers, his tongue licking at the seam of her lips until it plunged wetly inside. Julia gave a little "mmm" of pleasure as she twined her arms around his neck and pressed up flush against him, returning his kisses eagerly. She had to lift up on her toes a bit to slant her mouth fully against his, since for once she wasn't wearing heels. Her gold and coral jeweled flip flops coordinated with her

Matthew Williamson coral chiffon dress and its embellished gold belt. The floaty fabric of the dress was thin enough that she could feel the full imprint of Nathan's hands as they cupped her ass, lifting her so that he could nestle his hard cock into the notch of her thighs.

"If you don't want to lose another pair of those ridiculously overpriced panties, I suggest you decide quickly where you'd like to be fucked for the first time in this suite," he growled in her ear, even as he began to pull the hem of her dress up past her hips.

Julia groaned as his hand fondled her ass through the gossamer thin fabric of her pale apricot panties. His fingers slid along the back waistband to the cleft of her buttocks, slipping further down to briefly tease the puckered hole of her anus. At her gasp of surprise, he soothed her.

"Easy, baby. We're not going there today. But someday I'm going to claim this gorgeous little ass. Every part of you is going to belong to me. Now, since you haven't answered me yet, I think we'll be traditional and head over to that big bed in the next room."

He picked her up easily and carried her across the wide expanse of the living room to the large bedroom. He placed her gently on the vast bed, the cream colored duvet and pile of pillows matching the canopy that draped the four-poster frame. And then he proceeded to undress her slowly, deliberately. Instead of the wild, hungry fuck that she'd been breathlessly anticipating, he seduced her tenderly. Their lovemaking was sweet and slow, with long, drugging kisses, their hands gently stroking over every inch of the others body. Nathan entered her body with one long, slow thrust, wringing a gasp of pleasure from her throat.

"God, I love you," she murmured, her lips against the base of his throat as he stroked in and out of her with exquisite control. "And I love the way you love me."

Every part of their bodies were touching – arms and legs entwined, her breasts crushed to his chest, their lips clinging to the others, while he slid his cock in and out of her wet, clenching cunt with almost maddening slowness, savoring each sensation.

"I love you, too, baby," he whispered in her ear. "This is perfect. You and I are perfect. I wish we could freeze-frame this moment and stay just like this forever."

Julia felt tears well up in her eyes, her heart almost too full of emotion as she stared up at him. He was the man of her dreams, her soul mate, the other half of her. And she was so completely besotted with him, so utterly in love, that she would have done absolutely anything for him in that moment.

They took a long, decadent soak in the huge sunken bathtub, Nathan's hands soaping and teasing her swollen breasts before his fingers plunged inside her cleft and brought her to a quick, stunning orgasm. Then, despite his half-hearted protests at being spent, she stroked and pumped his cock until he was groaning, his hips thrusting upwards in rhythm with her strokes. Just before he climaxed, she took him inside her mouth and he came long and hard down her throat.

After drying each other off, they snuggled together on the bed, pleasantly exhausted, and took a short nap. It was the knock on the door to the suite that woke them, and Nathan sleepily pulled on one of the thick, white terrycloth hotel robes before stumbling to the door. Someone – most likely Stuart – had discreetly left a cloth covered cart just outside the private entryway to the suite. Julia, now swathed in her own robe, padded barefoot into the living room to help inspect the array of dishes on the cart as Nathan wheeled it inside.

There was a beautifully arranged platter of fine cheeses and pates, and a basket of crackers and thinly sliced baguette. There were also little dishes of nuts and olives, as well as juicy melon slices with paper thin strips of prosciutto wrapped around them.

She popped one of those in her mouth and sighed with pleasure. "Mmm. Salty and sweet. The perfect combination."

Nathan wrapped her in his arms, nuzzling the still damp tendrils of her hair. "That's exactly how you taste, baby," he whispered naughtily. "Salty and sweet. My very favorite dish."

She squeezed the firm cheek of his butt through the robe. "Yes, but man cannot live by pussy alone. Besides, you need to eat up. You'll be burning off a ton of calories tonight."

He chuckled and pinched her cheek. "You have great faith in my stud-like abilities, baby. What makes you think I have anything left after this afternoon?"

Julia slipped her hand inside the opening of his robe and latched onto his semi-erect penis. "Because you're Superman, lover. And I bought a bunch of new undies for this trip. You can help me pick out which ones to wear tonight."

He groaned as she continued to stroke his cock. "Ah, baby, you know me so well. But as good as you're making me feel, we should hold off for awhile. For what I have in mind for you tonight, you're going to need nourishment, too."

She kissed him, then reluctantly stepped back, continuing to inspect the cart. "Well, someone in this place must suspect what's going to happen in here tonight. Look what's in the ice bucket."

Nathan grinned as he extracted the bottle of Cristal champagne. "Liquid seduction. Let's get this opened and start getting you tipsy."

She accepted the flute of champagne he poured for her. "You don't have to get me tipsy to seduce me, you know."

He snagged her free hand and brought it to his lips. "Really? So what do I have to do?"

She turned her cheek into his palm. "Look at me. Say my name. Touch my hand. Basically, just be in the same room with me. That's all it takes to make me want to jump your bones."

"Wanton little hussy," he teased. "But so long as you're that way only with me you certainly won't hear me complain." He brushed her hair behind her ear. "And it's the same for me, baby. The sound of your voice makes me hard."

They walked out to sit on their private patio, nibbling on cheese and sipping champagne, and Julia couldn't help but think of that evening at the Plaza Hotel. It had been almost a full year since they'd met in New York, and so much had changed in her life during that time that it made her head spin to think about it. The journey to this point had certainly been filled with bumps and missteps, but the trip had been worth all the obstacles.

She reached out with her bare foot and tickled his calf. "You know how you were worried about me being too exposed in that new aqua bikini I bought?"

Nathan eyed her warily. "What about it?"

"Well, if we just swim naked in our own private pool you won't have to worry about it."

He burst out laughing. "Baby, some of the things that come out of that pretty mouth of yours knock me for a loop. I think I'm having a bad influence on you."

Julia stood up, only to straddle his lap and loop her arms around his neck. "Was that a complaint I heard?"

He pulled her down for a long, hungry kiss. "Oh, hell, no."

✳✳✳✳✳

They ate dinner at the four-star Mediterranean-style restaurant within the hotel. Nathan wore a pale gray Prada suit with an open-necked white shirt and no tie. Julia had chosen a Narciso

Rodriguez panel dress in a delicious shade of citron green with a pair of gold metallic sandals. In a restaurant filled with well-kept, well-to-do patrons, they stood out, easily the most attractive couple in the room. But the lovers seemed to ignore everyone else around them, more than content to stare at each other across the table, clearly enraptured with the other. They fed each other bites of food, shared sips of wine from the same glass, and kept their hands entwined during most of the meal.

They took a leisurely walk around the hotel grounds after dinner and dessert, not having had the opportunity to explore until now. From the back terrace, there were stairs down to the beach but Julia looked dubiously at her high heels and shook her head.

"Tomorrow, I think," she said regretfully.

Then she was squealing in surprise as Nathan swooped her up into his arms and carried her down the stairs to the sand below. She took off her shoes and carried them in one hand as he snagged the other in his.

"Thank you, baby. My knight in shining armor," she teased.

"My pleasure, my lady. It's such a beautiful night I couldn't resist walking along the beach with you."

They strolled up the hard packed sand for long, leisurely minutes, not speaking, just enjoying the balmy evening and each other's company. The tide was out so they didn't have to worry about getting splashed by an errant wave.

"This is an amazing place," she signed. "I haven't been to Santa Barbara since I was in high school. Have you been here before?"

He hesitated a moment before nodding. "Once, several years ago."

She grinned at him. "I'll bet it was with a woman and you don't want to talk about it because you think I'll be jealous."

Nathan shrugged. "It was a long time ago, and I'd almost forgotten about it. It was pretty casual. I didn't really have a serious long term relationship until – well-"

"Until Cameron," she finished for him. "So what you're trying to tell me was that you were something of a manwhore."

He laughed. "I am definitely *not* trying to tell you that. I admit I dated a lot during college and in my twenties, but even before I met Cameron I was really toning it down. There haven't been nearly as many women in my life as you might think."

Julia rested her head on his shoulder as they walked along. "That's a relief. And you already know about my previous relationships. Sam, of course, and then that total asshole whose name I refuse to mention again. Two others, very brief relationships, who meant less than nothing to me. And then you."

He kissed her forehead. "I still don't know how I lucked out. I've seen you completely ignore a room filled with men and somehow you chose me."

She ran a finger over his lips. "Hmm, must be that dirty mouth of yours. You say such nasty stuff but then do such delicious things to me with it at the same time."

Nathan chuckled and swatted her playfully on the butt. "Good thing all those other guys don't know the secret to your heart is a dirty mouth."

Julia shook her head. "That's only a small part of it, baby. While the sex is spectacular, and your body is the stuff girly dreams are made of, it's what's inside of you that I love the most. When I saw you for the first time in New York, I just – knew. I can't really explain it properly."

"You don't have to, because I get it." He wrapped his arm about her waist, holding her close. "It's exactly the same for me. It's like I was waiting my whole life for you and then one day there you were."

"Can we go back to our room now?" she whispered. "I'm feeling in need of some dirty talk."

He slid his hands into her hair and bent her head back for a deep, searing kiss. "Baby, I'll talk dirty to you all night long if that's what you crave. Do you want me to start now?"

She closed her eyes. "Yes, please."

Nathan trailed hot kisses down the side of her neck, cupping her breast in his hand. "I'm going to take you back to our room now, Julia, and you're going to undress for me. Very slowly. And then when you're beautifully naked, I'm going to eat out that delicious cunt of yours until you come."

She groaned as his thumb flicked over her nipple, and his lips continued their descent to the base of her throat. "Then you're going to return the favor and suck me off in that sexy mouth of yours until I shoot my load down your throat," he rasped.

Nathan ground his rapidly hardening erection against her cleft as he cupped her ass, holding her still for him. "And then I'm going to lick these pretty nipples and play with these gorgeous tits until I'm hard again.' He squeezed one round breast. "Then I'm going to fuck you hard. From behind. And you're going to let me do whatever I want."

Julia was panting now from excitement, fully aroused just by his words. "Yes, Nathan. Yes, whatever you want. I love you so much."

They were back near the staircase now, so he picked her up and carried her up to the terrace. Once they reached the top, Julia wiggled in his arms.

"You can put me down now," she teased.

Nathan smiled, but made no move to set her down as he continued walking. "I know. But I can walk faster than you, which means you'll be naked that much sooner."

＊＊＊＊＊

Nathan lowered his sunglasses and ogled Julia as she sunbathed on their private patio. The aqua bikini did a piss-poor job in covering up her curves, especially those tits that threatened to spill over the low-cut top or expose a nipple. He couldn't resist snapping a photo of her with his phone, adding it to the considerable album he'd already compiled of her.

She turned her head and gave him a mock glare behind her oversized sunglasses. "That picture had better not wind up on your Facebook page. The last picture you posted of me with some cleavage showing got some rather pervy comments from your buddies."

He grinned. "Just showing you off a little, baby. And every one of my friends is off the wall jealous of me."

"Aren't most of your friends married?"

He snapped another photo, this one a close up of her cleavage. "Yeah, and they're all eating their hearts out. And relax — there's no way I'd share a photo of you baring this much of your tits with anyone. These are for my eyes only, baby."

She took a drink of the ice-cold margarita that had been delivered along with Nathan's Corona just a few minutes ago. "Lucky for you. I've met a few of your friends, don't forget, and I can't say for one hundred percent certain that some of them wouldn't plaster photos like that all over the place."

"Well, I know my buddies a lot better than you do, and I *can* say with one hundred percent certainty that a few of them are perverted enough to do just that. And since I don't want my girl to be the next Internet sensation, the photos stay private. I don't share, Julia, and that includes a photo like this one."

She patted his hand and took another sip of her drink. "I know you don't. And I love how protective and possessive you get at times. You make me feel cherished."

He squeezed her hand in return. "That's because you are. I adore you, Julia. There isn't anything I wouldn't do for you."

She smiled at him saucily. "How about skinny dipping in the pool? Would you do that for me?"

He shot to his feet. "Absolutely, except I think that would be more for my benefit than yours."

Julia allowed him to help her to her feet, and then took a long drink of the margarita before divesting herself of the bikini in two swift motions. Nathan stared at her slack-jawed as she strode to the edge of the pool, proudly nude. She crooked a finger at him.

"What are you waiting for?"

He watched as she slid gracefully into the heated infinity pool, then yanked off his swim trunks and dove in after her. Julia gave a little yelp of alarm as he caught her around the waist, pressing his chest against her back.

"Temptress," he scolded. "Do you enjoy provoking me?"

She wiggled her bare buttocks against his rapidly hardening erection. "Of course. I mean, after all, you're so easy to provoke. But only with me, lover. I don't share either."

Nathan's hands slid up the side of her waist to cup her swollen breasts. "Like I'd have anything left to share after you had your way with me, wench. Keeping you satisfied is a lot of work."

"Mmm, sounds like you're due some overtime pay." She gasped as he pinched her nipples. "Could you be persuaded to accept your compensation with sexual favors?"

He groaned as she reached behind her and took hold of his throbbing cock. "Oh, hell yes."

They swam and played in the warm water for awhile, kissing and fondling each other in between. Julia splashed him and Nathan retaliated by diving beneath the surface to grab her ankle and tug her underwater. She was sputtering indignantly but giggling at the same time when they both surfaced, her arms looped around his neck and her legs wrapped around his waist.

"Having fun?' he asked her, grinning.

She gave him a wet, smacking kiss in reply. "Absolutely. This has been the best weekend of my life so far. And it's not even half over."

"I'm glad you're enjoying it. We both needed this break. And it's been the most fantastic time of my life, too. I owe Ian big time for this."

Julia ran her fingers through his wet hair. "Hmm, we should set him up with a nice girl. I can't believe someone as yummy as he is doesn't have a steady girlfriend or wife."

He tweaked her nipple playfully. "Yummy, huh? Just keep that particular observation to yourself, okay? I think if I wasn't in the picture – and he wasn't our client – that he'd be all over you, baby. He asked me jokingly if you had a twin sister."

She stared at him in dismay. "Oh, God, please tell me you did not offer to fix him up with Lauren."

Nathan gave a mock shudder. "Good Lord, no. Not that Ian wouldn't be able to hold his own against her, but he might come out with a few scratches. Worse, he might fire us."

"Trust me, he's not Lauren's type. She either likes the dangerous, tattooed bad boys, or the outdoorsy, adventure seeking guys. Somehow I don't think Ian has a tattoo or a piercing, nor can I picture him rock climbing or ocean kayaking."

He walked her over to the edge of the pool, with her legs still wrapped around his hips, and lifted her to sit on the patio, her feet dangling in the water. "Well, as it happens, I can vouch for both. No tattoos or piercings, and he prefers golf or tennis or swimming laps to anything more extreme."

Julia ran her hands over his shoulders. "You've seen him naked? Come on, I want details."

He glared. "Hey, I didn't exactly give him the once over, you know. He invited me to play a round of golf at his club once and we showered afterwards in the locker room. I can't give you any other details save that I did not notice any ink or jewelry. And stop sounding so interested in what Ian Gregson looks like naked."

"You're right. I mean, I've got my hands full here, don't I?" She squeezed his biceps.

He bent his head and licked a drop of water from her nipple. "I'll tell you what I'd like to have your hand full of. Not to mention what *I* want a handful of."

She gave a low sound of pleasure as he cupped her breasts, his thumbs rasping over the nipples.

"Except that my hands aren't big enough to hold all of you at once," he murmured huskily. "And by the feel of how hard I'm getting, it might be too much for you to handle as well."

"Why don't you let me be the judge of that?" she teased. "Come here, lover."

She slid her hand down his rock-hard, sculpted abs to find his fully erect cock. "Mmm, you're right," she breathed sultrily. "Way, way more than a handful. Have you ever fucked in a pool before?"

He nuzzled her neck. "No. And I'm not going to do it now, either. The footing is too slippery for as hard as I need to give it to you. Come on, I have an idea."

His idea was to pull the thick, dark blue cushions off their chaise lounges and lay them side by side on the patio. The warm sun beat down on their wet bodies, quickly drying them as they kissed and caressed each other boldly, hungrily. Nathan rolled to his knees, and then sat back on his heels, pulling her up to straddle his lap.

"I want to take you this way," he told her in hushed tones. "Tell me if it's too much."

In answer, she lowered herself slowly, impaling herself on his cock an inch at a time until he was buried to the balls inside of her. For long seconds they didn't move – Nathan savoring the incredible feeling of being so deep, and Julia letting her body adjust to accommodate his thick length. Then she began to move, slowly at first, and then with increasing speed, his hands at her hips guiding their movements. He bent his head and took a nipple into his mouth, sucking hard, and eliciting a moan from her.

"Christ, you feel so good," he rasped against her breast. "Lean back now, baby. My turn to ride you."

Julia obliged, her yoga-toned body giving her the flexibility to lower herself onto her back with her knees still bent beneath her. Nathan reared up onto his knees, and plunged into her hard.

She bit her lip to control the scream that would otherwise have escaped. "Ah, Nathan, oh, God," she panted, as he continued to fuck her relentlessly, his body pounding into her. The same hot sun that had dried the pool water from their bodies now caused a fine layer of perspiration to form on their skin. Sweat dropped from his forehead onto her bare torso as he worked her over, pushing her hard.

"I want your legs around my neck," he demanded. "Do it now."

Again she obeyed instantly, hooking her ankles behind his head as his hands slid beneath her buttocks, lifting and positioning her to the angle he desired. And still he continued to drive into her, each thrust somehow harder than the one before, until she was dizzy and almost incoherent from the intensity, half-afraid that it was more than she could take. He kept at her for what felt like forever, drawing out their mutual pleasure to the limits of their endurance. She didn't know how he was able to hold back for so long, for he felt harder and thicker and hotter than she could ever remember, his cock stroking into her again and again. She was so wet that she could vaguely hear slurping sounds where their bodies were joined as he continued to work her over. And then, when she feared she might pass out from his demanding, almost brutal possession, it took only the smallest flick of his thumb on her clit to send her crashing into orgasm, her pussy convulsing around his cock until he, too, came hard, his body shuddering over and over. Groaning, he collapsed next to her on the cushions, his breathing as labored as hers.

"I'm not sure I'm going to be able to walk after that." She stretched her arms and legs in opposite directions, giving a low groan as she did so.

He propped himself up on one elbow and grinned down at her. "I'll just have to carry you everywhere, then. Though my legs feel pretty shaky right now, too. Once again you've wiped me out."

Julia wiggled her toes, relieved to see she could move at least one body part. "I'll probably fall asleep during my massage this afternoon. Good thing I forced myself to get up early for that yoga class, because there's no way I could move a muscle after this."

"Hmm, I was just thinking I don't need a workout this afternoon after all. Think I just found the ultimate aerobic exercise. And it's a hell of a lot more fun than swimming laps or running five miles."

She trailed her fingers down his chest to his stomach. "We both worked up a sweat, that's for sure. Shower or bath?"

The glint in his eyes should have warned her, but she was still caught unawares when he stood, hefted her up into his arms, and strode towards the pool.

Julia kept her arms tightly locked around his neck. "You're not really thinking about throwing me in, are you?"

In answer he tossed her into the pool, grinning broadly at the sound of her shrieks and sputtering when she surfaced a moment later. She was glaring at him through the wet curtain of her hair.

"Just for that, I'm going to request that my masseuse be the tallest, hottest guy they have on staff," she threatened.

"Too late, baby," he smirked. "When I so nicely offered to make the reservation for you, I specifically asked for a female masseuse."

She stuck her tongue out at him. "Well, then, you don't get to pick my undies for tonight. I might decide to wear plain white cotton ones."

Nathan hooted. "Sweetie, you don't own any plain white cotton anything. But even if you did, you'd still look hot in it."

"Speaking of hot – you still look pretty sweaty. I think you need to cool off."

Then it was Nathan's turn to yelp as she splashed him from head to toe, just before tugging at his ankle and pulling him into the pool.

Chapter Twenty-One

Mid-September

"You are just about the luckiest SOB I've ever met, Atwood. No other explanation for how you snagged someone as hot as Julia."

Nathan grinned over the rim of his wine glass before taking a healthy swallow of the mellow Merlot. "You won't hear any arguments from me about that. I thank my lucky stars several times a day that she even considers me worthy to hold her hand."

Rick sighed. "Goddamn, she is really something, isn't she? Does she look that smokin' hot every day?"

The two men stared admiringly across the patio at the alluring sight Julia made tonight. She wore a black floral print dress with a corset styled bodice and slim fitting skirt. Nathan knew it was from one of her favorite designers – Dolce & Gabbana – and it showed her ample cleavage off without being too revealing. Her red patent platform stilettos were another pair of the sexy Louboutins she favored. Her glorious hair fell in its usual loose waves about her back and shoulders, and that lush mouth he longed to kiss right this very second was glossed over in bright scarlet. She looked so sexy and tempting that he didn't know how he was holding himself back from dragging her back to their room and fucking her again. But he'd already received a scolding from her once this evening, having made them a few minutes late for the party, and he didn't want to push his luck.

It really hadn't been his fault, though, he thought sheepishly. He couldn't name one man here tonight – married or otherwise – who could have resisted Julia once they'd seen her dressing for tonight's party. It had only taken one long, steamy look at the low-cut, strapless black lace bra and matching lace boy shorts she'd put on for him to grow instantly and almost violently aroused. And then, despite her protests that they were already running late, he'd picked her up and wrapped her legs around his waist before fucking her hard and fast against the hotel room wall.

The scolding had followed soon after that, as she'd had to quickly clean up and repair her makeup, and he'd been sufficiently chastised. But her annoyance with him had been well worth the deep sexual satisfaction that had hummed through his body after coming so thoroughly and so pleasurably.

He met Julia's eyes across the patio and they smiled at each other knowingly. And despite her initial displeasure with him at mussing her up, he knew damned well that she'd enjoyed their quick, sexy encounter just a short while ago. And she was hopefully looking forward to picking up where they'd left off just as soon as this party was over with.

They were spending this gorgeous September night at a resort in the Napa Valley to attend a thirtieth birthday party. The honoree was Jada Wright, whose husband Matt was an old water polo teammate of Nathan's. Matt worked at a tech firm in Silicon Valley and was raking in big bucks, so he was sparing no expense for this bash. There were at least a hundred and fifty guests gathered out here on the spacious patio, drinking fine wine and sampling hors d'oeuvres. A sit-down dinner would be following shortly, and then dancing and more drinking, probably into the wee hours. Nathan was doubly glad that he and Julia had decided to stay overnight so that they could both enjoy themselves freely and not have to worry about the long drive back to San Francisco.

And he was really, really enjoying showing Julia off to so many of his friends. The party was turning out to be a mini-reunion of his college buddies and water polo teammates, and very few of them had met Julia yet. She had, in fact, met hardly any of his friends, mostly because he'd been greedy about keeping her all to himself. Additionally, he hadn't wanted to seem totally insensitive to the fact that he'd recently broken off his engagement to Cameron by flaunting his hot new girlfriend too soon afterwards.

Fortunately, all of his friends plus their wives or girlfriends had all seemed very pleased to meet Julia, and everyone had been welcoming and friendly. Even now Julia was deep in conversation with Ryan and Sophie Latimer, the couple he'd last seen at the Design Awards dinner. Their new baby girl was less than two months old and currently being cared for by Sophie's parents. Nathan had gone to get another glass of wine for him and Julia only to be waylaid by Rick Marshall on the way back.

"So how come you didn't attend the convention this year?" asked Rick. The AIA Convention was due to start in a couple of days in Dallas. Rick was missing it because he was due to fly out to Hawaii on Monday to attend his sister's wedding later in the week. It had been a fortunate coincidence that this party had given him a reason for a layover in San Francisco.

Nathan shrugged. "Just way too busy at work this year. We've got this big resort hotel we're almost ready to break ground on, just a few miles away from here in fact. Besides," he added with a knowing grin, "I didn't want to leave my girl behind for five days. I think I'd have gone blind if I had to go without for that long."

Rick groaned. "You are such a lucky bastard. So, uh, how often do you guys, uh – "

"Daily. At least. Shit, I feel like a sixteen-year-old when I'm near her," marveled Nathan. "Constantly horny. And it's never enough, I always want more."

"Cut it out, Nate. Now you're making *me* horny just thinking about the two of you getting it on that often. And to think you didn't believe she was even interested in you."

Nathan shook his head. "Hard to imagine that was a whole year ago. A lot has happened since the last time I saw you in New York. Never thought I'd get this lucky. You were right, Rick – Julia's definitely a once in a lifetime kind of woman."

Rick snorted. "Took you long enough to figure that one out, dumbass. Speaking of which, you'd better get back to your woman. Jonathan is here solo tonight and he was really panting after Julia earlier."

Nathan scowled. "Jonathan can go piss off. And he'd better put his tongue back in his head and find his own girl."

He strode purposefully across the patio until he reached his girl, sliding a possessive arm around her waist and handing her a glass of wine.

She beamed at him. "Thanks. You were gone awhile."

"Miss me?" he asked, nuzzling her neck.

"Always. Sophie and Ryan were just showing me photos of Carina. She is the sweetest baby."

While Nathan also admired the photos of the baby, Matt breezed by, camera in hand.

"Gotta commemorate the occasion for Jada," he told them cheerfully. "So let's smile and say cheese, everyone!"

He took a photo of the four of them, then individual shots of each couple. Nathan wrapped his arms around Julia's waist, while she entwined hers about his neck, and then they smiled widely for Matt. Even after Matt moved on to the next group, they remained locked together tightly.

Ryan grinned. "I'd tell you two to get a room but I hear you already have one."

Julia flushed but merely rested her head on Nathan's shoulder while he squeezed her waist. Both of them sent a silent message to the other that the night couldn't go by fast enough until they could retire to the aforementioned room and take up where they'd left off a short while ago.

But despite their desire to be alone, the evening did turn out to be a great time and Nathan was thrilled that Julia got along so well with his friends. He didn't miss all the admiring, if not lustful, gazes the guys gave Julia and most of them whispered to him that he was the luckiest fucker in the universe.

The dinner was fabulous, and he took great enjoyment in watching Julia savor each bite. Both of them imbibed freely of the wine, and by the end of the meal they were each feeling more than a little tipsy.

Matt was making the rounds with his camera again, and this time Nathan impulsively tugged Julia onto his lap. She laughed in delight, wrapping her arms around his neck as Matt snapped their photo. Nathan kept her firmly in place once Matt walked away.

"Mmm, I like having you on my lap this way," he murmured in her ear. "Too bad this dress is so tight. There's no way I can slide my hand up underneath it discreetly. And it's really too bad that the weather is too warm for you to have worn stockings. The ones with the seam up the back that I love so much would have looked really hot with this dress."

She wiggled her derriere intentionally against his rapidly hardening erection. "Sorry to disappoint you, honey. But even for you I'm not putting on hosiery when it's eighty degrees outside."

He ran a hand up the back of her calf. "I'll just have to content myself with all this bare, silky skin. And look forward to the days getting colder soon."

Nathan reluctantly returned Julia to her own seat when dessert and coffee were served. Dessert was a fabulous red velvet birthday cake, and he watched his girl with a grin as she licked the thick glob of cream cheese frosting off her fork.

"Yum, this is *sooo* good," she groaned. "I wish I hadn't had so much to eat at dinner. Otherwise, I would totally get a second piece of that cake. Remind me to ask Jada what bakery they ordered it from."

He took a leisurely sip of his coffee. "You're going to have to find a way to work off all those calories, baby. I've got a great suggestion."

She rolled her eyes at him. "Yeah, I'll just bet you do. If I keep using your methods to burn off calories, I'm going to drop a dress size pretty soon."

Nathan snickered, running his hand up the side of her waist to brush teasingly against her breast. "Just as long as you don't drop a bra size. I like the girls just the way they are." He ran his tongue around the shell of her ear. "In fact, I like them so much I'm thinking seriously about fucking them later."

Julia gave a little shiver of arousal at the enticing picture he painted. "Um, I think they'd really, really like that," she murmured. "When can we duck out of here without seeming rude?"

His hand stroked the nape of her neck. "If we left now everyone at this party will know we're headed out to fuck. Ten of my buddies would follow us to our room and try to eavesdrop or call out lewd suggestions from outside the door."

"Oh." She took a sip of her coffee. "Guess we'll wait awhile longer, then."

He chuckled. "Probably a good idea. Besides, think of how much hotter it'll be if we have to wait for a couple more hours."

Julia leaned over and whispered naughtily, "But my panties are already wet. If we have to wait another two hours, it's going to take you forever to lick me dry."

Nathan threaded a hand in her hair and pulled her close for a long, deep kiss. She was panting when he finally lifted his mouth from hers, only to nuzzle the side of her neck. He completely ignored the cat calls and semi-obscene suggestions several of his buddies seated around their table made.

"You're always getting your underwear wet, baby," he purred low enough for only her ears. "Maybe you should just stop wearing them. Think how much money you'd save if you don't have to buy any more ridiculously overpriced panties."

She laughed along with him, even as he pulled her to her feet and then out to the area that had been cleared for dancing. Matt had gone all out and hired a six-piece band, and numerous pairs of eyes were drawn to Julia and Nathan as they tore up the dance floor. And Julia grew more and more turned on with each new song the band played – whether it was a slow, sultry number where they danced wrapped in the other's arms, her head on his shoulder, or a faster one where they dirty danced, grinding up against each other suggestively. She laughed at the whistles and cheers several of Nathan's friends gave in encouragement as his hands gripped her hips from behind, moving her in sync with his gyrating pelvis.

Then the music changed again, and Nathan pulled her close for another slow dance.

"I hope like hell this band starts winding down soon," he murmured in her ear. "I'm so fucking horny right now it's getting painful."

"Poor baby," she crooned. "I guess this would be a bad time to tell you about how wet I am."

He groaned. "Yeah, it really, really would. Jesus, all I want to do is slide inside that sweet cunt of yours and stay there for at least a couple of hours."

"Maybe the bandleader takes bribes. To stop playing, that is, not for requests."

Nathan chuckled. "I like the way you think." He bent his head and captured her mouth in a long, slow kiss, ignoring the cat calls as well as the flash of a camera. He lifted his head in time to see a grinning Matt, camera in hand yet again, and managed to discreetly flip him off.

✳✳✳✳✳

"Ah, God, that's so good, Nathan. Ohh, yes, just like that."

Julia's head thrashed back and forth on the pillow while Nathan's head was busy between her legs, his tongue licking at her soaking wet slit. She had already been so aroused, so needy, from their earlier cuddling and dancing, that it had taken the merest thrust of his fingers inside of her, while his talented mouth had sucked her nipple, for her to go off. But that hadn't been nearly enough for Nathan, and he was in the very enjoyable process of wringing another orgasm from her.

Her back bowed off the bed as his tongue thrust inside of her, his finger circling the hard nub of her clit over and over.

"Ohh, I'm going to come again. Ah, Nathan, I love you!"

He rested his head on her belly, placing kisses along her hipbone as she quivered uncontrollably from orgasm number two. It never failed to amaze Julia at how quickly and effortlessly he could make her come. He was so skilled, so knowledgeable about what she craved, and seemed to be more familiar with her body than she was.

But when he lowered his head to begin round three, she pulled on his hair, tugging him up.

"God, I can't," she breathed. "I'm still coming down to earth from the last one."

Nathan slid up beside her, wrapping her in his arms and kissing her slowly, his lips still shiny with her muskiness. "I love making you come. I could do that for hours, baby, just eat you out all night long."

"Mmm, but that hardly seems fair," she whispered, her hand slowly stroking his rock hard erection. At his groan, she began to gradually increase the rhythm of her strokes. "I mean, you need equal attention, after all. We could switch off – one orgasm for me, one for you."

He chuckled, tumbling her onto her back. "I doubt that I could keep up with you, baby. Though it would be a hell of a lot of fun to try. Now, as I recall, I promised my favorite girls a special treat."

Julia cupped her full, achy breasts and pushed them even closer together, until there was virtually no space in between them. Nathan gave an almost feral smile, his light blue eyes glittering with arousal.

"That's it, baby. Push those tits together so they're nice and tight for my cock."

He guided the tip of his penis between her breasts, and then slowly began to thrust up and down. With each upward thrust, Julia flicked her tongue over the broad head of his cock.

"Jesus," he gritted out. "That feels so fucking amazing. I'm going to come all over your tits if I keep this up."

She sucked the tip of his cock between her lips at the next thrust. "Do it," she urged, as he slid back down through her deep cleavage.

Then she was gasping, for in two swift movements he had slid down her body and thrust deep inside her dripping wet pussy. Her legs instantly wrapped around his hips as he rode her hard. Nathan laced his fingers with hers, drawing her arms over her head and pinning them in place. And then he slowed the pace of his movements to long, deliberate thrusts, pulling out of her nearly to the tip and then sliding back inside with exquisite control.

He nuzzled his face into the side of her neck, his sweat dampened hair brushing against her cheek. "God, I could stay just like this forever, Julia," he breathed. "I don't want to move because then it'll be over with too soon and I want to make this last as long as possible."

She turned her head to meet his deep, searching kiss, their tongues tangling together in a slow, erotic mating. "I want that, too," she whispered back. "I always want you. Too much, I think."

"No." He rose up, lifting his chest from her breasts and shaking his head as he gazed down at her. "Never too much. It's just right, baby."

Julia gasped as he began to move again, more quickly this time. Bracing himself on his hands, he used the leverage to do her hard, fucking into her over and over. A long, low moan began to rise up from her throat as she began to feel the stirring of yet another climax he was wringing from her body. Then he slid his hands to her thighs, lifting her knees and bending them towards her shoulders so that he could penetrate her even deeper.

"Oh, God, oh, God, oh, God," she chanted wildly, consumed with the half-pleasure, half-pain she was experiencing at having him buried so deeply inside of her. Tears were streaming down her cheeks at the intensity, the raw, primal beauty of their lovemaking, and she screamed his name as she came for long, shuddering moments.

"Ah, Christ, I want to make this last, feel this fucking good for hours yet, but I need to come so badly. Jesus, it hurts from being so hard," he grunted.

She pulled his head down to hers, kissing him long and deep, before murmuring in his ear, "Then come. I promise to get you hard again real fast."

Groaning, he gave in, finding the release his body so desperately craved. He continued to pump into her long after she would have imagined him empty. Even before he slowly, reluctantly, withdrew from her, she could feel the hot, wet trickle of his semen seeping down her thighs.

Nathan collapsed on the bed next to her, instantly drawing her close against him as their limbs entwined. Julia felt incredibly sated, her legs like wet noodles, but at the same time her body continued to react to his and her erect nipples poked into his chest, her hand rubbing up and down his hipbone.

"It's never enough, is it?" he rasped, caressing her cheek, his thumb brushing over her kiss-swollen lips.

She sucked his thumb into her mouth, loving the way his eyes darkened as she did so. "No, never. I'm glad you feel that way, too. I was starting to worry that I was abnormal or something, wanting you as much as I do."

He chuckled, sliding his hand down to cup her breast, tweaking the nipple. "Baby, there isn't one single abnormal thing about you." He licked the side of her neck. "Especially not your insatiable sex drive."

"Mmm." She purred like a kitten beneath the slow, sensual kiss he gave her. "You're just as insatiable."

Nathan splayed his hand over her soft belly, his fingers tickling the curls between her thighs. "Can you blame me? All I have to do is look at you and I get hard. And as soon as I come, all I can think about is fucking you again. I'm obsessed with you, Julia."

"It's the same for me," she confessed. "All day long at work all I can think about is when it will finally be time to go home so I can be with you again. Do you think we need therapy or something? I mean, is this really normal or healthy?"

He laughed, rolling onto his back and pulling her astride him. He caressed the bare curves of her ass before giving her a playful swat. "No, we definitely don't need therapy. We probably have the healthiest sex life in San Francisco. And I guarantee you that out of all the rooms in this hotel ours is getting the most action by far. I'm guessing my buddies have probably figured that out by now, too."

Julia gasped in indignation. "Please tell me that those perverts are not at the door listening."

"Oh, hell, no. Baby, I told you that I'm not into exhibitionism. Especially not with my horndog friends. But every one of them had their tongue hanging out after meeting you tonight, and told me what a lucky bastard I am. Not that I didn't already know that."

"Ohh, that's so good," she moaned, as his hand slid up the side of her waist to fondle one engorged breast, his thumb brushing over the nipple. Beneath her she could feel his cock starting to swell again, and she smiled at the sharp intake of his breath as she ran just the tip of her finger up and down his length.

"Christ, I'm already getting hard again," he hissed, as her hand closed over him fully, stroking him persuasively.

She lowered herself to lie on top of him, her breasts crushed to his chest. "I did promise you, didn't I?" she murmured naughtily, her teeth nipping at his earlobe.

Their lips met and clung in a wet, open-mouthed kiss. Nathan groaned beneath her sultry kiss, the feel of her full breasts as she rubbed them against his skin, and the slow, deliberate strokes of her hand on his cock.

"God, what you do to me, Julia," he uttered harshly. "I've never, ever been able to get this hard so fast, so soon. You're going to kill me with so much sex."

"Fucked to death." She nodded in amused agreement. "But what a way to go, huh?"

"Put me inside you. Real slow." He bit his lip as she followed his command to the tee, inserting just the tip of his cock inside her drenched slit before lowering herself a mere inch at a time until he was fully sheathed.

Sweat dripped from his forehead as he gazed up at her. Their hotel room was fully lit so that he could see her in exquisite detail – the pink flush on her cheeks, the way her lushly swollen mouth trembled in anticipation, the beads of sweat trickling ever so slowly between the heavy mounds of her breasts. His hands gripped her hips, guiding the motion as she screwed him slowly.

"Jesus, you look so fucking hot," he growled. "You're so beautiful, Julia, almost too beautiful to be real."

"But I am real," she breathed, rocking her pelvis to and fro, riding him in slow, measured movements. "Touch me, feel me, *own* me, Nathan. This is what I live for – to be with you just like this, every day, as many times as possible. I am *definitely* obsessed with you."

"Julia." Her name was a long, drawn-out moan that came from deep in his chest. He reared up to his knees, draping her thighs over his as he silently urged her to ride him harder. She clutched his shoulders, holding on tight as she did his bidding. His arms banded around her waist, his lips sucking at a tender spot on the side of her neck, and she recognized hazily that he was marking her. But her neck wasn't the only place he was leaving a brand – she belonged to him body and soul and the same was true for him. They were bound together in every way, and it was a sweet, intoxicating craving that never seemed sated, no matter how many times they were together this way.

They made love to each other all night long – using hands, mouths, bodies – until they were both exhausted. And even then – when Nathan knew he was physically incapable of summoning up one more erection, and Julia was raw and aching in every part of her body – they still craved the other. They lay cuddled together, too wrung out to even lift their heads, and when Julia spoke it was in a hoarse little whisper.

"I think – I need to sleep now," she told him weakly. "We might have finally managed to wear each other out."

He exhaled deeply, flinging an arm across her body and burying his face in her pillow. "Jesus, no kidding. I came so many times tonight I think it'll be days before I can get it up again."

"Really? Guess I'll have to forget about my idea of waking you up with a blowjob, then," she murmured teasingly, running her hands through the damp strands of his hair.

Nathan lifted his head from the pillow with some difficulty, squinting at her with one eye half-open. "Oh. Shit. Um, well, let's not give up hope just yet. I'll bet if we get a few hours of sleep I'd be as good as new. So don't put that idea by the wayside so soon."

She gave him one final, sweet goodnight kiss. "Sleep tight, baby. I'm so tired I feel like I could sleep for two whole days."

"Mmm, sounds good. But not nearly as good as that wake-up call you just mentioned."

Julia laughed softly. "See? I knew that would get your attention. I love you, Nathan."

He kissed the top of her head tenderly. "And God knows how much I love you, baby. Sleep now."

Chapter Twenty-Two

Late September

Cameron stared at her computer monitor, growing angrier and angrier as she paged through one photo after another. She'd been both pissed off and deeply hurt when Nathan had removed her from his list of Facebook friends, not to mention blocking her email address and changing his phone numbers. But she was still friends with several of their mutual acquaintances, including Matt and Jada Wright. The photos that Cameron was currently fuming over had been taken at Jada's thirtieth birthday party, and several of them featured Nathan and his little bitch Julia.

She snarled at the shot of them with their arms wrapped around each other, smiling happily for the camera. She cursed both of them vividly when she saw the photo of Julia sitting on Nathan's lap, her arms entwined around his neck. But the picture that caused her to throw her wine glass against the wall was a candid one that had caught the lovebirds kissing passionately.

"Fucking boyfriend-stealing bitch!" she screamed, her rage growing in leaps and bounds. "You are *so* going to pay for this, you skank!"

It had been almost three months now since Nathan had broken their engagement, and her heart along with it. But Cameron was no closer to getting over it today than she had been back in June. When her other two engagements had ended, she hadn't wasted any time in going back on the prowl, looking for a new boyfriend. This time was different.

Her sister and girlfriends had tried their best to cheer her up and help her get over the heartache. But nothing had helped –

dinners out, barhopping, shopping trips, spa days. Stephanie had convinced her to spend a long weekend in Palm Springs, but Cameron had been morose and despondent the whole time, and spent most of it drinking.

She'd been drinking a lot lately, truth be told, and it was starting to show in her puffy face and bloodshot eyes. At the same time she had no appetite and was skinnier than ever. She hadn't bothered to cut her hair or have the color touched up for weeks now, and her brown roots were really showing. She'd missed several manicure appointments, and her nails looked appalling. But none of that mattered to her. All she could dwell on, day after day, was how miserable she was, how betrayed she felt, how alone she was. She despaired of ever finding a man, of being married or being happy. She had no interest in dating, or even having a one-night stand. Instead, she was obsessed with finding a way to get Nathan back, and to exact her well-deserved revenge on Julia.

But since Nathan had virtually cut off all ties with her, and made it extremely difficult to see or talk to him, her frustration mounted daily. She had started toying with the idea of hiring a private detective to shadow Nathan's daily activities so that she would know where to find him. But even in her highly emotional state, Cameron realized just how desperate that idea was and had nixed it.

It wasn't out of the question, however, for her to follow him by herself. She could hang outside his condo undetected and wait for him to emerge, or linger outside his office building when he left work. If she was discreet, he would never notice her. And then, when the time felt right, she could approach him and tell him how much she still loved him, how much she needed to be with him, and how happy they could still be together.

Cameron felt a little calmer now that she had some semblance of a plan. It would mean spending even more time away from the gallery, but that was why she paid her employees so well. What was the point of being the boss if she couldn't make her own hours?

She would begin the next day, waiting outside the parking garage next to Nathan's office building for his car to exit. Then she would follow him in her own vehicle, and hope the opportunity presented itself to talk to him. One way or the other, she would find a way to get Julia out of his life and resume her rightful place as Nathan's fiancée.

✳✳✳✳✳

"I love to watch you eat."

Julia looked up self-consciously at Nathan's comment, aware that her cheeks were currently stuffed full of mushroom risotto. She swallowed carefully and took a sip of her wine to wash it down before asking him warily, "Uh, and why is that?"

He grinned, chucking her playfully on the chin. "Because you get such enjoyment from whatever you eat. It's almost like a sexual experience to watch you sometimes, the way you moan in pleasure and lick your lips. I'm more than a little turned on right now."

She laughed. "You want me to re-enact the famous orgasm scene from *When Harry Met Sally*? That's one of my favorite movies of all time. I think I know that scene word for word."

He glanced around the crowded restaurant uncertainly. "Um, better not. But you can have a real orgasm when we get back to my place."

"Is that a guarantee? You're very confident in your abilities, aren't you?" she challenged.

He clasped her hand. "Where you're concerned, yes. Just consider me your sex slave, baby. My sole purpose in life is to give you pleasure."

Her green eyes twinkled merrily. "Well, if that's the case, I want at least three orgasms tonight – slave."

"Ah, a tall order, my lady, but your loyal slave will do his utmost to satisfy you."

They laughed at their silly little role playing, before resuming their meal. Because they had worked so late, Julia hadn't argued for once when Nathan had insisted on going out to dinner. She cooked as often as possible, especially at his condo where she adored the spacious kitchen and professional grade appliances. His formerly austere kitchen now held an ever increasing inventory of pots, pans, utensils, spices and food. They divided their time almost equally between their two places, not having made much progress in finding a larger place so they could officially move in together.

Nathan made a mental note to contact one of his friends who was a property manager to see if he could help them find a larger place to rent. He had already decided to rent out his condo, and would eventually sell it when – and if – the dream home in Tiburon got built.

They were just finishing up their meal when Julia froze, an expression of alarm on her features. He frowned, but before he could ask what was wrong, the sound of an all-too-familiar voice answered his own question.

"Well, look who's here. My backstabbing ex-fiancé and his boyfriend-stealing little bitch."

Cameron's voice could have cut glass, and the look on her face was one of pure hatred. Nathan stared at her in shock, for the woman hovering menacingly over their table bore little resemblance to the sleek, sophisticated woman he'd dated for two years. Cameron was scary-skinny, her face gaunt with dark circles under her eyes. She wasn't wearing any makeup, or it had already worn off, and her hair was lank and limp, as though she hadn't washed it for days. Her skirt and blouse were wrinkled and hung loosely on her body. But what really concerned Nathan was the almost manic look in her eyes.

He tried valiantly to keep things calm, speaking in a soft, gentle voice. "Cameron, what are you doing here? Are you having dinner with someone?"

Cameron looked from him to Julia and back again, her agitation mounting. "No. I just walked by and saw you through the window."

Nathan frowned, for their table was set far back in a corner, and it would have been extremely difficult to see them from the sidewalk. Tactfully, though, he decided not to push the issue, especially since he now feared that Cameron had followed them here from the office.

"Was there something you wanted?" he asked politely.

Cameron's mouth curled up into an expression that resembled a snarl. "Yes. I want things to go back to the way they were before this whore stole you away from me. I want my fiancé back. And I'm going to make sure it happens."

Nathan flinched, especially when the ever-increasing volume of her voice started attracting stares from other diners. "Cam, this really isn't the time or place to have this discussion," he told her firmly. "Don't make a scene, okay?"

"A scene?" she screeched. "I'll make a goddamn scene if I goddamn feel like it! Here – how's this for a scene?"

In a flash, she'd picked up Nathan's half-empty wine glass and flung the liquid in Julia's face. Aware of all the gasps and stares coming from the surrounding tables, as well as the distress on Julia's face, he surged to his feet and grabbed Cameron's forearm.

"You need to get out of here now," he hissed. "You're way out of line. I don't want to see or hear from you ever again, Cameron. You need to leave us alone."

"Screw you both!" she screamed at the top of her lungs. "I'll leave when I'm fucking ready to leave. Let go of me, you bastard!"

Fortunately, the maitre'd and two waiters were hurriedly approaching the table, and Nathan was all too happy to have them forcibly escort an irate Cameron from the premises. His legs were shaking as he took his seat, and he could finally tend to Julia.

She was trembling, and tears had pooled in her eyes. She'd blotted up the wine from her face and dress, and had wrapped her arms around herself. Tenderly, he tilted her chin up.

"Are you okay, baby?" he murmured in concern. "God, what a disaster that was. I'm so sorry."

Julia shook her head. "It's okay, not your fault. How could you possibly have known she'd show up here?"

Nathan hesitated before sharing his concerns with her. "I think she might have followed us here after work," he admitted. "I didn't want to tell you this because frankly I thought I was probably just imagining it. But I think she's been stalking us a bit over the past couple of weeks."

"What?" Julia's eyes went wide with shock. "Oh, my God, that's crazy. Why do you think that?"

"Now that I think of it, I swear I've seen someone resembling her hanging outside both the office and the condo a few times recently. I put it down to coincidence or paranoia, but after this incident I'm pretty sure it was her."

"What can we do about it?" she asked in a worried tone.

"Not sure exactly. Tonight was the first time she's actually approached either of us, so hopefully she'll leave us alone from here on end. If she does start harassing us, though, we call the police and get a restraining order. Right now we can't do much, I'm afraid. Just be aware and if you do see her try your best to avoid a confrontation."

Julia glared. "She's damned lucky that was white wine she doused me with, not red. And the bitch had better hope the dry cleaner can get the stain out of this dress. It's Donna Karan, you know, and one of my new favorites."

He chuckled, admiring anew how hot she looked in the camel colored dress with its little cap sleeves and draped neckline that revealed a tantalizing bit of cleavage. "Baby, how do you keep track of all that stuff in your closet? Your aunt sends you stuff faster than you can wear it."

"Its Fashion Week time of year," she explained. "All of the designers are showing their spring collections, so Aunt Maddy is getting tons of stuff sent her way. Therefore, I'm getting tons of stuff sent my way."

"We're definitely going to need a separate room just for your clothes and shoes."

Julia was about to make a retort when the maître'd approached their table, apologizing profusely for having let Cameron slip past him.

"I'm so sorry, madam, sir," he told them earnestly. "I could sense that the lady was in something of a state, but I was busy helping other customers and she just walked in. Are you both all right? Can I offer you a glass of wine, perhaps, to calm the nerves?"

Julia shuddered. "Not wine, no."

"I think maybe just some hot tea for the lady. And a brandy for me," added Nathan. "And I apologize as well for the scene she caused. It was very unexpected."

The maître'd assured him it was no problem, and summoned a waiter to get their drinks.

"I didn't think to ask. Did you want dessert?"

She shook her head at Nathan's questions. "No. This pretty much ruined my appetite. And that's a real shame because I saw chocolate cream pie on the menu."

He grinned. "We'll get two slices to go. Hopefully your appetite will return later tonight. Otherwise the pie will keep until tomorrow."

Her eyes sparkled. "I knew there was a reason I loved you besides your hot body and your ability to give me multiple orgasms. Speaking of which – that particular appetite hasn't been affected."

He squeezed her hand. "Well, that's a relief. Good to know a crazy ex-girlfriend doesn't impair your libido."

"Honey, I think you'd have to go bald, gain fifty pounds, and eat whole cloves of garlic in order to impair my libido," she joked. "So let's order that pie so you can start working on those three orgasms you promised me."

Chapter Twenty-Three

October

Nathan had only been inside the McKinnon home in the Carmel Highlands for a few minutes, but still felt an instant connection to the place. The architect in him greatly admired the design of the spacious home and its abundance of natural light. Nearly every room had an ocean or cove view, and there was access to the wraparound deck from multiple locations.

And the homebody in him felt an immediate sense of peace and tranquility from the way the place had been decorated. It seemed that each piece of furniture, each sculpture or bowl or memento had been lovingly and carefully chosen. And of course, the house boasted some of Natalie Benoit's finest works hanging on the walls.

Because work had been so crazy these past few months, and factoring in the month Julia's parents had spent vacationing in South America, this weekend was the first time Nathan had met Robert McKinnon and his wife Natalie. He had been admittedly more than a little nervous to meet Julia's parents, especially her father who Nathan had hero-worshipped since deciding to become an architect. He had been pleasantly surprised at how warm and welcoming both of them had been, and how they had made him feel instantly at home.

It was late Friday afternoon, and the four of them were sitting on the main deck at the back of the house which had a spectacular ocean view. The weather was perfect – sunny, a little warm, and very little breeze – the sort of ideal Indian summer day that Northern California often enjoyed at this time of year. Natalie had opened a bottle of crisp, chilled Chardonnay and set out little dishes of olives, ceviche, mango salsa, and goat cheese with assorted breads and crackers.

Upon their arrival less than an hour ago, Nathan and Julia had been enthusiastically greeted by her parents' three Australian shepherds. Julia had called each of them by name – Gracie, Duncan and Mickey – and explained that the female was the mother to the two younger, friskier boys. All three dogs had followed Nathan in a pack, clearly enchanted by the newcomer and demanding his attention. They had finally mellowed out, retreating to their own corner of the deck, rousing now and then to bark at an errant seagull.

He was glad he'd followed Julia's instructions to dress casually in jeans and a gray Armani T-shirt, for both of her parents were equally casual. Both wore jeans, Robert in a white shirt with the sleeves rolled up to his elbows, while Natalie's floaty tunic was half a dozen shades of blue and lavender. Both were barefoot. Julia, of course, wore her version of casual – a dainty white ruffled chemise top paired with a tiered floral print cotton skirt. To Nathan's surprise, she actually kicked off her wedge sandals upon arrival and was now padding around barefoot like her parents.

It was clear that Julia and Lauren greatly resembled their mother, for Natalie had the same classically beautiful features and caramel colored hair. But the twins' huge mossy green eyes had been inherited from their father – a handsome, dark-haired man with touches of gray at the temples.

The peaceful serenity was abruptly interrupted by the arrival of Lauren. They could see her approach from the road below, and Nathan was not the least bit surprised to see her drive up in a four-wheel drive Jeep Wrangler. Given the tough-girl image she worked so hard to project, it was small wonder that she would be driving such a heavy duty vehicle. The dogs went nuts when they saw her, barking and running around excitedly before greeting her with enthusiastic licks. She dropped her backpack and an overstuffed canvas tote bag in her tracks, and gave everyone a hug, Nathan included.

"So you finally got the balls to meet the parents, huh?" she asked in her usual forthright manner.

Natalie rolled her eyes. "Lauren, darling, language."

Lauren merely gave her mother a resounding smack on the cheek in reply. "Nathan's a big boy. He can handle whatever I dish out."

Julia shook her head in exasperation as she greeted her twin with a hug. "One of these days that smart mouth of yours is going to get you into trouble."

Lauren hooted. "Baby sister, what makes you think it already hasn't? Remind me to tell you about the latest blow-up I had with my boss. I can still see the steam coming out of his ears."

Julia frowned. "Careful he doesn't fire your butt."

"Nah. It's way too cute a butt and besides, Ben knows how valuable I am to the magazine. Doesn't hurt to keep him on his toes every so often. So – you don't look a year older, baby girl."

Julia laughed. "Yeah, neither do you, big sis."

"That's because your birthday isn't until tomorrow," retorted Robert. "And both of my girls look beautiful. Though I can't believe you're already twenty-six. It seems like just yesterday you were small enough that your mother could still dress you alike."

Lauren shuddered. "Thank God Mom got over that whole notion by the time we were two."

"That's because Julia refused to wear anything but cute, frilly dresses and you would only wear pants or shorts," replied Natalie dryly. "Some things haven't changed."

"Hey, I wore a dress last month," protested Lauren. "It was at a dinner party that Jules and Nathan gave. One of their big clients attended so Julia dragged me into her closet and got me all girly."

Julia smiled. "And she looked gorgeous. Enough so that Ian stuck by your side all evening."

Lauren shrugged. "He's a sweetheart. Such a gentleman and really, really attractive. But nothing happening there, I'm afraid. Not my type."

"Honestly, Lauren?" asked Julia in exasperation. "Mom, you should see this guy. Six four, shoulders like a linebacker, Savile Row suits, British accent. And he's filthy rich. But Lauren would rather go out with some grungy guy in a two-bit rock band who lives above a garage somewhere."

"If Ian Gregson is so fabulous, why aren't you dating him?" challenged Lauren.

"Um, hey? Over here? Remember me – the boyfriend?" Nathan glared at Lauren. "I saw her first. And Ian is a client – our best client."

Lauren looked unimpressed. "So? You're Julia's boss – employer – whatever. How is that anymore appropriate?"

"Enough." Robert McKinnon's voice was brisk and authoritative, and both girls were instantly quiet. "It's like the two of you were back in high school with your arguing. Let's have a peaceful weekend, young ladies. I don't get to see both of my girls together very often so cease your bickering."

Nathan wasn't surprised when Julia obediently murmured, "Yes, Daddy," but he was startled when the ballsy Lauren also backed down and gave her father a hug. It was obvious that Robert adored his twin daughters and that they in turn doted on their father.

Julia helped Natalie get dinner together while Lauren fed the dogs. That left Nathan alone with Robert.

"I've been admiring this house since we drove up," admitted Nathan. "It's given me a few ideas about a project I'm working on. A personal project."

Robert nodded. "Julia mentioned that you're designing a home of your own. And that you've got designers block or some such thing."

Nathan grinned. "I'm not sure that's an actual condition but yes, nothing I've started so far feels right. There's something I'm missing, and it's been driving me mad for months now."

The older man finished his wine. "Did you bring any of your designs along?"

"I did, actually," admitted Nathan. "I thought spending time by the ocean might inspire me. I don't know how much Julia has told you about the lot but it's on the waterfront."

"Aye, she told me that much." A trace of Robert's Scottish brogue could be plainly heard now and then, though living in the U.S. for over forty years had erased most of it. "Perhaps after dinner we'll take a look at some of your ideas, brainstorm a bit. Natalie has a good eye for these things, too. Such a talent that woman has for art and design. Simply brilliant."

Nathan was almost speechless with surprise. "I - that's fantastic, Mr. McKinnon. But I don't want to intrude, especially since you don't get to see your daughters that often."

"Not to worry, young man. I see our Laurie quite a bit, and Natalie and I are planning to visit Julia at the end of the month. In fact, we can take a first-hand look at this property of yours, maybe refine any ideas we might come up with this weekend. And Nathan —" he paused until Nathan met his eye, then smiled reassuringly. "It's Robert. We're not much for formalities around here."

Nathan couldn't help but contrast the relaxed and informal atmosphere that filled the McKinnon home with the stiff, uncomfortable and stuffy feeling he'd always had when associating with Cameron's family. The Tollivers would never have dreamed of dining alfresco in bare feet, eating off Mexican pottery and enjoying a casual but delicious meal of clam chowder, cracked crab, and a huge green salad. The conversation around the dinner table was lively and stimulating, and Nathan never felt that he had to choose his words carefully or avoid particular topics. The McKinnons made him feel instantly welcomed and part of the family. Even the dogs liked him, judging by the fact that one rested a furry head in his lap, while another lounged at his feet.

"You've made some friends there, Nathan," observed Natalie with a smile.

Lauren snickered. "Don't flatter him, Mom. These mutts will hang around anyone they think will cave in and feed them. They must scent your susceptibility, Nathan."

"Hey, missy, these are purebred, pedigreed Aussies," said Robert in indignation. "Don't be calling my boys and my best girl here mutts." He scratched an adoring Gracie behind the ears.

"Dad's dogs got away with murder when we were growing up," groused Julia. "Far more spoiled and indulged than Lauren and I were."

"And more obedient, too," retorted Robert.

Julia tapped Mickey on the nose, his head still resting in Nathan's lap. "Hey, you, stop begging. Never mind that look. I stopped falling for those sorts of looks a long time ago." She looked curiously from the dog's pale blue eyes to Nathan's and smiled. "Look, you two have the same eyes."

Nathan grinned. "Maybe Mickey thinks I'm a long lost brother or cousin. He sees the family resemblance."

That comment brought a round of laughter from everyone at the table and made Nathan feel even more at ease.

When dinner was over, everyone did their part in clearing the table and tidying up the dishes. Robert took several shot glasses from a cabinet in the dining room.

"What say we hold off on coffee and dessert for a bit and break open this lovely bottle of Macallan that Nathan brought down?" he suggested.

There were no arguments to be heard as everyone settled around the spacious oak pedestal table in the dining room. The sun had set and with it the day's balmy temperatures, so it felt good to be inside the house. At Robert's urgings, Nathan fetched the house designs he'd brought with him and spread them out on the huge table. It didn't take long for all the McKinnons to jump into the discussion and offer up their opinions, in between shots of twenty-one year old single malt Scotch.

After listening to his wife's and daughters' ideas, Robert furrowed his brow and tapped a finger against his lips.

"Here's a thought, Nathan. What if you were to change this over here —" he drew a few lines, erased others. "And then, in this section, you tried something like this."

Fifteen minutes later, Nathan could only stare in wide-eyed admiration at the small but significant changes Robert had made. All of a sudden the missing pieces clicked into place, and he had a clear and vivid picture of what he wanted to do.

The two men worked on the design for another hour until the smell of freshly brewed coffee and warm cinnamon scented bread budding lured them away from their project. It was after midnight by the time he was cuddling in bed with Julia, and he offered up an apology.

"I'm sorry if I neglected you tonight, baby. I just couldn't believe how that design came together so easily with your dad's input. He really is a genius," marveled Nathan.

Julia entwined her legs with his, pressing a kiss to his throat. "I don't mind at all. I'm just happy you seem to get on so well with him. Daddy isn't always an easy one to get close to. But he likes you, I can tell."

He stilled her hand as it caressed his hip. "Well, he won't like me at all if he thinks we're getting it on in his house. As tempting as you are, I'm not going to ravish you with your parents' bedroom on one side, and your sister's on another. Not to mention our roommate here."

Julia laughed softly as Mickey's ears twitched in his sleep. The dog had followed them into their bedroom and promptly settled in for a long night's sleep at the foot of the bed.

"Don't mind Mickey. Not much wakes him – or the other two for that matter. But you're right – I'd be more than a little self-conscious with my parents and Lauren both within earshot. Guess we should have stayed at a hotel, huh?"

He cuddled her close, kissing her temple. "Don't be silly. I wouldn't have passed up the opportunity to sleep in a Robert McKinnon designed house. And it's been great meeting your parents and seeing where you grew up."

"I'll get to return the favor when we head to Michigan for Thanksgiving. I'm really looking forward to seeing your parents again and meeting the rest of your family."

"You're sure you don't mind not seeing your family then?"

Julia shook her head. "It's okay. My parents and Lauren always fly to New York to spend Thanksgiving with Aunt Maddy. With the holiday shopping season already in full swing, it's impossible for her to get away then. Besides, we'll get to spend Christmas with my family so it's a fair trade."

They fell asleep soon after, one of the very few times they'd slept together without having sex first. It took a great deal of self control on Nathan's part the next morning to gingerly extricate himself from her arms and slip out of bed. The temptation to wake her with a bout of sleepy sex was almost too much to resist, but the recollection that they were far from alone in this house greatly cooled his ardor. Not to mention the fact that Mickey suddenly bounced up like a jackrabbit, evidently well rested from his long sleep, and began licking Nathan happily, his tail wagging furiously. Nathan was barely able to struggle into some running clothes and pick up his shoes without the dog lavishing him with attention.

He'd figured to be the only one awake at this hour, but the smell of coffee dispelled that idea. Lauren was in the kitchen, sipping from her coffee mug, and also dressed in workout gear. The other two dogs were resting at her feet.

"So you survived the night with Mickey, I see," she said dryly. "He snores pretty loud."

Nathan accepted the mug she handed him and poured some coffee. "Yeah, well, he's also a very effective cockblocker."

Lauren snickered. "Like you would have really had the balls to hump my sister with our father in the next room anyway. Jules and I might be twenty-five – ah, twenty-six actually – but Daddy still thinks of us as his little girls. Do you know I still have to call him every time I'm on assignment? One time I was in a really remote locale with no cell or internet service, and he actually called my boss in New York because he hadn't heard from me yet. Ben had to reach me by satellite phone and tell me to call my Daddy. He still ribs me unmercifully about it, the bastard."

"He just cares about you. And he's right to worry, given some of the godforsaken places Julia's told me you've been to. You've got more guts than I do."

She grinned. "Yeah, and I'll bet I can kick your ass on this run, too. I hope you've been doing some hill training, because there aren't too many flat spots around here."

Nathan finished his coffee and gave her a mock glare. "Oh, it is on like Donkey Kong. Come on, let's see how tough you really are."

An hour later, he was grateful he hadn't eaten anything that morning for he was sure he'd be puking it up right now. Lauren had been merciless, running him up one ridiculously steep hill after another, until his lungs were ready to burst and his quadriceps shaking. The only satisfaction he got from the punishing workout was that Lauren, too, seemed more than a little spent.

They staggered up the outside stairs to the upper level deck just off the kitchen. Natalie was seated outside sipping coffee and sketching on a big pad. She smiled at them serenely.

"Lovely morning for a run. Lauren, I hope you weren't too tough on Nathan."

"He can take it," she replied without even a hint of compassion. "Where is everyone?"

"Your father's walking on the beach with the dogs as usual, and Julia is still asleep last I checked. She always was a much better sleeper than you were, Lauren."

Lauren snorted. "Lazy slug. I can't believe she actually drags her butt out of bed for a six a.m. yoga class."

"She does," verified Nathan. "Most mornings, anyway. But I've learned not to try and actually talk to her until after class. She's not much of a morning person."

Natalie smiled. "You're a wise man to have figured that out. But I did want to get breakfast started soon. We'll have our hands full as the day goes on getting ready for tonight's festivities."

There was a party planned to celebrate the twins' birthday, though Julia had told him not to expect anything too big or fancy. Maybe two dozen people, mostly family and old friends, and a very casual, laid-back buffet dinner. But it had been evident from last night's dinner that Julia had inherited her love of cooking from her mother, and Nathan was certain that Natalie had something special planned for tonight.

He finished the bottle of water that Natalie had thoughtfully had waiting for him and Lauren. "I'll go wake up Sleeping Beauty," he offered. "We'll be out after I shower."

He removed his shoes before entering the house, conscious of the beautiful white birch floors. They were a key element of the Nantucket style of the house, with its high wood-beamed ceilings and wainscoting in nearly every room.

He carefully shut the bedroom door behind him, and stripped off his sweaty workout clothes before kneeling beside the bed. Julia was still sleeping peacefully, her cheeks rosy and her mouth softly parted. With her hair tumbling around her shoulders, she looked very much like the fairytale princess he'd once compared her to, so beautiful she took his breath away. Gently, he pulled the covers off her, revealing her petite, curvy body garbed in a slip-style nightie of gold satin. One of the thin straps had fallen down her shoulder, baring half of her breast. Unable to resist, he slid the strap farther down, and groaned when her full, round breast popped out. He bent his head to lick the pink nipple before drawing it into his mouth.

Julia stirred beneath him, her legs moving restlessly. He pushed the short hem of her nightie up, baring the lower half of her body. She wasn't wearing panties and his nostrils flared at the sight of her naked cunt, and the musky scent of her female essence. He couldn't help nuzzling his face into her public hair, and then running his tongue over her satiny slit.

She gasped when he sucked at her clit, her eyes flying open as her hands tangled in his hair. "Oh, God, Nathan. God, that's good," she breathed.

He replaced his tongue with two long fingers, thrusting them in and out of her slickness. "Good morning, baby," he told her wickedly. "Sleep well?"

Julia panted as his fingers grew bolder. "You – ah, you should have woken me sooner. Especially if you're going to give me an orgasm."

Nathan chuckled. "That's the plan, baby. But I think we should continue this in the shower. I don't trust your sister not to eavesdrop. That girl needs to get laid more regularly. Maybe then she wouldn't be such a – "

She laid two fingers over his mouth, only to have him suck them hard. "You're right. Let's shower. Especially since I can tell you've been for a run. Please tell me you didn't go with Lauren."

He groaned. "Too late. Just don't tell her how badly she kicked my ass."

Minutes later they were happily ensconced in the en suite shower, soaping each other up and confident that the sound of the water running would drown out their amorous activities. They kissed wetly, Nathan's palms overflowing with Julia's lush breasts, while she stroked his rigid cock with both of her hands. When she reached further back to lightly squeeze his balls, he growled and spun her around, pressing the front of her body against the white and blue tiled shower wall.

"I haven't been inside you for over twenty-four hours," he rasped in her ear. "I think that's some sort of record for us. One I have no intention of ever trying to break."

He guided his cock inside of her, then held on to her hips as he began to move, his thrusts growing faster and harder. Julia's moans were muffled against the hand she thrust into her mouth, and his groans were stifled by burying his face in her neck. He slid one hand over her belly before dipping into her pubic hair and finding her swollen clit. Her head fell back against his shoulder as he continued to fuck her hard while flicking his thumb over her clit.

She came mere moments before he did, spilling himself deep inside of her. He held her back against him, steadying her while she quivered, and then turning her in his arms to meet his deep kiss.

"Now that's a proper good morning kiss," she whispered. "My very favorite way to start the day."

"Better than yoga class?" he teased. "And I can't believe it's better than a café au lait and a chocolate croissant."

Julia giggled. "Well, both of those are pretty close. But nothing says good morning like a big cock fucking your brains out."

He smacked her bare ass a little too hard to be considered playful. "You've become such a bad, dirty girl. We're going to have to start talking about punishments if you don't watch that filthy mouth."

"Hah. You love it and you know it."

Fifteen minutes later they were dressed and joining the others for breakfast on the deck. It was a simple but delicious meal of waffles, brown sugar-glazed bacon, fresh fruit and coffee. After the meal was served and the dishes cleared, everyone was tasked with doing their part to get ready for the birthday party. Lauren, who admittedly wasn't much of a cook, instead did some cleaning and rearranging of furniture. Natalie and Julia busied themselves in the kitchen to turn out platters and bowls of food. Nathan helped Robert set up the bar and the sound system, but after that there wasn't much else for them to do. But when Nathan suggested they help Julia and her mother with the food, Robert shuddered.

"It's a brave man – or a foolish one – who tries to invade Natalie's kitchen. It took years for her to get comfortable with Julia helping in there. Lauren is all too happy to stay out of there, as is my sister-in-law. Let's do some more work on those house plans of yours instead."

Nathan was thrilled at the opportunity to work alongside the architect he'd admired and emulated for more than a dozen years. And it didn't hurt that he was also forming a real rapport with Julia's father.

At some point, when they were looking at designs for the master bedroom, Robert lifted a brow in question. "I assume you've seen the contents of Julia's closet?"

Nathan nodded. "It's quite impressive, isn't it?"

Robert looked rather revolted. "More like obsessive. That's Madelyn's influence, not Natalie's. But be that as it may, all that stuff needs a place to reside. You'd best plan on making this walk in closet a whole lot bigger." He paused for long seconds before adding, "That is, assuming you intend for my Julia to live in this house one day."

Nathan flushed under the older man's intense regard. "Yes, of course. I mean, we haven't discussed marriage just yet, we haven't officially been dating all that long. But I'm crazy about her, she's everything I could ever want, and having her as my wife one day – well, it would be a dream come true."

Robert smiled, clearly pleased with this answer. "That's good enough for me, then. All in due time, I suppose." He returned his attention to the house plans. "On second thought, you may just want to build a whole separate room for her clothes. I don't know if a mere closet could hold them all."

✳✳✳✳✳

Guests began to arrive around six o'clock for the party, and within half an hour the upper deck was filled with people. Julia happily introduced Nathan to everyone – neighbors, old friends from school, friends of her parents, and Robert's younger brother Malcolm. Nathan learned that Julia's uncle lived in nearby Monterey and was also a renowned photographer. It was his influence that had set Lauren on her chosen career path.

To Nathan's surprise, another guest at the party was none other than Sam Patterson, the NFL quarterback and Julia's old high school sweetheart. His team was playing the San Francisco 49ers on Monday night, and thus he'd been able to break away for a quick visit to his parents, who were also at the party.

Nathan clenched his fists when he saw Sam sweep Julia into a fierce hug and plant a resounding smooch on her lips. But from the way both of them laughed as he let her go, Nathan felt reassured that the embrace had been a friendly one only.

Sam grinned at Nathan as they shook hands. "So you're the dude dating my Julia. You'd better be taking good care of my girl here."

Nathan scowled at him, not caring if he was one of the top sports figures in the country. "Actually, I think she's officially *my* girl now. You blew your chance a few years ago."

Sam chuckled. "Yeah, that's for sure. If I thought I stood a chance, I might try stealing her back from you, Nathan. But Jules seems pretty taken with you."

"There's always her identical twin," teased Nathan.

The look of horror on Sam's face was almost comical. "Oh, hell, no. I'd rather get sacked by a three hundred pound defensive lineman than tangle with Lauren. She scares the shit out of me."

Nathan nodded in agreement. "One of these days she'll meet her match. Kind of like *Taming of the Shrew.*"

Julia gave him a playful punch on the upper arm. "Hey, that's my sister you're dissing. And while Lauren may be a little intimidating she's a great girl. Any guy would be lucky to have her."

Sam gave a little shudder. "Not touching that one. I still haven't forgotten the roundhouse kick she landed on my head junior year. Almost knocked me out cold."

Nathan was pleasantly surprised to find that Sam was one of the most likeable guys he'd ever met, and they conversed easily. It turned out that Sam had actually met Jared a couple of years ago at some celebrity golf tournament, and the two of them had kept in touch. Sam's parents were also terrific people and spent quite a bit of time talking to Nathan.

Sam's mother – Wendy – gave Julia a fond hug. "I'm still not sure why my idiot son let this one slip away," she confided. "She's the sweetest girl. You're a lucky man, Nathan."

Nathan proudly admired the glowing picture Julia made tonight in a flowing gold chiffon Alexander McQueen dress belted at the waist. With her strappy gold sandals and long, curly hair, she positively shined.

"Don't I know it," he acknowledged. "Though I still don't know why she picked me."

Wendy winked at him. "Think I can guess. You two make a gorgeous couple. Meanwhile, my dimwit son is dating some vapid supermodel who never eats."

Everyone laughed at Wendy's half-joking comment, including Sam.

The rest of the party was as casual and relaxed as the McKinnons themselves. The platters of food were hungrily devoured, the wine and beer consumed in rather startling quantities, and the soft jazz and blues music that played through the speakers entirely appropriate to the surroundings. Nathan had a very pleasant buzz going on that was only partially due to the alcohol. The rest was from being completely content and blissfully happy, and he couldn't remember too many times in his life when he'd felt this way. Even though this was his first visit to Julia's childhood home, he felt welcomed and at ease, as though he'd been coming here for years. As for Julia, she looked happier than he'd ever seen her, and it made his heart ready to burst from how much he loved her.

It was far past midnight by the time all the guests had departed and the house cleaned up. Julia was yawning sleepily as she scrubbed off her makeup, and he forced himself to check his lust when she stripped down to her pale yellow lace bra and sheer panties.

"Not fair," he groaned, clenching his fists. "You shouldn't wear such sexy undies when I know you're too wiped out for sex. Not to mention the parents on one side of us, and the nosy, bossy sister on the other."

Julia tried to giggle, but another yawn escaped instead. "Sorry. I'll make it up to you tomorrow night."

Nathan growled as she stripped off her lingerie and quickly shimmied into her nightie. "Night? Hell no am I waiting that long. I'll warn you now, baby. The minute we get inside your place I'm tossing you on the sofa and having my wicked way with you."

She shivered. "Oh. I wonder how early we can get out of here tomorrow."

He guffawed as he slid into bed and he cuddled her close. "I have definitely corrupted you."

She nuzzled her face into his chest. "Complaining?"

"Not on your life." He kissed her long and deep before reluctantly lifting his mouth. "Let's get some sleep now, baby. And rest up for tomorrow. You'll need all the energy you can spare."

Chapter Twenty-Four

Late October

"Hey, baby. How's your day going?"

Julia smiled at the sound of Nathan's voice on the other end of the phone. "Kind of crazy, but in a good way. Very productive so far. How about yours?"

He sighed. "Not quite as productive as yours, I'm afraid. This site survey is taking a lot longer than I'd planned. Will you be mad if I can't make lunch?"

"You can make it up by buying me a really expensive dinner," she joked. "And, no, I'm not mad. It was going to have to be a quick lunch anyway since I'm meeting that new client at two-thirty at her home."

"I forgot about that. Tell you what – I'll definitely be back in the city by then. Give me the address and I'll pick you up there."

"Sounds great, let me get the address." She searched through her normally tidy desk for the form she needed. In the meanwhile, a beep sounded on the phone, signaling that Nathan had another call coming in.

"Damn," he muttered. "Look, just send me a text when you find the address. Gotta go, baby. Love you."

"Love you, too."

Sure enough, she located the form with all the contact information for her new prospective client mere seconds after Nathan ended the call. Before she forgot, she sent him a quick text with the address, adding that she'd likely be finished with the appointment by three-thirty.

She hadn't been too thrilled to take on this client – whom she'd yet to meet or even speak to personally. She'd received the call about a week ago from the woman's PA - a young woman who had been a little too pushy for Julia's liking - to set up an appointment as soon as possible. The client – a woman named Elizabeth Gardiner – wanted to have her entire condo redecorated, and had been referred to Julia via Jackson West. It was only because of her association with the winery owner that Julia had accepted the job. She was already so busy these days with all the projects Travis kept throwing her way that she really didn't have time for Ms. Gardiner. But the PA had been almost obnoxiously persistent, and Julia had finally relented just to get the woman off her back.

Not having enough hours in the day notwithstanding, life was pretty damned perfect these days. She loved her job and her co-workers; was really starting to adore San Francisco and learn her way around, making Manhattan a distant memory; and she was head over heels in love with her Nathan. They were always together, never spending a night apart, though still shuttling back and forth between his condo and her flat. Nathan had finally contacted a friend who was a leasing agent, and he was actively searching for a larger place for them to rent together. He was certain he could rent Nathan's condo out as well until the time was right to sell it.

And the most exciting development was that Nathan had almost finalized the plans for his dream home in Tiburon. After spending the weekend at her parents' house and soaking up her father's considerable experience, Nathan had found new inspiration to finish the plans. Her parents were due for a visit in less than a week's time, and they had already planned to see the Tiburon property up close.

Julia was also making plans for entertaining her parents during their visit. It had already been decided that they would stay at her flat while she and Nathan would bunk at his condo.

Nathan had also been after her lately to finally buy a car, and she was quickly running out of excuses. In fact, he was planning for them to go car shopping this weekend, and she had more or less resigned herself to canvassing car lots instead of browsing the sale at Neiman Marcus.

At two twenty-five, the cab let her off in front of the building where her new client lived. The building was located in a high-priced, high-class neighborhood, as evidenced by the bevy of luxury automobiles parked nearby, and the well-dressed residents who walked past. She was glad she'd chosen an elegant black Ralph Lauren dress. Paired with her go-to black Louboutins and a Prada tote, she more than fit in with this elite crowd.

The condo was in an older building and appeared to only have about a dozen units in all. It was nothing like the ultra-modern high-rise structure where Nathan lived, with its spacious lobby and 24-hour security. This small building had a keypad entry, for which Elizabeth Gardiner's pushy assistant had given Julia the code. She had thought that a bit odd, but had been anxious to get the obnoxious PA off the phone and hadn't questioned it. Checking her notes, she keyed in the security code and pushed the door open into the small lobby. There were only three floors in the building, and Ms. Gardiner lived on the top one. Julia contemplated taking the stairs, but decided instead on the elevator, given her four-inch heels.

She was further puzzled when she reached Elizabeth Gardiner's front door and found it slightly ajar. She knocked and called out. "Ms. Gardiner? It's Julia McKinnon, the interior designer."

Moments later, a somewhat muffled voice called out, "Yes, come in. I'll be right there."

Fighting off a growing sense of unease, Julia nonetheless stepped inside the condo and shut the door behind her. A quick glance around the living/dining space revealed sleek, modern furnishings, tasteful artwork, and a variety of carefully chosen sculptures, vases and pottery. It did not look in the least bit like a space that needed to be redecorated.

"Hello, Julia. So nice of you to stop by."

Julia froze at the sound of that familiar, menacing voice and her blood chilled as Cameron walked slowly into the room. Cameron looked even worse than she had in the restaurant a few weeks earlier – gaunt and thin, her clothes wrinkled and stained, and her hair unkempt. But what really, really concerned Julia was the pistol Cameron held in her hand – a pistol that was now pointed at Julia.

"Cameron." Julia expelled a long breath, trying to stay calm and rational, something that wasn't easy to do in the presence of a semi-crazed woman holding a gun. "I assume this Elizabeth Gardiner ruse was meant to get me here alone."

Cameron shrugged. "I gave my assistant a nice bonus for pushing so hard to get you here. You apparently weren't too eager to get my business. I told my assistant I was just trying to play an elaborate prank on a friend."

"Except that the joke's on me, I suppose," stated Julia flatly.

"You're a smart girl. Guess that fancy Ivy League education paid off," said Cameron with heavy sarcasm. "What a smug bitch you are, thinking you're better than I am because you went to Cornell and lived in New York and speak French. Big fucking deal."

Julia winced as Cameron's voice increased in volume. "I never thought I was better than you," she told her softly, trying to keep her calm.

Cameron's eyes blazed angrily. "Shut up! I don't want you to talk. You fucked up my life so badly, you little whore. Why didn't you just stay in goddamned New York and leave my fiancé alone? You've ruined everything – everything!"

Cameron was screaming at this point, and Julia began to gingerly start backing up towards the door. She wondered wildly if she could possibly hope to outrun Cameron and make it safely outside. She'd have to ditch her shoes, of course, and even then –

"Don't fucking move, bitch!" screeched Cameron. "I see what you're trying to do. You're not going anywhere, Julia. Not until you pay for what you did to me. You've ruined me, made me a fucking laughingstock with all my friends, made me an object of pity. Poor Cameron, dumped again. She'll meet the right guy one of these days. Fuck them! I *did* meet the right guy. Nathan was perfect for me, until you stole him away. You're not going to get away with it!"

Now Julia was really beginning to quiver with fear, especially when she noticed how Cameron's gun hand was waving around erratically. How in the world had Cameron obtained a gun anyway?

"Cameron, calm down, please. Let's talk about this rationally. And please put the gun down. You don't want it going off accidentally." Julia spoke with a calm she sure as hell didn't feel.

Cameron gave a hysterical laugh. "Accidentally? Oh, please. I've been handling guns since I was a child. Daddy is on the board of the NRA and he made sure all of us could shoot. I still go to the shooting range once or twice a month to stay in practice. No, Julia, there will be nothing accidental about shooting you. In fact, it will be quite intentional."

Julia was frozen with fear, and strove to keep her voice from breaking. "Cameron, that's crazy. You can't possibly think you could get away with something like that."

"Oh, but I have it all figured out," declared Cameron. "I'll say I thought you were an intruder and shot you in self-defense. My father will get me the best attorney in the state, and I won't even be charged with anything. Money talks, Julia."

Julia could only stare in horrified disbelief. "That – you're insane. Insane. Cameron, you can't do something like that. My God, I know you're angry and hurt but you aren't a cold-blooded murderer."

"Shut up!" shrieked Cameron. "You don't know fuck about me, Julia. I was the best fucking thing that ever happened to Nathan until you shoved those big tits in his face and wiggled your ass in those tight skirts and stole him away. He was in love with me, we were supposed to be married, were going to be so happy. And then you had to come along and fuck everything up. You need to pay for that, bitch."

"And how do you think Nathan is going to react when he knows what you've done?" asked Julia quietly. "You know he'll never believe your story."

Cameron's eyes looked glazed. "That's not true. He *will* believe me. And with you out of the picture he'll realize how much he still loves me and will come back to me. But he won't do that until you're not around anymore. So be prepared to die now, bitch."

As Julia recognized the sound of the trigger of the gun being pulled, she barely had time to react, ducking behind a cabinet filled with objects d'art. She could see the bullet ricochet off the cabinet, and then felt a sudden, searing pain on her upper left arm. Glancing down she saw blood begin to pour down her arm from where the bullet had grazed her, and she bit her lip to hold back the scream of terror bubbling up in her throat.

The sight of Julia's blood seemed to have caused Cameron to freeze in place, as though she couldn't believe she'd actually pulled the trigger. Julia reacted quickly, taking advantage of Cameron's sudden confusion, and grabbed an undoubtedly priceless sculpture from a nearby table, flinging it wildly at Cameron. The marble piece caught Cameron square on the arm, and she dropped the gun from her shaking fingers. As she fell to her knees, intent on retrieving the gun, Julia snatched a heavy crystal vase and smashed it over Cameron's head. Cameron groaned and slumped to the floor.

Julia's heart was racing so hard she feared she'd faint, but wasted no time in tearing madly out of the condo.

✳✳✳✳✳

Nathan was tired and irritable when he finally wrapped up surveying the site of a potential new office building. The site was in a community a few miles south of San Francisco, one he wasn't too familiar with, so he'd had to wait on the arrival of the city planner and civil engineer, and they had both been late. The builder who'd been selected for the project had had dozens of questions, and what should have been a relatively quick survey had taken far too long.

He was back in San Francisco now, and he debated whether he had time to return to the office before picking Julia up from her client's. It occurred to him that he didn't even know the address, and hoped that she'd sent him the promised text. While stopped at a red light, he quickly found the text and immediately felt his blood turn to ice.

Cameron. It was her address. Somehow she'd managed to lure Julia to her home, obviously under false pretenses, because there was no possible way Julia would have gone there willingly.

"Shit!" he cursed, and immediately started figuring out the absolute fastest route to Cameron's condo. He couldn't imagine that his ex-fiancée would actually harm Julia, until he recalled the hard slap Cameron had given her once, hard enough to leave a bruise and a cut.

The light turned green and he surged ahead, grateful he'd driven the BMW today for it was much faster and easier to maneuver than his SUV. He hoped fervently he didn't cross paths with a police car, because he was intent on breaking every speeding record in the book to get to Cameron's the fastest possible way. He ignored the honks from pissed-off drivers as he cut them off, veered into lanes without signaling, and tailgated unmercifully. All the while he was half-praying, half reassuring himself that nothing was wrong, that Julia was fine, that Cameron was probably doing nothing more than insulting her or screaming like the shrew she was. God, if that crazy bitch even dared to lift a finger against Julia, he'd wring her skinny neck until it snapped!

His heart was pounding like crazy, and he felt sick to his stomach as he drew ever closer to Cameron's condo. A glance at the clock revealed it to be two forty-five, only fifteen minutes past the time Julia was supposed to have arrived. Nathan thanked the powers that be that had made him check Julia's text before heading for the office instead.

His leg was shaking with fear as he came within three blocks of his destination. Parking was an absolute nightmare in this area no matter the time of day, and he only hoped he could find a space nearby.

He had circled the block twice already, cursing vividly when there was no parking to be found. He was going around for the third time when his blood chilled at the horrifying sight that greeted his eyes – a bloodied, disheveled, hysterical Julia stumbling out the front door of the condo building. Immediately, he double parked the car and raced over to the sidewalk to catch her as she collapsed tearfully in his arms.

"Jesus, baby, what the hell happened? Julia, my God – you're bleeding! Let me call 911. Jesus."

She was sobbing, clutching his arm as they sunk to the sidewalk together. "Oh, God, Nathan. It's Cameron – she has a gun – and she tried to kill me – I think it's just a graze, but – "

"Shh." He kept an arm wrapped around her while he searched for his phone, somehow managing to punch in 9-1-1 with badly shaking fingers. He ignored the gathering crowd of passers-by, most of whom just gawked in alarm before hurrying on their way, but a few who hovered in the background, and one man who hunkered down next to them. He introduced himself briefly as Charlie, and identified himself as an off-duty nurse. Charlie began checking Julia's arm as Nathan answered the 911 operator's questions rather brusquely, and ignored the woman's repeated admonishments to calm down. After barking out the required information, he was assured by the operator that both an ambulance and a police unit would arrive very soon.

Charlie, meanwhile, was doing his best to calm Julia down, and desperately searching for something to staunch the flow of blood, which seemed to Nathan to be substantial.

"Do you have a first aid kit in your car?" he asked Nathan, when he learned the BMW was his. "Or a towel, anything like that? I'm almost sure this is just a deep graze, but it's bleeding like crazy and I'm sure it must hurt her like hell."

Nathan was reluctant to leave Julia even for a second, especially when he saw how pale she was and how clammy her skin felt. But he dashed to his car, not giving a flying fuck if he got three tickets for double-parking, and found a towel inside the gym bag he always kept stashed in the trunk.

As Charlie began to wrap the towel around Julia's arm to staunch the flow of blood, Nathan heard the telltale sound of a siren nearby and felt a mild relief. He clutched Julia's hand tightly, and kept kissing her forehead, brushing her damp curls behind her ear.

"It'll be okay, baby. You're going to be just fine," he assured her even as her eyes shut and her head lolled back limply.

"Shit," muttered Charlie. "She's passed out. I sure hope that's the ambulance and not the cops I hear approaching. Here, let's rest her head on your lap."

Nathan felt a hot tear run down his cheek as he tenderly cradled Julia's head in his lap.

"Is she going to be okay? Christ, that's a helluva lot of blood."

Charlie nodded as he tightened the towel around her arm. "Yep, probably why she passed out. She might need a transfusion but I'm fairly sure she'll be okay. Ah, here's the ambulance."

Nathan bent and kissed Julia gently on the lips. "Hang on baby. Everything's going to be just fine."

※※※※※

Cameron staggered to her feet, her vision impaired by the sluggish trickle of blood that ran from her temple into her eye. She was more than a little woozy but still alert enough to find the gun she'd dropped earlier and picked it up. A quick glance around revealed that Julia had escaped, leaving the front door wide open behind her. Enraged, Cameron grabbed her keys from the entryway table and ran down the three flights of stairs. That bitch couldn't have gotten far, especially in those ridiculous fuck-me stilettos, and Cameron was certain she could overtake her. Julia wouldn't be so lucky to escape with just a flesh wound this time. She'd shoot the bitch in the brain, the heart, the gut, to make sure she was well and truly dead.

But when she stumbled unsteadily into the lobby, she froze in her tracks as she saw the scene unfolding just outside the front door of the building. A small crowd had gathered on the sidewalk, including two paramedics who were lifting Julia onto a gurney.

And Nathan was there, too, somehow. How in the world had he arrived so quickly? How had Julia managed to contact him since it appeared she was passed out cold? Cameron watched, her heart shattering into a thousand pieces, as Nathan tenderly bent over Julia, clutching her hand and kissing her forehead. He was crying, shaken, and looked absolutely devastated. And it was in that moment Cameron realized how completely in love with Julia he really was, and how she could never, ever hope to get him back. Her legs wobbled, and she fought the urge to sink to the floor and weep.

And then another siren sounded, and Cameron's despair turned to fear at the arrival of the police cruiser. Aware all of a sudden that she was clutching a gun, she turned and ran down the flight of stairs that led to the small underground parking garage.

Her hands were shaking as she unlocked the door to her Mercedes sedan, and then tore out of the garage as fast as she could. Her heart was racing as panic surged through her. With Julia still alive, there was no way now that anyone would believe the fabricated tale of Cameron mistaking her for an intruder. God, she'd be arrested and charged with who knew what and all of her father's money and connections wouldn't save her from jail. She would be destroyed socially, her family would cut her off, she'd lose her business – the list went on.

Tears poured down her cheeks, mingling with the blood and sweat already streaming from her forehead, and her vision grew blurry. In the distance she could hear sirens, and she panicked, assuming the police were after her. She drove faster, recklessly, swerving into lanes of traffic, at one point driving over a curb, and had no clear idea of where she was headed or what she would do when she got there.

Cameron was so terrified, so panic-stricken, and so bewildered that she didn't notice she'd turned down a dead-end street, still traveling at a reckless speed. The last thing she thought before the darkness claimed her was that this was a strange place for a concrete wall to be.

✳✳✳✳✳

"The doctor said you can leave tomorrow, baby."

Julia gave Nathan a weak smile and squeezed his hand. She was more than a little dopey from the pain meds they'd shot her up with, and still shocky from everything that had happened earlier today. Since she had apparently fainted from shock and blood loss, she'd had to rely on Nathan's recounting of what had happened after she'd managed to escape a crazed Cameron.

The bullet had indeed only been a graze, but it had cut a deep groove and she'd lost a lot of blood. She'd received a transfusion, plus antibiotics and a tetanus shot, and been bandaged up. Though in no danger, the doctor wanted to keep her overnight for observation. Nathan had already called her parents and Lauren, and they were understandably upset but also grateful that she was okay. Julia had managed a small smile through her woozy state when she'd heard that Lauren was ready to drive up tonight, round up three or four friends, and go on the hunt for Cameron until they found her and broke every bone in her skinny body.

"Travis should be here any minute," Nathan told her, brushing her tangled hair off her shoulders. He'd been hovering over her, fretting and pacing, as though he was afraid to let her out of his sight for even a second. Even through her drug-addled state, she could see how agitated he was, how his suit and shirt were hopelessly rumpled and stained with her blood. His hair was a mess, sticking up haphazardly and in total disarray.

"I hope he's bringing you dinner," she said sleepily. "It's after seven and I know you haven't had a thing to eat or drink. You also look kind of scary with all those bloodstains."

He brought her hand to his lips. "Imagine then how terrified I was when I saw you falling to the sidewalk with all that blood pouring from your arm. Jesus, if I'd lost you, Julia, if she'd managed to really hurt you – I'd want to die, too."

"Shhh." She tenderly ran her fingers over his lips. "I'm okay. Just sleepy. And I'm sure this arm will hurt like hell when the meds wear off. At least it's not my drawing hand so I won't miss any work."

"Your boss might have something to say about that."

Julia and Nathan looked up as Travis strode into the room, carrying a takeout bag in one hand and a fuzzy stuffed pink unicorn in the other. He handed the bag to Nathan, proclaiming it dinner, and then tucked the stuffed toy next to Julia's pillow as he bent to kiss her cheek.

"Even bloodied and bandaged and drugged up, with that appalling hospital gown on, you still manage to look gorgeous," he told her with a smile.

She managed a small chuckle as she cuddled the unicorn. "Yes, well, forgive me if I don't believe you at the moment."

Travis shooed Nathan away from the hospital bed as he carefully sat down on the edge. "But he looks twice as bad as you do. You should have told me to bring you a clean shirt, Nate. Ugh, glad I already had my dinner because you look very unappetizing right now. Go over to that chair and eat your dinner there, out of my sight."

Scowling, Nathan did as he bid and took out the to-go order of pasta vongole, green salad, and garlic bread that Travis had brought, along with a can of soda. When Travis was satisfied that

Nathan was digging into the food, he turned his attention back to Julia.

"I didn't think to ask, sweetie. Should I have brought something for you to eat?" he asked in concern.

She grimaced and shook her head. "For once in my life, I'm not the least bit hungry. The pain meds are making me a little nauseous, I think. They brought me some broth and Jell-O awhile ago. That was more than I could manage."

Travis shook his head as he gently clasped her hand. "Who'd have thought Cameron was actually capable of something like this? Jesus, when Nathan called me from the ER I thought I'd pass out. Why in the world were you at her condo to begin with?"

Yawning sleepily, Julia told him how Cameron's employee at the gallery had duped her. Nathan chimed in between bites of pasta, confirming that the police had talked to the tearful young woman, who'd had no idea of Cameron's real intent. She'd been under the impression that all she was doing was playing a little practical joke on a friend of Cameron's.

Travis expressed his sympathies, told her that Anton sent his love, and assured her that she was to take the rest of the week off from work and longer if needed. It was only when Nathan touched his arm and motioned him outside the hospital room with a tilt of his head that Travis realized Julia had fallen asleep.

"You really do look like shit," he told Nathan as they stepped into the hallway. "You're going to have to throw that shirt out, probably the tie, too."

Nathan shrugged. "Like I give a fuck. When I think about what Cameron was intending to do, what could have happened to Julia if she hadn't gotten lucky — what a fucking disaster. And I feel responsible. I knew how unhinged Cameron had become, how she was stalking us. I should have called the police. Or hired a bodyguard. Something."

"The police haven't located her yet?"

Nathan shook his head. "They've got patrols stationed by her condo, the gallery, her parents' home. Of course they're keeping a watch on her credit card and passport to make sure she doesn't try to get a flight out. But nothing yet."

"Unbelievable. I mean, I always knew she was a coldhearted bitch but I never thought she'd be capable of actually trying to kill someone," mused Travis. "Bet her old man is shitting a brick."

"Good. He deserves to suffer, the evil old dick," muttered Nathan. "Thank God I never had to suffer having him as my father-in-law. What the hell was I thinking?"

Travis gave him a reassuring pat on the back. "Hey, Cameron could certainly be charming and fun and engaging. That's the side of her she made sure you saw. Obviously, the breakup made something inside of her snap. And before you say anything," he pointed a warning finger, "that was *not* your fault. She's probably been a little crazy most of her life. It wouldn't have taken much at all to push her over the edge."

Nathan sighed. "I don't dare tell Julia this, at least not now. When the police interviewed her employees at the gallery, nearly every one of them expressed concern about her erratic behavior these past few months. Last week – Jesus – she slashed the two Benoits she owned, just destroyed two of the most valuable paintings in the whole gallery."

"Crazy fucking bitch," muttered Travis. "You're right – Julia doesn't need to know that, maybe not ever. And please tell me you weren't planning on going back to your condo tonight. Crazy bitch might be waiting there for you."

Nathan hesitated. "She'd have a hell of a time getting past security, especially since the police have already notified them to be on the alert. But I figured on staying at Julia's since its closer to the hospital."

"My place is even closer. You'll stay in our guest room, it's the most sensible solution. If the police haven't found Cameron by tomorrow, you should hire security. Thank God we took precautions at the office weeks ago and already have them in place."

Nathan nodded tiredly and was about to reply when his phone rang. He frowned when he didn't recognize the number but answered it anyway. Travis watched with concern as he paled, and then closed his eyes. Nathan turned away and walked down the hall a short distance, obviously intent on keeping the conversation private. It was several minutes later when he walked back to where Travis stood, visibly shaken.

"That was the detective in charge of this case," he told a concerned Travis. "They – Christ – they found Cameron. She rammed her car into a concrete wall at the end of a cul-de-sac about five miles from her place. She's dead – probably died on impact. Holy fuck, Travis."

As Nathan swayed slightly, Travis grabbed hold of his arm and steered him around the corner from the nurses' station to a visitors waiting area. Both men sank down to sit on the padded bench.

"I'm sorry, Nate," said Travis gently. "Despite all of her craziness, I realize she was still your girlfriend for two years. This must be upsetting for you."

Nathan waved a hand in dismissal. "Not in the way you think. Sorry, but that bitch deserved everything she got for what she tried to do to Julia. You won't see me mourning her or attending her funeral. Any feelings I had for her are long gone. No, I'm just relieved this whole fucking mess is over. Julia and I don't have to keep worrying about her any longer."

Travis winked. "And now you can ask Julia to marry you."

In spite of the hell he'd been through in the past several hours, Nathan grinned. "All in good time, my friend. All in good time."

Epilogue

New Year's Eve

"Have I thanked you for wearing that dress tonight? Especially since I know it's really not meant for New Year's Eve weather in Paris."

Julia smiled and took a sip of her French champagne. "You haven't thanked me but the look in your eyes is all the thanks I need. And yes, it's a little lightweight for winter in France, but you'll just have to make sure you keep me real warm."

Nathan chuckled. "Oh, baby, you have no idea how hot I'm going to make you tonight. We'll probably have to turn the air conditioner on to cool off."

She raised a dainty brow. "Mmm, I hope our suite is suitably soundproofed. We might get kicked out of the Plaza Athenee for making too much noise."

He clinked his champagne flute against hers. "If you're trying to challenge me, you should know better by now. Especially when it comes to making you scream during sex."

Julia's cheeks pinkened and she glanced around the restaurant uncertainly. "Shhh. I know we're in Paris but I'm guessing most of the people here understand English. Especially the S-E-X word."

Nathan leaned over the table, tipping her chin up and giving her a lingering kiss. "Don't worry, baby. I promise I won't embarrass you in a three-star Michelin restaurant."

They were dining at Le Meurice, one of the top dining establishments in Paris. Julia's head was still spinning at the blatant luxury he'd been showering on her with this surprise trip – the trip that had been part of her Christmas gift. They had arrived two days ago – via a first-class flight, of course – and would be spending a whole week in the fabulous suite at the Plaza Athenee.

God knew they needed this time away, given everything that had happened over the past two months. Fortunately, the office was closed for two weeks over the holidays so they would only be missing a few days of work.

Physically, Julia had recovered from the bullet graze quickly, returning to work after just a few days. There was still a scar from the wound, though it was continuing to fade. With the cool fall and winter weather she'd been wearing dresses or blouses that covered the scar, which she was quite self-conscious about. And even though Nathan insisted he hardly noticed it, she was still contemplating having some minor plastic surgery done to erase the scar.

Predictably, Cameron's father had gone to great lengths to have the real story behind his daughter's fatal accident covered up. There had been no mention in the news of the fact that Cameron had tried to kill Julia, or that she'd crashed her car while fleeing the crime scene. Nathan had been furious that the truth had been buried away, wanting people to know what an evil, twisted bitch Cameron had really been. But Julia had felt quite differently, convincing him that all she really wanted was to forget the whole awful mess.

Her parents had arrived for their scheduled visit just a few days after the incident, and both had hugged her tight, Natalie visibly weeping. They had spent the first day and night of their visit just hanging out at Julia's flat, not wanting to be separated from their precious daughter whom they'd come too close to losing.

Julia had indulged them for one day, and then insisted on sticking to their original plans after that. Going out and having fun had been the best medicine, taking her mind off the trauma she'd suffered.

With Robert's input, Nathan had finalized the plans for the Tiburon house, and just a few weeks earlier had decided on a contractor. Groundbreaking on the house was due to start sometime in February, and by this time next year they would hopefully be celebrating New Year's Eve at the new place.

They'd flown out to Michigan to spend Thanksgiving with his family, though Nathan had seen very little of Julia during their visit. His overjoyed mother had monopolized a great deal of Julia's time - taking her shopping, introducing her to friends, and spending hours just chatting. Julia had loved meeting the rest of Nathan's family – his sister-in-law Brooke and young nephew Damien, and his younger brother Greg. There were also a host of other relatives who stopped in for a visit during their stay – grandparents, uncles, aunts, and cousins as well as neighbors and old friends from school. Julia's head had been spinning from meeting so many people in such a short period of time. It was evident that the Atwoods were a very sociable, funloving family, and some of the larger gatherings were a bit overwhelming for her at times.

December had been a crazy month, between the demands of their jobs, a round of holiday parties, and Christmas shopping. They had set up two Christmas trees – one at each of their places. Nathan had decided to hold on to his condo for now, given that the Tiburon house would be ready in about a year's time, and they would just continue to split their time between their two residences until then.

They left for Carmel the day before Christmas Eve, having agreed to exchange their gifts before departing. Nathan had been touched by the things she'd chosen with such care for him – an Omega watch he'd looked at several times during shopping excursions; a pair of gold and onyx cufflinks; a black wool overcoat, and – his favorite – a charcoal sketch she'd drawn of him without his knowledge when they had visited her parents back in October.

He'd given her a lingering kiss. "You are so talented, Julia. I swear you missed your calling. You could be as successful as your mother if you really wanted to."

She'd shrugged. "*That* is not possible, but I must admit I'd love to find the time to draw more often. But, you see, I've got this employer who just works me like a slave."

"Mmm, especially after hours," he'd told her suggestively. "I'm not surprised you don't have more time or energy to draw. I hear that boss of yours is very demanding."

"Oh, he is," Julia had agreed mischievously. "Most days he's so demanding I can barely walk the next morning."

Nathan had grinned, drawing her onto his lap for a cuddle. "Thank you for such wonderful presents, baby. Now it's my turn."

Her first present had turned out to be a brand new silver BMW sedan. With Angela's help, he'd managed to smuggle it into the garage downstairs. Julia had been speechless upon seeing it, and he'd had to open the driver's door and urge her inside.

As they had taken the car for a test drive around the neighborhood, Nathan had told her, "I got tired of all the excuses you kept giving for why you didn't need a car. But when you move in with me to the new house, you'll definitely need wheels to commute back and forth every day."

That had provoked a raised brow from Julia. "Is that right? And here I wasn't sure I'd even be invited to this new place, much less live there."

Nathan had snorted in derision. "Oh, please. Your father made sure that the damned walk-in closet was big enough for all your stuff. It's certainly way too big for my paltry wardrobe. So you have to move in. Besides, you promised me free decorating advice, so the least I can do is give you free rent in return."

Stupidly, Julia had felt her eyes fill with tears, and had impatiently brushed them away. "I would love to live with you in your dream house."

"Correction, baby. *Our* dream house."

As over-the-top extravagant as the new car had been, it was his next gift that had really made her swoon.

"Paris!" she'd squealed in delight. "You're taking me to Paris for New Year's Eve?"

Julia had studied the itinerary – with the flight and hotel information – as well as the hotel brochure carefully, and this time the tears had indeed spilled from her eyes. She'd flung her arms around his neck, kissing him thoroughly, before resting her head on his shoulder.

"I can't imagine a more perfect way to celebrate the New Year than with my lover in the City of Love," she'd murmured. "Aunt Maddy took me to Paris when I was eighteen for Fashion Week, but I hardly got to see any sights. And seeing Paris with your aunt isn't anywhere near the same as being there with your man. Thank you, Nathan. I think this is the best gift ever."

He had grinned in delight. "Oh, I can think of a better gift. In fact, I'm holding it in my arms right now." He'd dropped a kiss on the tip of her nose. "Merry Christmas, baby. I love you so much, Julia. There isn't anything I wouldn't give you if it was in my power."

Her arms had tightened around his neck. "Well, since the only thing I really want is you, then I suppose your shopping list is complete."

The Christmas holidays at the McKinnons were a somewhat quieter but no less joyous affair than Thanksgiving in Michigan had been. There had been neverending dishes of some of the best food Nathan had ever tasted, lots of wine and spirits, and nonstop conversation. In addition to being one of the top architects of his generation, Robert was also an impressive vocalist, and kept the family entertained with his piano playing and singing.

Nathan met the much-mentioned Aunt Maddy at last, and it was quite obvious that Julia had acquired her exquisite fashion sense from the older woman. It was interesting to notice that Lauren more closely took after Natalie with their casual, semi-bohemian style, while Julia and Maddy both loved high end fashion.

Madelyn Benoit was a very attractive, poised and sophisticated woman, and quite probably what Julia would look like in about twenty-five more years. She arrived at her sister's home with no boyfriend tagging along, and when Nathan had asked Julia very casually if her aunt had ever been married or engaged, Julia had given a rather brusque shake of her head.

"That's not a topic we discuss with Aunt Maddy," she'd explained. "There's definitely a story there but not one she or my mother have ever shared."

It was hard to imagine that a woman as beautiful as Madelyn had never been seriously involved with a man at some point, so Nathan surmised there had been some ill-fated love affair at one time or another. Not to mention the fact that someone with a job as high-profile and demanding as hers must not have had much time to devote to a relationship. Her career was very likely the reason she'd never married or had a family of her own.

They had flown to Paris three days after Christmas, and had spent their first day mostly recuperating from jet lag. But yesterday they had done a whirlwind tour of the Louvre, Notre Dame, and the Champs-Elysees. Not to mention browsing in a variety of boutiques and buying rather large quantities of French pastries.

Julia had grinned as she'd licked whipped cream off her fingers. "This is such a great city. It has all of my favorite things in the whole world – incredible art, beautiful clothes, delicious food, and you. I think I would be very happy living here."

Nathan had grown pensive while sipping his espresso inside the little bakery café they'd escaped into after a chilly walk back towards their hotel. "And to think you might have had that opportunity if you'd pursued that job with Gregson Hotels. I'm sure Ian would have found the right spot for you here."

Julia had picked up his hand, running her thumb over his knuckles. "Is that why we aren't staying at the Gregson hotel here? You think I might change my mind or something?"

"Maybe. No sense putting thoughts into that pretty little head. Because you aren't moving to Paris, baby. The only place you'll be moving is into our new home in Tiburon." He placed his hand over hers. "I made the huge mistake of letting you go once. That isn't going to happen ever again."

And now here they were, celebrating New Year's Eve with a romantic dinner in one of the best restaurants in Paris, if not the entire world. Nathan had intentionally worn the suit and tie he'd had on that magical evening in New York, even though the suit was admittedly a bit lightweight for wintertime in Paris. Fortunately for both of them, it would only be a matter of walking between the restaurant's front door and a warm, waiting taxi. At least until their next stop of the evening.

The dinner was sumptuous, each course more delicious and beautifully prepared than the one before it. Julia relished each bite, closing her eyes in appreciation as she smacked her lips.

"Ohh, I could get used to eating like this every day," she told him with a satisfied smile.

He chuckled and pinched her cheek. "Baby, if you ate like this every day – not to mention what you've already put away for breakfast, lunch and coffee break – you'd need a whole new wardrobe. And that would be a real shame, because I'd be very upset if you couldn't fit into that beautiful pink dress any longer."

Julia pouted playfully. "Are you trying to tell me I'm getting fat?"

"Hell, no. After all, I'm planning on getting laid tonight. Several times. So I would never imply that you might put on a few pounds if you keep eating two pastries every afternoon."

The mischievous twinkle in his light blue eyes did not amuse her, and she gave him a little kick beneath the table.

"Ow." He grimaced. "Guess I should be grateful you aren't wearing a pair of those pointy-toed things. I'd have a bruise for sure."

Julia looked guiltily at her empty dinner plate. "You're right. I'm making a pig of myself. No dessert tonight and definitely no pastries tomorrow."

"Silly girl." He caressed her cheek gently. "How often are we in Paris? Have dessert. We'll figure out a way to burn off those extra calories later."

She made a little face at him. "But it's too cold to go for a long walk after dinner."

"Brat." He stuck his tongue out at her. "Let me clarify. The physical activity I had in mind was of the indoor variety. And I guarantee you'll work up a sweat."

Julia smiled impishly. "Okay, you twisted my arm. Let's have the waiter bring us the dessert menu."

They were both pleasantly full from the gourmet dinner, and more than a little tipsy from both the champagne and the fine French wine. They bundled up into their new winter coats – Nathan's the black wool one that she had bought him for Christmas, and Julia's a chic white cashmere that Maddy had shipped to her a few months ago. He kept an arm wrapped around her as they ducked into a waiting taxi, but she frowned in bemusement as he asked the driver to take them to the Eiffel Tower.

"I thought we were going there tomorrow," she reminded him.

He smiled mysteriously. "Change of plans. Trust me. And I know it's freezing outside but we won't be there very long."

Julia was intrigued now but decided to indulge Nathan and sit back for the short drive to the world famous landmark. He had, after all, been pampering and spoiling her rotten these past few days, so she could certainly cede to his wishes now.

There were throngs of people already gathering near the Eiffel Tower in anticipation of the fireworks display scheduled for midnight, even though it was barely nine o'clock. Julia began to have her doubts about this, given her overall dislike of large crowds. She'd always avoided Times Square on New Year's Eve during her time in Manhattan, and now Nathan was drawing her out of the taxi into an ever-growing sea of humanity.

Somehow, Nathan convinced the taxi driver to wait for them, and then grabbed her hand, tugging her along until they were standing as close as possible to the Tower.

And it was then, as he pulled something out of his coat pocket, took her hand, and sank to one knee, that she realized his purpose in dragging her here. The tears were already starting to well in her eyes even before he began to speak.

"Julia Elizabeth McKinnon," he began, in a less than steady voice. "I fell in love with you the moment I first saw you on a crowded New York street. You took my breath away then and every single time I've seen you since. You are the most beautiful, talented and loving woman I've ever known, and I want to spend the rest of my life with you. I want you to cook incredible dinners for me, to create amazing artwork, to decorate our dream home, and one day to give me babies – even if they're twins. But mostly, I just want you."

Nathan opened the small black velvet jewelry box with shaking fingers and held it up for her inspection. The diamond was exquisite, flawless; the square cut the perfect size and shape for her dainty fingers.

"Will you do me the greatest honor I can imagine and marry me?" he murmured hoarsely, his own eyes now shiny with tears.

Julia clapped a hand over her mouth, her legs trembling and the tears streaming down her cheeks in earnest. "Oh, God, Nathan," she whispered. "Yes, of course I'll marry you! I love you so much."

He slid the ring onto her finger, then rose and swept her into a fierce embrace. It was only then that they realized they'd attracted quite a crowd who'd been watching the romantic scene unfold before their eyes. As Nathan captured her lips in a long kiss, the crowd of people around them erupted into applause and shouts of encouragement and congratulations. At least that's what Nathan assumed they were all shouting, given his very limited command of the French language.

"Are those shouts of approval?" he whispered in Julia's ear, "Or did I spur a riot?"

She laughed, snuggling into his embrace. "They were definitely shouts of approval. Peppered with a few cruder suggestions, something like the French equivalent of 'get a room'."

He burst into laughter. "Well, we've already got a room. And I suggest we head there posthaste before this crowd gets much bigger."

They hurried back to their waiting taxi amid the continued shouts of congratulations. Once inside the taxi Julia launched into a stream of rapid French, and the rather dour driver grinned in response.

"I told him you finally decided to make an honest woman out of me," she whispered in Nathan's ear. "He approves."

He whispered back to her naughtily, "Ask him if he approves of me bending you over the sofa in our suite, and lifting that pretty pink dress up so I can fuck you from behind. Or would he be more likely to approve of you riding my cock?"

Julia gasped and gave him a playful swat on the chest. "Would you stop that? We don't know if he understands English or not. Now behave yourself."

He grinned broadly as he cuddled her close. "But I thought you like it when I misbehaved."

She nipped his earlobe. "Not in a taxi, lover boy. Keep that bad boy under control until we're in our room, okay? Then he can be as bad as he wants to be."

They laughed and snuggled during the drive to their hotel. Once at their destination, Nathan paid the driver, giving him a generous tip, and thanked him for his good wishes. They hurried inside the hotel, which was a warm and cozy contrast to the chill air outside where sleet was beginning to fall.

The elegantly appointed elevator was empty as they rode up to their suite, and Nathan took full advantage of the opportunity, pinning Julia against the back wall and kissing her senseless. By the time the elevator doors opened on their floor, they were both panting and fully aroused.

He kept his arms wrapped around her as they walked the short distance to their room. "You're sure you want to go back to our room already? It's barely ten p.m. on New Year's Eve. Shouldn't we be out dancing or partying somewhere?"

Julia shook her head as he unlocked the door to their suite. "It's too cold to be outside, you know I'm not much into crowds, and I figured we could have a much better party with just the two of us."

He locked the door behind him and hung up his coat. "I like the way you think, baby. May I take your coat?"

She winked at him suggestively. "For starters."

"Well, that goes without saying," he murmured, drawing the soft white coat down her arms, and hanging it up in the entry closet next to his. "Now, come here, future Mrs. Nathan Atwood. I need to hold my fiancée."

Julia went willingly into his embrace, twining her arms around his waist. "Should we be calling our families and sharing our happy news?"

His lips clung to her forehead. "It'll keep until tomorrow. If I call my folks now, my mother will keep you on the phone for over an hour, and that is definitely not on the agenda for this evening. And your parents already know."

She gasped, staring up at him. "How is that possible? How could they know before I did?"

He smiled, smoothing her long curls off her shoulders. "Because my mother raised me to be a gentleman and part of that includes formally asking my beloved's father for her hand in marriage. He said yes, by the way, but insisted I had to okay it with your mother, too. Apparently they have a very equal marriage."

Julia nodded. "That's for sure." Then a sudden thought caused her to sober. "Did you ask Mr. Tolliver for his approval?"

Nathan grimaced. "No. I told you how the whole thing went down. And considering I was Cameron's third fiancé, asking for her father's permission seemed a bit silly. Now, I thought we agreed to never mention her name again."

She caressed her cheek. "We did. I'm sorry. The last thing I want to do on this lovely evening is ruin it with bad memories. So, let's make some good memories instead."

Slowly he unzipped her dress, nuzzling her neck. "I thought you'd never ask."

Julia wore the same pink and cream lingerie she'd had on the first time they'd been together, including the infamous pink lace panties that he'd finally returned to her. And tonight she'd added the matching lacy pink garter belt and sheer, sexy stockings.

He ran his fingertips up and down her arms, causing her to shiver in reaction. Then, without further preliminaries, he shoved his hands into her hair, tilting her head back and kissed her savagely. Julia whimpered beneath the force of his kiss as he held her head still.

"You are so fucking sexy," he growled in her ear, as his hands caressed the curve of her hip. "My favorite time of the whole day is watching you put all these tempting bits of lace and silk on this perfect body. Because then I get to think all day long about how hot you look, and how much I'm going to enjoy undressing you at the end of the day."

"Ahh," she panted, as he cupped her breast, his thumb teasing her nipple through the fragile lace covering it.

He kissed a slow, seductive path down her throat and across the high, upper curves of her breasts before tugging a bra strap off her shoulder. Julia groaned as he pinched her nipple, and then cupped her full, swollen breast as he suckled her hard. He repeated the action on her other breast until both nipples were wet and glistening, her breasts achy and tender.

"Have I told you how much I love your tits?" he muttered hoarsely, burying his face in her cleavage.

"Hmm, maybe three times a day or so," she giggled, running her hands through his hair. "I don't think that's anywhere near often enough."

"Oh, I agree Mrs. Atwood-to-be." He kissed his way down her cleavage, dropping to his knees as his mouth dipped to her navel. "But that's probably because I'm too busy telling you how much I also love your ass. And your legs. And especially this sweet, juicy cunt."

"Nathan." His name escaped her lips on a long, drawn-out moan, as he pushed aside the crotch of her panties to slide two fingers deep inside her.

"Always wet, always ready for me," he crooned as his thrust his fingers in and out. "And once again you got these pretty panties soaked. You know what that means."

He slid the pink lace boy shorts down her legs, and then carefully set them aside.

"We don't want to lose them again, do we?" he asked with a smirk. "After all the trouble I went through retrieving them the first time."

"N-n-no," she agreed shakily, as he licked at her moist folds. Her legs were trembling unsteadily in the sky-high stilettos as he proceeded to savor her with almost maddening slowness. He ate her out with exquisite care, opening her for his tongue and fingers, stimulating her clit until her hips began to rock against his mouth and he could feel her core convulse.

Nathan wrapped his arms around her knees, resting his forehead on her thighs, holding her steady as her body quivered with the long, drawn-out release he'd brought her to. He slid back up her body, unhooking her bra, and then led her over to the sofa. He bent her over the edge, her ass sticking up in the air, and he gave her buttocks a lingering caress.

"Don't move. And leave the shoes on." He ordered. "Stay exactly like that or I'll spank you."

In response, Julia wiggled her butt back and forth, drawing a chuckle from him as he swiftly undressed. When he was naked, he stepped behind her, his foot wedging its way in between hers.

"Spread them."

She obeyed instantly, recognizing the command in his voice, and feeling the surge of excitement shimmer through her. She groaned as he rubbed his rock hard erection between the cleft of her buttocks.

"Mmm, I'd love to slide inside this tight, delicious little ass," he breathed. "But not tonight, baby. We'd need to take that real slow and gentle and I need to fuck you hard and fast."

Julie cried out as he suddenly thrust fully inside her wet, clenching pussy, and then commenced to ride her with deep, rapid strokes. He held her immobile, bent over the sofa, his hands on her hips and his thighs pressed against the back of her legs. Her breath escaped in short, audible gasps, overwhelmed by his total possession, and half-afraid she'd faint from the intensity. With each deep stroke of his cock, she whimpered with the near-painful pleasure, felt him butting against the entrance to her womb.

He reached his hand between her legs, his thumb finding her tender, swollen clit and flicked over it again and again until she felt her orgasm building.

"Oh, God, Nathan, yes, just like that. Ohhh, I'm so close, so close. Just — ahhh!" she cried, as her body was wracked with the strong spasms of her climax, even as he continued to pound into her fiercely.

"Christ, I love you, Julia!" he called out just seconds before he came, filling her with his hot seed. He wrapped his arms around her waist, holding her close against his chest as his body shook over and over again.

He carried her still trembling body — sans the stilettos - into the huge white marble bathroom. A short time later, the sunken tub was filled with hot, fragrant water and the room lit with a dozen vanilla scented candles. Nathan sat with his back against the tub, and Julia nestled in between his spread legs. She'd hastily piled her hair atop her head with a clip but several errant curls tumbled down her back to tease the surface of the water. He picked up one silky strand and wrapped it around his finger.

"We should order a bottle of champagne."

She shook her head at his suggestion. "I think we indulged plenty at dinner, between a full bottle of champagne and another one of wine. Any more booze tonight and I'll fall asleep right here in the tub."

"You're right. I'll call room service for a pot of coffee instead. Or a few espressos. I plan on keeping you up for hours yet."

Julia snickered, reaching between his legs to squeeze his semi-erect cock. "I believe that's supposed to be my line."

And then her snickers turned to gasps as he cupped her breasts, his fingers twisting the nipples.

"I haven't fucked these beauties for awhile," he murmured, licking the side of her neck. "Maybe we'll get around to that before sunrise."

"Hmm." Her head had lolled back against his shoulder as he continued to pluck her nipples. "If you're serious about having sex until dawn, maybe that pot of coffee isn't a bad idea."

Nathan laughed heartily, his arms wrapping around her waist as he nuzzled behind her ear. "Don't worry, baby. I'll allow you short naps in between. And last time I looked you had a stash of pastries inside the fridge in case you need nourishment."

She swatted him playfully on the forearm. "Fiend. Considering I've probably already burned off like a thousand calories I probably will need to replenish if you're going to ravish me all night long."

He pinched her ass, drawing a yelp of protest from her. "Let's get dried off. It's almost midnight and we should watch the fireworks from our balcony. Then we'll come back inside and set off our own fireworks."

Despite the frigid temperatures and the freezing sleet, they wrapped themselves in the thick, fleecy hotel bathrobes and stepped out on the balcony.

"Should be any minute now, baby. Watch just over there," he said, wrapping her tight in his arms to keep her warm.

"Hmm, this is much better than being out there with thousands of other people getting pushed and shoved. Best seat in the house," she joked.

And then they could only ooh and ahh at the majestic display of fireworks that lit the Paris sky far above the Eiffel Tower.

"Happy New Year!" they told each other simultaneously, and shared a long, deep kiss.

"I love you, Nathan," she murmured. "This is the most wonderful New Year's Eve of my life."

He kissed her sweetly. "Mine, too. And next year's will be even better because we'll be ringing in the New Year in our brand new home. As husband and wife."

Julia tugged on his hair teasingly. "Married that soon, huh? And here I figured we'd have a very long engagement."

She squeaked when he slid his hand inside her robe and gave her a pinch on the ass. "Brat. If you think I'm waiting more than a year to marry you, guess again. What's the weather like in Carmel in June?" he asked.

She laughed as he swung her around, lifting her bare feet off the chilly tiles of the balcony. "A lot warmer than Paris in January." Her eyes were shining as she planted a smacking kiss on his mouth. "And absolutely perfect for a wedding."

The End

Dear Readers:

I hope you enjoyed this first book in the Inevitable series. Each of the six books planned in the series are standalones, with their own individual hero/heroine, and readers will easily be able to read any of the books in the series without first having read any previous ones. There will also be additional novellas and some other bonus material published.

Please be sure to visit my website – https://www.janetnissenson.com – for information on my current and future releases, as well as my pages at Facebook and Goodreads – https://www.facebook.com/janetnissensonauthor, https://www.goodreads.com/author/show/7375780.Janet_Nissenson

These are the books currently planned for the Inevitable series:

#1 – Serendipity – (Julia and Nathan) – released December 2013

#2 – Splendor – (Tessa and Ian) – released June 2014

#1.5 – All You Need is Love (Julia and Nathan) – released November 2014

#3 – Shattered (Angela and Nick) – released May 2015

#4 – Sensational (Lauren and Ben) – anticipated release Fall 2015

#5 – Serenity (Sasha and Matthew) – anticipated release 2016

#6 – Stronger (Cara and Dante) – anticipated release 2016

Happy reading and please remember to continue to support indie authors!

All my best,

Janet Nissenson

18709721R00263

Printed in Poland
by Amazon Fulfillment
Poland Sp. z o.o., Wrocław